SHORT STORIES ON FILM AND VIDEO

SHORT STORIES ON FILM AND VIDEO

Second Edition

CAROL A. EMMENS

1985
Libraries Unlimited — Littleton, Colorado

Library of Congress Cataloging-in-Publication Data

Emmens, Carol A.
    Short stories on film and video.

    Rev. ed. of: Short stories on film. 1978.
    Includes indexes.
    1. Short stories--Film and video adaptations--
Catalogs. 2. Short stories, American--Film and video
adaptations--Catalogs. I. Emmens, Carol A. Short
stories on film. II. Title.
PN1997.85.E45 1985   791.43'75   85-13160
ISBN 0-87287-424-9

Contents

Story to Screen

Since its inception, the motion picture industry has relied heavily on literary works adapted for the screen, including short stories. Yet until the first edition of *Short Stories on Film* was compiled, no source listed all the films, both theatrical and nontheatrical, that are based on short stories.

This second edition, entitled *Short Stories on Film and Video,* includes all the films produced between 1920 and 1984 that are based on short stories by American authors or outstanding international authors well known in America. There are approximately 1,375 entries; about 75 are new, and all the films in television's acclaimed American Short Stories series have been included.

A major change in the second edition is the inclusion of video distributors, a reflection of how much the video field has grown since 1978, when the first edition was published. Because of the improvements in the hardware—1/2-inch equipment now provides nearly the same quality that 3/4-inch used to provide—and the continuing drop in prices, the number of videocassette recorders in homes and educational institutions has increased enormously: of approximately 82,000 public schools K-12, over 56,000 use video equipment according to Quality Education Data (QED). The proliferation of hardware has, of course, resulted in the multiplication of the number of titles available. Over 200 more titles are now available on video (often through more than one distributor, as well as through local stores) than were available at the time of the first edition. Because of the increased number of distributors, comparison shopping is recommended. There are also a significant number of changes in the listing of the distributors because many companies in the educational film field have merged or failed. Unless otherwise noted, the distributors are for 16 mm film. Keep in mind, however, that films are released on video at a very rapid rate, and *The Video Source Book* is a good text to consult. In addition, the majority of 16 mm nontheatrical distributors do make their titles available on video, if requested, and more companies are doing so daily.

Unfortunately, many films are not at this time available for distribution in 16 mm or videocassette. However, the reader is urged to remain undiscouraged by the absence of a distributor in an entry; the number of films that are available increases daily.

To find films based on short stories, many reference books and catalogs were searched, including the *Library of Congress Catalog—Motion Pictures and Filmstrips; Who Wrote the Movie?* compiled and published by the Writers' Guild of America (Los Angeles, 1970); *Title Guide to the Talkies* by Richard B. Dimmitt (Scarecrow Press), 1964-1974 supplement by Andrew A. Aros; reviews in the

New York Times and other trade publications; the American Film Institute catalogs of motion pictures, 1921-1930 and 1961-1970 (Bowker); and *The Video Source Book* (National Video Clearinghouse).

Compiling *Short Stories on Film and Video* was a monumental task because all too often the references merely said "based on a story by ——————." What I learned is that *story* is an all-encompassing word and is used to refer to books, novels, short stories, original screenplays, and even plays. To add to this problem, some authors wrote in several of these genres, especially during the 1920s and 1930s when prolific writers were lured to Hollywood to write for the screen. To further complicate research, the definition of a short story varies widely. *Short Story Index* covers brief narratives as well as 150-page stories; other sources define a short story as a work of less than 60 pages. Because of this ambiguity, a few works that generally are considered novelettes are included in this guide.

To provide as much accuracy as possible—movie records are notoriously poor—an attempt was made to check all the titles in at least two sources. But, as noted, the sources are sometimes ambiguous.

Publication data on the stories also were difficult to ascertain occasionally because during the 1920s and 1930s both pulp magazines and literary journals abounded. Stories published in a magazine generally were not copyrighted individually. In one case, the story apparently was published after the movie was released: the movie *The Patent Leather Kid*, based on a story by Rupert Hughes, was nominated for an Academy Award in 1927 as an original story, yet it appears in the book *The Patent Leather Kid and Other Stories*, which was not published until later in the year.

When the information was available, I have named the periodical in which the story was originally published (though sometimes no date is available) because tracking down such information is time consuming. But no attempt was made to provide a source for all the stories, particularly those that are found in scores of anthologies. That information can be obtained readily from the *Short Story Index*. Additional sources for locating short stories include *Readers' Guide* (H.W. Wilson); *Humanities Index* (H.W. Wilson); and the out-of-print work *Poole's Index to Periodical Literature*.

Short Stories on Film and Video, 2d edition, is arranged alphabetically by author and subdivided by an alphabetical list of the story titles; thus, all the films based on a story are listed in one place beginning with the earliest. The short story and film title indexes that follow the "Directory of Distributors" facilitate alternative access by title.

The following sample entry identifies the content of each bibliographic item: author's name, short story title, film title, source material note, technical information, production credits, cast credits, and annotation. The joint author's name, if there is one, follows the short story title, and a cross-reference is provided. Occasionally, several stories (named in the source material note) have served as the sources for a particular film; cross-references from the name of these stories to the appropriate bibliographic entry are also supplied. When an author has used a pseudonym, cross-references refer to the most commonly used form of the author's name, and this is where the entries are listed.

The following is a sample entry:

POE, EDGAR ALLAN———————————————————author's name

A Descent into the Maelstrom————————————————short story title

War Gods of the Deep (s.m. also "The Doomed City," a poem)———film title
85 min.　　　color　　　　　　1965
Dir: Jacques Tourneur. Sp: Charles Bennett. Dist: Kerr Film Exchange,
　　Modern Sound Pictures, Wholesome Film Center.
Cast: Vincent Price, Tab Hunter, Susan Hart.
A girl is kidnapped from her home on the Cornish coast, and two friends go
to her rescue. Their search for her leads through secret doorways and subterranean
passages to a strange city under the sea.

The distributors cited in the entries are not the original theatrical distributors
but rather the current distributors of 16 mm, 8 mm film or videocassette tapes or
discs. As noted earlier, not all films are in distribution. Unless otherwise noted, the
distributor listed is the source for 16 mm films; however, nearly all of the distributors associated with educational materials now make most of their products available on 3/4-inch or 1/2-inch videocassettes, if requested. The number of companies
distributing on video grows constantly. But sometimes feature films on video are
available only for rental.

For a more comprehensive and up-to-date listing of distributors, consult
James Limbacher's 8th edition of *Feature Films on 16 mm and Video* (Bowker),
scheduled for release in 1985. Supplements to his volume are listed in *Sightlines,*
the magazine published by the Educational Film Library Association (45 John St.,
New York, NY). For up-to-date video distribution information, consult the *Video
Source Book* or such magazines as *Video.*

Because the primary objective of this filmography is to identify the films
based on short stories, the descriptive annotations are brief, and occasionally,
when the information was not readily available, especially for "poverty row"
films, annotations were omitted. A surprising number of films were not listed in
the Library of Congress catalogs, so information is sketchy. In a few instances,
the annotations of two or more films, although based on the same short story,
are considerably different because different elements of the plot were used or
because little more than the title was used by the Hollywood producers. Occasionally, a film was based on a play or novel that in turn was based on a short story,
and that information is noted in the source material. The notes also provide information about characters, such as Sherlock Holmes, who originally appeared in short
stories and were subsequently used in original screenplays.

Frequently, a reference source such as the Library of Congress catalogs listed
the number of reels rather than the running time, and I was sometimes forced to
follow suit. The approximate running time of a reel is 12 minutes.

Short Stories on Film and Video, 2d edition, is as complete as possible and
will be highly useful for teachers, librarians, and movie researchers as well as short
story buffs.

I welcome any suggestions, additions, or corrections for future editions.

Carol A. Emmens

Abbreviations Used in the Text

Adap.	adaptation
AFI	American Film Institute
a.k.a.	also known as
b&w	black and white
Dir.	director
Dist.	distributor
'	feet
in.	inches
jt.	joint
min.	minutes
mm	millimeter
mus.	music
Prod.	producer
pseud.	pseudonym
rel.	released
sd.	sound
sil.	silent
s.m.	source material note
Sp.	screenplay
Univ.	university

Names of countries are also abbreviated in the text.

Alphabetical List of Short Story Authors

ADAMS, CLIFTON

The Desperado

Cole Younger, Gunfighter
78 min.   color   1957
Dir: R.G. Springsteen. Prod: Allied Artists. Dist: Hurlock Cine-World.
Cast: Frank Lovejoy, James Best.
Western. A couple of men cross the path of the notorious gunslinger Cole Younger.

ADAMS, EUSTACE L.

Loot Below

Desperate Cargo
69 min.   b&w   1941
Dir: William Beaudine. Prod: Producers Releasing Corp. Dist: Discount
    Video (video).
Cast: Ralph Byrd, Carol Hughes, Jack Mulhall.
Spies commandeer a giant clipper ship on which two girls are returning to America.

Sixteen Fathoms Under (in *American Magazine*)

Sixteen Fathoms Deep
82 min.   color   1948
Prod: Monogram. Dist: Ivy Films.
Cast: Lloyd Bridges, Lon Chaney.
Sponge divers discover a saboteur aboard a boat off the coast of Florida.

ADAMS, FRANK R.

The American Sex (in *Munsey's Magazine,* June 1925)

Meet the Prince
6 reels   b&w   1926   sil.
Dir: Joseph Henabery. Adap: Jane Murfin, Harold Shumate. Prod: Metro-
    politan Pictures.
Cast: Joseph Schildkraut, Marguerite De La Motte.
Comedy-melodrama. Prince Nicholas Alexnov, now living in a tenement
in New York, dreams of his elegant palace in Russia. He falls in love with Annabelle
Ford and eventually wins her.

Circus Girl (in *Cosmopolitan Magazine*)

> *Circus Girl*
> 54 min.   b&w   1937
> Dir: John H. Aver. Sp: Adele Buffington, Bradford Ropes. Prod: Republic
>   Picture Corp. Dist: Ivy Films.
> Cast: June Travis, Robert Livingston.
> Trapeze partners argue over a girl.

Miles Brewster and the Super Sex (in *Cosmopolitan Magazine,* July 1921)

> *The Super Sex*
> 60 min.   b&w   1922   sil.
> Dir. and Adap: Lambert Hillyer. Prod. Frank R. Adams.
> Cast: Robert Gordon, Charlotte Pierce.
> Comedy. Miles Brewster Higgins is jealous when a salesman captures the

attention of his sweetheart. He invests his money, becomes rich, and wins his girl
back.

Proxies (in *Cosmopolitan Magazine,* August 1920)

> *Proxies*
> 7 reels   b&w   1921   sil.
> Dir: George D. Baker. Prod: Cosmopolitan Pictures.
> Cast: Norman Kerry, Zena Keefe.
> Crook melodrama. A butler is recognized as a former convict by a visitor,

who tries to embroil him in a fraudulent stock scheme.

Skin Deep (in *Cosmopolitan Magazine*)

> *Almost a Lady*
> 5,702'   b&w   1926   sil.
> Dir: E. Mason Hopper. Prod: Metropolitan Pictures.
> Cast: Marie Prevost, Harrison Ford, George K. Arthur.
> Romantic comedy. A young lady is introduced at a party as a famous writer.

William, a young man who's also an imposter, falls in love with her. She's forced to
confess, but all ends happily.

ADAMS, SAMUEL HOPKINS

Night Bus

> *It Happened One Night*
> 105 min.   b&w   1934
> Dir: Frank Capra. Sp: Robert Riskin. Prod: Columbia Pictures. Dist: Budget
>   Films/Video, Modern Sound Pictures, Swank, RCA/Columbia Pictures
>   Home Video.
> Cast: Clark Gable, Claudette Colbert.
> An heiress forbidden by her millionaire father to marry a man she thinks she

loves manages to flee her father's yacht. While her father and a squad of detectives
are searching the nation for her, she joins forces with a wisecracking reporter in a
journey across the country.

You Can't Run Away from It
95 min.   color   1956
Dir: Dick Powell. Sp. Claude Binyon, Robert Riskin. Prod: Columbia
     Pictures
Cast: Jack Lemmon, June Allyson.
Musical comedy. A willful heiress escapes her father, who seeks to have her
marriage to a fortune hunter annulled. En route she falls for an unemployed
reporter.

The Perfect Specimen

The Perfect Specimen
10 reels   b&w   1937
Dir: Michael Curtis. Sp: Norman Reilly Raine, Lawrence Riley, Brewster
     Morse, Fritze Falkenstein. Prod: Warner Bros.
Cast: Edward Everett Horton.
A man raised to be the "perfect specimen" discovers the outside world.

ADDINGTON, SARAH

Bless Their Hearts

And So They Were Married
74 min.   b&w   1936
Dir: Elliott Nugent. Prod: Columbia Pictures. Dist: Hurlock Cine-World, Kit
     Parker Films.
Cast: Simone Simon, James Ellison.
Screwball comedy about a girl who gives out too many keys to her apartment
during wartime. Reissued in 1948 by Monogram.

ADE, GEORGE

Making the Grade (in *Hearst's International Cosmopolitan*)

Making the Grade
6 reels   b&w   1929   sil. (talking sequences, mus.)
Dir: Alfred E. Green. Prod: Fox Film. Dist: MGM/UA Home Video.
Cast: Edmund Lowe, Lois Moran, Lucien Littlefield.
Social comedy-drama. Wealthy Herbert Dodsworth tries hard to prove himself
as a man.

AGEE, JAMES

A Mother's Tale

A Mother's Tale
18 min.   color   1977
Dir: Rex Goff. Prod: Rex Goff. Dist: Simon & Schuster (16 mm and video).
Voices: Maureen Stapleton, Orson Welles.
A thought-provoking parable that uses animals as the protagonists in an ironic
commentary on human behavior. A mother cow tells her children the story of a
young bull who tried to warn the other cattle of the suffering they would endure at

the hands of man but met only skepticism. The young calves, like others before the them, refuse to accept the story and resolve to discover the truth for themselves.

AIKEN, CONRAD

Silent Snow, Secret Snow

> *Silent Snow, Secret Snow*
> 17 min.   color   1966
> Dir: Gene Kearney. Dist: Audio Brandon.
> A young boy withdraws more and more completely into his own private

world of fantasy.

ALBEE, GEORGE SUMNER

The Next Voice You Hear

> *The Next Voice You Hear*
> 83 min.   b&w   1950
> Dir: William Wellman. Prod: MGM. Dist: Films Inc.
> Cast: James Whitmore, Nancy Davis, Gary Gray.
> A mysterious voice (perhaps God's) heard on a radio broadcast causes strange

announcements all over the world.

ALEICHEM, SHOLOM

Mottele Peyse, the Cantor's Son

> *Laughter Through Tears*
> 82 min.   b&w   1933
> Dir: G. Gritcher. Dist: Audio Brandon.
> Cast: Michael Rosenberg, E. Kovenberg, S.J. Silberman.
> Filmed in America and the U.S.S.R., the film recreates the colorful life in

Kozedayevka, a poor Jewish village in old Russia.

Fiddler on the Roof

> *Fiddler on the Roof* (s.m. play by Joseph Stein, Sheldon Harnick, Jerry Bock,
>   and Jerome Robbins, in turn based on the story)
> 180 min.   color   1971
> Dir: Norman Jewison. Sp: Joseph Stein. Prod: Norman Jewison. Dist:
>   MGM/UA Home Video; CBS/Fox Video; RCA Video Discs (video).
> Cast: Topol, Norma Crane, Leonard Frey, Mollie Picon.
> Set in 1905 at the home of Tevye, a poor dairyman in a tiny Russian village.

Elsewhere in Russia the Czar's cavalry is attacking young street revolutionaries.

ALEXANDER, ELIZABETH·

Fifty-Two Weeks for Florette

> *You Belong to Me*
> 70 min.   b&w   1934
> Dir: Alfred M. Werker. Sp: Walter DeLone. Prod: Paramount.
> Cast: Lee Tracy, Helen Morgan.
> A six-year-old boy tries to protect his actress mother until she remarries

and he ends up being shipped off to school.

The Self-Made Wife (in *Saturday Evening Post,* 28 October-18 November 1922)

> *The Self-Made Wife*
> 5 reels   b&w   1923   sil.
> Dir: Jack Dillon. Prod: Universal.
> Cast: Ethel Grey Terry, Crawford Kent, Virginia Ainsworth.
> Melodrama. Lawyer Tim Godwin strikes it rich in oil and moves with his

family to the city, but his wife is unhappy there.

ALLEN, FRANCIS K.

Murder Stole My Missing Hours

> *Road to Alcatraz*
> 60 min.   b&w   1945
> Dir: Nick Grinde. Prod: Republic Pictures. Dist: Ivy Films.
> Cast: Robert Lowery, Grant Withers.
> A young attorney is haunted by the fear that he murdered his partner while

sleepwalking.

ALLEN, JANE

A Girl's Best Friend Is Wall Street

> *She Knew All the Answers*
> 9 reels   b&w   1941
> Dir: Richard Wallace. Sp: Harry Segall, Kenneth Earl, Curtis Kenyon. Prod:
>   Columbia Pictures.

AMEN, CAROL

The Last Testament

> *Testament*
> 90 min.   color   1983
> Dir: Lynne Littman. Rel: Paramount. Dist: Paramount Home Video (video).
> Cast: Jane Alexander, William Devane.
> The day begins in a humdrum fashion but ends in incredible disaster—nuclear

war.

ANDERSEN, HANS CHRISTIAN

The Shadow

> *The Shadow*
> 27 min.   color   1976
> Dir: Don Ham. Prod and Dist: LSB Productions.
> A live-action dramatization in which a philosopher fantasizes that his shadow

can slip inside rooms and discover the secrets within. His shadow does indeed enter
the rooms, and years later returns to attempt to become the man's master.

ANDERSON, FREDERICK IRVING

Sophie Lang (s.m. several stories)

> *The Return of Sophie Lang*
> 7 reels   b&w   1936
> Dir: George Archainbaud. Sp: Brian Marlowe, Patterson McNott. Prod: Paramount.
> Cast: Gertrude Michael, Sir Guy Standing.

Sophie, a charming former thief, is mixed up with the theft of a world-famous diamond.

> *Sophie Lang Goes West*
> 6 reels   b&w   1937
> Dir: Charles Riesner. Sp: Doris Anderson, Brian Marlowe, Robert Wyler. Prod: Paramount.

ANDERSON, SHERWOOD

I'm a Fool

> *I'm a Fool*
> 38 min.   color   1977
> Dir: Noel Black. Sp: Ron Cowen. Dist: Coronet (video).
> Cast: Ron Howard.

His job, relationship with his co-workers, and desire to impress those around him motivate Andy, a "swipe" doing manual labor on the Ohio racetrack circuit in the early 1900s. When Andy meets a beautiful young woman at the track, he tries to impress her by exaggerating his position in life.

ARLEN, MICHAEL

The Ace of Cads (in *Everybody's Magazine,* June 1924)

> *The Ace of Cads*
> 8 reels   b&w   1926   sil.
> Dir: Luther Reed. Prod: Famous Players-Lasky.
> Cast: Adelphe Menjou, Alice Joyce, Norman Trevor.

Chappel Maturin and Basil De Gramercy are officers in the Guards who are both in love with Eleanor. Basil betrays his friend, and Maturin begins drinking. Twenty years later, Basil, who married Eleanor, is killed in the trenches, and Maturin falls in love with Eleanor and Basil's daughter.

The Dancer of Paris

> *The Dancer of Paris*
> 7 reels   b&w   1926   sil.
> Dir: Alfred Santell. Prod: First National Pictures.
> Cast: Conway Tearle, Dorothy Mackaill.

Drama. Consuelo Cox falls in love with Sir Roy Martel, a wealthy Englishman and accepts his proposal, but she discovers his love is the basest kind and goes to Paris.

The Gay Falcon

The Gay Falcon (a.k.a. *A Date With the Falcon*)
66 min.　　　b&w　　　1941
Dir: Irving Reis. Prod: RKO. Dist: Films Inc.
Cast: George Sanders.
The Falcon, a debonair troubleshooter, reportedly appeared in 16 mystery movies during the 1940s. Here he hunts down gem thieves.

A Gentleman From America

The Fatal Night (Br.)
50 min.　　　color　　　1948
Dir: Mario Zampi. Sp: Gerald Butler. Prod: Anglofilm.
Cast: Lester Ferguson, Jean Short.
Story of a haunted house.

ARMSTRONG, CHARLOTTE

The Enemy

Talk About a Stranger (a.k.a. *The Enemy*)
65 min.　　　b&w　　　1952
Dir: David Bradley. Prod: MGM. Dist: Films Inc.
Cast: Nancy Davis, Billy Gray.
A drama about a family's mysterious neighbors.

ARTHUR, ROBERT

The Haunted Trailer

The Haunted Trailer
24 min.　　　color　　　1978.
Dist: MTI Teleprograms (video).
A tale about a quartet of ghosts who play chamber music at night. An ABC Weekend Special.

ASHWORTH, JOHN

High Diver (s.m. also "The Gossamer World" by Faith Baldwin and "Horsie" by Dorothy Parker)

Horsie (a.k.a. *Queen for a Day*)
107 min.　　　b&w　　　1951
Sp: Seton Miller. Prod: United Artists. Dist: Ivy Films.
Stories of the contestants on a radio show.

ASIMOV, ISAAC

The Ugly Little Boy

The Ugly Little Boy
26 min.　　　color　　　1978

Dir: Barry Morse, Don Thompson. Dist: Simon & Schuster (16 mm and
   video).
Cast: Kate Reid, Barry Morse.
   A story of science versus morality in which a group of scientists bring a
Neanderthal child through time to their world, 40,000 years in the future. The
scientists begin experimenting with the child, and in spite of herself, the dis-
passionate nurse caring for the child sympathizes with his plight and tries to sur-
mount the communication barriers. Then the scientists decide to send the child
back, and the nurse is faced with a difficult decision.

AUSTIN, FREDERICK BRITTEN

Buried Treasure

Buried Treasure
7 reels   b&w   1921   sil.
Dir: George G. Baker. Prod: Cosmopolitan Pictures.
Cast: Marion Davies, Norman Kerry.
A man in a trance recalls previous incarnations.

AVERY, STEPHEN MOREHOUSE

Head Over Heels

Hard to Get (s.m. the screenplay by Wally Klein and Joseph Shrank was based
   on this short story)
80 min.   b&w   1938
Dir: Ray Enright. Prod: Warner Bros. Dist: MGM/UA Home Video (video).
Cast: Dick Powell, Olivia de Havilland.
A musical about the taming of a wild heiress.

AYERS, JOHN H.

Missing Men (jt. author Carol Bird)

Bureau of Missing Persons
73 min.   b&w   1933
Dir: Roy Del Ruth. Prod: First National Pictures. Dist: MGM/UA Home
   Video (video).
Cast: Bette Davis, Pat O'Brien, Louis Stone.
A murderess is trapped into attending a "mock-up" of her own funeral.

AYME, MARCEL

Walker Through Walls

Mr. Peek-a-Boo
74 min.   b&w   1951
Dir: Jean Boyer. Sp: Michel Audiard and Jean Boyer. Prod: Arthur Sachson
   Enterprises.
   Government official discovers he can walk through walls. He catches a burglar
and reforms a girl.

ß

BAER, ARTHUR (BUGS)

Rufftown Stories

> *Battle Royal*
> 2 reels   b&w   1932
> Dir: Harry Sweet. Sp: Ralph Ceder. Prod: RKO.

BAINES, JOHN V.   (see *Dead of Night* under BENSON, E.F.)

BAKER, MELVILLE

Hundred Million Dollars (jt. author John S. Kirkland)

> *Mills of the Gods*
> 7 reels   b&w   1934
> Dir: Roy William Neill. Sp: Garrett Ford. Prod: Columbia Pictures.

BALDWIN, FAITH

Apartment for Jenny

> *Apartment for Peggy*
> 99 min.   b&w   1948
> Dir: George Seaton. Sp: George Seaton. Prod: Twentieth Century Fox.
>   Dist: Films Inc.
> Cast: Jeanne Crain, William Holden.
> Amusing comedy of young marrieds on a campus after World War II.

August Weekend

> *August Weekend*
> 7 reels   b&w   1936
> Dir: Charles Lamont. Sp: Paul Pere. Prod: Chesterfield Motion Pictures.
> Cast: Valerie Hobson, G.J. Huntley, Jr.
> A man's relentless struggle for power and social position.

Comet Over Broadway (in *Cosmopolitan Magazine*)

> *Comet Over Broadway* (former title was *Curtain Call*)
> 72 min.   b&w   1938
> Dir: Busby Berkeley. Prod: First National Pictures. Dist: MGM/UA Home
>   Video (video).
> Cast: Kay Francis, Ian Hunter.

A self-abnegating actress gives up the theater and returns to her husband and child.

The Gossamer World (see *Horsie* under ASHWORTH, JOHN)

Wife Versus Secretary

> *Wife Versus Secretary*
> 85 min.   b&w   1936
> Dir: Clarence Brown. Sp: Norman Krasna, Alice Duer Miller, John Lee
>   Mahlin. Dist: Films Inc.
> Cast: Jean Harlow, Clark Gable, Gay Robson.
> A man's mother ignites his wife's jealousy.

BALLARD, TODHUNTER

Red Horizon (in *Esquire*)

> *The Outcast* (s.m. also the novel, *Two-Edged Vengeance* [Macmillan, 1951])
> 90 min.   color   1953
> Dir: William Witney. Sp: John K. Butler, Richard Wormser. Prod: Republic
>   Pictures. Dist: Ivy Films.
> Cast: John Derek, Joan Evans.
> Western. A young man hires nine gunmen to try to regain his ranch, which
> was stolen by an unscrupulous uncle.

BALZAC, HONORE DE

La Grande Breteche

> *La Grande Breteche*
> 24 min.   color   1976
> Prod: Twentieth Century Fox. Dist: Encyclopaedia Britannica (16 mm and
>   3/4", Beta and VHS video).
> Orson Welles introduces this tale of revenge, set in France during the
> Napoleonic wars. It begins as a love story involving a French countess, a Spanish
> prisoner of war, and a jealous husband. On a visit to his wife's bedroom, the count
> tricks her into swearing the closet is empty, when he knows otherwise. Pretending
> to believe her, he calmly proceeds to have the closet sealed up behind an impene-
> trable brick wall while his wife looks on in horror.

The Maid of Thilouse

> *The Maid of Thilouse*
> 15 min.   b&w   1955
> Prod: Dynamic Films. Dist: Audio Brandon.
> Cast: Monty Woolley.
> An elderly Baron seeks the hand of a young peasant girl, and when she
> rejects him, he decides to court her mother.

La Peau de Chagrin

> *The Dream Cheater*
> b&w   1920
> Dir: Ernest C. Warde. Prod: Hodkinson.
> Cast: J. Warren Kerrigan.

> *La Peau de Chagrin*
> 10 min.   color   1971
> Dir: Vlado Kristl, Ivo Urbanic. Dist: International Film Bureau.
> A sardonic animated tale in which a gambler makes a pact with a croupier (the devil) for a magic skin that can fulfill his every wish. With every wish granted, the skin grows smaller. Finally the hero dies with a cry of panic on his lips, and the skin, now a mere scrap of leather, is blown away by the wind.

> *Slave of Desire*
> 7 reels   b&w   1923   sil.
> Dir: George D. Baker. Adap: Alice D.G. Miller. Prod: Goldwyn.
> Cast: George Walsh, Bessie Love.
> Allegorical drama. Poet Raphael Valentin meets the vampish Countess Fedora, who makes him successful overnight and then leaves him. An antiquarian gives him a magical piece of leather that grants his every wish.

BANNING, MARGARET CULKEN

Enemy Territory

> *Woman Against Woman*
> 6 reels   b&w   1938
> Dir: Robert Sinclair. Sp: Edward Chodorov. Prod: MGM.
> Cast: Mary Astor, Virginia Bruce, Herbert Marshall.
> First wife pitted against second wife.

BARNETT, S.H.

A Place of Dragons

> *Father Goose*
> 115 min.   color   1964
> Dir: Ralph Nelson. Sp: Peter Stone, Frank Tarloff, Prod: Universal. Dist:
>   Ivy Films, NTA Home Entertainment (video).
> Comedy. A WWII tale of a beach bum who watches a strategic South Seas isle where a French woman and seven girls are stranded.

BARRY, JEROME

Ice Storm

> *Ice Storm*
> 25 min.   color   1976
> Prod: Twentieth Century Fox. Dist: Encyclopaedia Britannica (16 mm,
>   3/4", Beta and VHS video).

Orson Welles narrates this tale, in which a librarian turned detective must pit her wits against a ruthless killer whose identity is unknown. As the assistant to the owner of a priceless book collection, the heroine finds herself alone in her employer's mansion during a violent storm, during which three visitors come to buy rare books. One of the visitors is an imposter who is willing to kill her to get a share of the collection.

BARTEAU, MORTON (jt. author) (see *Six Hours to Live* under MORRIS, GORDON)

BEACH, REX
Big Brother

Big Brother
7 reels   b&w   1923   sil.
Dir: Alan Dwan. Prod: Paramount.
Cast: Tom Moore, Edith Roberts, Raymond Hatton.
Crook melodrama. Gangster Jimmy Donovan is made guardian of 7-year-old Midge and decides to reform.

The Crimson Gardenia

The Crimson Gardenia
6 reels   b&w   1925   sil.
Dir: Reginald Barker. Prod: Metro-Goldwyn.

The Goose Woman

The Goose Woman
8 reels   b&w   1925   sil.
Dir: Clarence Brown. Prod: Universal. Dist: Cinema Concepts/Cinema Eight (8 mm).
Cast: Louise Dresser, Jack Pickford, Constance Bennett.
The tragic experiences of a proud opera star who falls into disgrace because of drinking.

The Past of Mary Holmes
4 reels   b&w   1933
Dir: Harlan Thompson. Sp: Marion Dix, Edward Doherty. Prod: RKO.

The Michigan Kid

The Michigan Kid
6 reels   b&w   1928   sil.
Dir: Irwin Willat. Prod: Universal Jewel.
Cast: Rene Adoree.

The Michigan Kid
70 min.   color   1947
Dir: Ray Taylor. Sp: Roy Chanslor. Prod: Universal.
Cast: Jon Hall, Victor McLaglen.

Western. A number of characters try to find the loot stolen from a stage-coach. Plot is far removed from the original story.

Quicksand

Guilty Conscience
b&w   1932
Prod: World Wide Pictures.

The Recoil

The Recoil
7 reels   b&w   1924   sil.
Dir: T. Hayes Hunter. Prod: Goldwyn.
Cast: Mahlon Hunter, Betty Blythe.
Romantic Melodrama. Gordon Kent's wife runs away with an admirer, and he and a detective pursue them.

Rope's End (in *Cosmopolitan Magazine,* May 1913)

A Sainted Devil
9 reels   b&w   1924   sil.
Dir: Joseph Henabery. Adap: Forest Halsey. Prod: Famous Players-Lasky.
Melodrama. On her wedding day, Julietta is kidnapped.

BEAHAN, CHARLES (see also *Murder by the Clock* under KING, RUFUS)

Rose of the Ritz (jt. author Garrett Ford)

Naughty Baby
7 reels   b&w   1929   sd. effects and mus.
Dir: Mervyn LeRoy. Prod: First National Pictures.
Cast: Alice White, Jack Mulhall.
Rosie McGill, a hat checker at a posh hotel, sets her cap for wealthy Terry Vandeveer and goes to Long Beach, where she poses as a society girl.

BEAUCHAMP, D.D.

A-Hunting We Will Go

Father's Wild Game
60 min.   b&w   1950
Prod: Monogram Pictures.
A father protesting the inflated prices at a meat market hunts wild game.

The Cruise of the Prairie Queen

Leave It to Henry
57 min.   b&w   1949
Dir: Jean Yarbrough. Prod: Monogram.
Cast: Raymond Walburn, Walter Catlett.
Comedy. A lawyer is accused of setting fire to a bridge.

Enough for Happiness

She Couldn't Say No
89 min.   b&w   1954
Dir: Lloyd Bacon. Sp: D.D. Beauchamp, William Bowers, Richard Flournoy.
    Prod: RKO. Dist: Films Inc., Blackhawk (video).
Cast: Robert Mitchum, Jean Simmons.
Comedy. A young oil heiress anonymously distributes gifts and money to
the inhabitants of a small Arkansas town.

Journey at Sunrise

Father Makes Good
61 min.   b&w   1950
Prod: Monogram Pictures.
Father purchases a cow to show his contempt for the new milk tax.

The Wonderful Race with Rimrock (in *Collier's Magazine,* 8 March 1946)

Feudin', Fussin', and a-Fightin'
78 min.   b&w   1948
Dir: George Sherman. Sp: D.D. Beauchamp. Prod: Universal.
Cast: Donald O'Connor, Marjorie Main.
Comedy. A fast-running salesman is captured by a whole town, which plans
to race him in the annual footrace with a rival community.

BEAUMONT, GERALD

Betty's a Lady (in *Redbook*)

The Count of Ten
6 reels   b&w   1928   sil.
Dir: James Flood. Prod: Universal.
Cast: Charles Ray, James Gleason, Jobyna Ralston.
An ambitious prizefighter falls in love with a salesgirl named Betty and
marries her. Ordered not to fight when he hurts his hand, he does so when his wife
tells him she's pregnant.

The Blue Ribbon (s.m. "The Dove," a play by Willard Mack based on the story)

The Girl and the Gambler
7 reels   b&w   1939
Dir: Lew Landers. Sp: Joseph A. Fields, Clarence Upson Young. Prod: RKO.
A Latin American caballero bets he can woo and win a maiden's heart within
24 hours.

Dixie (in *Redbook,* September 1924)

The Dixie Handicap
7 reels   b&w   1925   sil.
Dir: Reginald Barker. Adap: Waldemar Young. Prod: Metro-Goldwyn.
Cast: Claire Windsor, Frank Keenan.

Judge Roberts hides his true financial situation from his daughter. After major major financial reverses, he is left with only a horse, which dies soon after foaling. However, the foal turns out to be a champion.

Even Stephen (in *Redbook*, October 1925)

> *Just Another Blonde*
> 6 reels   b&w   1926   sil.
> Dir: Alfred Santill. Prod: Rockett Prod.
> Cast: Dorothy Mackaill, Jack Mulhall.
> Jimmy O'Connor and his pal Scotty share everything until Scotty falls in love with Diana.

The Flower of Napoli (in *Redbook*, March 1924)

> *The Man in Blue*
> 6 reels   b&w   1925   sil.
> Dir: Edward Laemmle. Prod: Universal.
> Cast: Herbert Rawlinson, Madge Bellamy, Nick DeRuiz.
> Tom Conlin falls in love with Tita. She loves him but believes he is already married. Later, when Tom rescues her from a man who kidnaps her, she discovers he is single.

Heavenbent (in *Redbook*)

> *The Rainmaker*
> 6,055'   b&w   1926   sil.
> Dir: Clarence Badger.
> Cast: William Collier, Jr., Georgia Hale.
> War wounds tell a jockey when rain is coming.

Jack O'Clubs (in *Redbook*, December 1923)

> *Jack O'Clubs*
> 5 reels   b&w   1924   sil.
> Dir: Robert F. Hill (uncredited). Adapt: Raymond L. Schrock. Prod: Universal.
> Cast: Herbert Rawlinson, Ruth Dwyer, Eddie Gribbon.
> Jack Foley, a tough cop, loses his nerve when he thinks he's hurt Tillie Miller, the girl he loves.

John McArdle, Referee (in *Redbook,* July 1921)

> *The Referee*
> 5 reels   b&w   1922   sil.
> Dir: Ralph Ince. Prod: Selznick Pictures.
> Cast: Conway Tearle, Anders Randolf.
> An ex-boxer falls in love, but the girl's father objects.

The Lady Who Played Fidele (in *Redbook,* February 1925)

> *Scarlet Saint*
> 7 reels   b&w   1925   sil.
> Dir: George Archainbaud. Prod: First National Pictures.
> Cast: Mary Astor, Lloyd Hughes.
> Fidele, who is betrothed to Baron Badrew, loves Phillip, who is wounded
by the Baron in a duel and sent to jail.

The Lord's Referee (in *Redbook,* July 1923)

> *The Blue Eagle*
> 7 reels   b&w   1926   sil.
> Dir: John Ford. Prod: Fox.
> Cast: George O'Brien, Janet Gaynor, William Russell.
> Rival leaders of neighborhood gangs become stokers and watertenders on a
U.S. battleship during WWI.

> *The Silk Hat Kid*
> 6,250'   b&w   1935
> Dir: H. Bruce Humberstone. Sp: Edward Eliscu, Lou Breslow, Dore Schary.
>   Prod: Fox.

The Making of O'Malley (in *Redbook,* October 1924)

> *The Making of O'Malley*
> 8 reels   b&w   1925   sil.
> Dir: Lambert Hillyer. Prod: First National Pictures.
> Cast: Milton Sills, Dorothy Mackerill.
> A tough police officer, assigned duty as a traffic cop, discovers the hideout
of a gang of bootleggers but doesn't arrest the leader when he learns that his friend
Lucille is engaged to him.

> *The Great O'Malley*
> 71 min.   b&w   1937
> Dir: William Dieterle. Prod: Warner Bros. and Vitaphone. Dist: MGM/UA
>   Home Video (video).
> Cast: Pat O'Brien, Ann Sheridan.
> A remake of *The Making of O'Malley.* A police officer who lives by the rule-
book learns a tough lesson.

The Money Rider (in *Redbook,* September 1924)

> *Down the Stretch*
> 7 reels   b&w   1927   sil.
> Dir: King Baggot. Adap: Curtis Benton. Prod: Universal.
> Cast: Robert Agnew, Marian Nixon.
> Jockey Marty Krugger falls in love with Katie while he is laid up by an
accident. When he returns to the track, he's overweight, and the strict diet he is
put on endangers his health.

The Rose of Kildare (in *Redbook,* December 1922)

    The Rose of Kildare
    7 reels   b&w   1927   sil.
    Dir: Dallas M. Fitzgerald. Adap: Harold Shumate.
    Cast: Helene Chadwick, Pat O'Malley.
    The owner of a dance hall in South Africa loves singer Eileen, but she dreams
of her former fiance, who later turns up married.

Said with Soap (in *Redbook,* April 1925)

    Babe Comes Home
    6 reels   b&w   1927   sil.
    Dir: Ted Wilde. Prod: First National Pictures.
    The up and down courtship of Babe Dugan, a baseball player whose uniform
is always dirty, and his laundress.

Thoroughbreds

    Silks and Saddles (originally released as *Thoroughbreds*)
    6 reels   b&w   1929   sil.
    Dir: Robert F. Hill. Prod: Universal Jewel. Dist: Mogull's Films.
    Jockey Johnny Spencer loses his job for throwing a race.

Two Bells for Pegasus (in *Redbook,* February 1922)

    The Victor
    5 reels   b&w   1923   sil.
    Cast: Herbert Rawlinson, Dorothy Manners.
    Dir: Edward Laemmle. Prod: Universal.
    The Honorable Waring comes to America to marry a rich girl to save the
family estate, but he falls in love with Teddy, a poor actress.

United States Smith

    Pride of the Marines
    64 min.   b&w   1936
    Prod: Columbia Pictures.
    Cast: Charles Bickford, Florence Rice.
    A Marine adopts an orphan.

BECHDOLT, JACK

Fogbound (in *Argosy,* 22 December 1921)

    Fogbound
    6 reels   b&w   1923   sil.
    Dir: Irwin Willat. Prod: Famous Players-Lasky.
    Cast: Dorothy Dalton, David Powell.
    Roger is suspected of killing his friend Gale.

BEDFORD-JONES, HENRY

Garden of the Moon (jt. author Barton Browne; in *Saturday Evening Post*)

> *Garden of the Moon*
> 94 min.   b&w   1938
> Dir: Busby Berkeley. Prod: Warner Bros. Dist: MGM/UA Home Video
>   (video).
> Cast: Pat O'Brien, John Payne, Jimmy Fidler, Jerry Colonna.
> Story of a cranky, objectionable nightclub owner.

BEHN, MARCH (jt. author) (see *Charade* under STONE, PETER)

BELLAH, JAMES WARNER

The Big Hunt (see *She Wore a Yellow Ribbon* under **War Party**)

Command (in *Saturday Evening Post*, 8 June 1946)

> *A Thunder of Drums*
> 97 min.   color   1961
> Dir: Joseph Newman. Sp: James Warner Bellah. Prod: MGM. Dist: Films Inc.
> Cast: Richard Boone, George Hamilton.
> Western. U.S. Cavalry officers fighting Apaches when not fighting each other.

Massacre

> *Fort Apache*
> 127 min.   b&w   1948
> Dir: John Ford. Prod: Argosy. Dist: Blackhawk (video).
> Cast: John Wayne, Henry Fonda.
> Western. A West Point officer's rigid adherence to Eastern military traditions
and his failure to adjust to the particular demands of an isolated Western fort
result in the massacre of his troop.

Mission with No Record

> *Rio Grande*
> 105 min.   b&w   1950
> Dir: John Ford. Prod: Republic. Dist: Blackhawk (video).
> Cast: John Wayne, Maureen O'Hara.
> Western. A tough cavalry officer awaits orders to cross the river to engage
in battle with the Indians.

War Party (in *Saturday Evening Post*, 19 June 1948; s.m. also "The Big Hunt" in
        Saturday Evening Post, 6 December 1947)

> *She Wore a Yellow Ribbon*
> 103 min.   color   1949
> Dir: John Ford. Prod: Argosy. Dist: Images, Nostalgia Merchant (video),
>   VidAmerica, King of Video.
> Cast: John Wayne, Joanne Dru.

Western. The Captain of the Cavalry and his sergeant are near retirement age, and the rules of the Cavalry are scrutinized and tested by the next generation.

BELLEM, ROBERT LESLIE
Stock Shot

Blackmail
71 min.   b&w   1947
Dir: Lesley Selander. Sp: Royal K. Cole. Prod: Republic. Dist: Ivy Films.
A detective is called in to protect a rich playboy from blackmail.

BEMELMANS, LUDWIG (jt. author) (see *Yolanda and the Thief* under THERY, JACQUES)

BENET, STEPHEN VINCENT
The Devil and Daniel Webster

The Devil and Daniel Webster (reissued and retitled *All That Money Can Buy*)
109 min.   b&w   1952   1941
Dir: William Dieterle. Prod: Astor Films. Dist: Alba House, Janus Films.
Cast: James Craig, Simone Simon, Walter Huston.

Everybody Was Very Nice (in *Saturday Evening Post,* 5 September 1936)

Love, Honor and Behave
7 reels   b&w   1938
Dir: Stanley Logan. Sp: Clements Ripley, Michel Jacoby, Robert Buckner, Lawrence Kimble. Prod: Warner Bros.
A young man grows up, still under his dominating mother's influence, but a young girl helps him straighten out.

Famous

Just for You
104 min.   color   1952
Dir: Elliott Nugent. Prod: Paramount. Dist: Films Inc.
Cast: Bing Crosby, Jane Wyman.
Comedy-Drama. A producer sets out to win the affection of his children after years of concentrating on his career.

The Sobbin Women

Seven Brides for Seven Brothers
102 min.   color   1954
Dir: Stanley Done. Prod: MGM. Dist: Films Inc., MGM/UA Home Video (video).
Cast: Jane Powell, Howard Keel.
When the eldest of seven brothers in the Oregon Territory brings a wife home to take care of the family and farm, the other six brothers want wives of their own, and they sneak into town and steal six girls they had met at a barn raising.

Uriah's Son

The Necessary Evil
7 reels   b&w   1925   sil.
Dir: George Archainbaud. Prod: First National Pictures.
On her deathbed, Frances Jerome secures David Devannt's promise to raise her son Frank, who grows into a wild young man. Frank is wrongly accused of stealing, but David pretends to believe he is guilty in order to send him to the tropics.

BENSON, EDWARD F.

The Bus Conductor (see *Dead of Night* under The Room in the Tower)

Mrs. Amworth

Mrs. Amworth
29 min.   color   1977
Dir: Alvin Rakoff. Sp: Hugh Whitemore. Dist: Simon & Schuster (16 mm and video).
Cast: Glynis Johns.
Doctors ascribe the mysterious epidemic attacking the quiet village of Maxley to the bite of venomous gnats. But they are puzzled by the disease, which seems to drain the body of blood. Then Mrs. Amworth is accused of being a vampire by Francis Urcombe, a former physiology professor.

The Room in the Tower (s.m. also "The Bus Conductor")

Dead of Night
104 min.   b&w   1945
Dir: Alberto Cavilcanti, Charles Crichton, Basil Dearden, Robert Hamer. Prod: Ealing Studios. Dist: Budget Films/Video, Em Gee Film Library, Trans-World (video), Thorn EMI.
Cast: Sir Michael Redgrave, Mervyn Johns, Roland Culver.
A horror film that consists of five sequences, including The Hearse Driver sequence by Benson; The Christmas Party sequence by Angus MacPhail; The Haunted Mirror sequence by John V. Baines; The Ventriloquist's Dummy sequence by John V. Baines; and The Golfing Story by H.G. Wells. An architect is invited to spend a weekend at the country house of a client in order to survey the house. He finds a small party in progress and realizes the guests have appeared in his recurring nightmare.

BENTHAM, JOSEPHINE

A Bride for Henry

A Bride for Henry
7 reels   b&w   1937
Dir: William Nigh. Adap: Marion Orth. Prod: Monogram.
Cast: Warren Hull, Anne Nagel.
When the groom fails to show up at the wedding, the bride marries the best man.

BERCOVICI, KONRAD

The Bear Tamer's Daughter

Revenge
7 reels   b&w   1928   mus. score and sd. effects
Dir: Edwin Carewe. Prod: Edwin Carewe Prod.
Cast: Delores Del Rio, James Marcus.
Rascha, the wild daughter of Costa, the Gypsy bear tamer, swears revenge on her father's enemy.

BIALK, ELISA

The Sainted Sisters of Sandy Creek (s.m. also an unpublished play of the same title by Elisa Bialk and Alden Nash)

The Sainted Sisters
90 min.   b&w   1948
Dir: William Russell. Prod: Paramount.
Cast: Veronica Lake, Joan Caulfield, Barry Fitzgerald.
Two con girls are reformed.

BIERCE, AMBROSE

Boarded Window

Boarded Window
17 min.   color   1973
Dir: Alan W. Beattie. Dist: Coronet Films (16 mm and video).
A cabin shared by a hunter and his wife has only one window. When she was alive, flowers grew in a windowbox; once she dies, nature takes over for a macabre ending.

The Boarded Window
15 min.   color   1978
Prod: International Instructional Television Coop. Dist: Indiana University (16 mm and video).

Chickamauga

Chickamauga
33 min.   b&w   1961
Dir: Robert Enrico. Sp: Robert Enrico. Dist: Wholesome Film Center.
A symbolic world of the horrors of war, as a little boy wanders away from home, reaches a battlefield, plays soldier among the dead and dying, and returns home to find his house burned and his family slain.

The Man and the Snake

The Man and the Snake
Dir: Sture Rydman. Dist: Pyramid Films (16 mm and video).
Loosely based on the above, this is the story of the unsettling struggle between the common sense of the day and the eerie effects of the night.

Middle Toe of the Right Foot

The Return (s.m. also a story entitled *Nobody's House* by A.M. Burrage)
30 min.   color   1976
Dir: Elizabeth McKay. Dist: Pyramid Films.
There are rumors a ghost inhabits a boarded-up mansion in Edwardian England.

The Mockingbird

The Mockingbird
39 min.   b&w   1966
Dir: Robert Enrico. Dist: Audio Brandon.
A private in the Union Army, standing night guard, sees an indistinct figure, panics, and fires. The next day, troubled by the experience, he goes in search of the victim and finds the body of his twin brother in a Confederate uniform.

An Occurence at Owl Creek Bridge

An Occurence at Owl Creek Bridge
Dir: Robert Enrico. Prod: Janus Films. Dist: Brigham Young University
    (16 mm rental); Hollywood Home Theater (video; coupled with *The
    Red Balloon*).
Cast: Roger Jacquet, Anne Cornaly, Anker Larsen.
Set during the Civil War, a spy is condemned to die by hanging. But at the last minute he may be saved by a near-miracle. Or is he?

The Spy
b&w   1932
Dir: Charles Vidor.
Cast: Nicholas Bela.
The instant before his death by hanging a spy imagines an elaborate escape.

One of the Missing

One of the Missing
56 min.   color   1971
Dist: Audio Brandon.
Cast: Talmadge Armstrong, Gordon Baxter.
A spellbinding tale of a Civil War sharpshooter, who is pinned down after an explosion with his own cocked rifle pointed at his face. Knowing that the slightest move will set the gun off, the man cautiously tries to free himself and reflects on the past.

One of the Missing
52 min.   color   1977
Dist: Educational Communications.
A chilling tale, set during the Civil War, of a bounty hunter caught in a cabin as the roof collapses.

Parker Adderson, Philosopher

Parker Adderson, Philosopher
20 min.   color   1970
Prod: Ching Kuai.
A Federal spy is questioned by a Confederate general.

Parker Adderson, Philosopher
38 min.   color   1977
Dir: Arthur Barron. Dist: Coronet Films (16 mm and video).
Captured behind enemy lines at the end of the Civil War, Parker Adderson confronts a weary Confederate general, and a vicious battle ensues in the general's tent.

BIGGERS, EARL DERR

Behind That Curtain (in *Saturday Evening Post,* 31 March and 5 May 1928)

Behind That Curtain
10 reels   b&w   1929
Dir: Irving Cummings. Prod: Fox.
Mystery melodrama. Eve Mannering, the daughter of a wealthy Englishman, marries a fortune hunter, who kills the investigator hired by her father.

Broadway Broke (in *Saturday Evening Post,* 7 October 1922)

Broadway Broke
6 reels   b&w   1923   sil.
Dir: J. Searle Dawley.   Prod: Murray W. Garrson.
Cast: Mary Carr, Percy Marmont.
Nellie Wayne, a retired theatrical star, saves her family from bankruptcy when she sells her plays.

The Deuce of Hearts

Take the Stand
9 reels   b&w   1934
Dir: Phil Rosen. Prod: Liberty.

The Girl Who Paid Dividends (in *Saturday Evening Post*, 23 April 1921)

Her Face Value
50 min.   b&w   1921   sil.
Dir: Thomas N. Neffron. Prod: Realart Pictures.
Cast: Wanda Hawley, Lincoln Plummer.
Chorus girl Peggy Malone, who supports her father and brother, marries press agent Jimmy Parsons. But his health is jeopardized, and she must go back to work. She becomes a star and must choose between her husband and a wealthy admirer.

Honeymoon Flats (in *Saturday Evening Post*, 2 July 1927)

> *Honeymoon Flats*
> 60 min.   b&w   1928   sil.
> Dir: Millard Webb. Prod: Universal.
> Cast: George Lewis, Dorothy Gulliver, Kathlyn Williams.
> Comedy-Drama. Lila Garland marries Jim Clayton against her parents wishes,

and her mother's interference almost causes a divorce.

Idle Hands

> *The Millionaire*
> 80 min.   b&w   1931
> Dir: John Adolfi. Prod: Warner Bros.
> Cast: George Arliss, James Cagney.
> A millionaire takes a job incognito and helps to straighten out several people's

affairs.

> *That Way with Women*
> 84 min.   b&w   1947
> Dir: Frederick de Cordova. Prod: Warner Bros. Dist: MGM/UA Home Video
>   (video).
> Cast: Dane Clark, Sydney Greenstreet.
> Comedy about an irascible, benign old man.

John Henry and the Restless Sex (in *Saturday Evening Post*, 5 March 1921)

> *Too Much Business*
> Dir: Jess Robbins. Prod: Vitagraph.
> Cast: Tully Marshall, Edward Everett Horton.
> The romance of a sales manager and his secretary and the consolidation of

their company with a rival company.

The Ruling Passion (in *Saturday Evening Post*, 1922)

> *The Ruling Passion*
> 7,000'   b&w   1922   sil.
> Dir: Harmon Weight. Prod: Distinctive Prod.
> Cast: George Arliss, Doris Kenyon.
> James Alden—machinist, designer, inventor, and millionaire—is told by his

daughter to retire. However, he can't remain idle, so he goes into partnership with
a young man in a garage.

Trouping With Ellen (in *Saturday Evening Post*, 8 April 1922)

> *Trouping With Ellen*
> 7 reels   b&w   1924   sil.
> Dir: T. Hayes Hunter. Prod: Eastern Prod.
> Cast: Helene Chadwick, Gary Thurman, Gaston Glass, Basil Rathbone.
> Romantic Comedy. Ellen, a chorus girl, is asked frequently by the orchestra

leader to marry him, but she refuses.

BIRD, CAROL (jt. author) (see **Missing Men** under AYERS, JOHN H.)

BLISH, JAMES

There Shall Be No Darkness

> *The Beast Must Die!*
> 93 min.   color   1975
> Dir: Paul Annett. Sp: Michael Winder. Dist: Swank (video), Nostalgia
>   Merchant.
> Cast: Peter Cushing, Calvin Lockhart, Charles Gray, Marlene Clark, Anton
>   Differing.

A millionaire sportsman invites an odd assortment of guests to his isolated
lodge, knowing that one of them is a werewolf.

BLOCH, ROBERT

The Cloak (see *The House That Dripped Blood* under **Method for Murder**)

Enoch (s.m. also "Terror Over Hollywood," "Mr. Steinway," and "The Man Who
    Collected Poe")

> *Torture Garden*
> 93 min.   color   1967
> Dir: Freddie Francis. Prod: Columbia Pictures. Dist: Modern Sound Pictures.
> Cast: Jack Palance, Peter Cushing, Burgess Meredith.

Horror thriller. A unique sideshow is presided over by a sinister-looking man
who calls himself Dr. Diablo.

Frozen Fear (see *Asylum* under **The Weird Taylor**)

Lucy Comes to Stay (see *Asylum* under **The Weird Taylor**)

The Man Who Collected Poe (see *Torture Garden* under **Enoch**)

Mannikins of Horror (see also *Asylum* under **The Weird Taylor**)

> *The Mannikin*
> 28 min.   color   1977
> Dir: Don Thompson. Dist: Simon & Schuster (16 mm and video).
> Cast: Ronnee Blakely, Keir Dullea.

A beautiful New York singer finds little relief from recurring back pains after
visits to her psychologist, a cynical young man who loves her. The pains disappear
only when she returns to her childhood home and the reclusive housekeeper who
helped raise her.

Method for Murder (s.m. also "Waxworks," "Sweets to the Sweet," and "The
    Cloak")

> *The House That Dripped Blood*
> 101 min.   color   1970
> Dir: Peter Duffell. Dist: Swank.

Cast: Christopher Lee, Peter Cushing.
Four fascinating and suspenseful short stories set in an eerie country mansion.

Mr. Steinway (see *Torture Garden* under **Enoch**)

The Skull of the Marquis de Sade

The Skull
85 min.   color   1965
Dir: Freddie Francis. Prod: Paramount. Dist: Films Inc.
Cast: Christopher Lee, Peter Cushing.
The skull of the infamous Marquis de Sade is purchased by a student of the supernatural, even though he knows its diabolic history.

Sweets to the Sweet (see *The House That Dripped Blood* under **Method for Murder**)

Terror Over Hollywood (see *Torture Garden* under **Enoch**)

Waxworks (see *The House That Dripped Blood* under **Method for Murder**)

The Weird Taylor (s.m. also "Lucy Comes to Stay," "Frozen Fear," and "Mannikins of Horror")

Asylum
88 min.   color   1972
Dir: Roy Ward Baker. Prod: Cinerama Releasing. Dist: Swank.
Cast: Peter Cushing, Britt Eklund, Herbert Lom.
A spine-tingling tale by the author of "Psycho" that takes place in a private asylum for the incurably insane. Consists of four horror stories told by inmates.

BLOCK, LIBBIE

Pin-Up Girl

Pin-Up Girl
74 min.   b&w   1944
Dir: Bruce Humberstone. Prod: Twentieth Century Fox.
Cast: Betty Grable, Martha Raye, Joe E. Brown.
The romance of a sailor.

BLOCKMAN, LAWRENCE C.

Death From the Sanskrit

Quiet Please, Murder
70 min.   b&w   1942
Dir: John Larkin. Prod: Twentieth Century Fox. Dist: Films Inc.
Cast: George Sanders, Gail Patrick.
Offbeat yarn of a master forger who passes off copies of original Shakespeare volumes he stole.

BOLL, HEINRICH

Dr. Murke's Collected Silences

Dr. Murke's Collected Silences
23 min.   b&w   1971
Dir: Per Berglund.

A sound editor, who collects "silences," which he makes by cutting out phrases from the soundtracks of various radio programs, is furious one day when he needs to delete the word God 26 times from a tape and replace it with an equivalent but pretentious-sounding phrase. Swedish dialogue with English subtitles.

BOND, LEE

Homesteads of Hate

Land of the Open Range
60 min.   b&w   1942
Dir: Edward Killy. Sp: Morton Grant. Prod: RKO.

A man leaves his land to crooks who served two or more years in prison.

BOYD, THOMAS ALEXANDER

The Long Shot

Blaze O'Glory
10 reels   b&w   1929
Dir: Renaud Hoffman, George J. Crone. Prod: Sono-Art Prod.
Cast: Eddie Dowling, Betty Compson.

On trial for murder, Eddie Williams tells his story.

BOYLE, JACK

An Answer in Grand Larceny (see *Missing Millions* under **A Problem in Grand Larceny**)

Boston Blackie, a character created by Boyle, also appeared in *After Midnight With Boston Blackie, Alias Boston Blackie, Boston Blackie and the Law,* and *Boston Blackie Booked on Suspicion* (Dist: Kit Parker Films); *Boston Blackie Goes to Hollywood, Boston Blackie Goes to Washington, Boston Blackie's Chinese Venture* (Dist: Wholesome Film Center); *Boston Blackie's Rendezvous* (Dist: Kit Parker Films); and *The Chance of a Lifetime, A Close Call for Boston Blackie, Trapped by Boston Blackie.*

Boston Blackie's Little Pal (in *Redbook*)

Boston Blackie's Little Pal
b&w   1919   sil.
Dir: E. Mason Hopper. Prod: Metro Pictures Corp.

Boston Blackie's Mary (s.m. also "Fred the Count")

> *Blackie's Redemption*
> 5 reels   b&w   1919   sd.
> Dir: John Ince. Prod: Metro Pictures Corp.

Debt of Dishonor (in *Redbook*)

> *Soiled*
> 7 reels   b&w   1924   sil.
> Dir: Fred Windemere. Prod: Phil Goldstone Prod.
> Cast: Kenneth Harlan, Vivian Martin.
> Wilbur Brown steals $2,500 from his employer, and his sister is almost
forced to compromise herself in order to get the money to repay the company.

The Face in the Fog (in *Cosmopolitan Magazine*, May 1920)

> *The Face in the Fog*
> 7 reels   b&w   1922   sil.
> Dir: Alan Crosland. Prod: Cosmopolitan Pictures.
> Cast: Lionel Barrymore, Seena Owen.
> Reformed crook Boston Blackie accidentally comes into possession of the
Romanov jewels.

Fred the Count (see *Blackie's Redemption* under **Boston Blackie's Mary**)

A Problem in Grand Larceny (in *Redbook,* December 1918-January 1919)

> *Missing Millions* (s.m. also "An Answer in Grand Larceny")
> 6 reels   b&w   1922   sil.
> Dir: Joseph Henabery. Prod: Famous Players-Lasky.
> Cast: Alice Brady, David Powell.
> Mary Dawson is determined to repay Jim Franklin for sending her father
to Sing Sing after he reneged on his promise to drop the charges.

Unidentified story (in *Cosmopolitan Magazine*)

> *The Return of Boston Blackie*
> 6 reels   b&w   1927   sil.
> Dir: Harry D. Holt. Adap: Leah Baird. Prod: Chadwick Pictures. Dist:
>   Mogull's Films.
> Vowing to go straight now that he is out of jail, Blackie tries to reform a
pretty blonde who he thinks just stole a necklace.

BOYLE, KAY

Maiden, Maiden (suggestion for)

> *Five Days One Summer*
> 108 min.   color   1982
> Dir and Prod: Fred Zinneman. Dist: Warner Bros. (video).
> Cast: Sean Connery.
> An odd relationship develops between a man and a young woman as they
go mountain climbing.

BRACE, BLANCHE

The Adventures of a Ready Letter Writer (in *Saturday Evening Post,* 13 November 1920)

Don't Write Letters
5 reels   b&w   1922   sil.
Dir: George D. Baker. Prod: Famous Players-Lasky.
Cast: Gareth Hughes, Bartine Burkett.
A small-statured Army man finds a letter from Anna May and begins a correspondence with her, pretending that he is a muscular, tall man, and they are married by proxy.

A Letter for Evie
9 reels   b&w   1945
Dir: Jules Dassin. Sp: De Vallon Scott, Alan Friedman, Prod: MGM.
Cast: Marsha Hunt, John Carroll, Hume Cronyn.
A remake of *Don't Write Letters* in which a shy man writes to a girl but assumes the identity of his handsome buddy.

BRACKETT, CHARLES WILLIAM

Interlocutory (in *Saturday Evening Post,* 14 March 1924)

Tomorrow's Love
6 reels   b&w   1925   sil.
Dir: Paul Bern. Sp: Howard Higgin. Prod: Famous Players-Lasky. Dist: Audio Brandon.
Cast: Agnes Ayres, Pat O'Malley.
Judith becomes annoyed by her husband's bad habits. When his car breaks down and an old girlfriend picks him up, his wife suspects the worst and asks for a divorce.

Pearls Before Cecily (in *Saturday Evening Post* 17 February 1923)

Risky Business
74 min.   b&w   1926   sil.
Dir: Alan Hale. Adap: Beulah Marie Dix. Prod: DeMille Pictures. Dist: Select Film Library (8 mm).
A pampered rich girl loves a struggling doctor, but her mother wants her to marry wealthy Coults-Browne.

BRADBURY, RAY

All Summer in a Day

All Summer in a Day
25 min.   color   1983
Prod: Learning Corp. Dist: Simon & Schuster (16 mm and video).
A group of schoolchildren on a planet other than Earth wait anxiously for the sunlight—an event that comes only once every nine years.

The Beast From 20,000 Fathoms

The Beast From 20,000 Fathoms
80 min.　　　b&w　　　1953
Dir: Eugene Lourie. Prod: Warner Bros. Dist: Select Film Library, Allan
　　Twyman Presents, Ivy Films, Video Communications (video).
Cast: Paul Christian, Paula Raymond.
The prehistoric past and the nuclear future meet in this monster epic.

I Sing the Body Electric!

The Electric Grandmother
48 min.　　　color　　　1983
Director: Noel Black. Prod: Learning Corp. Dist: Simon & Schuster (16
　　mm and video).
Cast: Maureen Stapleton.
A magical woman transforms a skeptical little girl in a motherless household
into a gentle and loving child.

The Invisible Boy

The Invisible Boy
20 min.　　　color　　　1982
Prod: Highgate Pictures. Dist: Simon & Schuster (16 mm and video).
Cast: Kate Reid.
An eccentric old aunt tries to make her nephew disappear.

The Long Rain

The Illustrated Man (s.m. also "The Veldt" and "The Last Night of the
　　World")
103 min.　　　color　　　1969)
Dir: Jack Smight. Prod: Warner Bros.
Cast: Rod Steiger, Claire Bloom, Robert Drivas.
Three stories are tied together by the presence of a traveling performer
whose strange tattoos come to life to act out lessons in human nature.

The Murderer

The Murderer
28 min.　　　color　　　1976
Dir & Prod: Andrew Silver. Dist: Phoenix/BFA (16 mm and video).
A comic story of Albert Brock who is surrounded in his futuristic world
by communications devices that constantly demand his attention.

The Pedestrian

The Pedestrian
6 min.　　　1960
Prod: USC.
In a repressive society of the future, a man who is out for a walk is stopped
by the incredulous police.

The Veldt (see *The Illustrated Man* under **The Long Rain**)

BRADSHAW, GEORGE

Memorial to a Bad Man

> *The Bad and the Beautiful* (s.m. also "Of Good and Evil")
> 118 min.   b&w   1952
> Dir: Vincente Minelli. Prod: MGM. Dist: Films Inc.
> Cast: Lana Turner, Kirk Douglas.
> When a producer finds his career almost finished, he calls on three former associates to help him out. They reflect on how he helped and then tormented them with his own destructive personality.

Of Good and Evil (see *The Bad and the Beautiful* under **Memorial to a Bad Man**)

Shoestring

> *New Faces of 1937*
> 12 reels   b&w   1937
> Dir: Leigh Jason. Sp: Nat Perrin, Philip G. Epstein, Irving S. Brecher. Prod: RKO.
> Cast: Joe Penner, Milton Berle.
> The launching of a Broadway show.

Venus Rising (Practice to Deceive)

> *How to Steal a Million*
> 127 min.   color   1966
> Dir: William Wyler. Prod: Twentieth Century Fox. Dist: Films Inc.
> Cast: Audrey Hepburn, Peter O'Toole, Hugh Griffith, Eli Wallach.
> A pair of elegant thieves steal a Cellini statue that belongs to one of the thieves' art collector father, who had long been foisting fraudulent old masters on the art world.

BRANCH, HOUSTON

Congo Crossing

> *Congo Crossing*
> 85 min.   color   1956
> Dir: Joseph Pevney. Sp: Richard Alan Simmons. Prod: Universal.
> A melodrama set in Africa in which a young woman unjustly accused of murder evades a man who has been hired to kill her.

BRAND, MAX (pseud. of Frederick Faust)

Dr. Gillespie, a character created by Brand, appeared in several films, including *Calling Dr. Gillespie, Dr. Gillespie's Criminal Case,* and *Dr. Gillespie's New Assistant.*

Dr. Kildare, another character created by Brand, appeared in a number of films, including *Dr. Kildare Goes Home, Dr. Kildare's Crisis, Dr. Kildare's Strangest Case, Dr. Kildare's Victory, Dr. Kildare's Wedding Day, The People Versus Dr. Kildare, The Secret of Dr. Kildare,* and *Young Dr. Kildare.*

Alcatraz

Just Tony
58 min.　　　　b&w　　　　1922　　　　sil.
Dir: Lynn Edwards. Prod: Fox. Dist: Blackhawk, Killiam Collections.
Cast: Tom Mix, Claire Adams, and Tony (a horse).
A wild horse saved by the hero from a cruel captor later saves the cowboy's
life.

Champion of Lost Causes (in *Flynn's Magazine*)

Champion of Lost Causes
5 reels　　　　b&w　　　　1925　　　　sil.
Dir: Chester Bennett. Prod: Fox.
Cast: Edmund Lowe, Barbara Bedford.
An author notices Joseph Wilbur at a gambling resort, and Wilbur is later
murdered.

Children of the Night (in *Argosy All-Story Weekly Magazine*)

Children of the Night
5 reels　　　　b&w　　　　1921　　　　sil.
Dir: Jack Dillon. Prod: Fox.
Cast: William Russell, Ruth Renick.
A clerk falls asleep in his office and dreams that he has an aggressive personal-
ity and when he awakens, he does.

Cuttle's Hired Man (in *Western Story Magazine*)

Against All Odds
5 reels　　　　b&w　　　　1924　　　　sil.
Dir: Edmund Mortimer. Prod: Fox.
Cast: Charles "Buck" Jones, Dolores Rousse, Ben Hendricks, Jr., William
　　Scott.
Western. Chick Newton's friend Bill is framed and arrested for murdering
his uncle. His friend rescues him from lynching.

Hired Guns (in *Western Story Magazine*, 10 March 1923)

The Gunfighter
5 reels　　　　b&w　　　　1923　　　　sil.
Dir: Lynn F. Reynolds. Prod: Fox.
Cast: William Farnum, Doris May.
Western. A feud between the Benchleys and the Camps arises when Lew
Camp learns that his daughter was kidnapped to replace a dead Benchley child.

The Secret of Dr. Kildare

The Secret of Dr. Kildare
9 reels　　　　b&w　　　　1939
Dir: Harold Bucquet. Prod: MGM. Dist: Classic Film Museum.

Drs. Gillespie and Kildare keep secrets from each other, supposedly for the good of the other.

Senor Jingle Bells (in *Argosy All-Story Weekly Magazine,* 7 March and 4 April 1925)

The Best Bad Man
5 reels   b&w   1925   sil.
Dir: J.G. Blystone. Prod: Fox.
Cast: Tom Mix, Buster Gardner.
Western. An absentee ranchowner visits his property disguised as a peddler.

Who Am I? (in *Argosy All-Story Weekly Magazine,* 3 February 1918)

Who Am I?
5 reels   b&w   1921   sil.
Dir: Henry Kolker. Prod: Selznick Pictures.
Cast: Claire Anderson, Gertrude Astor.
Ruth Burns didn't know her father was a professional gambler until after his death.

Unidentified story

Interns Can't Take Money
77 min.   b&w   1937
Dir: Alfred Santell. Prod: Paramount.
Cast: Joel McCrea, Barbara Stanwyck.
In this first Dr. Kildare movie, a woman sent to prison can be helped by the doctor—if he's willing.

BRANSTEN, RICHARD (jt. author) (see *Margie* under McKENNEY, RUTH)

BREN, J. ROBERT (jt. author) (see *The Band Plays On* under STUHLDREHER, HARRY)

BRENNAN, FREDERICK HAZLITT

The Matron's Report((in *Cosmopolitan Magazine,* March 1928)

Blue Skies
6 reels   b&w   1929   mus. score and sd. effects
Dir: Alfred L. Werker. Prod: Fox.
Cast: Carmencita Johnson, Freddie Frederick, Helen Twelvetrees, Frank Albertson.
Two children are eventually rescued from an orphanage. Note: *Variety* said (July 17, 1929) that this film is "Fox's kid version of 'Over the Hill.' "

Little Miss Nobody
6,620'   b&w   1936
Dir: John Blystone. Prod: Twentieth Century Fox.
Cast: Jane Withers, Jane Darwell.

A homeless harum-scarum has a heart so big she gives up her own happiness for another.

Miss Pacific Fleet

Miss Pacific Fleet
76 min.   b&w   1935
Dir: Ray Enright. Prod: Warner Bros. Dist: MGM/UA Home Video (video).
Cast: Joan Blondell, Glenda Farrell.
Chorus girls trying to win popularity with the Navy.

Perfect Weekend

St. Louis Kid
67 min.   b&w   1934
Dir: Ray Enright. Prod: Warner Bros. Dist: MGM/UA Home Video (video).
Cast: James Cagney, Patricia Ellis.
A truck driver in the dairy business fights crooked officials.

The Pumpkin Shell

My Pal Wolf
76 min.   b&w   1944
Dir: Alfred M. Werker. Prod: RKO Dist: Films Inc.
Cast: Sharyn Moffett, Jill Esmond.
A little girl deserted by her parents and cared for by a cruel governess befriends a stray dog.

BRESLIN, HOWARD

Bad Times at Hondo

Bad Day at Black Rock
81 min.   b&w   1955
Dir: John Sturges. Sp: Mildred Kaufmaan. Prod: MGM. Dist: Films Inc.
Cast: Spencer Tracy, Robert Ryan.
When a one-armed stranger gets off the train, he encounters hostility from the community's 37 inhabitants when he asks about a Japanese-American farmer to whom he is delivering a medal.

BRODIE, JULIAN (jt. author) (see *Love on the Run* under GREEN, ALAN)

BROMFIELD, LOUIS

The Life of Vergie Winters

The Life of Vergie Winters
90 min.   b&w   1934
Dir: Alfred Santell. Sp: Jane Murfin. Prod: RKO.

Single Night

Night after Night
75 min.   b&w   1932
Dir: Archie Mayo. Prod: Paramount.

Cast: Mae West, George Raft.
The owner of a high-class speakeasy wants to become educated.

BROOKE, EDGAR (see *It's a Big Country* under PETRACCA, JOSEPH)

BROWN, FREDERIC

Madman's Holiday

> *Crack-Up*
> 93 min.   b&w   1946
> Dir: Irving Reis. Prod: RKO.
> Cast: Pat O'Brien, Claire Trevor.
> An art curator is tricked by art forgers into thinking he was in a train wreck.

BROWN, GEORGE CARLTON

The Holy Terror

> *Big Punch*
> 80 min.   b&w   1948
> Dir: Sherry Shourds. Prod: Warner Bros. Dist: MGM/UA Home Video
>   (video).
> Cast: Wayne Morris, Gordon MacRae.
> Prizefight drama.

The Magic Garden

> *Penny Whistle Blues*
> b&w   1952
> Prod: Swan Film.
> Comedy. A thief loses the loot he stole.

BROWN, KARL

The Creep in the Dark

> *The Ape Man*
> 64 min.   b&w   1943
> Dir: William Beaudine. Prod: Monogram Pictures. Dist: Audio Brandon,
>   Budget Film/Video, Ivy Films (video), Discount Video Tapes, Cable
>   Films, Sheik Video.
> Cast: Bela Lugosi, Wallace Ford.
> A scientist experiments and becomes half-man and half-ape.

BROWN, WALTER C.

Prelude to Murder

> *The House in the Woods*
> 62 min.   b&w   1957
> Dir: Maxwell Munden. Prod: St. John's Woods Studios.
> Cast: Patric Roc, Ronald Howard, Michael Gough.
> The ghost of a murdered woman returns.

BROWNE, BARTON (jt. author) (see *Garden of the Moon* under BEDFORD-JONES, H.)

BRUCE, GEORGE (jt. author) (see *Baby Face* under OPPENHEIMER, GEORGE)

BRUSH, KATHERINE

Free Woman

My Love Is Yours (a.k.a. *Free Woman*)
95 min.   b&w   1939
Dir: Edward H. Griffith. Prod: Paramount. Dist: Cable Films (video), Penguin Video.
Cast: Fred MacMurray, Madeleine Carroll, Allan Jones.
Romantic comedy. A cold, calculating career girl falls for a man.

Maid of Honor

Lady of Secrets
b&w   1936
Dir: Marion Gering. Prod: Columbia Pictures.
Cast: Ruth Chatterton, Otto Kruger, Lloyd Nolan.
A woman's one love affair has turned her into a recluse.

BUCKLEY, FRANK R.

Peg Leg the Kidnapper (in *Western Story Magazine,* 26 September 1925)

The Gentle Cyclone
5 reels   b&w   1926   sil.
Dir: William S. Van Dyke. Prod: Fox.
Cast: Buck Jones, Rose Blossom.
Western comedy. The uncles of orphan June feud when they learn she has inherited valuable property between their lands.

BUCKNER, ROBERT

Moon Pilot (serialized story in *Saturday Evening Post,* 19 March-12 April 1960)

The Moon Spinners
119 min.   color   1964
Dir: James Neilson. Prod: Walt Disney. Dist: Roa's Films.
Cast: Hayley Mills, Joan Greenwood.
A search for valuable stolen jewels and the thief.

BUHLER, KITTY

Time Is a Memory

China Doll
88 min.   b&w   1958
Dir: Frank Borzage. Prod: Romaina Prod. Dist: MGM/UA Home Video (video).
Cast: Victor Mature, Stuart Whitman.
An Air Force captain in China during World War II combats aerial bombardment to protect his young bride.

BUNNER, HENRY C.

Zenobia's Infidelity

>*Zenobia's Infidelity*
>74 min.   b&w   1939
>Dir: Gordon Douglas. Prod: Hal Roach. Dist: Mogull's Films, Select Film
>   Library.
>Cast: Oliver Hardy, Harry Langdon.

BURKE, THOMAS

The Chink and the Child

>*Broken Blossoms*
>68 min.   b&w   1919   sil.
>Dir: D.W. Griffith. Sp: D.W. Griffith. Prod: United Artists. Dist: Budget
>   Films/Video (video); Hollywood Home Theater, Sheik Video.
>Cast: Lillian Gish, Richard Barthelmess, Donald Crisp.

A gentle, contemplative Chinese youth arrives in the squalid Limeshouse district of London hoping to spread his philosophy of peace and love. He is quickly disillusioned, but when Lucy, who has been beaten by her father, falls unconscious outside the door of his shop, he takes her in and cares for her until her sadistic father finds her and drags her home.

>*Broken Blossoms*
>b&w   1936
>Dir: Hans Brahm.
>Cast: Emlyn Williams.

Gina of Chinatown

>*Dream Street* (s.m. also "The Lamp in the Window")
>102 min.   b&w   1921   sil.
>Dir: D.W. Griffith. Dist: Audio Brandon.
>Cast: Carol Dempster, Ralph Graves, Charles Emmett Mack.

Love and romance affect the lives of three people living in the slums of London: Gypsy Fair, a vivacious young dancer; Spike McFadden, an aggressive Don Juan; and Billy, Spike's frail and gentle brother.

The Lamp in the Window (see *Dream Street* under **Gina of Chinatown**)

Twelve Golden Curls

>*Curlytop*
>5,828'   b&w   1924   sil.
>Dir: Maurice Elvey. Adap: Frederick Hatton, Fanny Hatton.
>Cast: Shirley Mason, Wallace MacDonald.
>Two girls love the same man.

BURNET, DANA

The Billings Spend His Dime (in *Redbook,* June-August 1920)

> *The Billings Spend His Dime*
> 6 reels   b&w   1923   sil.
> Dir: Wesley Ruggles. Prod: Famous Players-Lasky.
> Cast: Walter Hiers, Jacqueline Logan.
> Salesclerk John falls in love with Suzanne Juarez when he sees her picture

on a cigar band, so he goes to Santo Dinero to try to win her.

Private Pettigrew's Daughter

> *Private Pettigrew's Daughter*
> b&w   1919   sil.
> Dir: George Melford. Prod: Paramount.
> Cast: Ethel Clayton.

The Shopworn Angel

> *The Shopworn Angel*
> 8 reels   b&w   1928   sd.
> Dir: Richard Wallace. Prod: Paramount/Famous Players-Lasky.
> Cast: Nancy Carroll, Gary Cooper, Paul Lukas.
> Daisy, a sophisticated New York chorus girl with a "guardian," falls in love

with Bill, a naive Army private from Texas who goes A.W.O.L. to be with her.

> *Shopworn Angel*
> 80 min.   b&w   1938
> Dir: H.C. Potter. Prod: MGM. Dist: Films Inc.
> Cast: Margaret Sullivan, James Stewart.
> A kept woman has a bittersweet love affair with a naive soldier.

Technic (in *Saturday Evening Post,* 16 May 1925)

> *The Marriage Clause*
> 8 reels   b&w   1926   sil.
> Dir: Lois Weber. Prod: Universal-Jewell.
> Cast: Francis X. Bushman, Billie Dove, Warner Oland.
> A shy, timid girl auditions for a role in a New York play, and the director

accuses her of stealing a purse.

Those High Society Blues (in *Saturday Evening Post,* 23 May 1925)

> *High Society Blues*
> 10 reels   b&w   1930
> Dir: David Butler. Adap: Howard J. Green. Prod: Fox.
> Cast: Janet Gaynor, Charles Farrell.
> Eli Granger and his family move to a wealthy area of Scarsdale after selling

their business in Iowa, but they are scorned by their neighbors.

Wandering Daughters (in *Hearst's International Magazine,* July 1922)

> *Wandering Daughters*
> 6 reels   b&w   1923   sil.
> Dir: James Young. Prod: Sam E. Rork.
> Cast: Marguerite De La Motte, William V. Mong.

Bessie, Bowden, the daughter of straight-laced parents, finds fast-set member Austin more interesting than hard-working John.

BURNETT, WILLIAM RILEY

Across the Aisle

> *Thirty Six Hours to Kill*
> 5,700'   b&w   1936
> Dir: Eugene Forde. Prod: Twentieth Century Fox.

Dr. Socrates

> *Dr. Socrates*
> 69 min.   b&w   1935
> Dir: William Dieterle. Prod: Warner Bros. Dist: MGM/UA Home Video
>   (video).
> Cast: Paul Muni, Ann Dvorak.

A doctor becomes involved with hoodlums after they break into his home.

> *King of the Underworld*
> 69 min.   b&w   1939
> Dir: Lewis Saler. Sp: George Bricker. Prod: Warner Bros. Dist: MGM/UA
>   Home Video (video).
> Cast: Humphrey Bogart, Kay Francis, James Stephenson.

A distaff doctor seeks revenge against a hood who manipulated her husband.

Jail Break

> *The Whole Town's Talking*
> 86 min.   b&w   1935
> Dir: John Ford. Prod: Columbia. Dist: Budget Films/Video.
> Cast: Edward G. Robinson, Jean Arthur.

A meek little white-collar worker who wouldn't hurt a fly has a problem—he's a dead ringer for a cold-blooded hoodlum who is public enemy No. 1.

BURR, JANE

I'll Tell My Husband

> *The Arnelo Affair*
> 87 min.   b&w   1947
> Dir: Arch Oboler. Prod: MGM. Dist: Films Inc.
> Cast: George Murphy, John Hodiak, Lowell Gilmore, Eve Arden.

A murder web.

BURRAGE, A.M. (see *The Return* under BIERCE, AMBROSE)

BURT, KATHARINE NEWLIN

The Red-Haired Husband (in *Cosmopolitan Magazine,* January 1926)

> *The Silent Rider*
> 6 reels   b&w   1927   sil.
> Dir: Lynn Reynolds. Prod: Universal.
> Cast: Hoot Gibson, Blanche Mehaffey.
> Marian Faer, an assistant cook, wants a red-headed husband.

Summoned (in *Ainslee's,* February 1923)

> *The Way of a Girl*
> Dir: Robert G. Vignola. Prod: MGM.
> Cast: Eleanor Boardman, Matt Moore, William Russell.
> Society girl Rosamond craves the excitement her staid fiance won't provide.

BURTIS, THOMSON

War of the Wildcats

> *In Old Oklahoma* (a.k.a. *War of the Wildcats*)
> 102 min.   b&w   1943
> Dir: Albert S. Rogell. Prod: Republic Pictures. Dist: Ivy Films.
> Cast: John Wayne, Marsha Scott.

BUSCH, NIVEN (jt. author) (see *The Big Shakedown* under ENGELS, S.)

BYRNE, DONN

The Changelings

> *His Captive Woman*
> 8 reels   b&w   1929
> Dir: George Fitzmaurice. Prod: First National Pictures.
> Cabaret dancer Anna Janssen kills her sugar daddy and escapes to an island
in the South Seas, but a detective finds her and tries to bring her back.

Destiny Bay

> *Wings of the Morning*
> 87 min.   b&w   1937
> Dir: Harold Schuster. Prod: Twentieth Century Fox. Dist: Budget Films/
>   Video.
> Cast: Henry Fonda, Anabella, John McCormack.
> A Canadian trains a princess's horse to win the Derby.

C

CAIN, JAMES M.

Baby in the Icebox

> *She Made Her Bed*
> 8 reels   b&w   1934
> Dir: Ralph Murphy. Prod: Paramount.
> Cast: Richard Arlen, Sally Eilers.
> A two-timing husband meets disaster.

CALEF, NOEL

Rudolphe et le Revolver

> *Tiger Bay*
> 105 min.   b&w   1959
> Dir: J. Lee Thompson. Prod: Continental. Dist: Walter Reade 16.
> Cast: John Mills, Hayley Mills, Horst Buchholz.
> A little girl witnesses a murder when a sailor comes home on leave, discovers his girlfriend no longer loves him, and kills her in a blind rage.

CAMERSON, ANNE

Green Dice

> *Mr. Skitch*
> 62 min.   b&w   1933
> Dir: James Cruze. Sp: Sonya Levien, Ralph Spence. Prod: Fox.
> Cast: Will Rogers, ZaSu Pitts, Rochelle Hudson.
> A family's adventures as they travel to California by car.

CAMP, WADSWORTH

The Black Cap (in *Collier's Magazine,* 24 January 1920)

> *A Daughter of the Law*
> 5 reels   b&w   1921   sil.
> Dir: Jack Conway. Prod: Universal.
> Cast: Carmel Myers, Jack O'Brien.
> The daughter of a police inspector tries to retrieve her brother from an underworld gang.

Hate

Hate
5,500'   b&w   1922   sil.
Dir: Maxwell Karger. Adap: June Mathis.
Cast: Alice Lake, Conrad Nagel.
Gamblers are rivals for the love of Babe, a chorus girl. Hume, who is ill, kills himself and tries to make it look like Felton killed him.

CAMPBELL, EVELYN

Remorse (in *Redbook*)

Masked Angel
6 reels   b&w   1928   sil.
Dir: Frank O'Connor. Prod: Chadwick Prod.
Cast: Betty Compson, Erick Arnold.
Unjustly accused of stealing, a fleeing cabaret hostess ducks into a hospital and pretends to visit a blind soldier, with whom she falls in love.

Yesterday's Wife (in *Snappy Stories*, 1 May 1920)

Yesterday's Wife
6 reels   b&w   1923   sil.
Dir: Edward J. LeSaint. Prod: Columbia.
Cast: Irene Rich, Eileen Percy.
A quarrel causes a divorce, and the husband remarries, but when his second wife is accidentally killed, he reconciles with his first wife.

CAMPBELL, JOHN W., JR.

Who Goes There

The Thing
87 min.   b&w   1951
Dir: Christian Nyby. Prod: RKO. Dist: Swank (video), Nostalgia Merchant, King of Video, VidAmerica.
Cast: James Arness, Margaret Sheridan, Kenneth Tobey.
A U.S. Air Force research team, isolated in the Arctic, is attacked by a ferocious creature with the chemistry of a plant. Omitted from the movie is the creature's chameleon-like ability to duplicate the appearance of a human.

The Thing
108 min.   color   1982
Dir: John Carpenter. Dist: MCA/UA Home Video (video).
Cast: Kurt Russell, A. Wilfred Brimely.
A classic tale of a dozen scientists trapped in an Antarctic research station by the "thing."

CANFIELD, DOROTHY (pseud. of D.F.C. FISHER)

Eternal Masculine (suggestion for)

> *Two Heads on a Pillar*
> 8 reels   b&w   1934
> Dir: William Nigh. Prod: Liberty Pictures.

CAPOTE, TRUMAN

Among the Paths to Eden (s.m. also "A Christmas Memory" and "Miriam")

> *Truman Capote's Trilogy*
> 99 min.   color   1969
> Dir: Frank Perry. Prod: Allied Artists. Dist: Hurlock Cine-World.
> Cast: Mildred Natwick in No. 1, Maureen Stapleton, Martin Balsam in No. 2,
>   and Geraldine Page in No. 3.

No. 1: A lonely governess experiences a schizophrenic breakdown, and her delusions take the form of the child Miriam. No. 2: A spinster looks for a husband in the cemetery where widowers visit the graves of their dead wives. No. 3: A memory of Christmas in Alabama.

A Christmas Memory (see *Truman Capote's Trilogy* under **Among the Paths to Ede Eden**)

Miriam (see *Truman Capote's Trilogy* under **Among the Paths to Eden**)

CARLISLE, HELEN GRACE

Unidentified story

> *Live, Love and Learn*
> 8 reels   b&w   1937
> Dir: George Fitzmaurice. Sp: Charles Brackett, Cyril Hume, Richard
>   Maibaun. Prod: MGM.
> Cast: Robert Montgomery, Rosalind Russell, Robert Benchley, Monty
>   Woolley, Helen Vinson, Mickey Rooney.
> A story about a struggling artist and his rich wife living in Greenwich Village.

CARPENTER, JOHN J.

The Reluctant Hangman

> *Good Day for a Hanging*
> 85 min.   color   1959
> Dir: Nathan Juran. Prod: Morningside. Dist: Argus Films, Modern Sound
>   Pictures.
> Cast: Fred MacMurray, Robert Vaughan.

Ben Cutler watches as a smiling, blue-eyed, baby-faced youth brutally guns down the town marshal in cold blood, but no one believes him, including his daughter.

CARR, ALBERT H.Z.

Return from Limbo (in *Saturday Evening Post,* 22 February 1936)

> *Women Are Like That*
> 78 min.   b&w   1937
> Dir: Stanley Logan. Prod: Warner Bros. Dist: MGM/UA Home Video (video).
> Cast: Pat O'Brien, Kay Francis.
> A long-winded marital drama.

The Trial of Johnny Nobody (in *Ellery Queen's Magazine,* November 1950)

> *Johnny Nobody*
> 88 min.   b&w   1965
> Dir: Noel Patrick. Prod: Viceroy Films.
> Cast: Nigel Patrick, Yvonne Mitchell.
> Mulcahy, a drunken writer living in a small Irish town, is killed in front of
a church.

CARR, JOHN DICKSON

Gentlemen from Paris

> *The Man with a Cloak*
> 81 min.   b&w   1951
> Dir: Fletcher Markle. Prod: MGM. Dist: Films Inc.
> Cast: Joseph Cotten, Barbara Stanwyck.
> Set in 19th century New York. The hero's secret identity is Edgar Allan Poe.

CARRIER, ROCK

La Plage

> *La Plage*
> 4 min.   color   1981
> Prod: National Film Board of Canada. Dist: Phoenix Films (16 mm and
>   video).
> A non-narrated film about three men who amuse themselves on the beach;
in the background a woman sails as one man sees a drowning woman in his glass.

CARROLL, SIDNEY

Who Is Mr. Dean?

> *Gambit*
> 109 min.   color   1966
> Dir: Ronald Neame. Prod: Universal.
> Cast: Michael Caine, Shirley MacLaine, Herbert Lom.
> Comedy-thriller. A scoundrel and his Eurasian partner attempt to pull the
perfect heist.

CARSON, ROBERT
Aloha Means Goodbye

Across the Pacific
97 min.   b&w   1942
Dir: John Huston. Dist: MGM/UA Home Video (video).
Cast: Humphrey Bogart, Mary Astor, Sidney Greenstreet, Monte Blue.
A taut spy story of international intrigue about a secret service agent who pretends to sell out to the Japanese to foil a plot to blow up the Panama Canal.

Bedside Manner (in *Saturday Evening Post,* 8 July 1944)

Her Favorite Patient (a.k.a. *Bedside Manner*)
90 min.   b&w   1945
Dir: Andrew Stone. Prod: United Artists. Dist: Ivy Films, Mogull's Films.
Cast: Ruth Hussey, Charlie Ruggles, Ann Rutherford.
Can a woman physician with a charming bedside manner treat a handsome test pilot?

Come Be My Love

Once More, My Darling
94 min.   b&w   1949
Dir: Robert Montgomery. Prod: Universal International. Dist: Swank.
Cast: Robert Montgomery, Ann Blyth.
A young lady sets her cap for a somewhat older film matinee idol who is recalled to active duty in the Army.

The Reformer and the Redhead

The Reformer and the Redhead
90 min.   b&w   1950
Dir: Norman Panama, Norman Frank. Prod: MGM. Dist: Films Inc.
Cast: June Allyson, Dick Powell.

Third Girl From the Right

Ain't Misbehavin'
81 min.   b&w   1955
Dir: Edward Buzzell. Prod: Universal.
Cast: Rory Calhoun, Piper Laurie.
A chorus girl marries a wealthy tycoon.

You Gotta Stay Happy

You Gotta Stay Happy
100 min.   b&w   1948
Dir: H.C. Potter. Prod: Universal.
Cast: Jean Fontaine, James Stewart, Eddie Albert, Roland Young.
The richest girl in the world leaves her fiance at the altar and goes on a cross-country adventure with two veterans who started their own airline.

CARY, LUCIAN

Johnny Gets His Gun

> *Straight From the Shoulder*
> 7 reels   b&w   1936
> Dir: Stuart Heisler. Prod: Paramount.
> Cast: Ralph Bellamy, Katharine Locke.
> Drama of two people who witness a hold-up and murder.

White Flannels (in *Saturday Evening Post,* 27 June 1925)

> *White Flannels*
> 7 reels   b&w   1927   sil.
> Dir: Lloyd Bacon. Prod: Warner Bros.
> Cast: Louise Dresser, Jason Robards.

A domestic melodrama about Mrs. Politz, whose husband is a coal miner, who saves for years to send her son to college.

CASE, DAVID

Fengriffen in Fengriffen (Br.)

> *And Now the Screaming Starts!*
> 87 min.   color   1973
> Dir: Roy Ward Baker. Sp: Roger Marshall. Prod: Cinerama. Dist: Swank, Nostalgia Merchant (video).

Thriller. A curse on the baronet of Fengriffen for the rape of a woodman's bride results in the unleashing of a dead hand that crawls and kills.

CASE, ROBERT ORMOND

Golden Portage (in *Saturday Evening Post*)

> *The Girl From Alaska*
> 54 min.   b&w   1942
> Dir: Nick Grinde. Sp: Edward T. Lowe. Prod: Republic Pictures. Dist: Ivy Films.
> Cast: Ray Middleton, Jean Parker.

Disappointed because he did not strike gold, a young man prepares to leave Alaska. He accidentally shoots a law officer and falls in with a robber.

CASPARY, VERA

Gardenia

> *Blue Gardenia*
> 90 min.   b&w   1953
> Dir: Fritz Lang. Sp: Charles Hoffman. Prod: Warner Bros. Dist: Kit Parker Films.
> Cast: Anne Baxter, Richard Conte.

A telephone operator implicated in a murder is cleared by a reporter, who discovers the real killer.

CATHER, WILLA

Jack-a-Boy

Jack-a-Boy
28 min.   color   1980
Dir. & Prod: Carl Colby. Dist: Phoenix Films (16 mm and video).
Cast: Jean Marsh, Fred Gwynne.
Set in New Orleans in 1920. A piano teacher resides in a boarding house
into which Jack-a-Boy and his family move.

Paul's Case

Paul's Case
55 min.   color   1982
Dir: Lamont Jackson. Dist: Coronet Films (16 mm and video).
Cast: Eric Roberts.
Paul yearns to leave his grim ordinary life in industrial turn-of-the-century
Pittsburgh.

CHADWICK, JOSEPH

Phantom of the Canyon

Rim of the Canyon
65 min.   b&w   1949
Dir: John English. Prod: Gene Autry Pictures. Dist: Budget Films/Video,
     Roa's Films.
Cast: Gene Autry, Nan Leslie.
Musical western. Cowboy gets the girl and the outlaws.

CHAMBERLAIN, GEORGE AGNEW

The Phantom Filly (in *Saturday Evening Post*)

April Love
99 min.   color   1957
Dir: Henry Levin. Prod: Twentieth Century Fox. Dist: Films Inc.
Cast: Pat Boone, Shirley Jones.
Romance on the farm.

Home in Indiana
9,567'   b&w   1944
Dir: Henry Hathaway. Prod: Twentieth Century Fox. Dist: Films Inc.
Cast: Walter Brennan, Jeanne Crain, Lon McCallister.
Story of a blind harness-racing filly.

CHAMBERLAIN, LUCIA

Blackmail (in *Saturday Evening Post*)

Blackmail
6 reels   b&w   1920   sil.
Dir: Dallas M. Fitzgerald. Prod: Metro.

CHAMBERLAIN, WILLIAM

A Company of Cowards

Advance to the Rear
97 min.   color   1964
Dir: George Marshall. Prod: MGM. Dist: Films Inc.
Cast: Melvyn Douglas, Glenn Ford, Joan Blondell.
Comedy. Civil War officers in a troop of misfits are distracted from battle.

CHAMBERS, ROBERT W.

Pickets

A Time Out of War
22 min.   b&w   1954
Dir: Denis and Terry Sanders. Dist: Pyramid Films.
Two Union soldiers and a Confederate soldier form a tentative camaraderie during a one-hour truce that reveals the dignity and tension of each participant. Winner of an Academy Award for best short live-action film.

Spy 13

Operator 13 (s.m. other stories)
9 reels   b&w   1934
Dir: Richard Boleslawski. Prod: MGM.
Cast: Gary Cooper, Marion Davies, Marjorie Gateson..
Set during the Civil War. A Northern female spy assigned to kill a Southern officer falls in love with him instead.

CHANSLOR, ROY

Hi, Nellie

Hi, Nellie
79 min.   b&w   1934
Dir: Mervyn LeRoy. Prod: Warner Bros. and Vitaphone. Dist: MGM/UA
      Home Video (video).
Cast: Paul Muni, Glenda Farrell.
A lightweight newspaper story.

The House Across the Street
69 min.   b&w   1949
Dir: Richard Bare. Prod: Warner Bros. Dist: MGM/UA Home Video (video).
Cast: Wayne Morris, Janis Paige.
A newspaper editor crusades against crime and solves a murder.

Love Is on the Air
61 min.   b&w   1937
Dir: Nick Grinde. Prod: Warner Bros. Dist: MGM/UA Home Video (video).
Cast: Ronald Reagan, June Travis.
A radio commentator is forced to soft-pedal issues on the air when he exposes a racketeer.

You Can't Escape Forever
77 min.   b&w   1942
Dir: Jo Graham. Prod: Warner Bros. Dist: MGM/UA Home Video (video).
Cast: George Brent, Brenda Marshall, Gene Lockhart, Don DeFore.

CHARTERIS, LESLIE

The Million Pound Day

Saint in London (Br.)
72 min.   b&w   1939
Dir: John Paddy Carstairs. Prod: RKO. Dist: Nostalgia Merchant (video).
Cast: George Sanders, Sally Gray.
    The Saint picks up a wounded man on the road and is plunged into
mysterious doings.

CHASE, BORDEN

Blue, White and Perfect (s.m. also a character named Michael Shane, who was created by Brett Halliday)

Blue, White and Perfect
78 min.   b&w   1942
Dir: Herbert I. Leeds. Prod: Twentieth Century Fox. Dist: Films Inc.
Cast: Lloyd Nolan, Mary Beth Hughes.
    Shane chases foreign agents, who are stealing industrial diamonds during the
war.

Concerto (in *American Magazine*)

I've Always Loved You
95 min.   b&w   1946
Dir: Frank Borzage. Prod: Republic Pictures. Dist: Ivy Films.
Cast: Philip Dorn, Catherine McLeod.
    The protégée of a famous conductor receives more applause at their joint
concert at Carnegie Hall, which outrages him, so she gives up her career but resumes
it later.

Dr. Broadway

Dr. Broadway
60 min.   b&w   1942
Dir: Anthony Man. Prod: Paramount.
Cast: Macdonald Carey, Jean Phillips, J. Carrol Nash.
    A Times Square doctor with a motley assortment of patients is persuaded
to do a last favor for a dying gunman and runs into problems with a rival gang.

Midnight Taxi

Midnight Taxi
6,610'   b&w   1937
Dir: Eugene Forde. Prod: Twentieth Century Fox.
Cast: Brian Donlevy, Frances Drake.

A federal man, disguised as a taxi driver, must run down a band of counterfeiters.

Pay to Learn (in *Saturday Evening Post*, 14 January 1939)

> *The Navy Comes Through*
> 82 min.   b&w   1942
> Dir: A. Edward Sutherland. Prod: RKO.
> Cast: Pat O'Brien, George Murphy, Jane Wyatt.
> Merchant Marines in action during WWII.

CHEAVANS, MARTHA
Penny Serenade

> *Penny Serenade*
> 124 min.   b&w   1941
> Dir: George Stevens. Prod: Columbia Pictures. Dist: Ivy Films, Hollywood
>   Home Theater (video).
> Cast: Cary Grant, Irene Dunne.
> Told in flashbacks. A woman is on the verge of breaking up with her husband, but her memories make her want to reconcile.

CHEEVER, JOHN
The Five Forty-Eight

> *The Five Forty-Eight*
> 60 min.   color   1979
> Prod: Ivory/WNET. Dist: Films Inc.
> Cast: Laurence Luckinbill, Mary Beth Hurt.
> An ordinary man's daily routine is shattered when he meets a former employee with whom he once had an affair.

O Youth and Beauty

> *O Youth and Beauty*
> 60 min.   color   1979
> Prod: WNET/Bleckner. Dist: Films Inc.
> Cast: Michael Murphy, Kathryn Walker.
> Story of a man's fear of losing his masculinity.

The Sorrows of Gin

> *The Sorrows of Gin*
> 60 min.   color   1979
> Prod: WNET/Hofsiss. Dist: Films Inc.
> An eight-year-old girl's search for security amid her parents' social whirl.

The Swimmer (in *New Yorker*)

> *The Swimmer*
> 94 min.   color   1968
> Dir: Frank Perry. Prod: Columbia Pictures. Dist: Video Communications
>   (video).
> Cast: Burt Lancaster, Janet Landgard, Janice Rule, Marge Champion.

An advertising man in his 40s finds himself eight miles from home dressed in swimming trunks, so he decides to "swim" home, and as he does so, he finds out much about human nature.

CHEKHOV, ANTON

The Bass Fiddle

The Bass Fiddle
28 min.   b&w   1962
Dir: M. Frasquel. Dist: University of Nebraska - AV Center (rental).
A lighthearted and frolicsome tale of how a young man and woman face a most improbable and embarrassing situation when they discover that their clothes were stolen while they were swimming.

The Bet

The Bet
24 min.   color   1969
Dir: Ron Waller. Dist: Pyramid Films (16 mm and video).
An updated version of the story that captured the boredom, panic, and hysteria experienced by a young man who bets a wealthy friend he can isolate himself in a single room for five years.

The Bet
15 min.   color   1978
Prod: International Instructional Television Coop. Dist: Indiana University
    (16 mm and video).
A wager pits a lawyer and a banker against each other over the question of capital punishment versus life imprisonment.

The Boarding House

The Boarding House
27 min.   b&w   1977
Dist: Films Inc.
Narrated by John Gielgud. Love turns out to be an expensive proposition for a penniless young artist who answers a notice for a room and is surprised when the landlady turns out to be an attractive young widow.

The Boor

The Boor
15 min.   b&w   1955
Prod: Dynamic Films. Dist: Audio Brandon.
Cast: Monty Woolley.
A merry tenant farmer comes to collect a debt and matches wits with an attractive widow.

Desire to Sleep

Desire to Sleep
14 min.   b&w   1977 (release)
Dist: Brigham Young University (rental).

Domestic bliss turns to tragedy when an overwrought servant veers out of control, begins to hallucinate, and smothers her charge.

The Drop of Water

Black Sabbath (s.m. also "The Telephone Call" and "The Wurdlak")
99 min.   color   1964
Dir: Mario Bava. Dist: Audio Brandon, Budget Films/Video, Cine Craft,
        Roa's Films, Welling Motion Pictures.
Cast: Boris Karloff, Mark Damon, Michele Mercier.
Consists of three separate episodes, each involving a return from the dead. In "The Drop of Water," a nurse steals a diamond ring from the hand of a slain clairvoyant and is killed by a ghost. In "The Telephone Call," a prostitute kills a man who threatened her and later receives a call from him. In "The Wurdlak," a young nobleman falls in love with a girl whose father is a vampire and thirsts for the blood of his relatives.

An Event (or Proisshestviye)

An Event (Yugoslavia)
93 min.   color   1970
Dir: Vastroslav Mimica. Prod: Jadran Film. Dist: Walter Reade 16.
Cast: Paule Vujisic, Serdjo Mimica.
Upon returning from a fair, a boy and his grandfather are pursued by a gamekeeper.

The Fugitive

The Fugitive
15 min.   b&w   1977 (release)
Prod: Macmillan.
Terror turns to compassion as a small boy learns to cope with some of the harsh realities of life such as illness.

Grief

The Father
28 min.   b&w   1970
Dir: Mark Fine. Dist: New Line Cinema.
Cast: Burgess Meredith.
The driver of a horse-drawn cab tries to explain his son's death to his fares.

The Lady With the Dog

The Lady With the Dog (Russian with English subtitles)
86 min.   b&w   1960
Dir: Joseph Heifitz.
Cast: Iya Savvian, Alexei Batalov, Alla Chostakova.
Set in Yalta at the beginning of the century. A beautiful young woman and a middle-aged bank official encounter each other while she walks her dogs, and they drift into an affair.

Revenge

Revenge
26 min.   b&w   1977

Narrator: John Gielgud.

A jealous husband decides to avenge himself on his unfaithful wife by shooting her lover, but after realizing he will be arrested and she will be free, he decides not to do it.

Rothschild's Violin

Rothschild's Violin
23 min.   b&w   1977 (release)
Narrator: John Gielgud.

A miserly coffinmaker is the meanest man in the village. He is especially vicious to his wife and fellow violin player until she dies and he regrets what he did to her.

The Telephone Call (see *Black Sabbath* under **The Drop of Water**)

Volodya

Volodya
25 min.   b&w   1977

Seventeen-year-old Volodya broods over his father's suicide, which was brought on by an extravagant wife, but he falls for a similar woman and his life also ends tragically.

A Work of Art

A Work of Art: Satirical Shorts (Russian with English subtitles)
10 min.   b&w   1960
Dir: M. Kovalyov.

An inhibited provincial doctor receives a nude statue from one of his patients.

The Wurdlak (see *Black Sabbath* under **The Drop of Water**)

CHESTER, GEORGE RANDOLPH

The Head of the Family (in *Saturday Evening Post*, 26 December 1912)

The Head of the Family
7 reels   b&w   1928   sil.
Dir: Joseph C. Boyles. Prod: Gotham Prod.
Cast: William Russell, Mickey Bennett.

Henpecked Daniel Sullivan goes for a health cure and leaves Eddie, the plumber, in charge of his nagging wife, but Eddie and Alice fall in love.

CHESTERTON, GILBERT KEITH

Father Brown Stories

The Detective (originally titled *Father Brown*)
92 min.   b&w   1954
Dir: Robert Hamer. Prod: Facet Prod., London. Dist: Budget Films/Video,
     Roa's Films, Alan Twyman Presents.
Cast: Alec Guinness, Joyce Greenwood, Peter Finch.

As a hobby, a Roman cleric applies transcendental logic to solving puzzling crimes.

Father Brown, Detective
67 min.   b&w   1935

Dir: Edward Sedgwick. Prod: Paramount. Dist: "The" Film Center.
Cast: Walter Connolly, Gertrude Michael.
International crook Flambeau announces the time and date he will steal a famous jewel.

CHESTNUTT, CHARLES

Dave's Necklace

Dave's Necklace
15 min.   color   1978
Prod: International Instruction Television Coop. Dist: Indiana University (16 mm and video).
A tale of racial prejudice that uses such terms as "nigger."

CHETWYND-HAYES, R.

An Act of Kindness

From Beyond the Grave (s.m. also "The Gate Crasher," "The Elemental," and "The Door")
98 min.   color   1976
Dir: Kevin Connor. Sp: Robin Clarke, Raymond Christodoulou. Dist: Modern Sound Pictures.
Cast· Peter Cushing, Margaret Leighton, Donald Pleasance, Ian Carmichael, Diana Dors.
An anthology in which four stories revolve around the proprietor of the "Customers of Temptations Limited" antique shop: a malevolent spirit in a mirror; a chance friendship leading to voodoo; exorcism; and a strange door that keeps a sorcerer alive.

CHEYNEY, PETER

Calling Mr. Callaghan

The Amazing Mr. Callaghan
1960
Prod: Atlantis Films.

CHILD, RICHARD WASHBURN

The Game of Light (in *Everybody's Magazine,* July 1914)

The Live Wire
60 min.   b&w   1925   sil.
Dir: Charles Hines. Dist: EmGee Film Library, Mogull's Films.
Cast: Johnny Hines, Edmund Breese.
The great Maranelli is forced to quit the circus and takes to the open road, where he meets the daughter of a power company president and goes to work for him.

Here's How

The Mad Whirl
75 min.   b&w   1925   sil.
Dir: William S. Seiter. Prod: Universal. Dist: Griggs-Moviedrome.

John and Mary Herrington try to keep pace with their son Jack on an endless round of parties. When he falls in love with a childhood friend, her father objects to the match.

Whiff of Heliotrope (in *Famous Story Magazine,* December 1925)

> *Forgotten Faces*
> 76 min.   b&w   1928   sil.
> Dir: Victor Schertzinger. Prod: Paramount.
> Cast: Clive Brook.

Harry finds out that his wife cheated on him and kills her lover. Before surrendering to the police, he leaves his daughter on the steps of a wealthy couple's home.

> *Forgotten Faces*
> 79 min.   b&w   1936
> Dir: E.A. Dupont. Prod: Paramount.
> Cast: Clive Brook, Mary Brian, William Powell, Baclanova.

Harry Harlow finds out that his wife cheated on him, kills her lover, and then leaves his daughter on the doorstep of a wealthy couple, who raise her.

> *Gentleman After Dark*
> 77 min.   b&w   1942
> Dir: Edward L. Marin. Prod: Small. Dist: Walter Reade 16.
> Cast: Brian Donlevy, Miriam Hopkins, Preson Foster.
> A remake of *Forgotten Faces.*

> *Heliotrope*
> b&w   1920
> Dir: George D. Baker. Prod: Cosmopolitan Pictures.
> Cast: Fred Burton.

CHRISTIE, AGATHA

Philomel Cottage

> *Love from a Stranger* (s.m. also the play "Love from a Stranger" by Frank
>   Vosper, which in turn was based on the story)
> 90 min.   b&w   1937
> Dir: Rowland V. Lee. Prod: United Artists. Dist: Classic Film Museum.
> Cast: Basil Rathbone.

> *Love from a Stranger*
> 81 min.   b&w   1947
> Dir: Richard Whorf. Prod: Eagle Lion Films. Dist: Ivy Films.
> Cast: John Hodiak, Sylvia Sidney.
> After her marriage, a woman suspects that her husband is a mad strangler.

Witness for the Prosecution

> *Witness for the Prosecution* (s.m. also in play form)
> 114 min.   b&w   1957
> Dir: Billy Wilder. Prod: United Artists. Dist: MGM/UA Home Video (video).
> Cast: Tyrone Power, Marlene Dietrich, Charles Laughton.
> A sensational London murder trial.

CHURCHILL, ROBERT B.

Hell on Wheels

Born to Speed
61 min.   b&w   1947
Dir: Edward L. Chan. Prod: Releasing Corp. Dist: Ivy Films, Lewis Film
    Service.
Cast: Johnny Sand, Terry Austin.
Tale of auto racing men.

CLARK, KENNETH B.

The Girl Who Wasn't Wanted (in *Munsey's Magazine,* April 1928)

Rough Romance
60 min.   b&w   1930
Dir: A.F. Erickson. Prod: Fox.
Cast: George O'Brien, Helen Chandler.
The life and death struggle between two men.

CLARK, WALTER VAN TILBURG

The Portable Phonograph

The Portable Phonograph
24 min.   color   1977
Prod. and Dist: Encyclopaedia Britannica (16 mm and video).
Four survivors of a devastating war gather in a dugout built by a soldier to
hear the portable phonograph one of them has saved.

CLARKE, ARTHUR

The Sentinel (novel published after movie release)

2001: A Space Odyssey
139 min.   color   1968
Dir: Stanley Kubrick, Arthur C. Clarke. Prod: MGM. Dist: Films Inc.,
    MGM/UA Home Video (video).
Cast: Keir Dullea, Gary Lockwood, Douglas Rain, William Sylvester.
A strange monolith, throwing off unexplained rays, is found at the bottom
of an excavation and points the way to something more foreign and distant than
man can imagine. As they travel to a new time and place, the computer Hal takes
over. The sequel 2010 was released in 1984.

CLAUSEN, CARL

The Perfect Crime (in *Saturday Evening Post,* 25 September 1920)

The Perfect Crime
5 reels   b&w   1921   sil.
Dir: Allan Dwan. Prod: Allan Dwan Prod.
Cast: Monte Blue, Jacqueline Logan.
Wally Griggs, a timid bank messenger, lives another life as a dashing young
sport.

Poker Face

> *Killer at Large*
> b&w   1936
> Dir: David Selman. Prod: Columbia Pictures. Dist: Ivy Films, Mogull's Films.
> Cast: Robert Lowery, Annabel Shaw.

CLIFFORD, W. K.

Eve's Lover

> *Eve's Lover*
> 68 min.   b&w   1925   sil.
> Dir: Roy Del Ruth. Adap: Darryl Zanuck. Prod: Warner Bros.
> Cast: Irene Rich, Bert Lytell, Clara Bow.
> A business rival coveting Eve's steel mill convinces an impoverished count to
marry her, but the count falls in love and won't deceive her.

CLIFT, DENISON

Room 40, O.B.

> *Secrets of Scotland Yard*
> 7 reels   b&w   1944
> Dir: George Blair. Prod: Republic Pictures.
> Cast: Edgar Barrier, Lionel Atwill, Stephanie Bachelor.
> A twin is killed after deciphering a Nazi secret code message, and the other
twin becomes part of the British communications staff.

COBB, IRVIN SHREWSBURY

Boys Will Be Boys (in *Saturday Evening Post*)

> *Boys Will Be Boys* (s.m. also the play "Boys Will Be Boys" by Charles
>   O'Brien)
> 5 reels   b&w   1921   sil.
> Dir: Clarence G. Badger. Prod: MGM.
> Cast: Will Rogers, Irene Rich.
> Peep O'Day, an orphan, falls heir to a small fortune.

Brer Fox and the Briar Patch (see *Judge Priest* under **A Tree Full of Hoot Owls**)

The Lord Provides (see *The Sun Shines Bright*)

Mob from Massac (see *The Sun Shines Bright*)

The Sun Shines Bright

> *The Sun Shines Bright* (s.m. also "Mob from Massac" and "The Lord
>   Provides")
> 92 min.   b&w   1953
> Dir: John Ford. Prod: Republic Pictures. Dist: Ivy Films.
> Cast: Charles Winninger, Arlene Whelan.

A small-town judge has a hard time running for reelection. Note: This film supposedly is a remake of *Judge Priest,* although the reference sources indicate that each film is based on different stories.

A Tree Full of Hoot Owls

Judge Priest (s.m. also "Brer Fox and the Briar Patch" and "Words and Music")
80 min.   b&w   1934
Dir: John Ford. Prod: Fox. Dist: Films Inc., Budget Films/Video (video).
Cast: Will Rogers, Anita Louise.
Comedy-drama set in the old South.

Words and Music (see *Judge Priest* under A Tree Full of Hoot Owls)

The Young Nuts of America

The New Schoolteacher
6 reels   b&w   1924   sil.
Dir: Gregory La Cava. Prod: Burr Pictures.
Cast: Doris Kenyon, Charles "Chic" Sale.
A country schoolteacher's pupils play pranks on him until he wins their respect by saving a young boy from a burning schoolhouse.

COBURN, WALT

Black K. Rides Tonight

Return of Wild Bill
6 reels   b&w   1940
Dir: Joseph H. Lewis. Prod: Columbia Pictures.
Cast: Iris Meredith, Bill Elliot.

Burnt Ranch

The Westerner
6 reels   b&w   1934
Dir: David Selman. Prod: Columbia Pictures.
Western. Out West, a man must be quick on the draw.

COCKRELL, EUSTACE

Count Pete

Walking on Air
8 reels   b&w   1936
Dir: Joseph Santley. Prod: RKO.
Cast: Gene Raymond, Ann Sothern.
Comedy. A young heiress falls for a scoundrel.

Rocky's Rose

Fast Company
68 min.   b&w   1953
Dir: John Sturges. Prod: MGM. Dist: Films Inc.
Cast: Howard Keel, Polly Bergen.
A scheming horse trainer tries to buy a race horse at a fraction of its value.

COE, CHARLES FRANCIS

Ransom

Nancy Steele Is Missing
78 min.   b&w   1937
Dir: George Marshall. Prod: Twentieth Century Fox.

Repeal (suggestion for)

The Gay Bride
89 min.   b&w   1934
Dir: Jack Conway. Prod: MGM.
Cast: Carole Lombard, Chester Morris.
A chiseling showgirl meets her match in a gangster.

COFFE, LENORE

Miss Aesop Butters Her Bread (jt. author William Joyce)

Good Girls Go to Paris
80 min.   b&w   1939
Dir: Alexander Hall. Prod: Columbia Pictures. Dist: Kit Parker Films.
Cast: Joan Blondell, Melvyn Douglas.
A waitress who wants to go to Paris tries her wiles on the scion of a wealthy family.

COHEN, ROY OCTAVIUS

Marco Himself (in *Hearst's International Magazine*, September 1929)

The Social Lion
69 min.   b&w   1930
Dir: A. Edward Sutherland. Prod: Paramount.
Cast: Jack Oakie, Mary Brian.
Marco, a prizefighter, sets his sights on Gloria, a selfish society girl who leads him on for laughs.

Two Cents of Humaneness (in *Saturday Evening Post*)

Dollars and Sense
5 reels   b&w   1920
Dir: Harry Beaumont. Prod: Metro-Goldwyn.

COLLINS, RICHARD (jt. author) (see *Thousands Cheer* under JARRICO, PAUL)

COLLINS, WILKIE

The Terribly Strange Bed

The Terribly Strange Bed
15 min.   b&w   1955
Prod: Dynamic Films.
Cast: Monty Woolley.
A visitor at an inn wins money at gambling and then routs a pair of murderous scoundrels.

The Terribly Strange Bed
24 min.   b&w   1931
Prod: Twentieth Century Fox. Dist: Encyclopaedia Britannica (16 mm, 3/4", Beta, and VHS video).
A reckless young man-about-town patronizes a sleazy gambling house looking for excitement and finds more than he bargained for when he is put to bed in an ingenious death trap.

COLLISON, WILSON

Blondie Baby

Three Wise Girls
70 min.   b&w   1931
Dir: William Beaudine. Prod: Columbia Pictures.
Cast: Jean Harlow, Loretta Young.

There's Always a Woman

There's Always a Woman
80 min.   b&w   1938
Prod: Columbia Pictures.
Cast: Joan Blondell, Melvyn Douglas.
Mystery. A private eye and D.A. who are husband and wife are working on the same case.

COLTER, ELI

Something to Brag About

The Untamed Breed
79 min.   b&w   1948
Dir: Charles Lamont. Prod: Sage Western Pictures. Dist: Newman Film Library.
Cast: Sonny Tufts, Barbara Britton.
Western. The trials and tribulations of breeding cattle in old Texas.

COLTON, JOHN

Heat

Wild Orchids
11 reels   b&w   1928   mus. and sd. effects

Dir: Sidney Franklin. Prod: MGM. Dist: Films Inc.
Cast: Greta Garbo, Lewis Stone, Nils Asther.
A plantation owner and his wife visit Java, where she has an affair with a native prince.

CONDON, FRANK

Speed But No Control (in *Saturday Evening Post,* 21 June 1924)

> *No Control*
> 60 min.   b&w   1927   sil.
> Dir: Scott Sidney, E.J. Babille. Prod: Metro Picture Corp.
> Cast: Harrison Ford, Phyllis Haver.

Nancy Flood takes a business job to help her father's floundering one-ring circus, but she's fired when the boss' son flirts with her.

CONNELL, RICHARD

Brother Orchid

> *Brother Orchid*
> 91 min.   b&w   1940
> Dir: Lloyd Bacon. Prod: Warner Bros. Dist: MGM/UA Home Video (video).
> Cast: Humphrey Bogart, Edward G. Robinson, Ann Sothern, Donald Crisp, Ralph Bellamy, Allen Jenkins.

An ex-convict takes refuge in a monastery but then returns to clean up the rackets.

A Friend of Napoleon (in *Saturday Evening Post,* 30 June 1923)

> *Seven Faces*
> 89 min.   b&w   1929
> Dir: Berthold Viertel. Prod: Fox.
> Cast: Paul Muni, Marguerite Churchill.

Youthful lovers meet secretly, but when the young man's father discovers the truth, he sends the girl away.

If I Was Alone with You (in *Collier's Magazine,* 30 November 1929)

> *Cheer Up and Smile*
> 68 min.   b&w   1930
> Dir: Sidney Lanfield. Adap: Howard J. Green. Prod: Fox.
> Cast: Dixie Lee, Arthur Lake.

Musical comedy. For his fraternity initiation, Eddie must kick the first man and kiss the first female he meets.

Isles of Romance (in *Saturday Evening Post* 12 April 1924)

> *No Place to Go*
> 7 reels   b&w   1927   sil.
> Dir: Mervyn LeRoy. Prod: Henry Hobart Prod.
> Cast: Mary Astor, Lloyd Hughes.

Sally yearns for exotic romance, so she convinces her boyfriend to go to the South Seas, where they visit an island inhabited by cannibals.

A Little Bit of Broadway (in *Liberty Magazine* 6-27 September 1924)

Bright Lights
72 min.   b&w   1931
Dir: Michael Curtiz. Dist: MGM/UA Home Video.
Cast: Dorothy Mackaill, Frank Fay, Noah Berry.
Cabaret girl Patsy goes home to her mother. Her sweetheart tries to imitate the style of her former cabaret friends with disastrous results.

The Most Dangerous Game

A Game of Death
72 min.   b&w   1946
Dir: Robert Wise. Prod: RKO. Dist: Ivy Films.
Cast: John Loder, Edgar Barriel.
A hunter living on an island makes shipwrecked victims his prey.

The Hunt
30 min.   color   1970
Dir. and Prod: David Deverell. Dist: Encyclopaedia Britannica (16 mm and
     video).
An avid huntsman leaves his friend, who does not like shooting animals, and goes off by himself. He meets an older hunter who yearns for a real challenge—human prey.

The Hounds of Zaroff (Br. title)
65 min.   b&w   1932
Dir: Ernest B. Shoedsack, Irving Pichel. Prod: RKO. Dist: Classic Film
     Museum, Em Gee Film Library, Hollywood Home Theater (video).
Cast: Joel McCrea, Fay Wray.
Count Zaroff, an eccentric Russian who lives in isolation, loves to hunt but needs a new challenge—men.

$100 (in *Hearst's International Magazine,* August 1928)

New Year's Eve
7 reels   b&w   1929   sd. effects
Dir: Henry Lehrman. Prod: Fox.
Cast: Mary Astor, Charles Morton.
A young woman who has to care for her younger brother puts aside her scruples and goes to see a gambler who lusts after her. She finds him dead and is put on trial for his murder.

The Solid Gold Article (in *Collier's Magazine*, 11 May 1929)

Not Damaged
7 reels   b&w   1930
Dir: Chandler Sprague. Prod: Fox.
Cast: Lois Moran, Walter Byron.

Romantic comedy. A young lady, although engaged, loves wealthy Kirk Randolph and goes to his apartment for a wild time.

The Swamp Angel (in *Collier's Magazine,* 10 February–10 March 1923)

> *Painted People*
> 7 reels   b&w   1924   sil.
> Dir: Clarence Badger. Prod: Associated First National.
> Cast: Colleen Moore, Ben Lyon.

Ellie and Don want to marry wealthy people, but when they each become successful, they realize how much they mean to each other.

Tropic of Capricorn

> *East of Broadway*
> 6 reels   b&w   1924   sil.
> Dir: William K. Howard. Adap: Paul Schofield. Prod: Encore Pictures.
> Cast: Owen Moore, Marguerite De La Motte.

The son of Irish immigrants dreams of becoming a policeman but is rejected because he is not tall enough.

CONNOLLY, MYLES

Lady Smith

> *Palm Springs*
> 79 min.   b&w   1936
> Dir: Aubrey Scotto. Prod: Paramount.
> Cast: Frances Langford, Sir Guy Standing, David Niven.
> A nobleman becomes a gambler to pay for his daughter's expensive school.

CONRAD, JOSEPH

The Secret Sharer (see also *Face to Face* under CRANE, STEPHEN)

> *The Secret Sharer*
> 30 min.   color   1969
> Prod. and Dist: Encyclopaedia Britannica (16 mm and video).

Haunting tale of a young sea captain whose inner conflicts pit his conscience against the safety of the ship he commands and the men he leads.

COOK, WILLIAM WALLACE

The Old West Per Contract (in *Argosy*)

> *'49-'17*
> 50 min.   b&w   1917   sil.
> Dir. and Sp: Ruth Ann Baldwin. Dist: Kit Parker Films.
> Cast: Joseph Girard, Leo Pierson, Jean Hersholt.
> An action western.

COOPER, COURTNEY RYLEY

Christmas Eve in Pilot Butte (in *Redbook*, January 1921)

> *Desperate Trails*
> 50 min.   b&w   1921   sil.
> Dir: Jack Ford. Prod: Universal.
> Cast: Harry Carey, Irene Rich.
> Bart Carson accepts the blame for a crime committed by his girlfriend's "brother" and later learns that the "brother" is really her lover.

> *Desperate Trails*
> 60 min.   b&w   1939
> Dir: Albert Ray. Prod: Universal.
> Cast: Johnny Mack Brown, Frances Robinson.

CORT, VAN

Mail Order ... (in *Saturday Evening Post*, 11 August 1951)

> *Mail Order Bride*
> 83 min.   color   1964
> Dir. and Sp: Burt Kennedy. Prod: MGM. Dist: Films Inc.
> Cast: Lois Nettleson, Keir Dullea, Buddy Ebsen.
> A hell-raising friend is in need of a wife.

COWARD, NOEL

Pretty Polly Barlow

> *A Matter of Innocence*
> 102 min.   color   1968
> Dir: Guy Green. Sp: Keith Waterhouse. Prod: Universal.
> A lonely girl meets a gigolo while they are on a cruise to Singapore.

COXE, GEORGE H.

Return Engagement

> *Here's Flash Casey*
> 6 reels   b&w   1937
> Dir: Lynn Shores. Sp: John Kraft. Prod: Grand National Films.
> Cast: Eric Linden, Boots Mallory.
> A crime photographer solves a mystery.

The Shadow

> *The Shadow Strikes*
> 65 min.   b&w   1937
> Dir: Lynn Shores. Prod: Grand National Films. Dist: Budget Films/Video.

Women Are Trouble

> *Women Are Trouble*
> b&w   1936
> Dir: Errol Taggart. Sp: Michael Fessier. Prod: MGM.
> Cast: Florence Rice, Stuart Erwin, Paul Kelly.
> A crime thriller.

COZZEN, JAMES GOULD

S.S. San Pedro (in *Scribner's Magazine,* 28 August 1930)

> *S.S. San Pedro*
> 1932
> Prod: Universal.

CRAM, MILDRED

The Feeder (in *Redbook,* May 1926)

> *Behind the Make-Up*
> 8 reels   b&w   1930
> Dir: Robert Milton. Prod: Paramount/Famous Players-Lasky.
> Cast: Hal Skelly, William Powell, Fay Wray.
> Hap Brown, an easygoing, happy-go-lucky actor, falls in love with Marie,
a waitress in the French Quarter of New Orleans.

Navy Born

> *Mariners of the Sky* (a.k.a. *Navy Born*)
> 8 reels   b&w   1936
> Dir: Nate Watt. Prod: Republic Pictures.
> Cast: Claire Dodd, William Gargan, Douglas Fowley.
> A navy pilot raises an orphan.

Sadie of the Desert (in *Redbook,* October 1925)

> *Subway Sadie*
> 7 reels   b&w   1926   sil.
> Dir: Alfred Santell. Prod: Al Rockett Prod.
> Cast: Dorothy Mackaill, Jack Mulhall.
> Sadie dreams of going to Paris, but her big chance to go there as a buyer is
lost when her fiance is hospitalized.

Thin Air

> *Stars Over Broadway*
> 89 min.   b&w   1935
> Dir: William Keighley. Prod: Warner Bros. Dist: MGM/UA Home Video
>   (video).
> Cast: James Melton, Jane Froman.
> A spoof of grand opera.

Wings Over Honolulu (in *Redbook*)

> *Wings Over Honolulu*
> 78 min.   b&w   1937
> Dir: H.C. Potter. Prod: Universal.
> Cast: Wendy Barrie, Ray Milland, William Gargan.
> A navy pilot becomes involved in a romantic triangle.

CRANE, STEPHEN

The Bride Comes to Yellow Sky

> *Face to Face* (composite film that includes *The Secret Sharer*)
> 90 min.   b&w   1952
> Dir: John Brahm, Bretaigne Windust. Prod: Theasquare Prod.

In "The Bride Comes to Yellow Sky," a sheriff returning from his honeymoon must cope with a gunman who has terrorized the town in his absence. In "The Secret Sharer," a young ship captain comes to the aid of another ship.

The Blue Hotel

> *The Blue Hotel*
> 54 min.   color   1977
> Dir: Jan Kadar. Dist: Simon & Schuster (16 mm and video).

A young Swede arrives at the hotel of a moody, frontier Nebraska town during the 1880s expecting to find the wild West of dime novels.

The Monster

> *Face of Fire*
> 80 min.   b&w   1959
> Dir: Albert Band. Prod: Allied Artists. Dist: Hurlock Cine-World.
> Cast: Cameron Mitchell, James Whitmore.
> Disfigured in a fire, the local handyman becomes a social outcast.

Three Miraculous Soldiers

> *Three Miraculous Soldiers*
> 17 min.   color   1977
> Dir: Bernard Selling. Dist: Phoenix Films (16 mm and video).

During the Civil War, a young girl is forced to recognize the humanity of both Confederate and Union soldiers.

The Upturned Face

> *The Upturned Face*
> 10 min.   color   1972
> Prod: Changeling Prod. Dist: Pyramid Films (16 mm and video).

A young officer is killed during the Civil War and buried by his two hesitant comrades.

CRANSTON, CLAUDIA (see *It's a Big Country* under PETRACCA, JOSEPH)

CUMMINS, RALPH

The Badge of Fighting Hearts (in *Short Stories,* July 1921)

> *The Fire Eater*
> 5 reels   b&w   1923   sil.
> Dir: Reaves Eason. Prod: Universal.
> Cast: Hoot Gibson, Louise Lorraine.

Western. Smilin' Bob Corey and his partner Jim are forest rangers who are sent to make a peaceful expedition to Paradise Valley, slated for a national park.

Cherub of Seven Bar (in *Short Stories*, 16 December 1921)

> *The Loaded Door*
> 5 reels   b&w   1922   sil.
> Dir: Harry A. Pollard. Prod: Universal.
> Cast: Hoot Gibson, Gertrude Olmstead, Bill Ryno.

Western. Bert Lyons returns to the Grainger spread and finds his former employer dead and the ranch in the hands of a dope smuggler. He rescues the ranch and the girl named Molly.

Rattler Rock (in *Ace High Magazine,* 18 August 1923)

> *Rarin' to Go*
> 5 reels   b&w   1924   sil.
> Dir: Richard Thorpe.
> Cast: Buffalo Bill, Jr., Olin Francis.

Western. Bill's friendship with Dorothy helps resolve the irrigation difficulties of his employers.

CUNNINGHAM, JOHN M.

Raiders Die Hard

> *Day of the Badman*
> 81 min.   color   1958
> Dir: Harry Keller. Prod: Universal.
> Cast: Fred MacMurray, Joan Weldon.
> Western. A judge is confronted by the brother of a man he sentenced to die.

The Tin Star

> *High Noon*
> 85 min.   b&w   1952
> Dir: Fred Zinnemann. Prod: Stanley Kramer Prod. Dist: Clem Williams Films,
>   Ivy Films, Blackhawk (video), NTA Home Entertainment.
> Cast: Gary Cooper, Grace Kelly.

Western. In the hot and dusty western town of Hadleyville in 1870, three gunmen await the arrival of the twelve o'clock train. Their leader is returning from prison, where he was sent by the Marshal, whom they plan to kill. The Marshal tries to get help, but the citizens desert him.

CURWOOD, JAMES OLIVER
Back to God's Country

Back to God's Country
70 min.   b&w   1927   sil.
Dir: Irvin Willat. Prod: Universal International. Dist: MOMA.
Detained in Canada by an unscrupulous trader, a schooner captain and his wife try to escape by dogsled.

Back to God's Country
78 min.   color   1953
Dir: Joseph Pevney. Prod: Universal.
Cast: Rock Hudson, Marcia Henderson, Steve Cochran, Hugh O'Brien.
A sea captain and his wife battle man and nature for their fur cargo.

The Fatal Note

Phantom Patrol
b&w   1936
Prod: Maurice Conn Prod.

Footprints

The Fighting Trooper
87 min.   b&w   1934
Dir: Ray Taylor. Prod: Ambassador Pictures. Dist: Video Dimensions (video).
Cast: Kermit Maynard.
Mounties bring law to the northwest.

Four Minutes Late

Northern Frontier
6 reels   b&w   1935
Dir: Sam Newfield. Prod: Ambassador Pictures.
Cast: Kermit Maynard.
Story of a Mountie.

Hell's Gulch

Timber War
6 reels   b&w   1936
Dir: Sam Newfield. Prod: Ambassador Pictures.

In the Tentacles of the North (in *Blue Book,* January 1915)

In the Tentacles of the North
6 reels   b&w   1926   sil.
Dir: Louis Chaudet. Prod: Ben Wilson Prod. Dist: Sylvan Films (8 mm).
Two vessels are stuck in the ice; on one is a crewman and on the other the lone survivor, a girl.

Jacqueline or Blazing Barrier (in *Good Housekeeping,* August 1918)

Jacqueline or Blazing Barrier
7 reels   b&w   1923   sil.
Dir: Dell Henderson. Prod: Pine Tree Pictures.
Cast: Marguerite Courtot, Helen Rowland, Gus Weinberg.
A love triangle.

The Other Man's Wife

My Neighbor's Wife
6 reels   b&w   1925   sil.
Dir: Clarence Geldert. Prod: Clifford S. Elfelt Prod.
The son of a millionaire wants to make it on his own, puts his last dime
into a film, and hires Eric Von Greed to shoot it.

Peter God

The Destroyers
5 reels   b&w   1916   sil.
Dir: Ralph Ince. Prod: Vitagraph.

The Poetic Justice of Uko San (in *Outing,* June 1910)

I Am the Law
7 reels   b&w   1922   sil.
Dir: Edwin Carewe. Prod: Edwin Carewe Prod.
Cast: Alice Lake, Kenneth Harlan.
A Royal Mounted Policeman rescues a young lady, who then falls in love
with his brother.

Retribution

Timber Fury
63 min.   b&w   1950
Dir: Bernard B. Ray. Prod: Jack Schwarz Prod. Dist: Budget Films/Video,
     Lewis Film Services, "The" Film Center.
Cast: David Bruce, Laura Lee.
An outdoor adventure among the giant trees.

The Speck on the Wall

Law of the Timber
70 min.   b&w   1941
Dir: Bernard B. Ray. Prod: Producers Releasing Corp. Dist: Mogull's Films.
Cast: Marjorie Reynolds, Monte Blue.

Wapi, the Walrus

Back to God's Country
6 reels   b&w   1919
Dir: David M. Hartford. Prod: First National Pictures.
Cast: Nell Shipman.

When the Door Opened (in *Leslie's Weekly*, 13 November 1920)

When the Door Opened
7 reels   b&w   1925   sil.
Dir: Reginald Barker. Prod: Fox.
Cast: Jacqueline Logan, Walter McGrail.
Clive returns home unannounced and finds his wife in the arms of Henry. He shoots Henry and then hides out in the woods.

Yukon Manhunt

Yukon Manhunt
60 min.   b&w   1960
Prod: Monogram Pictures. Dist: Modern Sound Pictures.
Cast: Kirby Grant, Chinook (dog).
Corporal Webb of the Mounties sets out after the criminals behind a series of payroll robberies and finds himself in danger on all sides.

D

DAHL, ROALD

Beware of the Dog (in *Harper's,* October 1944; s.m. also a television play and
   unpublished stories by Carl K. Hittleman and Lois H. Vance)

   36 Hours
   115 min.   b&w   1965
   Dir: George Seaton. Prod: MGM.
   Cast: James Garner, Rod Taylor, Eva Marie Saint.
   Thirty-six hours before D-Day in 1944, an American intelligence officer is
drugged and kidnapped by the Nazis, who hope to learn the invasion plans from
him.

DANE. CLEMENCE

St. Martin's Lane

   Sidewalks of London (Br. title *St. Martin's Lane*)
   86 min.   b&w   1940
   Dir: Tim Whelan. Prod: Pommer-Laughton-Mayflower. Dist: Budget Films/
      Video, Mogull's Films.
   Cast: Charles Laughton, Vivien Leigh.
   A sidewalk entertainer takes in a homeless waif and helps her become a
famous personality.

DAUDET, ALPHONSE

The Elixir of Father Gaucher

   Letter from My Windmill (s.m. also "The Three Low Masses" and "The
      Secret of Master Cornilie")
   116 min.   b&w   1955
   Dir. and Prod: Marcel Pagnol.
   Cast: Henri Vilbert.
   Subtitles.

The Secret of Master Cornilie (see *Letters from My Windmill* under **The Elixir of
   Father Gaucher**)

The Three Low Masses (see *Letters from My Windmill* under **The Elixir of Father
   Gaucher**)

DAVIS, CHARLES BELMONT

The Octopus

Mother O'Mine
7 reels   b&w   1921   sil.
Dir: Fred Niblo. Prod: Thomas H. Ince Prod.
His mother's letter of introduction gets Robert a job with financier Thatcher, who is really his father. Thatcher uses Robert to cheat another banker.

When Johnny Comes Marching Home (in *Metropolitan Magazine,* October 1914)

The Home Stretch
55 min.   b&w   1911   sil.
Dir: Jack Nelson. Prod: Thomas H. Ince Prod. Dist: Blackhawk.
Cast: Doublas MacLean, Beatrice Burnham.
Johnny Hardwick inherits a thoroughbred and stakes his bankroll on him.

DAVIS, ELMER

The Old Timer

My American Wife
81 min.   b&w   1936
Dir: Harold Young. Prod: Paramount.
Cast: Francis Lederer, Fred Stone, Ann Sothern, Billy Burke.
A crisis develops when a count wants to live on a ranch, but his wife wants to live in New York.

DAVIS, FREDERICK C.

The Devil Is Yellow

Double Alibi
60 min.   b&w   1940
Dir: Philip Rosen. Prod: Universal.
Cast: Wayne Morris, Margaret Lindsay.
A woman's ex-husband is the prime suspect in her murder.

DAVIS, MAURICE

Twisted Road (suggestion for)

Race Street
79 min.   b&w   1948
Dir: Edward L. Martin. Prod: RKO.
Cast: George Raft, William Bendix, Marilyn Maxwell.
When bookie Dan Gannin falls in love, he decides to go straight. Then his friend is killed, and he vows revenge.

DAVIS, MEREDITH

When Smith Meets Smith

Beyond the Border
55 min.   b&w   1925   sil.

Dir: Scott R. Dunlap. Prod: Rogstrom Prod. Dist: Select Film Library.
Cast: Harry Carey, Mildred Harris.
Western. When Sheriff Bob Smith catches a man accused but innocent of murder, he discovers the man is his sweetheart's brother.

DAVIS, NORBERT

A Gunsmoke Case for Major Cain

> *Hands across the Rockies*
> 61 min.　　　　b&w　　　　1941
> Dir: Lambert Hillyer. Prod: Columbia Pictures.
> Cast: William Elliot.

DAVIS, RICHARD HARDING

The Adventures of the Scarlet Car (in *Collier's Magazine,* 15 December 1906; 23 March 1907; 14 June 1907)

> *The Scarlet Car*
> 5 reels　　　　b&w　　　　1923　　　　sil.
> Dir: Stuart Paton. Prod: Universal.
> Cast: Herbert Rawlinson, Claire Adams.
> Billy exposes Peabody, a candidate for mayor, as a double-crosser.

The Adventures of Van Bibber

> *The Kiss Doctor*
> 2 reels　　　　b&w　　　　1928　　　　sil.
> Prod: Fox.

The Bar Sinister

> *Almost Human*
> 6 reels　　　　b&w　　　　1927　　　　sil.
> Dir: Frank Urson. Prod: Pathe.
> Cast: Vera Reynolds, Kenneth Thomson.
> Maggie, a mongrel dog, lures champion Regent Royal to the barn.

> *It's a Dog's Life*
> 87 min.　　　　color　　　　1955
> Dir: Herman Hoffman. Prod: MGM.
> Cast: Edmund Gwenn, Dean Jagger, Jeff Richards.
> A remake of *Almost Human* in which a bull terrier from the Bowery ends up in a classy dog show.

The Exiles

> *The Exiles*
> 5 reels　　　　b&w　　　　1923　　　　sil.
> Dir: Edmund Mortimer. Prod: Fox.
> Cast: John Gilbert, Betty Bouton.
> Alice, accused of murder, flies to Tangiers, where she is found.

Fugitives
6 reels   b&w   1929   sil.
Dir: William Beaudine. Prod: Fox.
Alice's innocence in a murder case is not proven until she escapes from Sing Sing.

Gallagher

Gallagher
79 min.   color   1969
Prod: Walt Disney Prod. Dist: Modern Sound Pictures.
Cast: Roger Mobley, Edmond O'Brien, Ray Teal, Harvey Korman.
An energetic newspaper copyboy noses his way into the hottest newsbreaks in town to solve a murder and expose a confidence ring.

Let'er Go Gallagher
6 reels   b&w   1928   sil.
Dir: Elmer Clifton. Prod: DeMille Pictures.
Cast: Junior Coghlan, Harrison Ford.
A street urchin tips off Gallagher about a murder.

The Grand Cross of the Desert

Stephen Steps Out
6 reels   b&w   1923   sil.
Dir: Joseph Henabery. Prod: Famous Players-Lasky.
Cast: Douglas Fairbanks, Jr., Theodore Roberts, Noah Beery.
When Stephen Harlow, Jr., fails a course in the history of Turkey, his father sends him there.

The Men of Zanzibar

The Men of Zanzibar
5 reels   b&w   1922   sil.
Dir: Rowland V. Lee. Prod: Fox.
Cast: William Russell, Ruth Renick.
The American consul in Zanzibar receives notice that a fugitive is headed there.

DAWSON, PETER

Long Gone

Face of a Fugitive
81 min.   color   1959
Prod: Morningside. Dist: Modern Sound Pictures.
Cast: Fred MacMurray, James Coburn.
A man falsely accused of murder moves to a new town and assumes a new name, but his past catches up with him.

DAY, LILLIAN

Living Up to Lizzie (in *Saturday Evening Post,* 8 December 1934)

Personal Maid's Secret
58 min.   b&w   1935
Dir: Arthur G. Collins. Prod: Warner Bros. and Vitaphone. Dist: MGM/UA
    Home Video (video).
Cast: Margaret Lindsay, Warren Hull.
A maid guides her employers to personal and financial success.

DEAL, BORDEN

Antaeus

Antaeus
20 min.   color   1982
Prod: Highgate Pictures. Dist: Simon & Schuster (16 mm and video).
Set in the 1940s. The story of a boy who moves from the country to the
city and convinces his new friends to grow plants on the rooftops.

DELL, ETHEL MAY

Her Own Free Will

Her Own Free Will
6 reels   b&w   1924   sil.
Dir: Paul Scardon. Prod: Eastern Prod.
Cast: Helene Chadwick, Holmes Herbert.
To save her father from bankruptcy, Nan marries a wealthy man and
reluctantly goes with him to South America. On the way she meets an old lover.

DELMAR, VINA

Angie in Loose Ladies

Uptown New York
85 min.   b&w   1932
Dir: Victor Schertzinger. Prod: E.W. Hammons. Dist: Thunderbird Films.
Cast: Jack Oakie, Raymond Hatton, Shirley Grey, Alexander Carr, Lee
    Moran.
Shirley, a young girl, loses the man she loves because his parents have
arranged for him to marry into a wealthy family.

Bad Boy

Bad Boy
50 min.   b&w   1936
Dir: John Blystone. Prod: Twentieth Century Fox.
Cast: James Dunn, Louise Fazenda.
The hero warns the girl he loves that he is bad, but she won't give him up.

Dance Hall (in *Liberty Magazine,* 16 March 1929)

> *Dance Hall*
> 7 reels   1929   sil. or sd.
> Dir: Melville Brown. Prod: RKO.
> Cast: Olive Borden, Arthur Lake.
> Tommy loves Gracie, who loves Ted, who is not interested in her.

The Human Side

> *The Great Man's Lady*
> 90 min.   b&w   1942
> Dir: William A. Wellman. Prod: Paramount. Dist: Swank.
> Cast: Barbara Stanwyck, Joel McCrea, Brian Donlevy.
> Saga of the West in which the hero dreams of oil wells and loses his girl.

Playing Dead (in *Metropolitan Magazine,* March 1915)

> *Restless Souls*
> 40 min.   b&w   1922   sil.
> Dir: Robert Ensminger. Prod: Vitaphone.
> Cast: Earle Williams, Francelia Billington.
> James' wife is so attracted by a neosymbolist lecturer that he resolves to
fake a suicide.

Pretty Sadie McKee

> *Sadie McKee*
> 88 min.   b&w   1934
> Dir: Clarence Brown. Prod: MGM. Dist: Films Inc.
> Cast: Joan Crawford, Franchet Love, Edward Arnold, Gene Raymond.
> A poor girl must choose between a rich alcoholic and her true love.

DEMING, RICHARD

The Careful Man (suggestion for)

> *Arrivederci, Baby*
> 105 min.   color   1966
> Dir: Ken Hughes. Prod: Paramount. Dist: Audio Brandon.
> Cast: Tony Curtis, Rosanna Schiaffino, Lionel Jeffries, Zsa Zsa Gabor.
> Con artist does away with his adoptive mother and her suitor, his chatterbox
wife, and his too-energetic second wife. But when he meets and weds a gorgeous,
scheming wealthy widow, getting rid of her turns out to be a major problem.

DENEVI, MARCO

Secret Ceremony

> *Secret Ceremony*
> 109 min.   b&w   1968
> Dir: Joseph Losey. Prod: Universal. Dist: Alan Twyman Presents.
> Cast: Mia Farrow, Elizabeth Taylor.

An aged prostitute meets a wealthy but deranged girl, who insists the woman is her mother.

DETZER, KARL

Car Ninety-Nine (in *Saturday Evening Post*)

> *Car Ninety-Nine*
> 70 min.   b&w   1935
> Dir: Charles Barton. Prod: Paramount.
> Cast: Fred MacMurray, Ann Sheridan.
> A rookie trooper lets the bank robbers get away.

DICKENS, CHARLES

A Christmas Carol

Earlier film versions include *A Christmas Carol* (Essanay, 1908); *A Christmas Carol* (Edison, 1910); and *A Christmas Carol* (Great Britain, 1914).

> *A Christmas Carol*
> 68 min.   b&w   1938
> Dir: Edwin L. Marin. Prod: MGM. Dist: Films Inc.
> Cast: Reginald Owen, Terry Kilburn.
> Reformation of an old miser takes place through the influence of the ghosts of Christmas Past, Present, and Future.

> *A Christmas Carol*
> 86 min.   b&w   1951
> Prod: United Artists. Dist: Video Communications (video).
> Cast: Alistair Sim, Kathleen Harrison.

> *A Christmas Carol*
> 54 min.   b&w   1954
> Prod: United Films. Dist: Carousel Films.
> Cast: Frederic March, Basil Rathbone, Ray Middleton.
> A musical adaptation with a score by Bernard Herman and libretto by Maxwell Anderson.

> *Mr. Magoo's Christmas Carol*
> 60 min.   color   1964
> Dir: Abe Levitow. Prod: UPA. Dist: Audio Brandon.
> Mr. Magoo as Ebenezer Scrooge.

> *Scrooge*
> 67 min.   b&w   1935
> Dir: Henry Edwards. Prod: Paramount. Dist: Select Film Library, "The" Film Center, Blackhawk (video), Video Yesteryear.
> Cast: Sir Seymour Hicks, Donald Calthrop.

Scrooge
111 min.   color   1970
Dir: Ronald Neame. Prod: National General. Dist: Swank, CBS/Fox
    Video (CED disc).
Cast: Albert Finney, Alec Guinness.
Lively and lavish musical version.

A Christmas Carol
23 min.   color   1984
Prod: Chuck Jones. Dist: Center for the Humanities (3/4" video).
Animated.

Mickey's Christmas Carol (made for television)
52 min.   color   1984
Prod: Walt Disney. Dist: Walt Disney Ed. Media.
Animated version starring Mickey Mouse.

Cricket on the Hearth

Biograph made two versions of this story, one in 1909 and the other in 1914.

Cricket on the Hearth
7 reels   b&w   1923   sil.
Dir: Lorimer Johnston. Prod: Paul Gerson Pictures. Dist: Blackhawk (8 mm
    or 16 mm).
Cast: Josep Swickard, Fritz Ridgeway.
In a small village in England, John Perrybingle, the mail carrier, courts and marries Dot, but their trust in each other becomes shaken. A cricket restores it.

Cricket on the Hearth
45 min.   color   1968
Prod: UPA. Dist: "The" Film Center, Blackhawk (video).
Voices: Danny Thomas, Marlo Thomas, Ed Ames, Hans Conreid, Abbe Lane,
    Roddy McDowall.
An animated version about a cricket who unravels all the troubles of a blind girl who regains her sight at Christmastime.

The Signalman

The Signalman
15 min.   b&w   1955
Prod: Dynamic Films. Dist: Audio Brandon.
Cast: Monty Woolley.
A haunting tale of the vision of a lonely railroad signalman, which foretells disaster and his own death.

DINNEEN, JOSEPH F.

They Stole $2,500,000—and Got Away with It

Six Bridges to Cross
96 min.   b&w   1955
Dir: Joseph Pevey. Prod: Universal.
Cast: Tony Curtis, Julie Adams.
A rookie cop befriends a young hoodlum shot by a police officer during a robbery.

DINELLI, MEL

Beware My Lovely (s.m. also the play "The Man")

Beware My Lovely
77 min.   b&w   1952
Dir: Harry Horner. Prod: RKO. Dist: Ivy Films.
Cast: Ida Lupino, Robert Ryan.
A young war widow is menaced by a sinister handyman.

DINESEN, ISAK

The Immortal Story

The Immortal Story
63 min.   color   1968
Dir: Orson Welles. Dist: Audio Brandon.
Cast: Orson Welles, Jeanne Moreau, Roger Coggio, Norman Ashley.
An aging and wealthy merchant attempts to make reality out of a legend about an old man who pays a handsome sailor to sleep with his beautiful young wife in order to have an heir.

DOSTOEVSKY, FYODOR

The Crocodile

The Crocodile
29 min.   color   1969
Prod: Encyclopaedia Britannica. Dist: Brigham Young University (rental).
A crocodile stretches its jaws and swallows Ivan, who decides living in its belly is utopia.

The Gambler

The Great Sinner
110 min.   b&w   1949
Dir: Robert Siodmak. Prod: MGM. Dist: Films Inc.
A story about people whose gambling fever almost ruins their lives.

The Gentle Woman

Une Femme Douce
87 min.   color   1969
Dir: Robert Bresson, Dist: New Yorker Films.
Cast: Dominique Sanda.

A gentle wife commits suicide, and her husband reviews their past to try to retrace the paths that led up to it.

DOYLE, ARTHUR CONAN

Sherlock Holmes, a character created by Doyle, appeared in many short stories and novels. The popular films released in the United States and England that were based on actual stories are listed here. Several original screenplays also were based on the character, including *The Private Life of Sherlock Holmes, Pursuit to Algiers, Scarlet Claw, The Seven Per Cent Solution, Sherlock Holmes, Sherlock Holmes in Washington, Terror by Night* (Dist: Hollywood Home Theater); and *The Woman in Green.* Scores of films made abroad were based on the Holmes character.

The Adventure of Charles Augustus Milverton

The Strange Case of the Missing Rembrandt (Br.)
84 min. b&w 1932
Dir: Leslie S. Hiscott. Prod: First Division Films.
Cast: Arthur Wontner, Jane Welsh.
An unscrupulous American millionaire forces an opium addict to steal a Rembrandt from the Louvre.

The Adventure of the Beryl Coronet (Br.)

The Adventures of Sherlock Holmes (a series of 15)
33-43 min. b&w 1921 sil.
Dir: Maurice Elvey. Prod: Stoll Picture Prod.
Cast: Eille Norwood, Hubert Willis.
The titles include (in brief form): *The Dying Detective, The Devil's Foot, A Case of Identity, The Yellow Face, The Red-Headed League, The Resident Patient, A Scandal in Bohemia, The Man with the Twisted Lip, The Beryl Coronet, The Noble Bachelor, Copper Beeches, The Empty House, The Tiger of San Pedro, The Priory School,* and *The Solitary Cyclist.*

The Adventure of the Copper Beeches (see *The Adventures of Sherlock Holmes* under **The Adventure of the Beryl Coronet**)

The Adventures of the Dancing Men

Sherlock Holmes and the Secret Weapon
68 min. b&w 1942
Dir: Roy William Neill. Prod: Universal. Dist: Audio Brandon, Cable Films (Beta and VHS video), Nostalgia Merchant (coupled with *The Woman in Green*), Electric Video (coupled with *Terror by Night*).
Cast: Basil Rathbone, Nigel Bruce, Lionel Atwill.
Holmes and Watson are hot on the trail of Nazi agents who are planning to steal a newly invented bombsight and kidnap its Swiss inventor.

The Adventures of the Devil's Foot (see *The Adventures of Sherlock Holmes* under **The Adventure of the Beryl Coronet**)

The Adventure of the Dying Detective

The Return of Sherlock Holmes (s.m. also "His Last Bow")
79 min.   b&w   1929   sd.
Dir: Basil Dean, Clive Brook. Prod: Paramount/Famous Players-Lasky.
Cast: Clive Brook, H. Reeves-Smith.
Holmes attends the wedding of Watson's daughter Mary, at which the father
of the groom is poisoned.

The Adventure of the Empty House (see also *The Adventures of Sherlock Holmes*
        under **The Adventure of the Beryl Coronet** and *Sherlock Holmes' Fatal
        House* under **The Final Problem**)

The Woman in Green
68 min.   b&w   1945
Dir: Roy William Neill. Prod: Universal. Dist: Audio Brandon, Cable Films
        (Beta and VHS video), Kit Parker Films (video), Video Connection,
        Discount Video Tapes, Western Film and Video, Nostalgia Merchant
        (coupled with *Sherlock Holmes and the Secret Weapon*).
Cast: Basil Rathbone, Nigel Bruce, Henry Daniell, Hillary Brooke.
In this freely adapted version, Holmes hunts for the missing link in a series
of bizarre murders, and the trail leads to Professor Moriarty.

The Adventure of the Five Orange Pips

The House of Fear
69 min.   b&w   1945
Dir: Roy William Neill. Prod: Universal. Dist: RKO (video), Video
        Communications.
Cast: Basil Rathbone, Nigel Bruce, Paul Cavanagh, Dennis Hoey.
One after another, the members of the Good Comrades Club are murdered
in a gloomy mansion off the Scottish coast until only two members and Watson
remain.

The Adventure of the Noble Bachelor (see *The Adventures of Sherlock Holmes*
        under **The Adventure of the Beryl Coronet**)

The Adventure of the Priory School (see *The Adventures of Sherlock Holmes*
        under **The Adventure of the Beryl Coronet**)

The Adventure of the Six Napoleons (suggestion for)

Pearl of Death
69 min.   b&w   1944
Dir: Roy William Neill. Prod: Universal. Dist: Audio Brandon.
Cast: Basil Rathbone, Nigel Bruce, Evelyn Ankers.
Holmes discovers a series of mysterious killings while stalking the stolen
Borgia pearl. The murders are all committed in the same manner and share the same
baffling clue.

The Adventure of the Solitary Cyclist (see *The Adventures of Sherlock Holmes* under **The Adventure of the Beryl Coronet**)

The Adventure of the Speckled Band

> *The Speckled Band* (s.m. also the play "The Speckled Band")
> 90 min.   b&w   1931
> Dir: Jack Raymond. Prod: First Division Pictures. Dist: Thunderbird Films.
> Cast: Raymond Massey, Athole Stewart.
> Dr. Rylott murders two of his stepdaughters by a unique plan and plans to

murder a third.

The Adventure of Wisteria Lodge (film title: *The Tiger of San Pedro*) (see *The Adventures of Sherlock Holmes* under **The Adventure of the Beryl Coronet**)

Brigadier Gerard Stories

> *The Adventures of Gerard*
> 91 min.   color   1970
> Dir: Jerzy Skolinowski. Prod: United Artists. Dist: MGM/UA Home Video
>   (video).
> Cast: Peter McEnery, Eli Wallach, Jack Hawkins, Claudia Cardinale.
> The encounters of a British soldier with war and women. Note: Earlier

silent versions were produced in Great Britain in 1915 and 1916.

> *The Fighting Eagle*
> 65 min.   b&w   1927   sil.
> Dir: Donald Crisp. Prod: DeMille Pictures. Dist: Em Gee Film Library, Film
>   Classic Exchange.
> Cast: Phyllis Haver, Rod La Rocque.

A Case of Identity (see *The Adventures of Sherlock Holmes* under **The Adventure of the Beryl Coronet**)

The Final Problem (Br.)

> *Sherlock Holmes' Fatal Hour* (s.m. also "The Empty House")
> 84 min.   b&w   1931
> Dir: Leslie S. Hiscott. Prod: First Division Pictures.
> Cast: Arthur Wontner, Ian Fleming.
> A complex plot involving a young woman's concern about her brother's

gambling.

> *The Triumph of Sherlock Holmes* (s.m. also the novel "Valley of Fear")
> 84 min.   b&w   1935
> Dir: Leslie S. Hiscott. Prod: Real Art Prod. Dist: Budget Films/Video (Beta
>   and VHS video), Cable Films.
> Cast: Arthur Wontner, Lyn Harding, Ian Fleming.
> Holmes investigates the murder of a Pinkerton detective.

His Last Bow (see also *The Return of Sherlock Holmes* under **The Adventure of the Dying Detective**)

Sherlock Holmes and the Voice of Terror
65 min.   b&w   1942
Dir: John Rawlins. Dist: Audio Brandon.
Cast: Basil Rathbone, Nigel Bruce, Henry Daniell.
Loosely based on the story, Holmes and Watson comb wartime London for Nazi agents who are broadcasting accounts of successful espionage activities.

The Lost Special

The Lost Special (serialized in 12 chapters)
b&w   1932
Dir: Henry McRae. Prod: Universal.
Two college students and a girl reporter search for the Gold Special, a train that disappeared without a trace (Holmes is not in this film).

The Man with the Twisted Lip (see *The Adventures of Sherlock Holmes* under **The Adventure of the Beryl Coronet**)

The Musgrave Ritual

Sherlock Holmes Faces Death
68 min.   b&w   1943
Dir: Roy William Neill. Prod: Universal. Dist: Audio Brandon.
Cast: Basil Rathbone, Nigel Bruce, Hillary Brooke, Milburn Stone.
One of the most bizarre Holmes tales. This film features a number of unusual clues such as a clock that strikes thirteen before a murder.

The Red-Headed League (see *The Adventures of Sherlock Holmes* under **The Adventure of the Beryl Coronet**)

The Resident Patient (see *The Adventures of Sherlock Holmes* under **The Adventure of the Beryl Coronet**)

A Scandal in Bohemia (see *The Adventures of Sherlock Holmes* under **The Adventure of the Beryl Coronet**)

Silver Blaze

Silver Blaze (s.m. also the novel "The Hound of the Baskervilles")
66 min.   b&w   1941
Dir: Thomas Bentley. Prod: Astor Pictures. Dist: Video Yesteryear
   (Beta and VHS video).
Cast: Lyn Harding, Arthur Wontner, Ian Fleming.
Holmes investigates the disappearance of Colonel Russ's horse Silver Blaze.

Silver Blaze
31 min.   color   1977

Dir: John Davis. Dist: Simon & Schuster (16 mm and video).
Cast: Christopher Plummer, Thorley Walters.
A favorite horse disappears and his trainer is murdered.

Unidentified story

Dressed to Kill (Br. title *Sherlock Holmes and the Secret Code*)
72 min.   b&w   1946
Dir: Roy William Neill. Prod: Universal. Dist: Cable Films (Beta and VHS
     VHS), Hollywood Home Theatre, Video Yesteryear (VHS).
The Bank of England's engraving plates are stolen, and Holmes is captured
while hot on the trail.

The Yellow Face (see *The Adventures of Sherlock Holmes* under **The Adventure
     of the Beryl Coronet**)

DOYLE, LAIRD

The Heir Chaser

Jimmy the Gent (jt. author Ray Nazarro)
67 min.   b&w   1934
Dir: Michael Curtiz. Prod: Warner Bros. Dist: MGM/UA Home Video (video).
Cast: James Cagney, Bette Davis.
An enterprising businessman locates phony "missing" heirs to large fortunes.

DRAWBELL, J.W.

Love Story

A Lady Surrenders (Br.)
90 min.   b&w   1947
Dir: Leslie Arliss. Prod: Gainsborough Studios.
Cast: Margaret Lockwood, Stewart Granger.
A wartime love story about a concert pianist and an RAF pilot, each of who
whom conceals an unhappy secret. Originally called *Love Story.*

DREISER, THEODORE

The Lost Phoebe

The Lost Phoebe
30 min.   color   1983
Dir: Mel Damski. Prod: American Film Institute. Dist: Coronet Films (16
     mm and video).
Senile Henry searches throughout the town for his dead wife.

The Prince Who Was a Thief

The Prince Who Was a Thief
83 min.   color   1951
Dir: Rudolph Mate. Prod: Learning Corp. Dist: Simon & Schuster (16 mm
     and video).
Cast: Tony Curtis, Piper Laurie, Everett Sloane.

An Arabian Nights' fantasy of a prince raised by thieves and the beautiful urchin who loves him.

DU MAURIER, DAPHNE

The Birds

The Birds
119 min.   color   1963
Dir: Alfred Hitchcock. Prod: Universal. Dist: Swank, Alan Twyman Presents,
  MCA Home Video (video), RCA/Columbia Pictures (CED disc).
Cast: Rod Taylor, Suzanne Pleshette, Tippi Hedren.
Hundreds of people are victims of a mysterious mass attack by fierce birds.

Don't Look Now

Don't Look Now
110 min.   color   1973
Dir: Nicholas Roeg. Prod: British Lion. Dist: Paramount Home Video (video).
Cast: Donald Sutherland, Julie Christie.
Set in Venice. A young couple's daughter drowns, and the city is besieged by a series of bizarre murders.

DUNCAN, DAVID

The Lost Treasure of the Andes

Jivarro
91 min.   b&w   1954
Dir: Edward Ludwig. Prod: Paramount. Dist: Westcoast Films.
Cast: Fernando Lamas, Rhonda Fleming.
Two adventurers seek treasure in the jungle territory of head-hunters.

DUNN, ELIZABETH

Candy Takes a Job

Meet the Stewarts
73 min.   b&w   1942
Dir: Alfred E. Green. Prod: Columbia Pictures.
Cast: William Holden, Frances Dee.
An heiress marries a white-collar worker and tries to live on a budget.

DUNN, J. ALLEN

The Mascotte of the Three Star

Action
5 reels   b&w   1921   sil.
Dir: Jack Ford. Prod: Universal.
Cast: Hoot Gibson, Francis Ford.
Western melodrama. An orphan, heir to a ranch and a mine, falls under the influence of a saloon owner who tries to get her inheritance.

DURLAM, ARTHUR

State Trooper

Young Dynamite
60 min.   b&w   1937
Dir: Leslie Goodwins. Prod: Maurice Conn. Dist: Film Classics Exchange.
Cast: Frankie Darro.

DWYER, JAMES

Maryland, My Maryland (in *Collier's Magazine,* 20 March 1920)

Bride of the Storm
7 reels   b&w   1926   sil.
Dir: J. Stuart Blackton. Prod: Vitagraph.
Cast: Dolores Costello, John Harron.
An American ship is wrecked off the coast of the Dutch East Indies, and a little girl and her mother are washed ashore.

EBERHART, MIGNON

Dead Yesterday

> *The Great Hospital Mystery*
> 52 min.   b&w   1937
> Dir: James Tinling. Prod: Twentieth Century Fox.
> Cast: Jane Darwell, Sig Rumann.
> Mystery surrounds a corpse that was shot after it was already dead.

EDGELOW, THOMAS

It Isn't Being Done This Season (in *Breezy Stories,* August 1918)

> *It Isn't Being Done This Season*
> 5 reels   b&w   1921   sil.
> Dir: George L. Sargent. Prod: Vitagraph.
> Cast: Corinne Griffith, Sally Crute, Webster Campbell.
> A society melodrama in which Marcia marries for money instead of love.

EDGINGTON, MAY (pseud. of Helen Marion Edgington)

The Heart Is Young

> *The False Madonna*
> 60 min.   b&w   1932
> Dir: Arthur Kober (pseud. of Stuart Walker). Prod: Paramount Publix.
> Cast: William Boyd, Conway Tearle.
> Story of two couples who are cardsharps and blackmailers.

The Joy Girl (in *Saturday Evening Post,* 13 November-18 December 1926)

> *The Joy Girl*
> 7 reels   b&w   1927   sil.
> Dir: Alan Dwan. Prod: Twentieth Century Fox.
> Cast: Olive Borden, Neil Hamilton, Marie Dressler.
> Jewel marries for wealth but later learns her husband is really a chauffeur
posing as a millionaire.

Judgment (in *Saturday Evening Post,* August 1924)

> *Her Husband's Secret*
> 7 reels   b&w   1925   sil.
> Dir: Frank Lloyd. Prod: Frank Lloyd.

Cast: Antonio Moreno, Patsy Ruth Miller.

A wife goes to see a neighbor when her husband throws a wild party, and he then divorces her for spending the night with another man.

Purple and Fine Linen

Three Hours
6 reels   b&w   1927   sil.
Dir: James Flood. Prod: Corinne Griffith.
Cast: Corinne Griffith, John Bowers.
Madeleine, once married to a wealthy man, is reduced to poverty and stealing.

Adventure in Manhattan
8 reels   b&w   1936
Dir: Edward Ludwig. Prod: Columbia Pictures.
Cast: Jean Arthur.

A remake of *Three Hours* in which a newspaperman sets out to capture a thief.

ELLIN, STANLEY

The Best of Everything (in *Ellery Queen's Magazine,* November 1952)

Nothing But the Best
98 min.   color   1964
Dir: Clive Donner. Prod: David Deutsch. Dist: Audio Brandon, Cine Craft, Modern Sound Pictures.
Cast: Alan Bates, Denholm Elliott, Harry Andrews, Millicent Martin, Nigel Stock, Peter Madden.

A cheeky young real estate salesman is set to climb the ladder and marry the boss's daughter but ends up strangled by his own Etonian tie.

ELLISON, HARLAN

A Boy and His Dog

A Boy and His Dog
89 min.   color   1976
Dir: L.Q. Jones. Dist: Films Inc.
Cast: Don Johnson, Susanne Benton, Alvy Moore, Jason Robards.

A boy and his telepathic dog roam about the misogynistic society of post-World War IV in search of food and women.

ELLSTON, ALLAN VAUGHAN

The Belled Palm

Paradise Isle
8 reels   b&w   1937
Dir: Arthur Greville Collins. Prod: Monogram Pictures.
Cast: Movita, Warren Hull.
A white man who is blind loves a South Seas native.

EMERY, STUART M.

The Wild, Wild Child (in *Liberty Magazine,* 31 January 1925)

> *Wild, Wild Susan*
> 6 reels   b&w   1925   sil.
> Dir: Edward Sutherland. Prod: Famous Players-Lasky.
> Cast: Bebe Daniels, Rod LaRocque.
> An affluent New York girl in search of thrills goes to work in a detective

agency.

ENGELS, S.

Cut Rate (jt. author Niven Busch)

> *The Big Shakedown*
> 61 min.   b&w   1933
> Dir: John Francis Dillon. Prod: First National Pictures. Dist: MGM/UA
>   Home Video (video).
> Cast: Ricardo Cortez, Bette Davis.

ENGLISH, RICHARD

Follow the Band

> *Follow the Band*
> 61 min.   b&w   1943
> Dir: Jean Yarbrough. Prod: Universal.
> Romantic mix-ups ensue when a Vermont boy gets a job in New York as a

trombone player.

No Place to Go (in *Saturday Evening Post*)

> *Leather Gloves*
> 75 min.   b&w   1948
> Dir: Richard Quine, William Asher. Prod: Columbia Pictures.
> A down-and-out boxer regains his self-respect.

ENTERS, ANGNA

Tenth Ave. Angel

> *Tenth Ave. Angel* (s.m. also "Miracle at Midnight," a radio sketch by Craig
>   Rice)
> 74 min.   b&w   1948
> Dir: Roy Rowland. Prod: MGM. Dist: Films Inc.
> Cast: Margaret O'Brien.
> A young girl living in a tenement influences everyone by her faith.

ERICKSON, CARL

Competition

> *Stranger in Town*
> 66 min.   b&w   1932

Dir: Eric C. Kenton. Prod: Warner Bros. Dist: MGM/UA Home Video (video).
Cast: Chic Sale, Ann Dvorak, Noah Beery.
Story of a small-town grandfather and his general store.

ERNST, PAUL

The Old Gang (in *Saturday Evening Post,* 11 July 1942)

Kid Dynamite
70 min.   b&w   1943
Dir: Wallace Fox. Prod: Monogram Pictures. Dist: Budget Films/Video,
    Ivy Films.
Cast: The Bowery Boys.
Friction develops between two members of a gang.

When We Were Twenty-One

Truth about Youth
68 min.   b&w   1930
Dir: William A. Seiter. Prod: First National Pictures. Dist: MGM/UA Home
    Video (video).
Cast: Loretta Young, Myrna Loy.
Romantic drama of crossed love affairs.

ERSKINE, LAURIE YORK

Renfrew of the Royal Mounted

Sky Bandits
56 min.   b&w   1940
Prod: Monogram Pictures. Dist: Video Connection (video).
Cast: James Newill, Dave O'Brien.
Mounties uncover the mystery of the disappearance of a plane carrying gold
from a Yukon mine.

EVANS, LARRY

Judgment of the Hills (in *Cosmopolitan Magazine*)

Judgment of the Hills
6 reels   b&w   1927   sil.
Dir: James Leo Meehan. Prod: R-C Pictures.
Cast: Virginia Valli, Frankie Darro.
Brant, an alcoholic, refuses to go to war until the sheriff finds him and
sends him to boot camp. He returns home a hero but still an alcoholic.

The Painted Lady (in *Saturday Evening Post,* November 1912)

The Painted Lady
7 reels   b&w   1924   sil.
Dir: Chester Bennett. Prod: Fox.
Cast: George O'Brien, Dorothy Mackaill.
Violet, released from prison after being convicted of a crime committed by
her sister, is forced to become a prostitute. A 1917 version of this film also is
available.

Pursued
61 min.   b&w   1934
Dir: Louis King. Prod: Fox. Dist: Corinth Films.

EVERSON, RONALD

Scare (s.m. also "The Red Shadow Scare" and the radio show "Street and Smith's Detective Story Magazine Hour")

Story Magazine Hour
20 min.   b&w   1932
Dir: Kurt Newmann. Prod: Universal.
A Shadow Detective series short.

F

FAIRMAN, PAUL (see JORGENSON, IVAR)

FARAGO, SANDOR

The Boy, the Girl, and the Dog (jt. author Alexander G. Kenedi)

Marry the Boss's Daughter
52 min.   b&w   1941
Dir: Thornton Freeland. Prod: Twentieth Century Fox.

FAST, HOWARD

Rachel

Rachel and the Stranger
92 min.   b&w   1948
Dir: Norman Foster. Prod: RKO. Dist: Films Inc., Nostalgia Merchant
   (video).
Cast: William Holden, Loretta Young.
Western. A man's love for his wife is aroused when a stranger visits their
home.

FAULKNER, WILLIAM

The Barn Burning (s.m. also "The Spotted Horses" and "The Hamlet")

The Long Hot Summer
115 min.   color   1958
Dir: Martin Ritt. Prod: Twentieth Century Fox. Dist: Films Inc., Blackhawk
   (video).
Cast: Orson Welles, Paul Newman, Joanne Woodward, Lee Remick, Tony
   Franciosa.
Turbulent relationships exist between a wealthy, aggressive father and his two
grown children, one a frustrated, unmarried young woman and the other a weak-
willed, married son.

Barn Burning
41 min.   color   1980
Dir: Peter Werner. Dist: Coronet Films (16 mm and video).
A proud tenant farmer in the late nineteenth century South burns his
employer's barn, and his son is horrifed.

A Rose for Emily

A Rose for Emily
27 min.   color   1983
Dir: John Carradine. Dist: Pyramid Films (16 mm and video).
Cast: Anjelica Huston.
Set in the South after the Civil War, Emily is isolated from society and does not invite guests to her home until a brash Yankee comes for dinner and never leaves.

The Spotted Horses (see *The Long Hot Summer* under **The Barn Burning**)

Tomorrow

Tomorrow
102 min.   color   1972
Dir: Joseph Anthony. Dist: Monterey Home Video (video).
A young Mississippi farmer nurses a pregnant woman abandoned by her husband and raises her son.

Turn About

Today We Live
110 min.   b&w   1933
Dir: Howard Hawks. Prod: MGM.
Cast: Joan Crawford, Gary Cooper.
A war story filled with heroism and sacrifice.

FAUST, FREDERICK (see BRAND, MAX)

FAY, WILLIAM

The Disappearance of Dolan (in *Saturday Evening Post*)

Champ for a Day
90 min.   b&w   1953
Dir: Irving Shulman. Prod: Republic Pictures. Dist: Ivy Films.
Cast: Audrey Totter, Alex Nichol.
Investigating the disappearance of his manager, a young prizefighter is indirectly responsible for breaking up a gambling syndicate.

The Man Who Sank the Navy (in *Saturday Evening Post*)

The Guy Who Came Back
91 min.   b&w   1951
Dir: Joseph Newman. Prod: Twentieth Century Fox. Dist: Ivy Films.
Cast: Paul Douglas, Joan Bennett.
A football hero can't seem to make it after his career is halted by an injury.

A Rose for Emily
Photograph courtesy of Pyramid Films

FERBER, EDNA

Classified

Classified
7 reels   b&w   1925   sil.
Cast: Corinne Griffith, Jack Mulhall.
Comedy. A girl who works in the classified advertising section of a newspaper flirts with every wealthy man she meets but falls in love with a garage owner.

Hard to Get
8 reels   b&w   1929   sd. or sil.
Prod: First National Pictures.
Cast: Dorothy Mackaill, Charles Delaney.
A millionaire philanderer and an automobile mechanic are rivals for a mannequin in a fashionable shop.

Glamour

Glamour
75 min.   b&w   1934
Dir: William Wyler. Prod: Universal.
Cast: Paul Lukas, Constance Cummings.
A chorus girl who is married and a mother falls in love with a composer.

Mother Knows Best

Mother Knows Best
9 reels   b&w   1928   sd. and music
Dir: John Blystone. Prod: Fox.
Cast: Madge Bellamy, Louise Dresser.
A domineering mother controls her daughter's successful show business career until the daughter suffers a nervous breakdown.

Not a Day Over Twenty-One

Summer Resort
b&w   1932
Prod: Worldwide.

Old Man Minick

The Expert
69 min.   b&w   1932
Dir: Archie Mayo. Prod: Warner Bros. and Vitaphone. Dist: MGM/UA Home
   Video (video).
Cast: Chic Sale, Lois Wilson.
A neglected old man befriends a newspaper boy.

FESSIER, MICHAEL

The Sheriff Was Scared

The Boy from Oklahoma
88 min.   color   1953
Dir: Michael Curtiz. Prod: Warner Bros.
A homespun sheriff restores law and order to a crime-ridden town using a lariat as his weapon.

The Woman They Almost Lynched (in *Saturday Evening Post,* 1 June 1951)

The Woman They Almost Lynched
90 min.   b&w   1953
Dir: Allan Dwan. Prod: Republic Pictures. Dist: Ivy Films.
Cast: Joan Leslie, Brian Donlevy.
A young Yankee girl becomes involved with a Confederate guerilla leader, his unscrupulous wife, and a rebel spy.

FIELD, JULIAN

Tempermental Lady

Setting of the Moon
54 min.   b&w   1936
Dir: Ralph Staub. Prod: Republic Pictures. Dist: Ivy Films.
Cast: Roger Pryor, Grace Bradley.
A composer helps a vocalist until his ex-girlfriend shows up calling herself his wife.

FINDLEY, FERGUSON

The Waterfront

The Mob
87 min.   b&w   1951
Dir: Robert Parrish. Prod: Columbia Pictures. Dist: Kit Parker Films.
Cast: Broderick Crawford, Betty Buehler, Richard Kiley.
An undercover agent is sent back to the waterfront to catch a top mobster after failing the first time.

FINKEL, ABEN (jt. author) (see *The Deceiver* under MUNI, BELLE)

FINNEY, JACK

Five Against the House (in *Good Housekeeping,* July-August-September 1951)

Five Against the House
84 min.   b&w   1955
Dir: Phil Karlson. Prod: Dayle Prod. Dist: Kit Parker Films.
The prankish scheme of four college boys and a songstress to rob a casino in Reno ends in a grim clash with the law.

House of Numbers (in *Cosmopolitan Magazine,* July 1956)

> *House of Numbers*
> 92 min.   b&w   1957
> Dir: Russell Rouse. Prod: MGM. Dist: Films Inc.
> Cast: Jack Palance, Barbara Lang.
> A clever plan for a murderer's escape from prison.

FISHER, DOROTHY F.C. (see CANFIELD, DOROTHY)

FISHER, STEVE

If You Break My Heart (in *Liberty Magazine*)

> *Nurse from Brooklyn*
> 65 min.   b&w   1938
> Dir: S. Sylvan Simon. Prod: Universal.
> Cast: Sally Eilers, Paul Kelly.
> The wounded detective who allegedly shot a nurse's brother is brought
to the hospital where she works.

The Sea Nymph

> *September Storm* (a.k.a. *The Girl in the Red Bikini*)
> 99 min.   b&w   1961
> Dir: Byron Haskin. Prod: Twentieth Century Fox. Dist: Willoughby-Peerless.
> Cast: Joanne Dru, Mark Stevens.
> A model joins adventurers trying to recover a fortune in sunken Spanish
gold.

Shore Leave

> *Navy Secrets*
> 7 reels   b&w   1939
> Dir: Howard Betherton. Prod: Monogram Pictures.
> Cast: Fay Wray, Craig Reynolds.
> Daring girls versus a spy ring.

FITCH, GEORGE

Siwash Stories

> *Those Were the Days*
> 76 min.   b&w   1940
> Dir: Jay Theodore Reed. Prod: Paramount.
> Cast: Bill Holden, Bonita Granville.
> A college comedy set during the horse and buggy days.

FITZGERALD, F. SCOTT

Babylon Revisited

> *The Last Time I Saw Paris*
> 116 min.   color   1954

Dir: Richard Brooks. Prod: MGM. Dist: Films Inc., Discount Video Tapes (video).

A war correspondent married during a World War I victory celebration in Paris lives happily until he is unable to sell his novels, falls into debt, and seeks solace in love affairs.

Bernice Bobs Her Hair

Bernice Bobs Her Hair
48 min.   color   1977
Dir. and Sp: Joan Micklin Silver. Dist: Coronet Films (16 mm and video).

"Ugly duckling" Bernice is transformed by her cousin into a vamp and becomes so adroit at using social clichés and conventions that she wins her cousin's suitors.

Head and Shoulders

The Chorus Girl's Romance
6 reels   b&w   1920   sil.
Dir: William C. Dowlan. Prod: Metro Pictures.

Offshore Pirate (in *Saturday Evening Post,* 29 May 1920)

The Offshore Pirate
6 reels   b&w   1921   sil.
Dir: Dallas M. Fitzgerald. Prod: Metro Pictures.
Cast: Viola Dana, Jack Mulhall.

Romantic comedy. Society girl Ardita is held up in her roadster and rescued by a Russian in search of a rich wife.

FLEMING, BRANDON

The Pillory

Eleventh Commandment
8 reels   b&w   1933
Dir: George Melford. Prod: Allied Pictures.
Cast: Allan Hale, Marian March.

A stepfather opposes his daughter's lover and tries to break up the romance.

FLEMING-ROBERTS, G.T.

Blackmail with Feathers

Find the Blackmailer
55 min.   b&w   1943
Dir: Ross Lalerman. Prod: Warner Bros. Dist: MGM/UA Home Video (video).
Cast: Faye Emerson, Jerome Cowan.

Comedy mystery. A detective is hired by a man who is being blackmailed by a talking blackbird.

FLYNN, THOMAS T.

The Man from Laramie

The Man from Laramie
104 min.   color   1955
Dir: Anthony Mann. Prod: Columbia Pictures. Dist: Budget Films/Video,
    Modern Sound Pictures, Newman Film Library.
Cast: James Stewart, Arthur Kennedy, Cathy O'Donnell.
A man hunts the cowboy responsible for his brother's death in this taut
psychological western.

FOOTE, JOHN TAINTOR

The Song of the Dragon

The Convoy
8 reels   b&w   1921   sil.
Dir: Joseph C. Boyle. Prod: First National Pictures.
Cast: Lowell Sherman, Dorothy Mackaill.
Sylvia tries to help her brother, who is a secret service agent, find out
information about one of her German admirers, a spy.

FOOTNER, HULBERT

A New Girl in Town (in *Argosy All-Story Weekly Magazine,* 30 September-28 October 1922)

The Dangerous Blonde
5 reels   b&w   1924   sil.
Dir: Robert F. Hill. Prod: Universal.
Cast: Laura LaPlante, Edward Hearn.
Colonel Faraday asks his daughter Diana to recover some letters that he
once wrote to an adventuress.

FORD, COREY

College Hero

Start Cheering
79 min.   b&w   1938
Dir: Albert S. Rogell. Prod: Columbia Pictures.
Cast: Jimmy Durante, Gertrude Niesen.
An ambitious movie idol, leaving for college, finds that his ex-staff is trying
to get him expelled.

Echoes That Old Refrain

Winter Carnival
105 min.   b&w   1939
Dir: Charles Reisner. Prod: Walter Wanger Prod. Dist: Institutional Cinema,
    Mogull's Films.
Cast: Ann Sheridan, Richard Carlson, Helen Parrish, Robert Armstrong.
Dartmouth College is a parade of sports, thrills, and romance.

FORD, SEWELL

Tessie and the Little Sap (in *Saturday Evening Post,* 28 March 1925)

> *Tessie*
> 7 reels   b&w   1925   sil.
> Dir: Dallas M. Fitzgerald. Prod: Arrow Pictures.
> Cast: May McAvoy, Bobby Agnew.
> A triangle involving an older woman.

FORESTER, CECIL SCOTT

The Commandoes (in *Cosmopolitan Magazine*)

> *Commandoes Strike at Dawn*
> 100 min.   b&w   1943
> Dir: John Farrow. Prod: Columbia Pictures.
> Cast: Paul Muni.
> The people of Norway resist the Nazis and pave the way for a commando

strike.

Eagle Squadron (in *Cosmopolitan Magazine*)

> *Eagle Squadron*
> 109 min.   b&w   1942
> Dir: Arthur Lubin. Prod: Universal.
> Cast: Robert Stack, Diana Barrymore.
> An American in the RAF falls in love with an English girl.

FORNEY, PAULINE

Boarding House Blues (jt. author Dudley Murphy)

> *Jazz Heaven*
> 7 reels   b&w   1929
> Dir: Melville Brown. Prod: RKO.
> Cast: John Mack Brown, Sally O'Neil.
> A young woman who works in a music publishing house helps a struggling

songwriter.

FORRESTER, IZOLA

The Gray Path (in *Ainslee's,* September 1922)

> *Youth for Sale*
> 6 reels   b&w   1924   sil.
> Dir: William Christy Cabanne. Prod: C.C. Burr Pictures.
> Cast: May Allison, Sigrid Holmquist.
> Molly is blinded by her first drink of alcohol.

FORSYTH, FREDERICK

A Careful Man

> *2 X Forsyth* (made for television)
> 60 min.   color   1984

Adap: Michael Feeney Callan. Prod: Tara Productions and Mobil Oil.
Cast: Dan O'Herlihy, Shirley Ann Field, Milo O'Shea.

A compilation of two stories: In "A Careful Man," a rich, childless widower wants to make sure his fortune does not go to his greedy sister. In "Privilege," a mild-mannered rare stamp dealer is unwittingly caught in an unfortunate transaction.

Privilege (see *2 X Forsyth* under **A Careful Man**)

FORT, GARRETT (jt. author) (see *The Prince of Headwaiters* under SHORE, VIOLA BROTHERS)

FOSTER, BENNETT

The Outlaws Are in Town (in *Saturday Evening Post,* 28 May 1949)

> *The Desperados Are in Town*
> 78 min.   b&w   1956
> Dir: Kurt Neuman. Prod: Regal Films.
> Cast: Rex Reason, Kathy Nolan.
> Western. A penitent young man, who was once involved with outlaws in
Texas, goes home.

Trail Town Fever

> *Flame of the West*
> 55 min.   b&w   1945
> Dir: Lambert Hillyer. Prod: Monogram Pictures. Dist: Hurlock Cine-World.
> Cast: Johnny Mack Brown.
> Western. A doctor helps clean up a small Western town.

FOSTER, MAXIMILLAN

The Silent Partner (in *Harper's Monthly,* May 1908)

> *The Silent Partner*
> 6 reels   b&w   1923   sil.
> Dir: Charles Maigne. Prod: Famous Players-Lasky.
> Cast: Beatrice Joy, Owen Moore.
> Lisa Coburn becomes a "silent partner" for her husband in his Wall Street
financial speculations.

FOX, PAUL HARVEY

Goddess

> *The Stars Are Singing*
> 99 min.   b&w   1953
> Dir: Norman Taurog. Prod: Paramount. Dist: Films Inc.
> Cast: Rosemary Clooney, Lauritz Melchoir.
> A broken-down opera singer, a struggling singer, a vaudeville entertainer,
and an unemployed dancer aid a Polish soprano in legal difficulties.

Masterpiece

Gentleman at Heart
66 min.   b&w   1942
Dir: Ray McCarey. Prod: Twentieth Century Fox. Dist: Films Inc.
Cast: Cesar Romero, Milton Berle.
Comedy. A racketeer goes into the art business.

Tall, Dark and Handsome
78 min.   b&w   1941
Dir: Bruce Humberstone. Dist: Films Inc.
Cast: Cesar Romero.
A story about a soft-hearted gangster and an orphan.

FRANCE, ANATOLE   *[handwritten: NOT ANATOLE FRANCE, BUT RENÉ FAUCHOIS]*

Boudu: Sauve Des Eaux

Boudu: Saved from Drowning (Fr. with English subtitles)
87 min.   b&w   1932
Dir: Jean Renoir. Dist: Budget Films/Video, Kit Parker Films, Cinema
     Concepts (video).
Cast: Michel Simon, Charles Grandval.
"It's about time that someone of our class did something heroic," remarks
a bystander as Lestingois pulls Boudu from the Seine. A thousand people who
miraculously appear on the bridge over the troubled waters nod their agreement;
of course, they have no intention of pushing their "class" forward to the point of
being helpful.

Juggler of Notre Dame

Juggler of Notre Dame
30 min.   color   1968
Prod: Craven/Dimka. Dist: Pyramid Films (16 mm and video).
A puppet-type animated story about a kind-hearted little juggler who travels
from town to town in medieval France.

FRANCIS, OWEN

Big

The Magnificent Brute
77 min.   b&w   1936
Dir: John G. Blystone. Prod: Universal.
Cast: Victor McLaglen, Binnie Barnes, William Hall.
A blast furnace boss becomes involved in a romantic triangle and stolen
money.

FRANKEN, ROSE

Twenty-Two

The Secret Heart (s.m. also "Holiday," a play)
97 min.   b&w   1946

Dir: Robert Z. Leonard. Prod: MGM.
Cast: Patricia Medina, June Allyson, Marshal Thompson.
Love triangles.

FRANKLIN, EDGAR

Poker Faces (in *Argosy All-Story Weekly Magazine,* 18 August-25 September
1923)

Poker Faces
8 reels   b&w   1926   sil.
Dir: Harry A. Pollard. Prod: Universal.
Cast: Edward Everett Horton, Laura LaPlante.
A struggling office worker is given a big chance to land an important
contract but complications ensue.

Protecting Prue (in *Argosy All-Story Weekly Magazine,* 16 August-13 September
1924)

My Lady of Whims
70 min.   b&w   1925   sil.
Dir: Dallas M. Fitzgerald.
Cast: Clara Bow, Donald Keith.
A young man is hired to keep an eye on the Bohemian daughter of a wealthy
man, and they fall in love.

Stay Home (in *Argosy All-Story Weekly Magazine,* November-December 1921)

I Can Explain
5 reels   b&w   1922   sil.
Dir: George D. Baker. Prod: Famous Players-Lasky.
Cast: Gareth Hughes, Bartine Burkett.
The boss's wife confides in his junior partner that she is planning to open
a rival business in South America.

Whatever She Wants (in *Argosy All-Story Weekly Magazine,* 11 June-9 July, 1921)
(s.m. also "White Collars," a play by Edith Ellis, which in turn is based on
the story)

The Idle Rich
9 reels   b&w   1929
Dir: William DeMille. Prod: MGM.
Cast: Conrad Nagel, Leila Hyams.
A typist's family refuses to share her husband's money until he offers to give
it to charity.

Rich Man, Poor Girl
8 reels   b&w   1938
Prod: MGM.
Cast: Lew Ayres, Ruth Hussey, Robert Young.
A remake of *The Idle Rich* in which a rich man carries off one of the
daughters of a middle-class family.

Whatever She Wants
5 reels   b&w   1921   sil.
Dir: C.R. Wallace. Prod: Fox.
Cast: Eileen Percy, Herbert Fortier.
Enid secretly gets a job in the office of the manufacturing company owned by her fiance.

Where Was I? (in *Argosy All-Story Weekly Magazine,* 1-22 November 1924)

Where Was I?
7 reels   b&w   1925   sil.
Dir: William A. Seiter. Prod: Universal-Jewell.
Cast: Reginald Denny, Marion Nixon.
A successful young businessman becomes engaged to the daughter of his rival.

FRANKLIN, GEORGE CORY

Into the Crimson West

Prairie Schooners
6 reels   b&w   1940
Dir: Sam Nelson. Prod: Columbia Pictures.

FRAZEE, STEVE

Death Rides This Trail

Wild Heritage
78 min.   color   1958
Dir: Charles Haas. Prod: Universal.
Cast: Will Rogers, Jr., Maureen O'Sullivan.
Western. Two pioneer families meet while traveling West.

Many Rivers to Cross

Many Rivers to Cross
92 min.   color   1955
Dir: Roy Rowland. Prod: MGM. Dist: Films Inc.
Cast: Robert Taylor, Eleanor Parker, Victor McLaglen, Russ Tamblyn.
Western. A good-natured spoof about the customs of a husband-hunting tomboy and a frontiersman.

My Brother Down There

Running Target
83 min.   color   1956
Dir: Marvin R. Weinstein. Prod: United Artists. Dist: MGM/UA Home Video (video).
Cast: Arthur Franz, Doris Dowling, Richard Reeves, Myron Healey.
Western. A trigger-happy marksman joins a posse on the getaway trail of four escaped convicts through the Rocky Mountains.

FREEMAN, EVERETT

$1,000 a Minute (in *Saturday Evening Post,* 26 January 1925)

One Thousand Dollars a Minute
54 min.   b&w   1935
Dir: Aubrey Scott. Prod: Republic Pictures. Dist: Ivy Films.
Cast: Edgar Kennedy, Edward Brophy.
A reporter wins romance by proving to two crooks that he can spend
$1,000 a minute for 12 hours.

FREEMAN, MARY WILKINS

One Good Time

One Good Time
20 min.   color   1983
Prod: Auburn Television. Dist: AIT (video).

The Village Singer

The Village Singer
15 min.   color   1978
Prod: International Instructional Television Coop. Dist: Indiana University.
A village church vocalist seeks revenge against her successor.

FRIEDMAN, BRUCE JAY

Black Angels

Bruce Jay Friedman
40 min.
Prod. and Dist: Authors on Videotape (video).
Friedman reads his stories: "Black Angels," about race relations, and "Change
of Plan," about a man who meets the girl of his dreams on his honeymoon.

A Change of Plan (see also *Bruce Jay Friedman* under **Black Angels**)

The Heartbreak Kid
104 min.   color   1973
Dir: Elaine May. Prod: Twentieth Century Fox. Dist: Films Inc., Media Home
     Entertainment (video).
The story of a Jewish boy from New York City who falls in love with an
attractive blonde while on his honeymoon in Miami.

G

GABINEAU, ARTHUR

Adelaide

Adelaide (French with English subtitles)
86 min.   color   1968
Dir: Jean-Daniel Simon. Dist: Audio Brandon.
Cast: Ingrid Thulin, Jean Sorel, Sylvie Fennec.
Following the death of her husband Elisabeth marries a research engineer
10 years her junior, but her daughter has also fallen in love with him and continues
to have an affair with him.

GABY, ALEX

Fifty-Two Miles to Terror (in *Saturday Evening Post,* 14 January 1956)

Hot Rods to Hell
92 min.   b&w   1967
Dir: John Brahm. Prod: MGM. Dist: Films Inc.
Cast: Jeanne Crain, Laurie Mock, Dana Andrews.
A family is menaced on the road.

GADDIS, PEGGY

The Part-Time Wife (in *Snappy Stories,* August 1925)

The Part-Time Wife
6 reels   b&w   1925   sil.
Dir: Henry McCarty. Prod: Gotham Prod.
Cast: Alice Calhoun, Robert Ellis.
Melodrama. A poor newspaperman marries a screen star, and her success
hurts his pride.

GAINES, ERNEST

The Sky Is Gray

The Sky Is Gray
47 min.   color   1982
Dir: Stan Lathan. Sp: Charles Fuller. Dist: Coronet Films (16 mm and video).
An eight-year-old black boy living in rural Louisiana in the early 1940s gets
a new perspective when he has to go to town to have a toothache treated.

GALE, ZONA

The Way

> *When Strangers Meet*
> 8 reels   b&w   1934
> Dir: William Christy Cabanne. Prod: Liberty Pictures.

GALLAND, VICTORIA

The Golden Gallows (in *Snappy Stories,* 1 October 1921)

> *The Golden Gallows*
> 5 reels   b&w   1922   sil.
> Dir: Paul Scardon. Prod: Universal.
> Cast: Miss Du Pont, Edwin Stevens.
> A chorus girl is left a fortune, which makes her boyfriends suspicious of her.

GALLICO, PAUL

The Adventure of Joe Smith, American (in *Cosmopolitan Magazine*)

> *Joe Smith, American*
> 63 min.   b&w   1942
> Prod: MGM. Dist: Films Inc.
> Cast: Robert Young, Marsha Hunt.
> A story of a munitions factory worker and his unglamorous wife.

> *The Big Operator*
> 91 min.   b&w   1959
> Dir: Charles Haas. Prod: MGM.
> Cast: Mickey Rooney, Mamie Van Doren.
> A remake of *Joe Smith, American.*

Under the Clock

> *The Clock*
> 90 min.   b&w   1945
> Dir: Vincente Minelli. Prod: MGM. Dist: Films Inc.
> Cast: Judy Garland, Robert Walker.
> A New York girl meets and marries a soldier on a 48-hour leave in New York.

The Man Who Hated People (in *Saturday Evening Post*)

> *Lili*
> 81 min.   color   1953
> Dir: Charles Walters. Prod: MGM. Dist: Films Inc., MGM/UA Home Video
>   (video).
> Cast: Leslie Caron, Mel Ferrer, Zsa Zsa Gabor, Jean-Pierre Aumont.
> Joining a carnival puppet show, a shy sixteen-year-old French orphan girl
becomes infatuated with a magician who keeps his marriage a secret for "business
reasons."

The Enchanted Hour

Next to No Time (Br.)
89 min.   b&w   1960
Dir: Henry Cornelius. Prod: Snow-Corp.
Cast: Kenneth More, Betsy Drake, Roland Culver.
A shy factory worker tries to put his automation plan into action.

Little Miracle (Br.)

Never Take No for an Answer
90 min.   b&w   1952
Prod: Souvaine Selective Pictures. Dist: Roa's Films.
Cast: Vittorio Manunta, Dennis O'Dea.
Peppino, the little seven-year-old businessman, takes Violette, his sick
donkey, to the crypt of St. Francis, where he is sure she will recover.

The Night before Christmas

No Time to Marry
68 min.   b&w   1937
Dir: Harry Lachman. Sp: Paul Gallico. Prod: Columbia Pictures.
Cast: Richard Arlen, Mary Astor.
Assignments keep an ace reporter and journalist from getting to the altar.

Tight Wad

Wild Money
7 reels   b&w   1937
Dir: Louis King. Prod: Paramount.
Cast: Marguerite Roberts, Eddie Welch.
A skinflint auditor spends freely when he hits the trail of a good story.

GALSWORTHY, JOHN

The First and the Last (Br.)

21 Days Together
8 reels   b&w   1940
Dir: Basil Dean. Prod: Columbia Pictures.
Cast: Laurence Olivier, Vivien Leigh.
A young lawyer and a girl decide to live a lifetime in 21 days.

GARDNER, ERLE STANLEY

Granny Get Your Gun

Granny Get Your Gun
56 min.   b&w   1939
Dir: George Amy. Prod: First National Pictures. Dist: MGM/UA Home
     Video (video).
Cast: May Robson, Harry Davenport, Margot Stevenson, Hardie Albright.
Western comedy.

GARLAND, HAMLIN

Mrs. Ripley's Trip

Mrs. Ripley's Trip
15 min.   color   1978
Prod: International Instructional Television Coop. Dist: Indiana University.
A poor farm woman realizes a 23-year-old ambition by leaving the farm for a trip to New York.

GARTH, DAVID

Don't Forget to Remember

There Goes the Groom
70 min.   b&w   1937
Dir: Joseph Santley. Prod: RKO.
Cast: Burgess Meredith, Ann Sothern.
A man, blessed with sudden riches, has in-law troubles.

GARVEY, STANLEY

Three on a Mike

Every Night at Eight
80 min.   b&w   1935
Dir: Raoul Walsh. Prod: Paramount.
Cast: George Raft, Alice Faye, Frances Langford, Patsy Kelly.
Three office girls go on the radio and win fame and fortune.

GELZER, JAY

The House of the Flock (in *Cosmopolitan Magazine,* September 1921)

Driven
6 reels   b&w   1923   sil.
Dir: Charles J. Brabin. Prod: Charles J. Brabin.
Cast: Emily Fitzroy, Burr McIntosh.
Two brothers, both bootleggers, want the same girl.

GIBBS, PHILIP HAMILTON

Darkened Rooms (in *Cosmopolitan Magazine,* March-June 1928)

Darkened Rooms
7 reels   b&w   1929
Dir: Louis Gasnier. Prod: Paramount/Famous Players-Lasky.
Cast: Evelyn Brent, Neil Hamilton.
Mystery melodrama. A young girl is saved from a false seeress.

Fellow Prisoners

Captured
72 min.   b&w   1933
Dir: Roy DelRuth. Prod: Warner Bros. Dist: MGM/UA Home Video (video).

Cast: Leslie Howard, Douglas Fairbanks, Jr., Paul Lukas.

A dramatic story set in a German prison camp, where a husband learns that his best friend, also in prison, was his wife's lover.

GIDE, ANDRÉ

La Symphonie Pastorale

Symphonie Pastorale
105 min.   b&w   1948
Dir: Jean Delanney. Prod: William Marshall, Inc.
Cast: Michele Morgan, Pierre Blanchar.
French with subtitles.

GILFORD, C.B.

Unidentified story (in *Ellery Queen's Magazine*)

Joy Ride
60 min.   b&w   1958
Dir: Edward Bernds. Prod: Allied Artists. Dist: Budget Films/Video, Hurlock
    Cine-World.
Cast: Regis Toomey, Ann Doran.
An "average man" is terrorized by young punks until he turns the tables on them.

GILL, THOMAS

In the Mexican Quarter

Border Cafe
7 reels   b&w   1937
Dir: Lew Landers. Prod: RKO.
Cast: John Beal, Harry Carey.
Western. Staid son settles in the West and fights a gang to protect his parents.

GILLESE, JOHN PATRICK

Kirby's Gander

Wings of Chance
76 min.   color   1961
Dir: Edward Dew. Prod: Universal.
Cast: James Brown, Frances Rafferty.
A pilot is stranded when his plane crashes in an uncharted wilderness.

GILMAN, CHARLOTTE PERKINS

The Yellow Wallpaper

The Yellow Wallpaper
15 min.   color   1978
Prod: International Instructional Television Coop. Dist: Indiana University.
A woman suffers a gradual mental breakdown as a result of her confinement by her husband and doctors.

GILROY, FRANK D.

The Last Notch

> *The Fastest Gun Alive* (s.m. also a television play)
> 91 min.   b&w   1956
> Dir: Russell Rouse. Prod: MGM. Dist: Films Inc.
> Cast: Glenn Ford, Jeanne Crain.
> Western. A peace-loving shopkeeper tries to keep his marksmanship a secret,

but his town is threatened by a desperado.

GLASPELL, SUSAN

Jury of Her Peers

> *Jury of Her Peers*
> 30 min.   color   1981
> Prod: Texture Films. Dist: Brigham Young University (rental).
> Story about the isolation and oppression of a farm woman in 1900.

GLASMAN, KUBEC

Nothing Down

> *Saleslady*
> 8 reels   b&w   1938
> Dir: Arthur Greville Collins. Prod: Monogram Pictures.
> Cast: Anne Nagel, Harry Davenport.
> An heiress gets a job as a saleslady working for the man who is ruining her

father's business.

GLIDDEN, FRED DILLEY (see SHORT, LUKE)

GOGOL, NIKOLAI

Christmas Slippers

> *Christmas Slippers*
> 1946
> Dist: Corinth Films.

Diary of a Madman

> *Diary of a Madman* (s.m. also the play "Diary of a Madman," which in turn
>   is based on the story)
> 87 min.   1967
> Dir: Robert Carlisle. Prod: Robert Carlisle.
> Cast: Tom Troupe.
> A study of the mental disintegration of a man living in nineteenth-century

Europe.

Il Coppotto

> *Il Coppotto* (It.)
> 93 min.   b&w   1953

Dir: Alberto Lattvada. Prod: Farro.
Cast: Renato Fascel, Yvonne Sanson.

Der Mantel

Der Mantel (Gr.)
35 min.   color   1955
Dir: Wolfgang Schieff.
Cast: Marcel Marceau.

May Night

May Night
59 min.   b&w   1952
Dir: A. Rou. Dist: Corinth Films.
Operatic version of a Ukranian folk story.

Shinel

The Overcoat (Russian)
70 min.   b&w   1926
Dir: Grigori Kozintsev, Leonid Trauberg. Dist: MOMA.
Cast: Andrei Dostrichkin, Sergei Gerasimov, Anna Zheimo.
A poor clerk's coat is stolen, he dies, and his ghost steals other coats.

The Overcoat
73 min.   b&w
Dir: Alexei Batalov. Prod: Lenfilm Studios. Dist: Corinth Films.
A pathetic little clerk in a grotesque world gets a new overcoat that changes
his destiny. Russian with English subtitles.

GOLDMAN, RAYMOND LESLIE

Battling Bunyon Ceases to Be Funny (in *Saturday Evening Post,* 15 March 1924)

Battling Bunyon
60 min.   b&w   1925   sil.
Dir: Paul Hurst. Prod: Crown. Dist: Blackhawk (video).
Cast: Wesley Barry, Molly Malone, Frank Campeau.
Arken Bunyon is matched with a professional boxer because he wants to try
to raise $1,000 to buy a partnership in a garage.

GOLDSMITH, L.S.

Man Who Stole a Dream

Manhandled
97 min.   b&w   1949
Dir: Lewis R. Foster. Prod: Paramount. Dist: Video Communications (video).
Cast: Dorothy Lamour, Dan Duryea.
Murder drama.

GOMBERG, SY

When Leo Came Marching Home

When Willie Comes Marching Home
82 min.   b&w   1950
Dir: John Ford. Prod: Twentieth Century Fox. Dist: Films Inc.
Cast: Dan Dailey, Corinne Calvet.
The story of a West Virginian lad who goes into the Army during World
War II and has a series of adventures, including a love affair with a beautiful French
leader of the underground.

GOODEN, ARTHUR HENRY

Below the Deadline

Below the Deadline
72 min.   b&w   1920
Dir: J.P. McGowan. Prod: Ascher Prod. Dist: Modern Sound Pictures.
Cast: William Beaudine.

GOODLOE, ABBIE C.

Claustrophobia

I Live My Life
10 reels   b&w   1935
Dir: W.S. Van Dyke. Prod: MGM.
Cast: Joan Crawford, Brian Aherne.
A hate-at-first-sight romance of a debutante and an archeologist.

GOODMAN, JACK

Magazine Story (jt. author Albert Rice)

Gay Blades
7 reels   b&w   1946
Dir: George Blair. Prod: Republic Pictures. Dist: Ivy Films.

GORDIMER, NADINE

Six Feet of the Country

Six Feet of the Country
30 min.   color
Dir: Lynton Stephenson. Dist: Coronet Films.
The troubled marriage of South Africans.

GORKY, MAXIM

Her One True Love

Her One True Love
24 min.   color   1977
Dir: Henry Comor. Prod: Bruce Raymond. Dist: Simon & Schuster (16 mm
    and video).
Cast: Kate Reid, John Horton.

Two agonizingly lonely people make fleeting contact: aging, illiterate Mae tries gamely to fill the loveless void in her life by entertaining gentlemen callers; next door, her rooming-house neighbor John passes his days in solitude.

Twenty-Six and a Girl

Nine and a Girl
24 min.   b&w
Dir. and Prod: Michael Weiskopf. Dist: Viewfinders.
The story of nine pretzel bakers and a young girl who comes each day to pick up an order. They see her as the most ideal of women until a new baker arranges a tryst with her.

GOULDING, EDMOND

Put and Take

Applause
80 min.   b&w   1929
Dir: Rouben Mamoulian. Prod: Tiffany-Stahl Prod. Dist: MOMA.
Cast: Helen Morgan.

GRAND, GORDON

Major Denning's Trust Estate

Sport of Kings
68 min.   b&w   1947
Dir: Robert Gordon. Prod: Columbia Pictures.
Cast: Paul Campbell, Gloria Henry.

GRANT, JAMES EDWARD

Big Brown Eyes

Big Brown Eyes (s.m. also "Hahsit Babe")
78 min.   b&w   1936
Dir: Raoul Walsh. Prod: Paramount. Dist: Universal 16.
Cast: Cary Grant, Joan Bennett, Walter Pidgeon, Lloyd Nolan.

Full Measure (see *Great Guy* under **Johnny Cave Stories**)

Johnny Cave Stories (in *Saturday Evening Post;* s.m. also "Johnny Cave Goes Subtle," "Larceny on the Right," and "Full Measure")

Great Guy
73 min.   b&w   1937
Dir: John G. Blystone. Prod: Grand National Films. Dist: Budget Films/ Films/Video, Em Gee Film Library, Cable Films (video), Penguin Video, Discount Video Tapes, Video Connection.
Cast: James Cagney, Mae Clark.
As a live-wire operative in the City Department of Weights and Measures, Jimmy sets out to find the persons who beat his boss savagely and put him in the hospital.

Journal of Linnett Moore

Proud Rebel
90 min.   color   1958
Prod: Formosa Prod. Dist: Roa's Films, Embassy Home Entertainment
    (video).
Cast: Alan Ladd, Olivia De Havilland, David Ladd.
A "proud rebel" seeks aid for his son, who has been mute since seeing his
mother die in the Battle of Atlanta.

A Lady Came to Burkburnett

Boom Town
120 min.   b&w   1940
Dir: Jack Conway. Prod: MGM. Dist: Films Inc.
Cast: Clark Gable, Spencer Tracy, Claudette Colbert, Hedy Lamarr.
Two rough and tough wildcatters on the prowl for oil and women.

Larceny on the Right (see *Great Guy* under **Johnny Cave Stories**)

Unidentified stories

She Had to Eat (jt. author Morris Musselman)
70 min.   b&w   1937
Dir: Malcolm St. Clair. Prod: Twentieth Century Fox.

Whipsaw (in *Liberty Magazine*)

Whipsaw
9 reels   b&w   1935
Dir: Sam Wood. Prod: MGM.
Cast: Spencer Tracy, Myrna Loy.
A jewel-robbing gang.

GRANT, MAXWELL

The Fox Hound

International Crime
87 min.   b&w   1938
Dir: Charles Lamont. Prod: Grand National Films. Dist: Wholesome Film
    Center, Admit One Video (video).
A dashing reporter outwits the Police Commission, which doesn't recognize
that blowing up a safe was really a cover for murder.

The Shadow

Invisible Avenger (s.m. also the character from the radio series and "Street
    and Smith Magazine Stories")
60 min.   b&w   1958
Dir: James Wong Howe, John Sledge. Prod: Republic Pictures.

The Shadow (serialized in 15 parts)
2 reels each   b&w   1940
Dir: James W. Horne. Prod: Columbia Pictures.

The Shadow Returns
61 min.   b&w   1946
Dir: Phil Rosen. Prod: Monogram Pictures.

GRASHIN, MAURI

Chatauqua

The Trouble with Girls (s.m. also a novel by Day Keene and Dwight Babcock,
    which in turn is based on the story)
104 min.   b&w   1969
Dir: Peter Tewksbury. Prod: MGM. Dist: Films Inc.
Cast: Marilyn Mason, Nicole Jaffe, Sheree North.
Set in the 1920s. The manager of The Tolling Canvas College has the usual
irritations of placating small-town politicians who think they have relatives with
talent.

GRAY, HUGH (jt. author) (See *River Gang* under DAVID, CHARLES)

GREEN, ALAN

Beauty on the Beat (jt. author Julian Brodie)

Love on the Run
80 min.   b&w   1936
Dir: W.S. Van Dyke. Prod: MGM.
Cast: Clark Gable, Joan Crawford, Franchot Tone.
Foreign correspondents in love travel around the world, fleeing from spies.

GREENE, GRAHAM

Across the Bridge

Across the Bridge
103 min.   b&w   1958
Dir: Ken Annakin. Prod: Rank. Dist: Budget Films/Video, Kit Parker Films.
Cast: Rod Steiger, David Knight.
A crooked tycoon on the lam from Scotland Yard is cornered in Mexico.

The Basement Room

The Fallen Idol
94 min.   b&w   1948
Dir: Sir Carol Reed. Dist: Budget Films/Video, Em Gee Film Library, Holly-
    wood Home Theater (video).
Cast: Ralph Richardson, Michelle Morgan, Sonia Dresdel, Bobby Henrey.
The story of a lonely young boy who is left in the care of the family butler,
whom he idolizes, while his parents are on a trip. He witnesses the butler's love
affair and the accidental death of his wife.

A Shocking Accident

A Shocking Accident
25 min.　　　　color　　　　1983
Dir: James Scott. Dist: Direct Cinema (16 mm and video).
An English schoolboy learns that his father has been killed in a bizarre
accident, and his friends tease him. Academy Award (1982) for Best Short Film.

GREEN, HAROLD

Hide and Seek

Hide and Seek
90 min.　　　　b&w　　　　1964
Dir: Cy Endfield. Prod: Albion Films.
A chemist tries to find his missing friend.

GREENE, WALTER

He Was One of the Boston Bullertons

Private Affairs
80 min.　　　　b&w　　　　1940
Dir: Albert S. Rogell. Prod: Universal Studios. Dist: Mogull's Films, "The"
　　　Film Center.
A young woman with problems goes to her father for advice, although he
hasn't seen her since her birth.

GREY, ZANE

Canyon Walls

Smoke Lightning
54 min.　　　　b&w　　　　1933
Dir: David Howard. Prod: Fox.
Western.

The Last of the Duanes (in *Argosy All-Story Weekly Magazine* September 1914)

The Last of the Duanes
7 reels　　　　b&w　　　　1924　　　　sil.
Dir: Lynn Reynolds. Prod: Fox.
Cast: Tom Mix, Marion Nixon.
Western. Cal Bain's insults force Duane to shoot him and then flee.

The Last of the Duanes
51 min.　　　　b&w　　　　1930
Dir: Alfred L. Werker. Prod: Fox.
Cast: George O'Brien, Lucille Brown, Myrna Loy.
A musical version.

Last of the Duanes
6 reels　　　　b&w　　　　1941
Dir: James Tinling. Prod: Twentieth Century Fox.

Lightning

Lightning
7 reels   b&w   1927   sil.
Dir: James C. McDay. Prod: Tiffany.
Cast: Jobyna Ralston, Margaret Livingston, Robert Frazier.
Western. Famed horse-breakers Lee and Coon fail to capture the wild stallion Lightning and their girls—until the end.

The Water Hole (in *Collier's Magazine* 8 October-24 December 1927)

The Water Hole
7 reels   b&w   1928   sil.
Dir: F. Richard Jones. Prod: Paramount/Famous Players-Lasky.
Cast: Jack Holt, Nancy Carroll, John Boles.
Western. Judith vamps Philip Randolph when he comes East to discuss business with her father, but she is only teasing and he gets quite angry.

GRIFFIN, ELEANORE

Be It Ever So Humble   (jt. author William Rankin)

Hi, Beautiful
66 min.   b&w   1944
Dir: Leslie Goodwins. Prod: Universal.
Cast: Martha O'Driscoll, Noah Beery, Jr., Hattie McDaniel.
Two young people win the "Happiest GI Couple" award, but they are not married. Note: A remake of *Love in a Bungalow* (1937), which, according to the Library of Congress catalogs, was based on an original screenplay. I was unable to confirm that it was later written as a short story, although the Library of Congress gives this story title as the source of the later movie.

Class Prophecy

When Love Is Young
76 min.   b&w   1937
Dir: Hal Mohr. Prod: Universal.
Cast: Virginia Bruce, Kent Taylor, Walter Brennan.
Ambitious press agent takes a plain girl and turns her into a gorgeous singer.

GROSS, CORDELIA BAIRD

It's Hard to Find Mecca in Flushing (see **Protection for a Tough Racket**)

Protection for a Tough Racket

This Could Be the Night (s.m. also "It's Hard to Find Mecca in Flushing")
104 min.   b&w   1957
Dir: Robert Wise. Prod: MGM.
Cast: Jean Simmons, Paul Douglas.
An innocent among the wolves of the Broadway night life.

GRUBER, FRANK

Dog Show Murder

Death of a Champion
7 reels   b&w   1939
Dir: Robert Florey. Prod: Paramount. Dist: Universal.
Cast: Lynne Overman, Virginia Dale.
Comedy mystery about the death of a champion dog.

GUITRY, SACHA

Bonne Chance

Lucky Partners
102 min.   b&w   1940
Dir: Lewis Milestone. Prod: RKO. Dist: Films Inc.
Cast: Ronald Colman, Ginger Rogers.
An artist shares a sweepstakes ticket with a girl and they win.

GULICK, BILL

Man from Texas (in *Saturday Evening Post,* 15 April 1950)

The Road to Denver
90 min.   color   1955
Dir: Joseph Kane. Prod: Republic Pictures. Dist: Ivy Films.
Cast: John Payne, Lee J. Cobb.
Set in Colorado at the turn of the century. One brother owns a stagecoach
line, and the other joins a gang of hijackers.

H

HALE, EDWARD EVERETT

Man without a Country

> *As No Man Has Loved* (a.k.a. *The Man without a Country*)
> 10 reels b&w 1925 sil.
> Dir: Rowland V. Lee. Prod: Fox.
> Cast: Edward Hearn.
> The hero, Philip Nolan, is sentenced to never see his country again.

> *Man without a Country*
> 21 min. color 1938
> Prod: Warner Bros. Dist: Syracuse University.

> *Man without a Country*
> 25 min. b&w 1953
> Prod: Bing Crosby Prod.

HALL, BLAIR

Easy Street

> *The Easy Road*
> 5 reels b&w 1921 sil.
> Dir: Tom Forman. Prod: Famous Players-Lasky.
> Cast: Thomas Meighan, Gladys George, Grace Goodall.
> Leonard Fayne, a novelist, marries wealthy Isabel, but her silliness interferes with his creativity.

HALL, WILBUR (pseud. of Rudolph Edgar Block)

Johnny Cucabod (in *Saturday Evening Post,* 12 June 1920)

> *Broken Doll*
> 5 reels b&w 1921 sil.
> Dir: Allan Dwan. Prod: Allan Dwan Prod.
> Cast: Monte Blue, Mary Thurman.
> A cowhand is mistaken for a thief.

On the Threshold (in *Saturday Evening Post*)

> *On the Threshold*
> 6 reels b&w 1925 sil.
> Dir: Renaud Hoffman. Prod: Hoffman Prod.

Cast: Gladys Hulette, Henry B. Walthall.

When his wife dies in childbirth, Andrew Masters swears he will prevent his daughter from marrying.

HALLIDAY, BRETT (see also *Blue, White and Perfect* under CHASE, BORDEN)

Three on a Ticket

Three on a Ticket (s.m. a character named Michael Shayne)
64 min.   b&w   1947
Dir: Sam Newfield. Prod: Releasing Corp. Dist: Ivy Films, Mogull's Films.
Cast: Hugh Beaumont.
The plans for a secret weapon are on their way to a foreign power.

HAMLIN, JOHN HAROLD

Painted Ponies (in *Western Story Magazine*)

Painted Ponies
6 reels   b&w   1926   sil.
Dir: Reeves Eason.
Cast: Hoot Gibson, William Dunn.
Western. Buck Sims drops into town and tries to win Mary from her suitor, who is the town bully.

HADLEY, DOROTHY CURNOR

Room for Two

Rosie the Riveter
75 min.   b&w   1944
Dir: Joseph Santley. Prod: Republic Pictures. Dist: Ivy Films.
Cast: Jane Frazee, Frank Albertson.
A wacky rooming house is the home of wacky defense plant workers.

HANLON, BROOKE

Delicatessen (in *Saturday Evening Post,* 24 August 1925)

It Must Be Love
7 reels   b&w   1926   sil.
Dir: Alfred E. Green. Prod: John McCormick Prod.
Cast: Colleen Moore, Jean Hersholt, Malcolm McGregor.
Fernie, who hates her father's delicatessen/home, ends up married to a man who tells her he's in stocks and then buys a delicatessen.

HARMON, DAVID

The Man Who Owned the Town

Johnny Concho
84 min.   b&w   1956
Dir: Don McGuire. Prod: United Artists.
Cast: Frank Sinatra, Keenan Wynn.
Western. A cowboy must face a fast gun.

HARRIS, KENNETH

Junk (in *Saturday Evening Post,* 25 December 1920)

> *The Idle Rich*
> 5 reels   b&w   1921   sil.
> Dir: Maxwell Karger. Prod: Metro Pictures.
> Cast: Bert Lytell, Virginia Valli.

Young, rich Sam is suddenly broke because of the business speculations of his executor, and his friends reject him.

HARRISON, WILLIAM C.

Petticoat Brigade

> *The Guns of Fort Petticoat*
> 82 min.   color   1957
> Dir: George Marshall. Prod: Brown-Murphy Pictures. Dist: Modern Sound
>   Pictures, Roa's Films.
> Cast: Audie Murphy, Kathryn Grant, Hope Emerson.

Western. In the Texas territory during the Civil War, women and children were left to defend themselves against the Indians.

Rollerball Murders

> *Rollerball*
> 123 min.   color   1975
> Dir: Norman Jewison. Prod: United Artists. Dist: CBS/Fox Video (video).
> Cast: James Caan, Ralph Richardson, John Houseman.

A futuristic combination of rugby, roller-skating, and gladiator fight-to-the-death spectacles.

HART, WILLIAM S.

O'Malley of the Mounted

> *O'Malley of the Mounted*
> 6 reels   b&w   1921   sil.
> Dir: Lambert Hillyer. Prod: Paramount.
> Cast: William S. Hart, Eva Novak.

Sergeant O'Malley of the Royal Northwest Mounted Police tracks down a killer and then falls in love with the killer's sister.

> *O'Malley of the Mounted*
> 70 min.   b&w   1936
> Dir: David Howard. Prod: Twentieth Century Fox. Dist: Lewis Film Service.
> Cast: George O'Brien, Irene Ware.

HARTE, BRET

The Idyll of Red Gulch

> *The Man from Red Gulch*
> 6 reels   b&w   1925

Dir: Edmund Mortimer. Prod: Hunt Stromberg.
Cast: Harry Carey, Harriet Hammond.
Western. At the time of the California Gold Rush, a woman runs off with the man who killed her husband.

The Luck of Roaring Camp

The Luck of Roaring Camp
28 min.   color   1984
Prod: Learning Corp. of America. Dist: Simon & Schuster (16 mm and video).
Cast: Randy Quaid.
A baby boy, suddenly orphaned, is "adopted" by a group of miners, and for a while he seems to bring them good luck.

M'liss, an Idyll of Red Mountain

The Girl Who Ran Wild
5 reels   b&w   1922   sil.
Dir: Rupert Julian. Prod: Universal.
Cast: Gladys Walton, Marc Robbins.
M'liss, a tomboy, is persuaded to tidy herself up and to get an education by the schoolmaster, with whom she falls in love. (Note: In 1915 and 1918, two versions were produced by World Film Corp. and Famous Players-Lasky.)

M'liss
7 reels   b&w   1936
Dir: George Nicholls, Jr. Prod: RKO.

The Outcasts of Poker Flats

Man Hunt
61 min.   b&w   1931
Dir: William Clemens. Prod: Pictures Co., rel. Warner Bros. Dist: MGM/UA Home Video (video).
Cast: Ricardo Cortez, Marguerite Churchill.

Outcasts of Poker Flats
68 min.   b&w   1952
Dir: Christy Cabanne. Prod: RKO.
Cast: Preston Foster.

Outcasts of Poker Flats
81 min.   b&w   1952
Dir: Joseph Newman. Prod: Twentieth Century Fox. Dist: Budget Films/Video, Select Film Library.
Cast: Dale Robertson, Anne Baxter, Miriam Hopkins.
In Poker Flats, one of the roaring camps of the California Gold Rush days, the townspeople, enraged by robbery and murder, drive four "undesirables" out of town. The outcasts and a young man and his girl are later forced to seek shelter together in a cabin, high in the Sierras, when a blizzard approaches.

Saint of Calamity Gulch (in *Hutchinson's Magazine,* July 1925)

> *Taking a Chance*
> 5 reels   b&w   1929   sil.
> Dir: Norman Z. McLeod. Prod: Twentieth Century Fox.
> Cast: Rex Bell, Lola Todd.
> Western melodrama.

Salomy Jane's Kiss

> *Salomy Jane* (s.m. also "Salomy Jane," a play by Paul Armstrong)
> 7 reels   b&w   1923   sil.
> Dir: George Melford. Prod: Famous Players-Lasky.
> Cast: Jacqueline Logan, George Fawcett.
> Salomy saves a stranger from hanging, who is later cleared of his crime.
Note: A silent version was made in 1914 by Alco.

> *Wild Girl*
> 70 min.   b&w   1932
> Dir: Raoul Walsh. Prod: Fox.

Tennessee's Partner (in *Booklover's Magazine,* July 1903)

> *The Flaming Forties*
> 6 reels   b&w   1924   sil.
> Dir: Tom Forman. Prod: Stellar Prod.
> Cast: Harry Carey, William Norton.
> Bill Jones saves Jack from drowning after he jumps off a steamboat that is
taking him to be hanged.

> *Tennessee's Partner*
> 87 min.   color   1955
> Prod: RKO. Dist: Audio Brandon, Cinema 8 (super 8 sound), Weiss Global
>   Enterprises (video).
> Cast: Ronald Reagan, John Payne, Rhonda Fleming.
> Western. A gambling queen, a gambler, and a cowpoke are all involved in a
shooting and a double-crossing.

> *Tennessee's Partner*
> 15 min.   color   1978
> Prod: International Instructional Television Coop. Dist: Indiana Univ. (16
>   mm and video).
> Genuine friendship between two men whose characters and appearances
belie their sentimental hearts.

> *Tennessee's Partner*
> 20 min.   color   1983
> Prod: Auburn Television. Dist: AIT (video).
> Coupled with Mary Wilkins Freeman's story "One Good Time."

HARTLEY, L.P.

The Island

The Island
30 min.   color   1977
Dir: Robert Fuest. Dist: Simon & Schuster (16 mm and video).
Cast: John Hurt.
A sophisticated young World War I army officer on overnight leave visits
the mansion where the wealthy woman with whom he was having an affair lives.
A series of peculiar events begins to take place.

HARVEY, WILLIAM FRYER

The Beast

The Beast with Five Fingers
88 min.   b&w   1946
Dir: Robert Florey. Dist: MGM/UA Home Video (video).
Cast: Robert Alda, Peter Lorre, Andrea King, Victor Francen, J. Carol
      Nash.
Horror thriller. A hand with an invisible body commits murder and terrorizes
the entire household of a dead pianist.

HATTON, FANNY (jt. author) (see HATTON, FREDERIC)

HATTON, FREDERIC

The Azure Shore (in *Harper's Bazaar,* March 1923)

The Rush Hour (jt. author Fanny Hatton)
7 reels   b&w   1927   sil.
Dir: E. Mason Hopper. Adap: Zelda Sears.
Cast: Marie Prevost, Harrison Ford.
Margie, a ticket agent, dreams of adventure and travel, but her fiance dreams
only about business.

With the Tide (in *Young's Magazine,* March 1923)

South Sea Love
7 reels   b&w   1927   sil.
Dir: Ralph Ince. Prod: R-C Pictures.
Cast: Patsy Ruth Miller, Lee Shumway.
While Fred slaves on an island to send money to Charlotte, she is seeing
another man.

HAVILAND-TAYLOR, KATHERINE

The Failure

A Man to Remember
79 min.   b&w   1938
Dir: Garson Kanin. Sp: Dalton Trumbo. Prod: RKO.
Cast: Edward Ellis, Anne Shirley.
The son of the richest man in town wounds the doctor's daughter.

One Man's Journey
b&w   1933
Dir: John Robertson. Sp: Lester Cohen, Sam Ornitz. Prod: RKO.

HAWKINS, DAVID (jt. author) (see *Shadow on the Window* under HAWKINS, JOHN)

HAWKINS, JOHN
Criminals Mark

Crime Wave (jt. author Ward Hawkins)
73 min.   b&w   1953
Dir: Andre de Toth. Sp: Crane Wilbur. Prod: Warner Bros.
Cast: Sterling Hayden, Gene Nelson, Phyllis Kirk.
Parolee Steve Lacey wants to go straight, but three crooks pressure him into robbing a bank.

The Missing Witness

Shadow on the Window (jt. author David Hawkins)
105 min.   b&w   1957
Dir: William Asher. Prod: Columbia Pictures. Dist: Institutional Cinema
    Service.
Cast: John Barrymore, Jr., Betty Garrett, Peter Carey.
A young boy wanders about in a daze after having witnessed a brutal murder. The police question the boy and gradually put together the clues from his incoherent story to solve the crime.

HAWKINS, WARD (see *Crime Wave* under HAWKINS, JOHN)

HAWTHORNE, NATHANIEL
The Birthmark

The Birthmark
15 min.   color   1978
Prod: International Instructional Television Coop. Dist: Indiana University
    (16 mm and video).
A scientist, obsessed with a desire for perfection, tries to remove a birthmark from his new wife and in the process kills her.

Dr. Heidegger's Experiment

Dr. Heidegger's Experiment
15 min.   b&w   1954
Prod: Dynamic Films. Dist: Audio Brandon.
Cast: Monty Woolley.
The search for an elixir of youth.

Twice Told Tales (s.m. also "Rappaccini's Daughter" and the novel *The
    House of the Seven Gables*)
119 min.   color   1963

Dir: Sidney Salkow. Sp: Robert E. Kent. Prod: United Artists. Dist: Audio Brandon.

Cast: Vincent Price, Sebastian Cabot, Brett Halsey.

A compilation of three of Hawthorne's works, including "Dr. Heidegger's Experiment," "Rappaccini's Daughter," in which a jealous father turns his daughter's blood to poison, killing any man who touches her, and *The House of the Seven Gables,* which was cursed by an innocent man who was burned for witchcraft.

Dr. Heidegger's Experiment
22 min.   color   1970
Dist: Audio Brandon.

Rappaccini's Daughter (see also *Twice Told Tales* under **Dr. Heidegger's Experiment**)

Rappaccini's Daughter
57 min.   color   1980
Dir: Dexso Magyar. Dist: Coronet Films.
Cast: Kristoffer Tabori, Kathleen Beller.

Dr. Rappaccini grows deadly plants, and like theirs, his daughter's touch is deadly.

Young Goodman Brown

Young Goodman Brown
30 min.   color   1973
Dir: Donald Fox. Dist: Pyramid Films (16 mm and video).

An enigmatic story of man's propensity for evil and the Puritan method of handling evil. Cine Golden Eagle. Special jury award, Atlanta International Film Festival.

HAY, JACOB

Fractured Jaw (Br.)

The Sheriff of Fractured Jaw
102 min.   b&w   1959
Dir: Raoul Walsh. Prod: Twentieth Century Fox. Dist: Films Inc.
Cast: Kenneth Moore, Jayne Mansfield.

A British gentleman tries to establish a gun business in the wild and woolly West in this humorous western.

HAYCOX, ERNEST

Canyon Passage

Canyon Passage
92 min.   color   1946
Dir: Jacques Tourneur. Sp: Ernest Pascal. Prod: Universal.
Cast: Dana Andrews, Brian Donlevy, Susan Hayward.

Western. Set in Oregon during frontier times. An owner of a general store clashes with an outlaw.

Stage Coach to Lordsburg (in *Collier's Magazine,* 10 April 1937)

> *Stagecoach*
> 114 min.   b&w   1939
> Dir: John Ford. Prod: John Ford Prod. Dist: Films Inc., Kit Parker Films,
>   Vestron Video (video), RCA Video Discs (CED).
> Cast: John Wayne, Claire Trevor, Thomas Mitchell, George Bancroft, Andy
>   Devine.

Western. The personalities of a group of passengers and stagecoach hands—
a medicine man, a gambler, a prostitute, a crooked banker, a drunkard, a sheriff
and his prisoner, and two Southern aristocrats—are revealed while they are under
Indian attack.

> *Stagecoach*
> 115 min.   color   1966
> Dir: Gordon Douglas. Prod: Twentieth Century Fox.
> Cast: Ann Margaret, Alex Cord, Bing Crosby, Red Buttons.

A remake of Ford's *Stagecoach.* A handful of passengers go through a great
deal before the final shootout.

Stage Station

> *Apache Trail*
> 7 reels   b&w   1942
> Dir: Richard Thorpe. Sp: Maurice Geraghty. Prod: MGM.
> Cast: Lloyd Nolan, Grant Withers, Gloria Holden.
> Western.

> *Apache War Smoke*
> 76 min.   b&w   1952
> Dir: Harold Kress. Sp: Jerry David. Prod: MGM. Dist: Films Inc.
> A remake of *Apache Trail.*

HAYNES, MANNING

Man at the Gate

> *Men of the Sea*
> 5 reels   b&w   1944
> Dir: Norman Walker. Prod: Releasing Corp. Dist: Mogull's Films.
> Cast: Sir Carol Reed.

HECHT, BEN

Actor's Blood (see *Actors and Sin* under **Concerning a Woman of Sin**)

Concerning a Woman of Sin

> *Actors and Sin* (s.m. also "Actor's Blood" in the same collection)
> 90 min.   b&w   1952
> Dir: Ben Hecht. Prod: United Artists. Dist: Budget Films/Video.
> Cast: Edward G. Robinson, Marsha Hunt, Eddie Albert.

A compilation of two stories. "Woman of Sin" satirizes the film industry, and "Actor's Blood" is the story of a has-been performer who tries to save his daughter's career.

Crime without Passion

Crime without Passion
72 min.   b&w   1934
Dir: Ben Hecht, Charles MacArthur. Prod: Paramount.
Cast: Claude Rains, Margo Whitney Bourne.
A Nietzchean defense lawyer with a flashy courtroom technique murders his mistress and attempts to concoct the perfect alibi.

Specter of the Rose

Specter of the Rose
90 min.   b&w   1946
Dir. and Sp: Ben Hecht. Prod: Republic Pictures. Dist: Ivy Films.
Cast: Judith Anderson, Ivan Kirov.
A story about a young ballet dancer who is slowly losing his mind and the girl who loves him.

HECKELMAN, CHARLES N.

The Last Outpost to Hell

Frontier Feud
54 min.   b&w   1945
Dir: Lambert Hillyer. Sp: Jess Bowers. Prod: Monogram Pictures. Dist: Hurlock Cine-World.
Cast: Johnny Mack Brown.
Western. A story about claim jumping.

HELLINGER, MARK

On the Nose

Broadway Bill
94 min.   b&w   1934
Dir: Frank Capra. Sp: Robert Riskin. Prod: Columbia Pictures.
Cast: Myrna Loy, Warner Baxter, Lucille Ball.
Story of a man, a maid, and a Cinderella racehorse named Broadway Bill.

Riding High
112 min.   b&w   1950
Dir: Frank Capra. Prod: Paramount.
Cast: Bing Crosby, Colleen Gray.
A remake of *Broadway Bill.*

HEMINGWAY, ERNEST

The Killers
The Killers
105 min.   b&w   1946

Dir: Robert Siodmak. Sp: Anthony Veiller. Prod: Universal.
Cast: Edmond O'Brien, Ava Gardner, Burt Lancaster.
Former fighter Swede is double-crossed by hoodlums and his girl; he lies in bed thinking about what happened while two hired killers wait for him.

The Killers
95 min.   color   1964
Dir: Don Siegel. Prod: Universal. Dist: Alan Twyman Presents, Universal, MCA/UA Home Video (video).
Cast: Lee Marvin, Angie Dickinson.
An updated version in which the plot also involves auto racing and a $1,000,000 post office robbery.

My Old Man

My Old Man
27 min.   color   1969
Prod. and Dist: Encyclopaedia Britannica.(16 mm and video).
Joe Butler must settle a conflict between reality and the preservation of his illusions.

Under My Skin
86 min.   b&w   1950
Dir: Jean Negulesco. Prod: Twentieth Century Fox. Dist: Films Inc.
Cast: John Garfield, Micheline Presle.
A jockey tries to go straight.

Nick Adams Stories

Hemingway's Adventures of a Young Man
96 min.   color   1962
Dir: Martin Ritt. Prod: Jerry Wald Prod., rel. 20th Century Fox. Dist: Films Inc.
Cast: Richard Beymer, Diane Baker, Paul Newman, Jessica Tandy, Eli Wallach, Dan Dailey.
To escape small-town life, Nick joins an ambulance unit in the Italian Army during World War I. Wounded and discouraged, he falls in love with a nurse, who restores his will to live.

The Short Happy Life of Francis Macomber

The Macomber Affair
89 min.   b&w   1947
Dir: Zoltan Korda. Prod: Award Prod.
Cast: Gregory Peck, Joan Bennett, Robert Preston.
A love triangle involving a man, his wife, and a guide on an African hunting expedition.

The Snows of Kilimanjaro

The Snows of Kilimanjaro
117 min.　　b&w　　1952
Dir: Henry King. Prod: Twentieth Century Fox.
Cast: Gregory Peck, Susan Hayward, Ava Gardner, Hildegarde Neff.
A war melodrama.

Soldier's Home

Soldier's Home (American Short Story Series)
42 min.　　color　　1977
Dir: Robert Young. Sp: Robert Geller. Dist: Coronet Films (16 mm and video).
When Harold Krebs returns home after World War I, he is unappreciated by the local townsfolk, and he feels alienated from the community.

HENDERSON, JESSIE

The Mouth of the Dragon (in *Ainslee's* March-April 1923)

The Perfect Flapper
7 reels　　b&w　　1924　　sil.
Dir: John Francis Dillon. Prod: Associated First National.
Cast: Colleen Moore, Sydney Chaplin.
Wallflower Tommie Lou becomes unconventional to achieve more attention.

HENRY, O.

During the early years of film (1900-1920), scores of films by Broadway Star Film Co., Biograph, Vitaphone, and other companies were based on O. Henry's stories, often uncredited. Space dows not allow the inclusion of films produced before 1920.

The Badge of Policeman O'Roon

Doctor Rhythm
81 min.　　b&w　　1938
Dir: Frank Tuttle, Prod: Paramount.
Cast: Bing Crosby, Beatrice Lillie, Mary Carlisle, Andy Devine.
A Park Avenue doctor serves as the bodyguard of the daughter of a screwy socialite to prevent her from marrying a smooth-talking heel.

Caballero's Way

In Old Arizona
7 reels　　b&w　　1929
Dir: Raoul Walsh, Irving Cummings. Prod: Fox.
Cast: Edmund Lowe, Dorothy Burgess.
The Caballero Cisco Kid, infatuated by a woman, is almost double-crossed by her, but she is shot instead of him. Note: The Cisco Kid was a character created by O. Henry who appeared in a number of films. This is the most important Cisco Kid movie; the others were made for the Saturday kiddie shows. Among the Cisco

Kid movies are *The Gay Amigo, The Gay Cavalier, Beauty and the Bandit, The Cisco Kid and the Lady, The Gay Caballero, The Cisco Kid in Old Mexico, The Cisco Kid Returns, The Daring Caballero, Girl from San Lorenzo, King of the Bandits, South of Monterey, South of the Rio Grande, The Valiant Hombre, Viva Cisco Kid, The Return of the Cisco Kid, Lucky Cisco Kid, Ride on Vaquero, Riding the California Trail,* and *Satan's Cradle.*

The Chaparral Prince

The Chaparral Prince
20 min.   color   1982
Prod: Highgate Pictures. Dist: Simon & Schuster (16 mm and video).
Cast: John Shea.
   A small girl, Lena, is forced to work in the kitchen of a demanding innkeeper and escapes the drudgery by identifying with characters from fairy tales.

The Clarion Call (see *O. Henry's Full House* under **The Cop and the Anthem**)

The Cop and the Anthem

O. Henry's Full House (s.m. also "The Clarion Call," "The Ransom of Red Chief," "The Last Leaf," and "The Gift of the Magi")
117 min.   b&w   1952
Dir: Jean Negulesco. Prod: Twentieth Century Fox. Dist: Films Inc.
Cast: Charles Laughton, Marilyn Monroe, David Wayne, Dale Robertson, Richard Widmark, Anne Baxter, Jean Peters, Fred Allen, Oscar Levant, Jeanne Crain, Farley Granger.

The Cop and the Anthem
23 min.   color   1982
Prod: Highgate Pictures. Dist: Simon & Schuster (16 mm and video).
Cast: Robert Morse.
   Soapy, a likable tramp, wants to spend the winter in jail but has trouble trying to get arrested—until he changes his mind.

Double-Dyed Deceiver (in *Everybody's Magazine,* December 1905)

The Llano Kid
8 reels   b&w   1939
Dir: Edward D. Venturini. Sp: Wanda Tuchock. Prod: Paramount.
Cast: Tito Guizar, Gale Sondergaard.
   The heroine refuses to turn in the Llano Kid, even though she thinks he is a bandit.

The Texan
79 min.   b&w   1930
Dir: John Cromwell. Prod: Paramount.
Cast: Gary Cooper, Fay Wray.

Fortune's Mask

Fortune's Mask
5 reels   b&w   1922   sil.
Dir: Robert Ensminger. Prod: Vitagraph.
Cast: Earle Williams, Patsy Ruth Miller.
A newcomer to a Central American town successfully leads a revolution.

The Gift of the Magi (see also *O. Henry's Full House* under **The Cop and the Anthem**)

The Gift of Love (television movie)
105 min.   color   1978
Cast: Marie Osmond, Timothy Bottoms.

The Last Leaf (see *O. Henry's Full House* under **The Cop and the Anthem**)

The Passing of Black Eagle

Black Eagle
8 reels   b&w   1938
Dir: Robert Gordon. Sp: Edward Huebsch, Hal Smith. Prod: Columbia Pictures.
Cast: William Bishop, Virginia Patton, Gordon Jones.
A hobo becomes involved in a quarrel between a female rancher and a group of swindlers.

The Ransom of Red Chief (see also *O. Henry's Full House* under **The Cop and the Anthem**)

The Big Chief
98 min.   b&w   1960
Dir.: M. Verneuil. Prod: Continental Dist. Corp.
Cast: Fernandel, Gino Cervi, Papouf.
A French version of the story in which the kid devastates his kidnappers.

The Ransom of Red Chief
27 min.   color   1977
Dir: Tony Bill. Sp: Michael Kane. Prod: Learning Corp. Dist: Simon & Schuster (16 mm and video).
Cast: Harry Dean Stanton, Joe Spinell, Robbie Rist.
A humorous story of a small boy whose kidnappers learn to regret their actions.

A Retrieved Reformation

Jimmy Valentine
55 min. (30 min. edited)   color   1985
Dir: Paul Saltzman. Prod: Learning Corp. of America. Dist: Simon & Schuster (16 mm and video). (In production at press time.)
Former safecracker Jimmy reforms when he falls in love with Annabel, but in order to save a child locked in a vault, he must reveal his past.

The Romantic Rogue

The Cisco Kid
65 min.   b&w   1931
Prod: Fox. Dist: Budget Films/Video.

The Two Thanksgiving Day Gentlemen

The Two Thanksgiving Day Gentlemen
15 min.   color   1978
Prod: International Instructional Television Coop. Dist: Indiana University
     (16 mm and video).
Two old men tied to tradition give a special Thanksgiving day feast for a
seemingly less fortunate man. Unexpected ending.

Whistling Dick's Christmas Stocking

An Unwilling Hero
5 reels   b&w   1921   sil.
Dir: Clarence Badger. Prod: Metro-Goldwyn.
Cast: Will Rogers, Molly Malone.
A hobo discovers other tramps are planning to rob a plantation.

HERBERT, F. HUGH (see also *People Will Talk* under KERR, SOPHIE)

A Guy Could Change (in *Saturday Evening Post,* 9 January 1943)

A Guy Could Change
65 min.   b&w   1946
Dir: William K. Howard. Prod: Republic Pictures. Dist: Ivy Films.
Cast: Bobby Blake, Gerald Mohr.

HERGESHEIMER, JOSEPH

Tol'able David

Tol'able David
8 reels   b&w   1921   sil.
Dir: Henry King. Prod: Inspiration-First National Pictures. Dist: Blackhawk
     (video), Sheik Video (video), Video Yesteryear.
Cast: Richard Barthelmess.
A young man takes care of his mother after his father and older brother are
killed by a ruthless gang of murderers, whom he eventually meets.

Tol'able David
8 reels   b&w   1930
Dir: John Blystone. Prod: Columbia Pictures.
Cast: Richard Cromwell, Henry B. Walthall.

HERRICK, KIMBALL

Night Patrol

Trouble at Midnight (s.m. also the screenplay "Midnight Raider")
69 min.   b&w   1938

Dir: Ford Beebe. Sp: Ford Beebe, Maurice Geraghty. Prod: Universal.
Cast: Noah Beery, Jr., Catherine Hughes, Larry Blake.
Mystery about the theft of dairy cows.

HERVEY, HARRY

Burnt Offering

> *A Passport to Hell*
> 68 min.　　　b&w　　　1932
> Dir: Frank Lloyd. Prod: Fox.

Shanghai Express

> *Peking Express*
> 84 min.　　　b&w　　　1932
> Dir: Joseph Von Sternberg. Prod: Paramount Publix. Dist: Alan Twyman
> 　　Presents.
> Cast: Marlene Dietrich, Clive Brook, Anna May Wong, Warner Oland, Eugene
> 　　Palette.

Adventure aboard a speeding train with a doctor and a woman nicknamed
Shanghai Lily.

> *Peking Express*
> 95 min.　　　b&w　　　1951
> Dir: William Dieterle. Prod: Paramount.
> Cast: Joseph Cotten, Corinne Calvet, Edmund Gwenn.
> A remake of the earlier movie.

HICHENS, ROBERT SMYTHE

Snake-Bite

> *The Lady Who Lied*
> 8 reels　　　b&w　　　1925　　　sil.
> Sp: Edwin Carewe. Prod: First National Pictures.
> Cast: Lewis Stone, Virginia Valli, Louis Rayne.

When Fay finds Horace in a seemingly compromising situation with another
woman, she breaks her engagement to him and marries an alcoholic doctor, who is
later called on to help Horace.

HICKS, EDWIN P.

Capital Offense

> *Hot Summer Night*
> 86 min.　　　b&w　　　1957
> Dir: David Friedkin. Sp: Morton Fine. Prod: MGM.
> Cast: Leslie Nielson, Colleen Miller.

An unemployed newspaperman is kidnapped in the Ozarks after he inter-
views a gangster.

HILLMAN, GORDON MALHERBE
The Great Man Votes

The Great Man Votes
70 min.   b&w   1939
Dir: Garson Kanin. Prod: RKO. Dist: Films Inc.
Cast: John Barrymore, Virginia Weidler.
A scholar who drinks too much reforms when the Children's Society threatens to take his children away from him.

Here I Am a Stranger

Here I Am a Stranger
77 min.   b&w   1939
Dir: Roy Del Ruth. Sp: Milton Sperling. Prod: Fox.
Cast: Richard Greene, Brenda Joyce.

HITTLEMAN, CARL K. (see *36 Hours* under DAHL, ROALD)

HOFFMAN, CHARLES
Untitled

It Could Happen to You
54 min.   b&w   1939
Dir: Alfred Werker. Prod: Twentieth Century Fox. Dist: Ivy Films.

HOLDING, ELIZABETH SANXAY
The Bride Comes Home

The Bride Comes Home
85 min.   b&w   1935
Dir: Wesley Ruggles. Prod: Paramount.
Cast: Claudette Colbert, Fred MacMurray, Robert Young.
Comedy about a love triangle.

HOLMES, MILTON
Bundles for Freedom

Mr. Lucky
100 min.   b&w   1943
Dir: H.C. Potter. Prod: RKO. Dist: Films Inc., Nostalgia Merchant (video).
Cast: Cary Grant, Lorraine Day.
A professional gambler seeks to raise money by operating a war-drive bazaar.

HOPPER, JAMES MARIE
Father and Son (in *Saturday Evening Post,* 25 October 1924)

Win That Girl
6 reels   b&w   1928   sd. effects and mus.

Dir: David Butler. Prod: Fox.
Cast: David Rollins, Sue Carol, Tom Elliot.
Comedy of a football rivalry between two families.

HORTON, ROBERT J.

A Man of Action (in *Western Story Annual*)

Rip Roarin' Roberts
5 reels   b&w   1924   sil.
Dir: Richard Thorpe. Prod: Approved Pictures.
Cast: Buddy Roosevelt, Brenda Lane.
To collect a reward, a man has himself appointed sheriff.

HOUGH, DONALD

Calaboose

Calaboose
b&w   1943
Dir: Hal Roach, Jr. Sp: Arnold Belgard. Prod: Hal Roach Studios.
Cast: Noah Beery, Jr.
A situation comedy about screwballs in the calaboose.

HOUSTON, NORMAN

Private Property

A Royal Romance
62 min.   b&w   1930
Dir: Erle C. Kenton. Prod: Columbia Pictures.

HOWARD, GEORGE BRONSON

Black Room

Man from Headquarters
65 min.   b&w   1928
Dir: Duke Warne. Prod: Rayart Pictures. Dist: Select Film Library.
Cast: Cornelius Keefe, Edith Roberts

HOWELL, DOROTHY

Black Sheep

Guilty
71 min.   b&w   1930   sil. or sd.
Dir: George B. Seitz. Prod: Columbia Pictures.
Cast: Virginia Valli, John Holland.
The daughter of a senator sentenced to prison for bribery is ostracized by
her friends. Note: According to the AFI, publication of the story was not verified.

HUGGINS, ROY

Now You See It

The Fuller Brush Man
93 min.   b&w   1948
Dir: S. Sylvan Simon. Prod: Columbia Pictures. Dist: Modern Sound
    Pictures.
Cast: Red Skelton, Janet Blair.
A streetsweeper, rejected as unworthy by his girlfriend, decides to earn his
living as a Fuller brush salesman.

HUGHES, LANGSTON

Thank You, M'am

Thank You, M'am
12 min.   color   1976
Dir: Andrew Sugerman. Dist: Phoenix Films. (16 mm and video).
A night nurse at a large city hospital is on her way home early in the morning
when a ten-year-old attempts to grab her purse. She grabs him and takes him to
her apartment.

HUGHES, LLWELLYN

Chap Called Bardell (in *Liberty Magazine,* 23 February 1929)

Sky Hawk
7 reels   b&w   1929
Dir: John G. Blystone. Prod: Fox.
Cast: Helen Chandler, John Garrick.
Pilot Jack Bardell, accused of crashing his plane to avoid serving on the
French front, proves his bravery.

HUGHES, RUPERT

Bitterness of Sweets

Look Your Best
6 reels   b&w   1923   sil.
Prod: Metro-Goldwyn.
Cast: Colleen Moore, Antonio Moreno.
A poor girl is given a chance to replace a chorus girl who has grown too fat.

Canavan, the Man Who Had His Way

Hold Your Horses
5 reels   b&w   1921   sil.
Dir: E. Mason Hopper. Prod: Goldwyn.
Cast: Tom Moore, Sylvia Ashton.
Dan Canavan, an immigrant from Ireland, goes from being a street cleaner
to the husband of society belle Beatrice.

It Had to Happen
7,184' b&w 1936
Dir: Roy Del Ruth. Prod: Twentieth Century Fox.
Cast: George Raft, Rosalind Russell.
An Italian immigrant becomes a big political boss and falls for the banker's
wife.

Don't You Care (in *Saturday Evening Post,* 4 July 1914)

Don't
5 reels b&w 1925 sil.
Dir: Alf Goulding. Prod: MGM.
Cast: Sally O'Neil, John Patrick.
A story about a flapper who defies her parents.

From the Ground Up (in *Cosmopolitan Magazine,* October 1921)

From the Ground Up
5 reels b&w 1921 sil.
Dir: E. Mason Hopper. Adap. Rupert Hughes. Prod: Metro-Goldwyn.
Cast: Tom Moore, Helen Chadwick.
Philena refuses to marry the man her father picked out because he needs
a loan from him.

The Girl on the Barge (in *Hearst's International Magazine,* October 1927)

The Girl on the Barge
8 reels b&w 1929
Dir: Edward Sloman. Adap: Charles Kenyon, Nan Cochrane. Prod:
   Universal.
Cast: Jean Hersholt, Sally O'Neill.
Erie McCadden, the daughter of a mean barge captain, falls in love with a
tugboat pilot.

Money Talks

Money Talks
6 reels b&w 1926 sil.
Dir: Archie Mayo. Prod: MGM.
Cast: Ned Sparks, Owen Moore, Claire Windsor.
A gun-running villain is thwarted by a gun-toting hero.

Obscurity

Breach of Promise
7 reels b&w 1932
Dir: Paul L. Stein. Prod: E.W. Mannons.

The Old Nest (in *Saturday Evening Post,* 3 June 1911)

The Old Nest
8 reels b&w 1921 sil.

Dir: Reginald Barker. Prod: Metro-Goldwyn.
Cast: Dwight Crittenden, Mary Alden.
The saga of a large family.

The Patent Leather Kid

The Patent Leather Kid
127 min.   b&w   1927
Dir: Alfred Santell.
Cast: Richard Barthelmess, Molly O'Day, Arthur Stone.
The love story of two fiery people who are caught up in war.

She Goes to War

She Goes to War
70 min.   b&w   1929
Prod: Henry King. Dist: Em Gee Film Library, Glenn Video Vistas.
Cast: Eleanor Boardman, Alma Rubens.

True as Steel (in *Cosmopolitan Magazine,* December 1923)

True as Steel
7 reels   b&w   1924
Dir: Rupert Hughes. Prod: Goldwyn.
Cast: Aileen Pringle, Huntley Gordon, Cleo Madison.
Frank Parry becomes infatuated with another woman while on a business trip to New York.

Unidentified story

FBI Girl
74 min.   b&w   1951
Dir: William Berke. Prod: Lippert. Dist: Mogull's Films.
Cast: Audrey Totter, George Brent.
A clerk is the bait to obtain evidence on a mob trying to uncover the governor's former criminal record.

HUMPHREY, WILLIAM

The Last of the Caddoes

The Last of the Caddoes
29 min.   color   1982
Prod. and Dist: Phoenix Films (16 mm and video).
A twelve-year-old boy goes through a summer of self-discovery and learns that he has Indian ancestors.

HUNYADY, SANDER

The Girl Downstairs

The Girl Downstairs
8 reels   b&w   1938

Dir: Norman Taurog. Prod: MGM.

Cast: Franciska Gaal, Franchot Tone.

The heroine is a naive domestic who wins the affections of a man-about-town from her rich employer.

HURST, FANNIE

Back Pay

Back Pay
7 reels   b&w   1922   sil.
Dir: Frank Borzage. Prod: Cosmopolitan Pictures.
Cast: Seena Owen, Matt Moore, J. Barney Sherry, Ethel Duray.

Country girl Hester Bevins is in love with delivery boy Jerry but doesn't want to live a dull, poor life.

Back Pay
77 min.   b&w   1930
Dir: William A. Seiter. Prod: Warner Bros. Dist: MGM/UA Home Video (video).
Cast: Montagu Love, Corinne Griffith.

A girl rebels against her small-town background.

Four Daughters

Young at Heart
117 min.   color   1954
Dir: Gordon Douglas. Prod: Warner Bros. Dist: NTA Home Entertainment (video).
Cast: Frank Sinatra, Doris Day, Gig Young, Ethel Barrymore, Dorothy Malone.

A cynical, hard-luck musician gets a new outlook on life when he meets and falls for a small-town girl.

Give This Little Girl a Hand

The Painted Angel
7 reels   b&w   1929
Dir: Millard Webb. Prod: First National Pictures and Vitaphone.

A violinist stops the bullet that is intended for an entertainer.

The Good Provider (in *Saturday Evening Post,* 15 August 1914)

The Good Provider
8 reels   b&w   1922
Dir: Frank Borzage. Prod: Cosmopolitan Pictures.
Cast: Vera Gordon, Dore Davidson.

Jewish immigrants struggle with changing business practices and city life before returning to the country.

Humoresque

Humoresque
6 reels   b&w   1920   sil.
Dir: Frank Borzage. Prod: Cosmopolitan Pictures.
Cast: Alma Rubens.

Humoresque
125 min.   b&w   1947
Dir: Jean Negulesco. Dist: MGM/UA Home Video (video).
Cast: Joan Crawford, John Garfield, Oscar Levant.
A poor but gifted musician is sponsored by a wealthy society woman who loves him, but he decides that his career is more important than she is.

Just Around the Corner

Just Around the Corner
7 reels   b&w   1921   sil.
Dir. and Adap: Frances Marion. Prod: Cosmopolitan Pictures.
Cast: Margaret Seddon, Lewis Sargent, Sigrid Holmquist.
Ma Birdsong's daughter Essie cannot get her fiance, a crooked ticket speculator, to visit her mother and hires an impersonator, whom she later marries.

The Nth Commandment

The Nth Commandment
8 reels   b&w   1929   sil.
Dir: Frank Borzage. Prod: First National Pictures.
Cast: Colleen Moore, James Morrison.
Flattered by the attentions of a sophisticated man, Sarah breaks her engagement to another man.

Roulette

Wheel of Chance
7 reels   b&w   1929   sil.
Dir: Alfred Santell. Adap: Gerald C. Duffy.
Cast: Richard Barthelmess, Warner Oland.
During the Czarist regime, a Russian family, saddened by the death of a son, comes to America, only to learn later that he is alive.

HUTCHINSON, BRUCE

Park Avenue Logger (in *Saturday Evening Post,* 29 November 1935)

Tall Timber (a.k.a. *Park Avenue Logger*)
67 min.   b&w   1937
Dir: David Howard. Prod: George A. Hirliman. Dist: Film Classics Exchange, Mogull's Films.
Cast: George O'Brien, Marjorie Reynolds.
A young man in society exposes the foreman of a lumber camp to be a crook.

HUXLEY, ALDOUS

The Giaconda Smile

A Woman's Vengeance
96 min.   b&w   1948
Dir: Zoltan Korda. Sp: Aldous Huxley. Prod: Universal.
Cast: Jessica Tandy, Charles Boyer, Ann Blyth.
A man who falls in love with a shopgirl is put on trial for poisoning his wife.

Young Archimedes

Prelude to Fame
78 min.   b&w   1942
Prod: Two Cities Films; rel. Universal.
A professor saves a young Italian conductor from exploitation.

HYDE, ROBERT

Just Another Dame

Not a Ladies Man
6 reels   b&w   1942
Dir: Lew Landers. Sp: Rian James. Prod: Columbia Pictures.

HYMER, JAMES

The Lost Game

Law of the Underworld (jt. author Samuel Shipman; s.m. also a stage production by John B. Hymer)
60 min.   b&w   1938
Dir: Lew Lander. Prod: RKO. Dist: Films Inc.
Cast: Chester Morris, Anne Shirely, Walter Abel.
A ruthless gang leader has a change of heart and saves a young couple from harm.

I

INGHAM, TRAVIS
Biddy

Most Precious Thing in Life
7 reels   b&w   1934
Dir: Lambert Hillyer. Sp: Ethel Hill, Dore Schary. Prod: Columbia Pictures.
Cast: Jean Arthur, Donald Cook.
A charwoman is really the mother of a spoiled young aristocrat.

IRISH, WILLIAM (see *Rear Window* under WOOLRICH, CORNELL)

IRVING, WASHINGTON
The Adventure of the German Student

The Adventure of the German Student
20 min.   color   1983
Prod: Auburn Television. Dist: AIT (video).
Set in the French Revolution. A shy young man sees the woman of his
dreams whose head was cut off the previous day. Coupled with Poe's story "The
Black Cat."

The Bold Dragon

The Bold Dragon
15 min.   b&w   1954
Prod: Dynamic Films.
Cast: Monty Woolley.
An innkeeper rids himself of a bothersome guest by giving him a haunted
room.

The Legend of Sleepy Hollow

Biograph, Selig, and Thanhouser are among the companies that produced
early silent versions of this story.

The Headless Horseman
8 reels   b&w   1922   sil.
Dir: Edward Venturini. Dist: Blackhawk (video).
Cast: Will Rogers, Lois Meredith.
Set along the Hudson River. Ichabod Crane encounters the headless
horseman.

Ichabod and Mr. Toad
(s.m. for Mr. Toad is also "The Wind in the Willows" by Kenneth Grahame)
68 min.   color   1949
Prod: Walt Disney.
Voices: Basil Rathbone, Bing Crosby.
Animated.

The Legend of Sleepy Hollow
13 min.   color   1972
Prod: Pyramid/Bosustow. Dist: Pyramid Films (16 mm and video).
Animated.

Tales of Washington Irving
45 min.   color
Prod: Dist: Twyman Films.
"The Legend of Sleepy Hollow" and "Rip Van Winkle" are the two stories
that are highlighted.

Rip Van Winkle

Rip Van Winkle
1 reel   1924   sil.
Prod: Universal.
Cast: Charles Dudley, Fay Holderness.

Rip Van Winkle
27 min.   color   1979
Prod: Will Vinton. Dist: Billy Budd Films.
Narrator: Will Geer.
A clay animated version of the story about a man who preferred telling
stories to tilling the soil. Academy Award Nomination. Also available in French.

IRWIN, WALLACE

American Beauty (in *Saturday Evening Post*, 8 January 1927)

American Beauty
7 reels   b&w   1927
Dir: Richard Wallace. Prod: First National Pictures.
Cast: Billie Dove, Lloyd Hughes, Walter McGrail.
A young, beautiful, but poor girl attempts to win a wealthy man for a
husband, but she is discovered.

Sophie Semenoff (in *Saturday Evening Post*, 27 November 1920)

Making the Grade
5 reels   b&w   1921   sil.
Dir: Fred J. Butler.
Cast: David Butler, Helen Ferguson.
A wealthy, freewheeling American lad marries a Russian schoolteacher and
takes her back to the U.S., only to find that she is really a princess escaping the
Bolsheviks.

ISHERWOOD, CHRISTOPHER

Berlin Stories (s.m. also a musical play by Jose Masteroff and the play "I Am a Camera" by John Van Druten, both of which are based on "Goodbye to Berlin")

Cabaret
123 min.   color   1972
Dir: Bob Fosse. Prod: Allied Artists and ABC Pictures. Dist: Hurlock Cine-World.
Cast: Liza Minelli, Michael York, Helmut Griem, Joel Gray.
A singer in pre-Hitler Germany leads a fun-filled life.

I Am a Camera
98 min.   b&w   1955
Dir: Henry Cornelius. Dist: Budget Films/Video, Video Communications (video).
Cast: Julie Harris, Laurence Harvey, Shelley Winters.
Sally Bowles is a zany nightclub singer in pre-Hitler Germany.

J

JACCARD, JACQUES

Hard Rock

The Galloping Ace
5 reels   b&w   1924   sil.
Dir: Robert North Bradbury. Prod: Universal.
Cast: Jack Hoxie, Margaret Morris.
War hero Jim Jordon takes a job on a ranch and falls in love with the woman who owns it.

JACKSON, FRED

High Speed (in *Argosy*, 1 June 1918)

High Speed
5 reels   b&w   1924
Dir: Herbert Blance. Prod: Universal.
Cast: Herbert Rawlinson, Carmelita Geraghy.
Athlete Hi Moreland tries to win the hand of the daughter of a bank president, but he is framed by a competitor.

Morocco Box (in *Argosy*, 6 January 1923)

Love Letters
5 reels   b&w   1924
Dir: David Soloman. Prod: Fox.
Cast: Shirley Mason, Gordon Edwards.
Two sisters try to retrieve passionate love letters they wrote to a notorious rake when they were young girls.

JACKSON, JOSEPH

The Champ

Be Yourself
67 min.   b&w   1930
Dir: Thorton Freeland. Prod: United Artists. Dist: Blackhawk, Mogull's
    Films.
Cast: Fanny Brice, Robert Armstrong.
The hero challenges a champion.

JACKSON, SHIRLEY

The Lottery

The Lottery
18 min.   color   1969
Prod. and Dist: Encyclopaedia Britannica (16 mm and video).
The inhabitants of a small town in America choose a person to be stoned to death each year.

JACOBS, WILLIAM WYMARK

The Interruption

Footsteps in the Fog
90 min.   b&w   1955
Dir: Arthur Lubin. Prod: Film's Locations Ltd. Dist: Modern Sound Pictures, Roa's Films.
Cast: Stewart Granger, Jean Simmons.
Set in London at the turn of the century. A patrician householder poisons his wife, and a servant blackmails him.

The Monkey Box

Our Relations
70 min.   b&w   1936
Dir: Harry Lachman. Prod: MGM. Dist: Blackhawk (video).
Cast: Laurel and Hardy, Alan Hale.
Long-lost twin brothers turn up, and a series of mistaken identity problems arise.

The Monkey's Paw

The Monkey's Paw
27 min.   color   1983
Prod: Stillife-Gryphon. Dist: Simon & Schuster (16 mm and video).
A grizzly old sailor gives a family a monkey's paw, said to grant wishes, but he advises against its use. The family fails to listen to him, with disastrous results.

The Monkey's Paw
19 min.   color   1979
Prod: Martha Moran. Dist: Phoenix Films (16 mm and video).
A monkey's paw opens the door to a family's desires.

Monkey's Paw (s.m. also the play by Louis Napoleon Parker)
56 min.   b&w   1932
Dir: Wesley Ruggles. Sp: Graham John. Prod: RKO.
Cast: C. Aubrey Smith, Ivan Simpson, Louis Carter.
Everything turns out to be a dream.

Monkey's Paw
64 min.   b&w   1948
Dir: Norman Dee. Sp: N. Lee, Barbara Toy. Prod: Butchers Films. Dist: Swank.
Cast: Milton Rosmer, Megs Jenkins, Joan Seton, Norman Shelley.

A couple obtains a monkey's paw that grants wishes but always at great cost.

Tales from the Crypt (s.m. also the comic book series "All Thru the House," "Reflection of Death," "Poetic Justice," "Blind Alleys," and "Wish You Were Here," which in turn is based on "The Monkey's Paw" by William M. Gaines, Albert B. Feldstein, and Johnny Craig).
92 min.   color   1972
Dir: Freddie Francis. Prod: Cinerama. Dist: Swank.
Cast: Sir Ralph Richardson, Joan Collins, Martin Boddey.
On a tour through a subterranean burial ground, five unrelated sightseers find themselves locked in a crypt where various horrific experiences from the future (or past?) are exposed to them.

JAMES, HENRY

The Altar of the Dead

The Green Room
90 min.   color   1978
Dir: Francois Truffaut. Dist: Warner Bros. Home Video (video).
Cast: Francois Truffaut, Nathalie Baye, Jean-Pierre Moulin.
A man haunted by the memory of his dead wife is unable to respond to the present.

The Jolly Corner

The Jolly Corner
43 min.   color   1977
Dir. and Sp: Arthur Barron. Dist: Simon & Schuster (16 mm and video).
Cast: Fritz Weaver, Salome Jens.
Brydon, an expatriate American who fled from the Civil War, returns to New York 35 years later. He is at once repelled and enticed by the lust for profit and power and wonders what would have happened had he remained.

The Real Thing

The Real Thing
15 min.   color   1978
Prod: International Instructional Television Coop. Dist: Indiana University (16 mm and video).
Reality is the theme of a story about an artist who decides to use a real lord and lady as models.

JAMES, MONTAQUE R.

Casting the Runes

Curse of the Demon (Br., a.k.a. *Night of the Demon*)
95 min.   b&w   1958
Dir: Jacques Tourneur. Prod: Columbia Pictures.
Cast: Dana Andrews, Peggy Cummins.
A fearsome monster from the past returns to wreak havoc in London.

JANIS, ELSIE (jt. author) (see *Close Harmony* under MARKEY, GENE)

JARRICO, PAUL

Private Miss Jones (jt. author Richard Collins)

> *Thousands Cheer*
> 126 min.   color   1944
> Sp: George Sidney. Prod: MGM. Dist: Films Inc.
> Cast: Kathryn Grayson, Gene Kelly, Mary Astor.
> A musical about a soldier and the colonel's daughter.

JENKINS, WILL F.

The Purple Hieroglyph (in *Snappy Stories,* 1 March 1920)

> *Murder Will Out*
> 7 reels   b&w   1930
> Dir: Clarence Badger. Prod: First National Pictures.
> Cast: Jack Mulhall, Lila Lee, Noah Beery, Jr.
> A young couple in the upper crust of Washington, D.C. society are plagued
by blackmail, attempted murder, and kidnapping.

JEWETT, SARAH ORNE

The White Heron

> *The White Heron*
> 26 min.   color   1978
> Prod: Jane Morrison. Dist: Simon & Schuster (16 mm and video).
> Sylvy is caught between her admiration for a young hunter who wants her to
help him catch a heron and her love of nature.

JOHNSON, DOROTHY

Man Called Horse (in *Collier's Magazine,* 7 January 1950)

> *A Man Called Horse*
> 114 min.   color   1970
> Dir: Elliot Silverstein. Prod: Cinema Center. Dist: Swank, CBS/Fox Video
>   (video).
> Cast: Richard Harris, Dame Judith Anderson.
> An English aristocrat, captured by the Sioux Indians in the 1700s, has only
one chance of survival: to prove his manhood in their savage ritual "Vow to the
Sun."

The Man Who Shot Liberty Valance

> *The Man Who Shot Liberty Valance*
> 122 min.   b&w   1962
> Dir: John Ford. Prod: Paramount. Dist: Films Inc., Paramount Home Video
>   (video).
> Cast: James Stewart, John Wayne, Lee Marvin, Edmond O'Brien.
> An Eastern lawyer is determined to rid a Western town of its resident terror,
Liberty Valance, by organizing the citizens, holding elections, and so forth. The
leading strong gun watches in amusement and then does the job himself by shooting
Liberty.

JOHNSON, NUNNALLY

Rough House Rosie (in *Saturday Evening Post,* 12 June 1926)

> *Rough House Rosie*
> 59 min.   b&w   1927   sil.
> Dir: Frank Strayer. Sp: Louis Long, Ethel Doherty. Prod: Famous Players-
>   Lasky.
> Cast: Clara Bow, Reed Howes.
> In this society comedy, a young woman wants to be a dancer and boxer.

JOHNSON, OWEN

The Lawrenceville Stories

> *The Happy Years*
> 110 min.   color   1950
> Dir: William Wellman. Prod: MGM. Dist: Films Inc.
> Cast: Dean Stockwell, Darryl Hickman, Leo G. Carroll, Scotty Beckett,
>   Leon Ames.

The exasperating experiences of a pint-sized terror to teachers and parents
who is sent to the Lawrenceville, New Jersey, prep school in the 1890s.

JOHNSTON, CALVIN

Temple Dusk (in *Saturday Evening Post,* 16 October 1920)

> *Without Limit*
> 7 reels   b&w   1921
> Dir: George D. Baker. Prod: S-L Pictures.
> Cast: Anna Q. Nilsson, Robert Frazer.
> The son of a clergyman gambles away his money.

JONES, HERBERT A.

The Mystery Ship

> *Suicide Fleet*
> 9 reels   b&w   1931
> Dir: Albert Rogell. Sp: Lew Lipton. Prod: RKO.
> Cast: William Boyd, Ginger Rogers, Robert Armstrong.
> Two brawling sailors fight over the same girl.

JORDAN, ANNE

Kitchen Privileges

> *Luckiest Girl in the World*
> 68 min.   b&w   1936
> Dir: Edward Buzzell. Sp: Herbert Fields, Henry Myers. Prod: Universal.
> Cast: Jane Wyatt, Louis Hayward, Nat Pendleton.

A wealthy society girl must live on $150 a month to prove to her father that
she can stand being married to a poor man.

JORGENSON, IVAR (pseud. of Paul Fairman)

Deadly City

> *Target Earth*
> 75 min.   b&w   1954
> Dir: Sherman A. Rose. Sp: William Raynor. Prod: Allied Artists.
> Cast: Richard Denning, Virginia Grey, Kathleen Crowley.

A girl awakens alone in the city because everyone else has fled the giant robots with death rays that arrived from Venus.

JOSSELYN, TALBERT

Navy Bound (in *Collier's Magazine,* 14 December 1935)

> *Navy Bound*
> 61 min.   b&w   1951
> Dir: Paul Landres. Prod: Monogram Pictures. Dist: Institutional Cinema
>   Service.

Action-packed drama of a Navy boxing champion and the touching gratitude he feels for his foster father.

KAFKA, FRANZ

The Hunger Artist

> *The Hunger Artist*
> 10 min.   color   1976
> Dir: Fred Smith, Maura Smith. Prod: Paramount Oxford.

The hero is engaged in the crowd-gathering spectacle of starving, attracting the curious and the scornful.

The Woman Who Came Back

> *The Woman Who Came Back* (s.m. also a story suggested by Philip Yordan)
> 69 min.   b&w   1945
> Dir: Walter Colmer. Prod: Republic Pictures. Dist: Ivy Films.
> Cast: John Loder, Nancy Kelly.

Fool's First (in *Saturday Evening Post,* 20 November 1920)

> *Fools First*
> 6 reels   b&w   1922   sil.
> Dir. and Prod: Marshall Neilan.
> Cast: Richard Dix. Claire Windsor.

Once released from prison, Tommy robs a bank with his girlfriend but then tries to return the money.

Once a Peddler (in *Saturday Evening Post,* 3 September 1921)

> *The Little Giant*
> 7 reels   b&w   1926   sil.
> Dir. and Adap: William Nigh. Prod: Universal.
> Cast: Glenn Hunter, Edna Murphy.

Elmer, the sales manager of a large manufacturing company, launches a successful sales campaign, which is sabotaged by the son of the company's president.

KALEY, J.

Deuces Wild

> *Saddle Aces*
> 57 min.   b&w   1935
> Prod: Republic Pictures. Dist: Thunderbird Films.
> Cast: Rex Bell.

KAMSOFF, MANUEL

The $1000 Bill

The $1000 Bill
24 min.   color
Dist: MTI Teleprograms (video).
Sudden wealth changed Henry from a timid salesman to a hero, but the money is counterfeit. An ABC Weekend Special.

KANTOR, MACKINLEY

Gun Crazy (in *Saturday Evening Post,* 3 February 1940)

Gun Crazy (a.k.a. *Deadly Is the Female*)
87 min.   b&w   1948
Dir: Joseph Lewis. Prod: United Artists. Dist: Hurlock Cine-World.
Cast: Peggy Cummins, John Dall.
A gangster and his gun moll.

Mountain Music

Mountain Music
8 reels   b&w   1937
Dir: Robert Florey. Sp: John C. Moffett, Duke Atteberry, Russell Crouse,
     Charles Lederer. Prod: Paramount.
Cast: Bob Burns, Martha Raye.
Slapstick comedy about an amnesiac.

KAUFFMAN, REGINALD WRIGHT

Our Undisciplined Daughters

School for Girls
8 reels   b&w   1934
Dir: William Nigh. Prod: Liberty Pictures.

Relative Values (in *Saturday Evening Post,* 27 January 1923)

Young Ideas
5 reels   b&w   1924   sil.
Dir: Robert Hill. Prod: Universal.
Cast: Laura La Plante, T. Roy Barnes.
Octavia supports a large family, all of whom pretend ailments to avoid work.

Sweetie Peach

The House That Jazz Built
6 reels   b&w   1921   sil.
Dir: Penrhyn Stanlaws. Prod: Realart Pictures.
Cast: Wanda Hawley, Forrest Stanley.
Frank and Cora Rodham live in a modest suburb, where he acquires a good position and she becomes fat. He becomes infatuated with another woman.

KEEFE, FREDERICK L.

The Interpreter

Before Winter Comes
108 min.   color   1969
Dir: J. Lee Thompson. Prod: Columbia Pictures. Dist: Budget Films/Video,
    Charard Motion Pictures, Modern Sound Pictures, Welling Motion Pictures.
Cast: David Niven, Anna Karina, Topol.

A refugee camp in occupied Austria after World War II is run by British
Major Giles Burnside, a stickler for regulations. He must assign displaced persons of
the border camp to either the American or Russian zones. The camp is a shambles
until a refugee steps forward to help.

KEELER, HARRY STEPHEN

Twelve Coins of Confucius

Mysterious Mr. Wong
56 min.   b&w   1935
Dir: William Nigh. Prod: Monogram Pictures. Dist: Budget Films/Video,
    Classic Film Museum, Em Gee Film Library, Wholesome Film Center,
    Cable Films (video), Discount Video Tapes, Penguin Video.
Cast: Bela Lugosi, Wallace Ford.

Twelve coins, given by Confucius on his deathbed to his friends, were circu-
lated and lost over the years. According to legend, if one man could amass all of
them, he would gain extraordinary power, so Wong stops at nothing to try to
locate the last coin.

KELLAND, CLARENCE BUDINGTON

Knots and Windshakers (in *Everybody's Magazine,* April 1920)

French Heels
7 reels   b&w   1922   sil.
Dir: Edwin L. Hollywood. Adap: Eve Unsell. Prod: Holtre Prod.
Cast: Irene Castle, Ward Crane.

A soldier returning home from the war must tell a young girl that her brother
was killed. She goes to work in a cabaret to support herself, and his parents object.

Scattergood Baines stories (suggestion for)

Scattergood Baines
68 min.   b&w   1941
Dir: Guy Kibbee. Prod: Pyramid Pictures, rel. RKO. Dist: Roa's Films.
Cast: Christy Cabanne.

The sage of Coldriver selects a new teacher, keeps control of his community
railroad, defeats the syndicate, and stills gossipy tongues. Other films featuring the
character include *Scattergood Meets Broadway* (1941), *Scattergood Pulls the String*
(1941), and *Scattergood Rides High* (1942).

Stand-In (in *Saturday Evening Post,* 13 February 1937)

Stand-In
90 min.   b&w   1937
Dir: Tay Garnett. Prod: United Artists. Dist: Mogull's Films, Monterey Home
    Video (video).
Cast: Leslie Howard, Joan Blondell.
An alcoholic producer and a ravishing former child star come to the aid of a
befuddled financial expert who is trying to save a movie studio from bankruptcy.

Thirty-Day Princess (in *Ladies Home Journal,* July 1933)

Thirty-Day Princess
76 min.   b&w   1934
Dir: Marion Gering. Prod: Paramount.
Cast: Sylvia Sidney, Cary Grant.
A princess on a goodwill tour gets the mumps and a replacement must be
found.

KELLY, T. HOWARD

His Buddy's Wife

His Buddy's Wife
6 reels   b&w   1925   sil.
Dir: Tom Teriss. Prod: Associated Exhibitors.
Cast: Glenn Hunter, Edna Murphy.
A war buddy asks Jim to look after his family if anything happens to him.
When Bill does not return from a patrol, Jim goes to Bill's farm to care for his
family until the neighbors begin to gossip.

Lover's Island

Lover's Island
5 reels   b&w   1925   sil.
Dir: Henri Diamont-Berger. Prod: Encore Pictures.
Cast: Hope Hampton, James Kirkwood.
Clemmy, who has been attacked, names Avery as her attacker, and her
father vows he will make him marry her.

KENEDI, ALEXANDER G. (jt. author) (see *Marry the Boss's Daughter* under
    FARAGO, SANDOR)

KENT, ROBERT E.

Assigned to Danger

Assigned to Danger
66 min.   b&w   1948
Dir: Oscar Boetticher. Sp: Eugene Ling. Dist: Budget Films/Video, Ivy
    Films.
Cast: Gene Raymond, Noreen Nash.
The adventure of an insurance investigator who brings about the capture
of a gang of payroll bandits.

KEOUN, ERIC

Sir Tristram Goes West

> *The Ghost Goes West* (Br.)
> 85 min.   b&w   1936
> Dir: Rene Clair, Prod: London Film. Dist: Audio Brandon, Mogull's Films.
> Cast: Robert Donat, Jean Parker.

When the castle of Lord Tristram is moved stone by stone to America, its resident spirit follows and lives with a young, pretty lady who soon becomes aware of her "guest."

KERR, SOPHIE

Beauty's Worth (in *Saturday Evening Post,* 14 February 1920)

> *Beauty's Worth*
> 7 reels   b&w   1922
> Dir: Robert G. Vignola. Prod: Cosmopolitan Pictures.
> Cast: Marion Davies, Forest Stanley.

A sophisticated neighbor flirts with a Quaker girl, even though he is really not interested in her.

Kayo, Oke

> *People Will Talk* (s.m. also the story *Such a Lovely Couple* by F. Hugh
>   Herbert)
> 7 reels   b&w   1935
> Dir: Alfred Santell. Sp: Herbert Fields. Prod: Paramount.
> Cast: Cary Grant, Jeanne Crain.

A physician falls in love with a pregnant girl and is accused of malpractice by a jealous colleague.

KETCHUM, PHILLIP

The Town in Hell's Backyard

> *The Devil's Trail*
> b&w   1941
> Dir: Lambert Hillyer. Prod: Columbia Pictures.
> Cast: Bill Elliott, Tex Ritter.
> Western.

KEYES, DANIEL

Flowers (short story and later a novel)

> *Charly*
> 103 min.   color   1968
> Dir: Ralph Nelson. Prod: Cinerama. Dist: Films Inc.
> Cast: Cliff Robertson, Claire Bloom.

Charly, a thirty-year-old with the mental capabilities of a six-year-old, undergoes experimental treatment in a mental retardation clinic and achieves normal intelligence, only to learn that he will soon revert to his former state.

KILBOURNE, FANNIE

The Girl Who Was the Life of the Party (in *American Magazine,* December 1923)

> *Girls Men Forget*
> 6 reels   b&w   1924   sil.
> Dir: Maurice Campbell. Prod: Principal Pictures.
> Cast: Johnnie Walker, Patsy Ruth Miller.
> Kitty Shayne, the life of the party, learns that the men in her life marry

the quiet girls.

Sunny Goes Home (in *Saturday Evening Post*)

> *The Major and the Minor* (s.m. also "Connie Goes Home," a play by Edward
>   Childs Carpenter)
> 100 min.   b&w   1942
> Prod: Paramount. Dist: Universal.
> Cast: Ginger Rogers, Ray Milland, Rita Johnson, Robert Benchley, Diana
>   Lynn.
> A career woman impersonates a twelve-year-old girl in order to save on train

fare and then must continue the masquerade while biding time in a boys' military
academy.

> *You're Never Too Young*
> 102 min.   b&w   1955
> Dir: Norman Taurog. Prod: Paramount. Dist: Audio Brandon.
> Cast: Dean Martin, Jerry Lewis.
> A wacky barber is forced to pose as a child because a murderer is on his

trail. Supposedly a remake of *The Major and the Minor.*

The Ghost's Story

> *Earthbound*
> 60 min.   b&w   1940
> Dir: Irving Pichel. Sp: Samuel G. Engle, John Howard Lawson. Prod:
>   Twentieth Century Fox.
> Cast: Warner Baxter, Andrea Leeds.
> The spirit of a man returns to earth.

KING, RUFUS

The Case of the Constant God

> *Love Letters of a Star*
> 66 min.   b&w   1936
> Dir. and Sp: Lewis R. Foster, Milton Carruth. Prod: Universal.
> Cast: Henry Hunter, Polly Rowles, C. Henry Gordon.
> A girl commits suicide because she was blackmailed over letters she wrote to

a stage star.

Murder by the Clock

Murder by the Clock (s.m. also "Murder by the Clock," a play by Charles
Beahan)
74 min.   b&w   1931
Dir: Edward Sloman. Sp: Henry Myers. Prod: Paramount.
Cast: William Boyd, Lilyan Tashman, Irving Pichel, Regis Toomey.

Museum Piece Number 13 (in *Redbook*)

Secret Beyond the Door
99 min.   b&w   1948
Dir: Fritz Lang. Sp: Silvia Richards. Prod: Diana Prod. Dist: Ivy Films,
NTA Home Entertainment (video).
Cast: Joan Bennett, Michael Redgrave.
A beautiful woman married after a whirlwind romance suspects that her
husband wants to kill her.

KING, STEPHEN

Children of the Corn

Children of the Corn
94 min.   color   1984
Dir: Fritz Kiersch. Dist: Embassy Home Entertainment (VCR, LV, CED)
Cast: Peter Horton, Linda Hamilton.
A couple stumbles on a town in which the children killed their parents
because spirits told them to do it.

The Crate

Creepshow (s.m. several short stories by King)
120 min.   color   1982
Dir: George Romero. Prod. and Dist: Warner Bros. Home Video
(videocassette, LV, CED).
Cast: Hal Holbrook, Adrienne Barbeau, Fritz Weaver, Leslie Nielson.
A collage of several stories, including "The Crate," which features a professor who encounters the unspeakable horror of an ancient creature imprisoned
in a box. Also includes "Something to Tide You Over" and "They're Creeping Up
on You."

Something to Tide You Over (see *Creepshow* under KING, STEPHEN)

They're Creeping Up on You (see *Creepshow* under KING, STEPHEN)

KIPLING, RUDYARD

The King's Ankus

Jungle Book (s.m. also other Mowgli stories)
115 min.   color   1942
Dir: Zoltan Korda. Sp: Laurence Stallings. Dist: Embassy Home Entertainment (video), Hollywood Home Theater.

Cast: Sabu, Joseph Calleia, John Qualen.

A boy strays from his village as an infant and is raised by a she-wolf. He then discovers a vast treasure in the jungle and must protect it from the villagers.

Just So Stories
12 min. ea.   color   1982
Prod: Marble Arch Film. Dist: Coronet Films (16 mm and video).
A ten-part animated series.

The Man Who Would Be King

The Man Who Would Be King
127 min.   color   1976
Dir: John Huston. Sp: Gladys Hill, John Huston. Prod: Columbia Pictures, Allied Artists. Dist: Hurlock Cine-World, CBS/Fox Video (video).
Cast: Sean Connery, Michael Caine, Christopher Plummer.

Tongue-in-cheek version in which boyhood heroes teach the tribesmen to slaughter enemies like civilized men.

Mowgli Stories

The Jungle Book
78 min.   color   1967
Dir: Wolfgang Reitherman. Prod: Buena Vista.
Voices: George Sanders, Phil Harris, Sebastian Cabot, Louis Prima.
Animated.

Mowgli's Brothers
26 min.   color   1977
Prod: Chuck Jones. Dist: Xerox Films.
Wolves adopt and raise a human baby, and from them he learns about love, justice, and loyalty in this animated version.

The Jungle Book
105 min.   color   1941
Prod: United Artists. Dist: Budget Films/Video (video), VidAmerica.
Cast: Sabu, Joseph Calleia, Rosemary de Camp.

Rikki-Tikki-Tavi

Rikki-Tikki-Tavi
26 min.   color   1977
Prod: Chuck Jones. Dist: Xerox Films.
Voice: Orson Welles.

An animated tale of a mongoose who is saved from drowning by an Indian family and who protects them from two dreaded cobras.

Soldiers Three

Soldiers Three
95 min.   b&w   1951

Dir: Tay Garnett. Prod: MGM. Dist: Films Inc.
Cast: Stewart Granger, Walter Pidgeon.
Soldiers in India.

Toomai of the Elephants

Elephant Boy
80 min.   b&w   1937
Dir: Robert Flaherty, Zoltan Korda. Prod: London Film. Dist: Budget
    Films/Video, Roa's Films.
Cast: Sabu.
Because of his friendship with Kala Nag, a tremendously large elephant,
Toomai saves his village from stampeding wild elephants.

The White Seal

The White Seal
26 min.   color   1977
Prod: Chuck Jones. Dist: Xerox Films.
Narrator: Roddy McDowall.
Kotick, the white seal, learns to survive in the Bering Sea and puts his
knowledge to work to protect his friends in this animated version.

Without the Benefit of Clergy

Without the Benefit of Clergy
6 reels   b&w   1921   sil.
Dir: James Young. Prod: Pathe.
Cast: Percy Marmont.
English engineer John Holden rescues a woman from an unwelcome suitor
in Lahore.

KIRK, LAWRENCE

A Cargo of Innocents

Stand by for Action
109 min.   b&w   1942
Dir: Robert Z. Leonard. Sp: George Bruce, John Balderston, Herman
    Mankiewicz. Prod: Loew's.
Cast: Robert Taylor.
A group of mothers and their children, stranded on a boat, are rescued.

KIRK, RALPH G.

Malloy Campeador (in *Saturday Evening Post,* 17 September 1921)

The Scrapper
5 reels   b&w   1922   sil.
Dir: Hobart Henley. Prod: Universal.
Cast: Herbert Rawlinson, Gertrude Olmstead.
A construction engineer falls in love with the contractor's daughter.

United States Flavor (in *Saturday Evening Post,* 14 June 1924)

> *Men of Steel*
> 10 reels   b&w   1926   sil.
> Dir: George Archainbaud. Prod: First National Pictures.
> Cast: Milton Sills, Doris Kenyon.
> A fugitive mine laborer rises to leadership among the workers at a steel mill

and becomes engaged to the mill owner's daughter, only to have his past catch up
with him.

KIRKLAND, JACK

Honor Bright (jt. author Melville Baker)

> *Now and Forever*
> 82 min.   b&w   1934
> Dir: Henry Hathaway. Prod: Paramount. Dist: Swank.
> Cast: Carole Lombard, Gary Cooper.
> A jewel thief tries to go straight for the sake of his daughter, but

circumstances lead him into committing another robbery and violating his promise.

KOMROFF, MANUEL

The Thousand Dollar Bill

> *The Small-Town Boy*
> 6 reels   b&w   1937
> Dir. and Sp: Glenn Tryon. Prod: Grand National Films.
> Cast: Stuart Erwin, Joyce Compton.
> A small, timid boy is an easy mark for everyone.

KUTTNER, HENRY (see PADGETT, LEWIS [pseud.])

KYNE, PETER B.

All for Love

> *Valley of Wanted Men*
> b&w   1935
> Prod: Maurice Conn Prod.

Back to Yellow Jacket

> *Back to Yellow Jacket*
> 6 reels   b&w   1922   sil.
> Dir. and Prod: Ben Wilson.
> Cast: Roy Stewart, Kathleen Kirkham, Earl Metcalf.
> Carmen, wife of Sunny Jim, a prospector, is dissatisfied with her life and

attends a public dance with gambler Flush Kirby.

Blue Blood and the Pirates (in *Saturday Evening Post,* 30 March 1912)

> *Breed of the Sea*
> 6 reels   b&w   1926   sil.

Dir: Ralph Ince. Adap: J.G. Hawks. Prod: R-C Pictures.
Cast: Ralph Ince, Margaret Livingstone.
Two brothers are in love with the same girl.

Bread Upon the Waters (in *Hearst's International Magazine*)

A Hero on Horseback
6 reels   b&w   1927   sil.
Dir: Del Andres. Adap: Mary Alice Scully, Arthur Statter. Prod:
     Universal.
Cast: Hoot Gibson, Ethlyne Clair.
A happy-go-lucky cowboy loses almost $500 gambling but invests $50
in a grubstake with an old prospector who finds a mine.

Brothers Under Their Skins (in *Cosmopolitan Magazine,* December 1921)

Brothers Under Their Skins
6 reels   b&w   1922   sil.
Dir: E. Mason Hopper. Prod: Goldwyn.
Cast: Pat O'Malley, Helene Chadwick.
Newton Craddock, a shipping clerk, and the vice president of the company
have similar marital problems—suspicious, spendthrift wives.

Cappy Ricks stories (Cappy Ricks is a character that appeared in some of Kyne's novels and short stories)

The Affairs of Cappy Ricks
61 min.   b&w   1937
Dir: Ralph Staub. Prod: Republic Pictures. Dist: Ivy Films.
Cast: Walter Brennan, Lyle Talbot.
Cappy, an old codger, sends his family to a desert island to teach them a
lesson.

Cappy Ricks
6 reels   b&w   1921
Dir: Tom Forman. Prod: Paramount.
Cast: Thomas Meighan, Agnes Ayres.
Sea melodrama in which Cappy objects to the man his daughter loves.

Cornflower Cassie's Concert (in *Cosmopolitan Magazine,* February 1924)

Beauty and the Bad Man
6 reels   b&w   1925   sil.
Dir: William Worthington. Adap: Frank E. Woods. Prod: Penisual Studios.
Cast: Mable Ballin, Forrest Stanley, Russell Simpson.
An orphan marries the organist of the church but leaves him because of his
low character.

Dog Meat

Blue Blood
72 min.   b&w   1951

Dir: Lew Landers. Prod: Monogram Pictures. Dist: Hurlock Cine-World.
Cast: Bill Williams, Jane Nigh.
A veteran trainer convinces a wealthy girl to let him train a horse headed for oblivion.

Flaming Guns

Flaming Guns
57 min.   b&w   1932
Dir: Arthur Rosson. Sp: Jack Cunningham. Prod: Universal.
Cast: Tom Mix.
Western.

The Great Mono Miracle (suggestion for)

A Face in the Fog
60 min.   b&w   1936
Dir: Robert Hill. Prod: Victory Pictures. Dist: Mogull's Films.
Cast: June Clude, Lloyd Hughes.
A female reporter joins the search for a murderer.

The Harbor Bar (in *Redbook,* April 1914)

Loving Lies
7 reels   b&w   1924   sil.
Dir: W.S. Van Dyke.
Cast: Evelyn Brent, Monte Blue, Joan Lowell.
Hazards in the line of duty cause marital problems for the captain of a harbor tugboat.

Humanizing Mr. Winsby (in *Redbook,* April-May,1915)

Making a Man
6 reels   b&w   1922   sil.
Dir: Joseph Henabery. Prod: Famous Players-Lasky.
Cast: Jack Holt, J.P. Lockney, Eva Novak.
A rich man from California falls on hard times in New York, only to be redeemed by the love of the girl who had spurned him at home.

The Light to Leeward

Homeward Bound
7 reels   b&w   1923   sil.
Dir: Ralph Ince. Prod: Paramount.
Cast: Thomas Meighan.
First mate Jim Beford wins his girl and her father's blessing when he proves his bravery.

Lionized

Racing Blood
61 min.   b&w   1936

Dir. and Prod: Maurice Conn. Dist: Select Film Library, Willoughby-Peerless.
Cast: Frankie Darro.

A boy rescues a crippled horse about to be slaughtered and turns it into a racehorse.

The Man in Hobbles (in *Saturday Evening Post,* 29 March 1913)

The Man in Hobbles
6 reels   b&w   1928   sil.
Dir: George Archainbaud. Prod: Tiffany-Stahl.
Cast: John Harron, Lila Lee.

A young photographer has to contend with his wife's shiftless family until he makes good.

A Motion to Adjourn (in *Saturday Evening Post*)

A Motion to Adjourn
6 reels   b&w   1921   sil.
Dir: Roy Clements. Prod: Ben Wilson.
Cast: Harry Rattenberry, Roy Stewart.

Comedy about the disinherited playboy son of a wealthy New York broker and his induction into a western mining community group.

The New Pardner

Hot Off the Press
6 reels   b&w   1935
Dir: Al Herman. Sp: Victor Potel, Gordon S. Griffith. Prod: Victory Pictures.
Cast: Jack LaRue, Monte Blue.

A story about rival newspapers, one backed by crooks.

On Irish Hill

Kelly of the Secret Service
73 min.   b&w   1936
Prod: Principal Prod.
Cast: Lloyd Hughes, Sheila Manners.

A bomb is perfected to keep the enemy fleet from U.S. shores.

One Day's Work

Rio Grande Romance
7 reels   b&w   1936
Dir: Bob Hill. Sp: Al Martin. Prod: Victory Pictures.

One Eighth Apache (in *Redbook*)

Danger Ahead
6 reels   b&w   1935
Dir: Al Herman. Sp: Al Martin. Prod: Victory Pictures.
Cast: Lawrence Gray, Sheila Manners.

A gang tries to swindle a sea captain out of $40,000.

One Eighth Apache
6 reels   b&w   1922   sil.
Dir: Ben Wilson. Prod: Berwilla Films.
Cast: Roy Stewart, Kathleen Kirkham.
A man uses murder and scandal to prevent the marriage of his former sweetheart to the son of a cattle and oil baron.

The Parson of Panamint

The Parson of Panamint
84 min.   b&w   1941
Dir: William McGann. Prod: Paramount.
Western. In a wild town that grew up with a gold strike, a gentle parson is almost executed as a murderer.

While Satan Sleeps
60 min.   b&w   1922   sil.
Dir: Joseph Henabery. Prod: Famous Players-Lasky.
Cast: Jack Holt, Wade Boteler, Mabel Van Buren.
Western. Phil Webster, alias Slick Phil, escapes from prison and disguises himself as a minister.

Rustling for Cupid (in *Hearst's International Magazine,* February 1926)

Rustling for Cupid
5 reels   b&w   1926   sil.
Dir: Irving Cummings. Prod: Fox.
Cast: George O'Brien, Anita Stewart.
Western. A young man returns from college to his father's ranch and discovers his father engaging in cattle rustling.

Shipmakes

Taming the Wild
6 reels   b&w   1936
Dir: Bob Hill. Sp: Al Martin. Prod: Victory Pictures.
Cast: Brian Washburn, Rod LaRocque.
A family lawyer protects a headstrong heiress from gangsters.

Ten Dollar Raise (in *Saturday Evening Post,* 4 December 1909)

He Hired the Boss
65 min.   b&w   1942
Dir: Thomas Z. Loring. Sp: Ben Markson, Irving Cummings, Jr. Prod:
    Twentieth Century Fox. Dist: Films Inc.
Cast: Stuart Erwin, Evelyn Venable.
A bookkeeper wants a raise and is sold options instead.

Ten Dollar Raise
6 reels   b&w   1921   sil.
Dir: Edward Sloman. Prod: J.L. Frothingham.

Cast: William V. Mong, Marguerite De La Motte.

Wilkins, a bookkeeper for 20 years, does not receive an expected raise and can't marry Emily until he strikes oil on his property.

$10 Raise
6 reels   b&w   1935
Dir: George Marshall. Sp: Henry Johnson, Louis Breslow. Prod: Twentieth
     Century Fox.
Cast: Edward Everett Horton, Karen Morley.
A timid bookkeeper invests in property sold to him by a con man.

Thoroughbreds (in *Hearst's International Magazine,* September 1925)

The Golden Strain
6 reels   b&w   1925
Dir: Victor Schertzinger. Prod: Fox.
Cast: Hobart Bosworth, Kenneth Harlan.
Western. A newly commissioned lieutenant assigned to a cavalry post fails to lead his men in the first attack by the Indians but later redeems himself.

The Three Godfathers

Bronco Billy and the Baby
1 reel   b&w   1908   sil.
Cast: G.M. Anderson.
Western. Bronco Billy, an outlaw, gives up his freedom to help a lost child and is reformed by love. Reissued by Essanay in 1915 as *The Three Outlaws.*

Hell's Heroes
7 reels   b&w   1930
Dir: William Wyler. Adap: Tom Reed. Prod: Universal.
Cast: Charles Bickford, Raymond Hatton.
Western. Three bandits, escaping from the sheriff, come upon a woman dying during childbirth. She asks them to be the godfathers of her child and to take the baby to New Jerusalem to its father.

The Three Godfathers
8 reels   b&w   1936
Dir: Richard Boleslawski. Sp: Edward E. Parmore, Jr., Manuel Seff. Prod:
     MGM.
Cast: Chester Morris, Lewis Stone, Walter Brennan.
Western. A trio of fugitive gunmen rescue a newborn baby found in a covered wagon with its dying mother.

Three Godfathers
105 min.   color   1948
Dir: John Ford. Sp: Laurence Stallings, Frank S. Nugent. Prod: Argosy
     Pictures.
Cast: John Wayne, Pedro Armadariz.
Set in nineteenth century Arizona. Three robbers become godfathers.

The Godchild (made-for-television movie)
72 min.   color   1974
Dir: John Badham.
Cast: Jack Palance, Jack Warden, Jose Perez.
A remake of *The Three Godfathers.*

Tidy Toreador (in *Cosmopolitan Magazine,* April 1927)

Galloping Fury
6 reels   b&w   1927   sil.
Dir: Reaves Eason. Prod: Universal.
Cast: Hoot Gibson, Otis Harlan.
Western. A ranch foreman infected with poison ivy, treats it with mud from a marsh, which also improves his looks, so the whole town wants to buy the mud.

The Tie That Binds (suggestion for)

Flaming Frontiers (serials)
2 reels ea.   b&w   1938
Dir: Ray Taylor, Alan James. Sp: Wyndham Gittens, George Plympton,
    Basil Dickey, Paul Perez. Dist: Thunderbird Films.
Cast: John Mack Brown, Eleanor Hansen.
Western. A young Indian scout aids a beautiful girl whose brother, the owner of a gold mine, has been framed for murder.

Vengeance of the Lord

Bars of Hate
6 reels   b&w   1936
Dir: Lew Landers. Sp: J. Robert Bren, Edmund L. Hartmann. Prod: RKO.
Cast: Robert Armstrong, Sally Eilers.
A story about the responsibility of airline pilots for their crews.

L

LACROSSITT, HENRY

The Mob

> *Homicide Squad*
> 70 min.   b&w   1931
> Dir: George Melford. Prod: Universal.
> Cast: Leo Carrillo, Noah Beery, Jr.
> The police hunt a big-time gangster, whose own son is forced to frame him.

LAMBERT, RIETA

Clipped Wings

> *Hello Sister*
> 62 min.   b&w   1930
> Dir: Alan Crosland, Erick von Stroheim. Prod: Sono Art World Wide Pictures.
> Cast: ZaSu Pitts, James Dunn.

L'AMOUR, LOUIS

The Gift of Cochise (in *Collier's Magazine*)

> *Hondo*
> 93 min.   color   1955
> Dir: John Farrow. Prod: Wayne-Fellows Prod.
> Cast: John Wayne, Geraldine Page.
> Western. In 1874, Hondo Lane, a dispatch rider for the U.S. Cavalry, comes
upon a woman and her son who have been deserted by her husband after an Apache
attack.

> *Hondo and the Apaches*
> color   1967
> Dir: Lee Katzin. Sp: Andrew Fenady. Prod: MGM.
> Cast: Robert Taylor, Ralph Taeger, Noah Beery, Jr.
> A remake of *Hondo* for television and overseas markets.

Plunder

> *The Tall Stranger*
> 81 min.   color   1957
> Dir: Thomas Carr. Prod: Allied Artists. Dist: Ivy Films.
> Cast: Joel McCrea, Virginia Mayo.
> Western. A wagon train of settlers fights off desperados.

Unidentified story

> *Four Guns to the Border*
> 83 min.   color   1954
> Dir: Richard Carlson. Sp: George Van Marter, Franklin Coen. Prod:
>   Universal.
> Cast: Rory Calhoun, Colleen Miller, George Nader.
> Western. After a bank robbery, an outlaw gang helps an ex-gunslinger and

his beautiful daughter fight off Apaches.

LANGELAAN, GEORGE

The Fly

> *The Fly*
> 95 min.   color   1958
> Dir: Kurt Neumann. Prod: Twentieth Century Fox. Dist: Budget Films/
>   Films/Video, Roa's Films, Select Film Library.
> Cast: Vincent Price, Patricia Owens.
> A scientist discovers a method of disintegrating objects and then materializing

them at a distance. When he experiments on himself, a housefly intrudes and their
atoms become confused. *The Return of the Fly,* based on the characters in the
original, was produced in 1959, and *The Curse of the Fly* was produced in 1965,
both by Twentieth Century Fox.

LANHAM, EDWIN

The Senator Was Indiscreet

> *The Senator Was Indiscreet*
> 81 min.   b&w   1947
> Dir: George S. Kaufman. Sp: Charles MacArthur. Prod: Universal.
> Cast: William Powell, Ella Raines.
> A boisterous senator, who wants to be the next President, decides that the

way to win the nomination is to state that he is not a candidate for the office.

Unidentified story

> *It Shouldn't Happen to a Dog*
> 6,279'   b&w   1946
> Dir: Herbert I. Leeds. Sp: Eugene Ling, Frank Gabrielson. Prod: Twentieth
>   Century Fox. Dist: Films Inc.
> Cast: Carol Landis, Allyn Joslyn.
> A reporter flirts with a lady cop to get an exclusive story.

LARDNER, JOHN (jt. author) (see *Finger Man* under LIPSIUS, MORRIS)

LARDNER, RING

Alibi Ike

> *Alibi Ike*
> 72 min.   b&w   1935
> Dir: Ray Enright. Prod: Warner Bros. Dist: MGM/UA Home Video.

Cast: Joe E. Brown, Olivia De Havilland.

A modest baseball player nearly forfeits his team's chances by modestly denying his real love.

Champion

Champion
99 min.   b&w   1948
Dir: Mark Robson. Prod: Screen Players. Dist: Budget Films/Video, Ivy
    Films, Kit Parker Films, Video Communications (video).
Cast: Kirk Douglas, Arthur Kennedy.

A young man's ruthlessness takes him to the top of the prizefighting pro-
fession. Winner of an Academy Award for best editing.

The Golden Honeymoon

The Golden Honeymoon
52 min.   color   1980
Dir: Noel Black. Dist: Coronet Films.
Cast: James Whitmore, Teresa Wright.

Charlie Tate and his wife go to St. Petersburg to celebrate their 50th
anniversary. There he meets the man who was previously engaged to his wife,
and he feels that he has to win her all over again.

LARKIN, JOHN FRANCIS

Customer's Girl

She Had to Say Yes
64 min.   b&w   1933
Dir: Busby Berkeley. Prod: First National Pictures and Vitaphone. Dist:
    MGM/UA Home Video.
Cast: Loretta Young, Lyle Talbot.

A girl entertains an out-of-town buyer and gets into trouble.

LAWRENCE, DAVID HERBERT

The Rocking Horse Winner

The Rocking Horse Winner
91 min.   b&w   1950
Dir: Anthony Pelessier. Prod: Two Cities Films. Dist: Janus Films.
Cast: John Mills, Valerie Hobson.

Paul Grahame, a sensitive ten-year-old boy, hears his parents fighting about
money. He is given a toy rocking horse and soon begins to find out the winners
of actual horse races by rocking on it, but the strain proves to be too much.

The Rocking Horse Winner
30 min.   color   1977
Dir: Peter Medak. Adap: Julian Bond. Prod: Highgate Pictures. Dist: Simon
    & Schuster.
Cast: Kenneth More.

A young boy is disturbed by the arguments between his father and mother over money, and he becomes obsessed by the need to be lucky. On his rocking horse, he suddenly learns how to predict the outcome of the races, but the results are disastrous.

LEA, FANNY HEASLIP

The Peacock Screen

Cheaters
68 min.   b&w   1934
Dir: Phil Rosen. Prod: Liberty Pictures.

LE FANU, SHERIDAN

Carmilla

Vampyr (Gr.; a.k.a. *The Strange Adventure of David Gray*)
66 min.   b&w   1931
Dir: Carl Dreyer. Sp: Christen Jul, Carl Dreyer. Dist: Hollywood Home
    Theater (video).
Cast: Julian West, Sybille Schmitz, Maurice Schutz.
The story of David Gray and his misadventures in vampire-laden Eastern
Europe.

Blood and Roses
74 min.   color   1961
Dir: Roger Vadim. Prod: Paramount. Dist: Audio Brandon.
Cast: Mel Ferrer, Elsa Martinelli, Annette Stroyberg.
Vampire-spirit Carmilla, who has been dormant for several hundred years, takes over the body and soul of a look-alike relative when an Army mine frees her spirit.

Terror in the Crypt (Br. title *Crypt of Horror*)
84 min.   b&w   1960
Dir: Thomas Miller. Dist: Audio Brandon.
A father must deal with the spirit of a vampire, which has been reincarnated into the body of his daughter.

The Vampire Lovers (Br.)
88 min.   color   1970
Dir: Roy Ward Baker. Sp: Tudor Gates.
Cast: Ingrid Pitt, Pippa Steel.
Carmilla befriends and kills young women. Two sequels were made: *Lust for a Vampire* (1970) and *Twins of Evil* (1971).

LEIGHTON, FLORENCE (pseud. of FLORENCE LEIGHTON PFALZGRAF)

Heaven's Gate

Our Little Girl
63 min.   b&w   1935

Prod: Fox.
Cast: Shirley Temple, Joel McCrea.
A troubled only child tries to patch up her parents' differences.

LEIGHTON, WILL R.

The Able-Minded Lady (in *Saturday Evening Post*)

The Able-Minded Lady
5 reels   b&w   1922   sil.
Dir: Ollie Sellers. Prod: Pacific Films.
Cast: Henry B. Walthall, Elinor Fair, Helen Raymond.
Western. A cowboy bachelor works for a three-time widow, who eventually
wins him too.

LEINSTER, MURRAY (see WILL F. JENKINS)

LE NOIR, PHILLIP

The Man Who Wouldn't Take Off His Hat (in *Argosy All-Story Weekly Magazine,* 19 August 1922)

The Devil's Bowl
5 reels   b&w   1923   sil.
Dir: Neal Hart. Prod: William Steiner Prod.
Cast: Catherine Bennett, W.J. Allen, Neal Hart.
Sam rescues his sister from marriage to a horse thief. Reissued in 1924
under the title *Branded a Thief.*

LEONARD, ELMORE

The Captives

The Tall T
78 min.   1957
Dir: Budd Boetticher. Prod: Columbia Pictures. Dist: Kit Parker Films,
   Westcoast Films.
Cast: Randolph Scott, Richard Boone.
Western.

3:10 to Yuma

3:10 to Yuma
92 min.   b&w   1957
Dir: Delmer Daves. Prod: Columbia Pictures. Dist: Audio Brandon.
Cast: Glenn Ford, Van Heflin, Felicia Farr.
A rancher is faced with the responsibility of putting a notorious killer on the
gallows-bound train to Yuma and is unable to obtain help.

LEWIS, HERBERT CLYDE

D-Day in Las Vegas

Lady Luck
97 min.   b&w   1946

Dir: Edwin L. Marin. Prod: RKO. Dist: Films Inc.

Cast: Robert Young, Barbara Hale.

Comedy-drama. A nice girl tries to tame a high-rolling gambler by marrying him.

LEWIS, SINCLAIR

Bongo (s.m. also the fairy tale "Jack and the Beanstalk")

Fun and Fancy Free
73 min.　　　　　color　　　　　1947
Prod: Walt Disney Prod. Dist: Films Inc., Roa's Films.
Narration: Dinah Shore.
An animated story of Bongo the circus bear and other Disney characters.

The Ghost Patrol

The Ghost Patrol
5 reels　　　　　b&w　　　　　1923　　　　　sil.
Dir: Ralph Graves. Prod: Universal.
Cast: Ralph Graves, Bessie Love, George Nichols.
A kind police officer helps Terry go straight and win the girl he wants.

Let's Play King

Forbidden Adventure
6,950'　　　　　b&w　　　　　1931
Dir: Norman Taurog. Sp: Edward E. Paramore, Jr., Joseph L. Mankiewicz.
　　Prod: Paramount.
Cast: Mitzi Green, Jackie Searl.
A story of the enmity between two jealous women.

LIEBE, HAPSBURG

Trimmed and Burned (in *Collier's Magazine,* September 1921)

Trimmed
5 reels　　　　　b&w　　　　　1922　　　　　sil.
Dir: Harry Pollard. Prod: Universal.
Cast: Hoot Gibson, Patsy Ruth Miller.
A sheriff expected by the political boss to be easy to manipulate remains honest.

LINDNER, ROBERT M.

Destiny's Tot

Pressure Point
89 min.　　　　　b&w　　　　　1962
Dir: Hubert Cornfield. Prod: Larcus.
Cast: Sidney Poitier, Bobby Darin, Peter Falk.
A tense drama of a Nazi Bundist in America in the 1930s and the black prison psychiatrist who tries to straighten out his mind.

LINDSEY, JUDGE BEN

Little Colored White Cloud

One Mile From Heaven
7 reels   b&w   1937
Dir: Allan Dwan. Prod: Twentieth Century Fox.
Cast: Clair Trevor, Sally Blane.
A young black woman brings up a white child and battles in court to keep
her.

LIPSIUS, MORRIS

Finger Man (jt. author John Lardner)

Finger Man
82 min.   b&w   1955
Dir: Harold Schuster. Sp: Warren Douglas. Prod: Allied Artists. Dist: Ivy
    Films.
Cast: Frank Lovejoy, Forrest Tucker.
To avoid prison, an ex-convict turns informer and assists the FBI in breaking
up a syndicate.

LITTLETON, SCOTT

Inside Story

Night Editor (s.m. also the radio show "Night Editor")
68 min.   b&w   1946
Dir: Henry Levin. Prod: Columbia Pictures.
Cast: William Gargan, Janis Carter.
A story about a crooked cop and a luscious but mean woman.

LOCKRIDGE, FRANCIS (see LOCKRIDGE, RICHARD)

LOCKRIDGE, RICHARD

Mr. and Mrs. North stories (jt. author Frances Lockridge)

Mr. and Mrs. North (s.m. also a play by Owen Davis based on these
    characters)
7 reels   b&w   1942
Dir: Robert B. Sinclair. Prod: MGM.
Cast: Gracie Allen, William Post, Jr.
A mystery farce.

LOFTS, NORA

Chinese Finale

Seven Women
93 min.   color   1966
Dir: John Ford. Sp: Janet Green, John McCormick. Prod: MGM. Dist:
    Films Inc.
Cast: Anne Bancroft, Sue Lyon, Margaret Leighton.

Set in China during the turbulent 1930s. An isolated missionary post is headed by a straightlaced spinster who eagerly awaits the new resident doctor—a breezy, profane, drinking, chain-smoking woman dressed in riding breeches.

LONDON, JACK

The Abysmal Brute

Conflict
63 min.   b&w   1936
Dir: David Howard. Sp: Charles A. Logue, Walter Weems. Prod: Universal.
Cast: John Wayne, Jean Rogers.
A beautiful female reporter tries to discover if a lumberjack is actually in cahoots with a fake fight racket.

All Gold Canyon

All Gold Canyon
21 min.   color   1973
Prod: Kratsky Film, Prague. Dist: Indiana University.
A prospector discovers gold, works his claim, and is ambushed.

Brown Wolf

Brown Wolf
30 min.   color   1972
Dir: George Kaczender. Prod: Highgate Pictures. Dist: Simon & Schuster.
Two people attempt to possess a wild and beautiful dog after it is separated from its master, who later returns.

Demetrios Cantos

Devil's Skipper
6 reels   b&w   1928   sil.
Dir: John G. Adolfi. Prod: Tiffany Prod.
Cast: Belle Bennett, Montagu Love.
The female commander of a slave ship lures aboard a man who caused her suffering and has him tortured. She turns over the young girl with him to the crew and later learns she's her own daughter.

Finis

Finis
54 min.   color   1983
Prod: Norwalk. Dist: Encyclopaedia Britannica (16 mm and video).
His partner and sled dogs dead, a man suffering from frostbite and scurvy desperately struggles to survive.

Flush of Gold

Alaska
76 min.   b&w   1944
Dir: George Archainbaud. Sp: George Wallace Sayre, Harrison Orkow. Prod: Monogram Pictures. Dist: Hurlock Cine-World.

Gold Hunter of the North

North to the Klondike (s.m. also an adapted story by William Castle)
70 min.   b&w   1941
Dir: Erle C. Kenton. Sp: Clarence Upson Young, Lew Sarecky, George
   Bricker. Prod: Universal. Dist: "The" Film Center.
Cast: Broderick Crawford, Lon Chaney, Jr.
Gold is discovered on the land of a beautiful girl.

In a Far Country

In a Far Country
54 min.   color   1983
Prod: Norwalk Prod. Dist: Encyclopaedia Britannica (16 mm and video).
Unwilling to travel 1,000 miles, two men on the gold rush trail choose to
spend the arctic winter in a deserted cabin but lack the discipline to overcome
their fears and survive.

Love of Life

Love of Life
30 min.   color   1981
Prod: Norfolk Communications. Dist: Simon & Schuster.
In the Klondike wilderness, two weary prospectors push toward civilization,
suffering several mishaps along the way.

The Mexican

The Fighter
78 min.   b&w   1952
Dir: Herbert Kline. Prod: G.H. Prod. Dist: Budget Films/Video.
Cast: Richard Conte, Lee J. Cobb.
A poor Mexican patriot comes to America at the turn of the century to
obtain money for guns so that his people can free themselves from a dictatorship.

The One Thousand Dozen

The One Thousand Dozen
54 min.   color   1983
Prod: Norwalk Prod. Dist: Encyclopaedia Britannica (16 mm and video).
David Rasmussen faces a hazardous journey with a fragile cargo—eggs—which
he believes he can sell to the hungry prospectors for outrageous sums of gold.

Race for Number One

Race for Number One
54 min.   color   1983
Prod: Norwalk Prod. Dist: Encyclopaedia Britannica (16 mm and video).
Two prospectors—Olaf and Smoke—engage in a grueling dogsled race to the
claim office in Dawson.

A Raid on the Oyster Pirates

Tropical Nights
6 reels   b&w   1928   sil.
Dir: Elmer Clifton. Prod: Tiffany-Stahl.
Cast: Patsy Ruth Miller, Malcolm MacGregor.
A young woman thinks she is responsible for the death of a salesman dealing in pearls.

The Scorn of Women

The Scorn of Women
52 min.   color   1983
Floyd Vanderlipp, a manly hero, is admired for his prowess in overcoming the perils of the North, and three women attempt to ensnare him.

The Siege of the Lancashire Queen

Prowlers of the Sea
6 reels   b&w   1928   sil.
Dir: John G. Adolfi. Prod: Tiffany-Stahl.
Cast: Carmel Myers, Ricardo Cortez.
An honest man is put in charge of the Coast Guard, but he succumbs to the charms of a beautiful, dishonest woman.

Son of the Wolf

Son of the Wolf
5 reels   b&w   1928   sil.
Dir: Norman Dawn. Prod: Tiffany-Stahl.
Cast: Wheeler Oakman, Edith Roberts.
Scruff Mackenzie falls in love with his Indian ward, Chook-Ra, but he must prove he loves her to her people.

The Story of Jess Uck

The Mohican's Daughter
5 reels   b&w   1922   sil.
Dir: S.E.V. Taylor. Prod: PTB Inc.
A half-breed girl defies Indian law by getting medicine for a sick child and flees to the trading post manager for help.

That Spot

Sign of the Wolf
80 min.   b&w   1941
Dir: Howard Bretherton. Prod: Monogram Pictures. Dist: Mogull's Films.
Cast; Michael Whelan, Grace Bradley.
Two dogs battle in the Canadian wilds.

A Thousand Deaths

Torture Ship
57 min.   b&w   1939
Prod: Producers Releasing Corp.
Cast: Lyle Talbot, Sheila Bromley.

To Build a Fire

To Build a Fire
56 min.   color   1969
Dir: David Cobham. Dist: Audio Brandon.
Cast: Ian Hogg.
Narrator: Orson Welles.
A lone man travels through the -75 degree weather of the Alaskan wilderness.

To Build a Fire
15 min.   color   1975
Dir: Robert Stitzel. Dist: Phoenix/BFA Films and Video.
The encounter between man and nature in freezing cold weather.

The Unexpected

By the Law (U.S.S.R.)
61 min.   b&w   1926   sil.
Dir: Lev Kuleshov. Dist: Budget Films/Video, Em Gee Film Library.
A psychological drama in which a member of a party goes on a killing rage in a log cabin in Alaska.

The Unexpected
53 min.   color   1983
Prod: Norwalk Prod. Dist: Encyclopaedia Britannica (16 mm and video),
A campsite is thrown into chaos when one of the gold miners runs amok, killing two of his comrades.

White and Yellow

Romance of the Redwoods
63 min.   b&w   1939
Dir: Charles Vidor. Prod: Columbia Pictures.
Cast: Jean Parker, Charles Bickford.
Men and women in a logging camp find romance.

Wife of the King

Wife of the King
b&w   1928   sil.
Prod: Tiffany-Stahl.

Yellow Handkerchief

Stormy Waters
6 reels   b&w   1928   sil.

Dir: Edgar Lewis. Adap: Harry Dittmar. Prod: Tiffany-Stahl.
Cast: Eve Southern, Malcolm MacGregor, Roy Stewart.
Although David is engaged to be married, he succumbs to the temptation of
Lola, a barfly, while on a seafaring trip to Buenos Aires.

LONG, AMELIA REYNOLDS

The Thought-Monster

Fiend Without a Face
75 min.   b&w   1958
Dir: Arthur Crabtree. Dist: Budget Films/Video, Modern Sound Pictures,
    Blackhawk (video).
Cast: Marshall Thompson, Kim Parker, Terence Kilburn.
In a small Canadian town, the U.S. Air Force has set up a secret radar station,
which results in agonizing deaths.

LOVECRAFT, H.P.

Case of Charles Dexter Ward

The Haunted Palace
85 min.   color   1963
Dir: Roger Corman. Prod: Roger Corman. Dist: Audio Brandon.
Cast: Vincent Price, Debra Paget, Lon Chaney, Jr.
Although the title is taken from Poe's story, the film is based almost entirely
on Lovecraft's story in which a warlock who was burned at the stake returns to
possess the body of his sole descendant.

The Colour Out of Space (in *Amazing Stories,* September 1927)

Die, Monster, Die!
80 min.   color   1965
Dir: Daniel Haller. Prod: American International. Dist: Budget Films/Video,
    Clem Williams Films, Ivy Films, Wholesome Film Center.
Cast: Boris Karloff, Nick Adams, Patrick Magee.
Because of a radioactive meteor, the ancient lord of a mouldering estate is
slowly transformed into a monster, gradually losing his sanity and human qualities.

The Dreams in the Witch-House (uncredited)

The Crimson Cult
87 min.   color   1970
Dir: Vernon Sewall. Dist: Budget Films/Video, Ivy Films, Roa's Films.
Cast: Boris Karloff, Christopher Lee, Mark Eden, Barbara Steele.
A young man seeking his brother goes to Grey Marsh Lodge, and at the
family graveyard he finds a witches' shrine with a crimson sacrificial altar.

The Dunwich Horror

The Dunwich Horror
90 min.   color   1970
Dir: Daniel Haller. Sp: Curtis Lee Hanson. Dist: Audio Brandon, Wholesome
    Film Center.

Cast: Sandra Dee, Dean Stockwell, Sam Jaffe.

The town of Dunwich turns into a haven for the practice of the black mass and black magic, and a young woman is lured to the Devil's estate.

The Shuttered Room

The Shuttered Room (Br.)
100 min.   color   1968
Dir: David Greene. Prod: Warner Bros. Dist: Kerr Film Exchange, Roa's
    Films.
Cast: Gig Young, Carol Lynley, Oliver Reed, Flora Robson.

An attractive couple assume their inheritance and insist on seeing their house, including the shuttered room.

LOWDES, MRS. BELLOC

Shameful Behavior

Shameful Behavior
6 reels   b&w   1926   sil.
Dir: Albert Kelley. Prod: Preferred Pictures.
Cast: Edith Roberts, Richard Tucker.

A young flapper poses as Sally, an escapee from an insane asylum, but the joke wears thin.

LOWRY, MALCOLM

Under the Volcano (later expanded into a novel, which served as the source of the movie)

Under the Volcano
112 min.   color   1984
Dir: John Huston. Prod: Moritz Borman and Wieland Schulz-Keil.
Cast: Albert Finney.

A 24-hour period in the life of Geoffrey Firman, an alcoholic and former British Consul living in a small town in Mexico.

LUTHER, BARBARA

Moon Walk (in *Ladies Home Journal,* February 1962)

A Ticklish Affair
89 min.   color   1963
Dir: George Sidney. Sp: Ruth Brooks Flippen. Prod: MGM. Dist: Films Inc.
Cast: Shirley Jones, Gig Young, Red Buttons.
The escapades of a widow, her three sons, and a naval officer.

LYLE, EUGENE P., JR.

The Ringtailed Galliwampus (in *Saturday Evening Post,* 15 July 1922)

Try and Get It
6 reels   b&w   1924   sil.
Dir: Cullen Tate. Adap: Jules Furthman.
Cast: Bryant Washburn, Billie Dove.
Two young bill collectors at work.

LYNCH, JAMES CHARLES

Battle of Pilgrim Hill (in *Saturday Evening Post*)

> *Hurricane at Pilgrim Hill*
> 65 min.   b&w   1953
> Dir: Richard Bare. Prod: Howco. Dist: National Film Service.
> Cast: Clem Bevans, Cecil Lellaway, David Bruce.
> Pop Snedly, a cantankerous old screwball, visits his son in the quiet town of
Pilgrim Hill and sets the town on its ear.

LYNDON, BARRE

Unidentified story (in *Saturday Evening Post*)

> *Sundown*
> 90 min.   b&w   1941
> Dir: Henry Hathaway. Prod: United Artists. Dist: Films Inc.
> Cast: Gene Tierney, Bruce Cabot, George Sanders.
> A British settlement in Africa is helped to defeat the Nazis by a jungle girl.

MACAULAY, RICHARD

Ready, Willing and Able

> *Ready, Willing and Able*
> 93 min.   b&w   1937
> Dir: Ray Enright. Prod: Warner Bros. Dist: MGM/UA Home Video (video).
> Cast: Jane Wyman, Ruby Keeler.
> A stage-struck girl pretends to be a London musical star.

Special Arrangement

> *Melody for Two*
> 60 min.   b&w   1936
> Dir: Louis King. Prod: Warner Bros. and Vitaphone. Dist: MGM/UA Home
>   Video (video).
> Cast: James Melton, Patricia Ellis.
> A clash between rival singers.

MacDONALD, JOHN D.

Taint of the Tiger (in *Cosmopolitan Magazine,* March 1958)

> *Man-Trap*
> 93 min.   b&w   1961
> Dir: Edmond O'Brien. Sp: Ed Waters. Prod: Tiger Prod.
> Cast: Jeffrey Hunter, David Janssen.
> Matt Jameson becomes involved in the recovery of $3,500,000 for a Central
American dictator.

MacGRATH, HAROLD

You Can't Always Tell (in *Redbook,* December 1925)

> *Womanpower*
> 7 reels   b&w   1926   sil.
> Dir: Harry Beaumont. Prod: Fox.
> Cast: Ralph Graves, Kathryn Perry.
> A rich, young idler becomes a fighter.

MACHARG, WILLIAM BRIGGS

The Price of a Party (in *Cosmopolitan Magazine*)

> *The Price of a Party*
> 6 reels   b&w   1924   sil.

Dir: Charles Giblyn. Prod: Howard Estabrook Prod.
Cast: Hope Hampton, Harrison Ford.
A broker hires a poor but beautiful cabaret dancer to prevent a hated business rival from exercising a valuable option.

Wine (in *Hearst's International Magazine,* March 1922)

> *Wine*
> 7 reels   b&w   1924   sil.
> Dir: Louis J. Gasnier. Prod: Universal.
> Cast: Clara Bow, Forrest Stanley.
> Facing financial ruin, John joins up with bootleggers.

MACK, WILLARD

The Public Be Damned

> *Night of Terror*
> 65 min.   b&w   1933
> Dir: Benjamin Stoloff. Prod: Columbia Pictures. Dist: Buchan Pictures.
> Cast: Bela Lugosi, George Meeker, Tully Marshal.
> A maniac killer is on the loose.

MACORLAN, PIERRE

Port of Shadows

> *Port of Shadows*
> 90 min.   b&w   1939
> Dir: Marcel Carne. Prod: Film Alliance. Dist: Budget Films/Video.
> Cast: Jean Gabin, Michele Morgan.

MAGRUDER, MARY

Courage (in *Young's Magazine*)

> *Satan and the Woman*
> 7 reels   b&w   1928   sil.
> Dir: Burton King. Prod: Excellent Pictures.
> Cast: Claire Windsor, Cornelius Keefe.
> A ruthless old woman tries to crush the romance of her heir and a grand-daughter whose blood relationship she had refused to acknowledge.

MALAMUD, BERNARD

Angel Levine (in *Commentary,* December 1955)

> *The Angel Levine*
> 107 min.   color   1970
> Dir: Jan Kadar, Chiz Schultz. Dist: Audio Brandon, Budget Films/Video, Welling Motion Pictures.
> Cast: Zero Mostel, Harry Belafonte, Ida Kaminska.
> Down on his luck, a tailor finds a black man sitting in his kitchen who claims that he can work a miracle if the tailor has faith in him.

MALLOY, DORIS (jt. author) (see *Mad Parade* under ORR, GERTRUDE)

MANN, E.B.

Stampede

> *Stormy Trails*
> 59 min.   b&w   1936
> Prod: Grand National. Dist: Video Communication (video).
> Cast: Rex Bell.
> A fighting cowpoke.

MANN, THOMAS

Tonio Kroger

> *Tonio Kroger* (Fr./W. Ger. with English subtitles)
> 90 min.   b&w   1968
> Dir: Rolf Thiele. Prod: Pathe.
> Cast: Jean-Claude Brialy, Nadja Tiller, Gert Frobe.
> A story about growing up in Germany in the late nineteenth century.

MANNES, MARYA

The Woman Who Was Scared

> *Forever Darling*
> 91 min.   color   1956
> Dir: Alexander Hall. Prod: MGM. Dist: Films Inc.
> Cast: Lucille Ball, Desi Arnaz.
> A guardian angel,who looks like a movie star, saves the marriage of a scatter-
brained wife and her long-suffering husband.

MANSFIELD, KATHERINE

The Garden Party

> *The Garden Party*
> 24 min.   color   1974
> Prod: Gurian/Sholder Prod.
> After World War II, a young girl makes her first acquaintance with death
when a neighboring farmer is killed in an accident the day of her mother's party.

MARCIN, NATALIE

You Can't Fool a Marine

> *Anchors Aweigh*
> 140 min.   color and b&w   1945
> Dir: George Sidney. Prod: MGM. Dist: Films Inc.
> Cast: Gene Kelly, Frank Sinatra.
> Two prowling gobs on a damsel-hunting expedition in Hollywood: one is
a seagoing Don Juan, the other a slightly backward, gawky chump.

MARKEY, GENE

Blinky (in *Blue Book,* January 1923)

> *Blinky*
> 6 reels   b&w   1923
> Dir: Edward Sedgwick. Prod: Universal.
> Cast: Hoot Gibson.
> Blinky proves his worth to the cavalry.

Close Harmony (jt. author Elsie Janis)

> *Close Harmony*
> 7 reels   b&w   1929
> Dir: John Cromwell, Edward Sutherland. Adap: Percy Heath. Prod:
>   Paramount/Famous Players-Lasky.
> Cast: Charles Rogers, Nancy Carroll.
> A girl interferes with a band's big chance.

MARMUR, JACLAND

No Home of His Own (in *Saturday Evening Post*)

> *Return from the Sea*
> 80 min.   b&w   1954
> Dir: Lesley Selander. Prod: Allied Artists. Dist: Hurlock Cine-World.
> Cast: Neville Brand, Jan Sterling.
> A chief mate finds romance in San Diego before shipping out again.

MARQUAND, JOHN PHILLIPS

Only a Few of Us Left (in *Saturday Evening Post*)

> *High Speed Lee*
> 5 reels   b&w   1923   sil.
> Dir. and Adap: Dudley Murphy. Prod: Atlantic Features.
> Cast: Reed Howes.
> A wealthy, idle young man falls for a young girl, but she is unhappy because
he does not take an interest in the family tire business.

The Right That Failed

> *The Right That Failed*
> 5 reels   b&w   1922   sil.
> Dir: Bayard Veiller. Prod: Metro Pictures.
> Cast: Bert Lytell, Virginia Valli.
> A boxing champ, resting at a summer resort, falls in love with a society girl
with the approval of her father and the opposition of her stuffy fiance.

That Girl and Mr. Moto

> *Think Fast, Mr. Moto*
> 5,961'   b&w   1937
> Dir: Norman Foster. Prod: Twentieth Century Fox. Dist: Warner Bros.

Cast: Peter Lorre.
A suave, sinister man solves baffling crimes.

MARTIN, THORNTON (jt. author) (see *The Band Plays On* under
STUHLDREHER, HARRY)

MASON, FRANK VAN WYCK

International Team

The Spy Ring
70 min.   b&w   1938
Dir: Joseph H. Lewis. Prod: Trem Carr.
Cast: William Hall, Jane Wyman.
Spies are hot on the trail of a young inventor.

MASON, GRACE SARTWELL

Clarissa and the Post Road (in *Saturday Evening Post,* 14 July 1923)

Man Crazy
6 reels   b&w   1927   sil.
Dir: John Francis Dillon. Adap: Perry Nathan. Prod: Charles R. Rogers
Prod.
Cast: Dorothy Mackaill, Jack Mulhall.
Against her grandmother's wishes, the carefree daughter of an aristocratic
New England family falls for a handsome truckdriver and aids him in a fight against
bootleggers.

Speed (in *Saturday Evening Post,* 18-25 October 1924)

Speed
6 reels   b&w   1925   sil.
Dir: Edward J. Le Saint. Prod: Banner Prod.
Cast: Betty Blythe, Pauline Garon.
Jazz-mad young people pursue pleasure recklessly until the heroine is
kidnapped.

MATSON, NORMAN

Larger than Life

He Couldn't Say No (s.m. also "Larger than Life," a play by Joseph Shrank,
which in turn is based on the story; a.k.a. *Larger Than Life*)
7 reels   b&w   1937
Dir: Lewis Seiler. Prod: Warner Bros. Dist: MGM/UA Home Video.
Cast: Jane Wyman, Frank McHugh.
An office clerk is harrassed by his girlfriend's mother.

MATTIESSON, PETER

Travelin' Man (in *Harper's,* February 1957)

The Young One (Mex.)
96 min.   b&w   1961

Dir: Luis Bunuel. Prod: Olmec Prod.
Cast: Zachary Scott, Bernie Hamilton, Kay Meersman.
A black man fleeing the law is drawn into a web of danger.

MAUGHAM, W. SOMERSET

The Alien Corn (see *Quartet* under Facts of Life)

The Ant and the Grasshopper

Encore (s.m. also "Winter Cruise" and "Gigolo and Gigolette")
90 min.   b&w   1951
Dir: Pat Jackson. Prod: Two Cities Films.
Cast: Glynis Johns, Kay Walsh, Nigel Patrick.
In one story, a playboy tries to get money from his brother; in the second
story, a spinster makes things rough on a ship, and a high-dive artist fears an
accident in the third story.

The Colonel's Lady (see *Quartet* under Facts of Life)

Facts of Life

Quartet (Br.; s.m. also "The Alien Corn,""The Kite," and "The Colonel's
    Lady")
108 min.   b&w   1949
Dir: Ken Annakin, Arthur Crabtree, Harold French, Ralph Smart. Prod:
    J. Arthur Rank. Dist: Walter Reade 16.
Cast: Mai Zetterling, Cecil Parker, George Cole.
Four stories ranging from the dramatic to the comic.

Gigolo and Gigolette (see *Encore* under The Ant and the Grasshopper)

The Kite (see *Quartet* under Facts of Life)

The Letter (a short story and a play)

The Letter
97 min.   b&w   1940
Dir: William Wyler. Prod: Warner Bros. Dist: MGM/UA Home Video (video).
Cast: Bette Davis, Herbert Marshall, Gale Sondergaard.
A wife, on trial for murdering her lover, must retrieve an incriminating letter.

The Letter
1963
Prod: MGM.

Theatre

Adorable Julia (Fr./Aust. with subtitles; s.m. also unidentified short stories)
106 min.   b&w   1963
Dir: Alfred Weidenman. Dist: Budget Films/Video, Video Communications
    (video).
Cast: Lili Palmer, Charles Boyer, Jean Sorel, Jeanne Valerie.

An actress fighting an apparently losing battle with middle age pretends that her eighteen-year-old son is fifteen and then takes a very young lover.

Lord Mountdrago

> *Three Cases of Murder* (s.m. also "In the Picture" by Roderick Wilkinson)
> 99 min.   b&w   1955
> Dir: George More O'Ferrall ("Lord Mountdrago"), Wendy Toye ("In the Picture")
> Cast: Orson Welles, Alan Badel in "Lord Mountdrago"; Alan Badel, Hugh Pryse in "In the Picture."

A trio of tales, two based on short stories: in "Lord Mountdrago," a hex is put on a man who is placed in embarrassing situations in his dreams. "In the Picture" is about a mad artist who lives within a painting at a museum. He entices people to enter, and they never leave.

Mr. Know All (see *Trio* under The Verger)

Rain

> *Sadie Thompson* (s.m. also "Rain," a play by John Colton and Clemence Randolph)
> 9 reels   b&w   1929   sil.
> Dir: Raoul Walsh. Prod: Gloria Swanson Prod.
> Cast: Gloria Swanson, Lionel Barrymore, Raoul Walsh.
> A minister saves a woman from her immorality but later tries to seduce her.

> *Rain*
> 91 min.   b&w   1932
> Dir: Lewis Milestone. Prod: Feature Prod. Dist: Cable Films (video), Discount Video, Penguin Video, Video Communications, Video Magic.
> Cast: Joan Crawford, Walter Huston, Guy Kibbee.

The most celebrated version of the story, which vividly captures the lives of several very different people during a fierce monsoon, including a prostitute and a minister, who tries to reform and then seduce her.

> *Miss Sadie Thompson*
> 91 min.   1953
> Dir: Curtis Bernhardt. Sp: Harry Kleiner. Prod: Columbia Pictures. Dist: RCA Home Video (video).
> Cast: Rita Hayworth, Jose Ferrer.

The Verger

> *Trio* (Br.; s.m. also "Mr. Know All" and "The Sanitorium")
> 91 min.   b&w   1951
> Dir: Ken Annakin. Prod: Gainsborough Pictures. Dist: Walter Reade 16.
> Cast: Jean Simmons, Michael Rennie.

Three separate stories about a church verger, an obnoxious passenger on a ship, and a romance in a sanitorium.

The Vessel of Wrath

Beachcomber
88 min.   b&w   1939
Dir: Erich Pommer. Prod: Laughton Pommer-Mayflower Prod. Dist: Budget
    Films/Video, Classic Film Museum, Reel Images, Cable Films (video),
    Video Connection.
Cast: Charles Laughton, Elsa Lanchester.
A delightful nonconformist finds that his life takes a somersault when a prim
reformer invades his South Sea Island home.

The Beachcomber
82 min.   color   1955
Dir: Muriel Box. Prod: United Artists.
Cast: Robert Newton.
A bum meets a missionary's sister on a tropical island, and his life is changed.

Winter Cruise (see *Encore* under **The Ant and the Grasshopper**)

MAUPASSANT, GUY DE

Angel and Sinner (Boule de Suif)

Angel and Sinner (Fr.)
90 min.   b&w   1946
Dist: Film Classic Exchange.

The Woman Disputed (subtitles)
9 reels   b&w   1928   sil.
Dir: Henry King, Sam Taylor. Prod: United Artists.
Cast: Norma Talmadge, Gilbert Roland.
An Austrian and a Russian soldier reform a prostitute who helps save the
lives of 10,000 men.

He

He (Fr. with subtitles)
85 min.   b&w   1933
Prod: Astor Pictures.
Cast: Fernandel.

The Horla (in *Gil Blas,* 26 October 1886)

Diary of a Madman (s.m. based on three stories, primarily "La Horla" and
    two unidentified)
96 min.   color   1962
Dir: Reginald Le Borg. Sp: Robert E. Kent. Dist: MGM/UA Home Video
    (video).

The House of Madame Tellier (see *Le Plaisir* under **The Mask**)

Cast: Vincent Price, Nancy Kovack, Ian Wolfe.

A possessed man is forced to kill.

The Job

Boccaccio '70

145 min.   color   1962

Dir: Frederico Fellini, Luchino Visconti, Vittorio de Sica. Prod: Concordia
     cia cinematographie-Cineraz.

Cast: Sophia Loren, Romy Schneider.

Three episodes; the second, based on the story, is about an aristocrat's wife
who takes a job as his mistress.

Mademoiselle Fifi

Mademoiselle Fifi

68 min.   b&w   1944

Dir: Robert Wise. Prod: RKO. Dist: Films Inc.

Cast: Simone Simon, Jason Robards, Sr.

A young laundress repulses a German officer and joins the French
underground.

The Mask

Le Plaisir (Fr.; s.m. also "The Model" and "The House of Madame Tellier")

95 min.   b&w   1953

Dir: Max Ophuls. Prod: Stera Films. Dist: Kit Parker Films.

Cast: Danielle Darrieux, Claude Dauphin.

In "The Mask," a wife describes to a doctor how her aging husband visits a
dance hall wearing a mask to hide his wrinkles. "The House of Madame Tellier"
concerns a woman who closes her brothel so that she and her girls can attend her
niece's first communion. "The Model" is about a young painter who has an affair
with a model. She throws herself from a window because of her love for him and
breaks her legs.

The Model (see *Le Plaisir* under The Mask)

The Necklace

The Necklace

23 min.   color   1979

Dir: Mark Baer, Mark O'Kane. Dist: FilmFair Communications.

A haughty wife loses the diamond necklace she borrowed and must sell all
she has to buy a duplicate, but she learns the necklace was nothing more than
paste.

The Necklace

21 min.   color   1981

Prod: Bernard Wilets. Dist: Phoenix Films (16 mm and video).

Set in nineteenth century Paris. Mathilde borrows a necklace, which
she loses and must replace.

Paul's Mistress (La Femme de Paul)

Masculine-Feminine (s.m. also "The Sign")
103 min.   b&w   1966
Dir: Jean Luc-Godard. Prod: Columbia Pictures. Dist: Swank.
Cast: Jean-Pierre Leaud.
An updated portrayal of youthful Paris, mingling sex with violence, in the story of a callow young man and a freewheeling young woman.

The Sign (see *Masculine-Feminine* under Paul's Mistress)

The Two Little Soldiers

The Two Little Soldiers
15 min.   color   1978
Prod: International Instructional Television Coop. Dist: Indiana University (16 mm and video).
Explores the consequences of friendship betrayed.

Unidentified stories

End of Desire (Fr.)
86 min.   1962
Dir: Alexander Astruc. Prod: Continental.
Cast: Maria Schell, Christian Marquand.
A wealthy girl discovers that her husband married her so he could pay off his debts.

McCALL, MARCY C., JR.

Fraternity

On the Sunny Side
69 min.   b&w   1941
Dir: Harold Schuster. Prod: Twentieth Century Fox. Dist: Select Film Library.
Cast: Roddy McDowall, Jane Sarwell.
A London lad whose family was bombed out by the blitz comes to live with an American family, and the son becomes jealous of him.

Revolt

Scarlet Dawn
58 min.   b&w   1932
Dir: William Dieterle. Prod: Warner Bros. Dist: MGM/UA Home Video (video).
Cast: Douglas Fairbanks, Jr., Nancy Carroll, Lilyan Tashman.
During the height of the Russian Revolution, a prince who is saved by a devoted female servant marries her, and together they flee to Paris.

McCULLEY, JOHNSTON

The Brute Breaker (in *Argosy All-Story Weekly Magazine,* 10 August 1918)

The Ice Flood
70 min.   b&w   1926   sil.
Dir: George B. Seitz. Prod: Universal. Dist: Mogull's Films (16 or 8 mm)
Cast: Kenneth Harlan, Viola Dana.
Jack cleans up the tough timber camps on his northwest property.

El Torbellino

The Black Pirates
73 min.   color   1954
Dir: Allen H. Miner. Sp: Fred Freiberger. Prod: Salvador Films. Dist: Film
   Classic Exchange, "The" Film Center.
Cast: Anthony Dexter.
A band of pirates force terrorized villagers to dig for buried treasure.

King of Cactusville

Outlaw Deputy
60 min.   b&w   1935
Dir: Otto Brower. Prod: Puritan Pictures.
Cast: Tim McCoy.
Western. A reformed outlaw becomes a sheriff.

Various stories

The Sign of Zorro (s.m. the Zorro stories and "The Curse of Capistrano,"
   a magazine serial later published as a novel)
90 min.   b&w   1960
Dir: Norman Forster, Lewis R. Foster. Prod: Walt Disney Prod. Dist: Roa's
   Films.
Cast: Guy Williams, Henry Calvin.
Reedited from the television shows, these are the daring escapades of the
romantic rogue who righted the wrongs of evil-doers in early Spanish California.

Unidentified stories

Mark of the Renegade
81 min.   color   1951
Dir: Hugo Fregonese. Prod: Universal.
Cast: Ricardo Montalban, Cyd Charisse, J. Carrol Naish.
Set in 1824. A renegade in the West is forced to romance a beautiful girl.

McGIBNEY, DONALD

Two Arabian Nights (in *McClure's Magazine*)

Two Arabian Nights
9 reels   b&w   1927   sil.
Dir: Lewis Milestone. Prod: Caddo Co.
Cast: William Boyd, Mary Astor.

Two Army men are imprisoned by the Germans but escape disguised as Arabs in this romantic comedy.

When the Desert Calls (in *Ladies Home Journal,* May 1920)

> *When the Desert Calls*
> 6 reels   b&w   1922   sil.
> Dir: Ray C. Smallwood. Prod: Pyramid Pictures.
> Cast: Violet Heming, Robert Frazer.

Discredited, a man feigns suicide, and his wife finds shelter with a sheik's widow.

McGIVERN, WILLIAM

The Big Heat (serialized in the *Saturday Evening Post* beginning 27 December 1952)

> *The Big Heat*
> 90 min.   b&w   1953
> Dir: Fritz Lang. Prod: Columbia Pictures. Dist: Audio Brandon, Kit Parker
>   Films, RCA Home Video (video).
> Cast: Glenn Ford, Lee Marvin, Gloria Grahame.

Dave Bannion, a police detective, is determined to expose the circumstances surrounding a fellow officer's suicide, although he is warned by his superiors to give up the investigation.

McGRATH, HAROLD

Beautiful Bullet (in *Redbook,* November 1927)

> *Danger Street*
> 6 reels   b&w   1928   sil.
> Dir: Ralph Ince. Sp: Enid Hibbard. Prod: FBO.
> Cast: Warner Baxter, Martha Sleeper.

A society clubman, weary of life, purposely gets involved in a gunfight with local gangs.

McGUINESS, JAMES K.

Pearls and Emeralds

> *Cocktail Hour*
> 80 min.   b&w   1933
> Dir: Victor Schertziner. Sp: Gertrude Purcell. Prod: Columbia Pictures.
>   Dist: Kit Parker Films.
> Cast: Bebe Daniels, Randolph Scott.

McHUGH, MARTIN J. (jt. author) (see *The Rising of the Moon* under O'CONNOR, FRANK)

McKENNEY, RUTH

Several unidentified stories

>*Margie* (jt. author Richard Bransten)
>94 min.   b&w   1946
>Cast: Jeanne Crain, Glenn Langan.
>Comedy about high school life in the 1920s.

McNEILE, H.C. (see SAPPER [pseud.])

McNUTT, WILLIAM SLAVENS

His Good Name (in *Collier's Magazine*, 22 July 1922)

>*Trifling With Honor*
>8 reels   b&w   1923   sil.
>Dir: Harry A. Pollard. Prod: Universal.
>Cast: Rockliffe Fellowes, Fritzi Ridgeway.
>A former convict makes good as a baseball player.

Leander Clicks

>*Hot Tip*
>7 reels   b&w   1935
>Dir: Ray McCarey, James Gleason. Sp: Hugh Cummings, Olive Cooper,
>   Louis Stevens. Prod: RKO.
>A man risks his family fortune at the racetrack.

McSHERRY, GARY

Good Boy

>*Scandal at Scourie*
>90 min.   color   1953
>Dir: Jean Negulesco. Sp: Leonard Spigelgass, Karl Tunberg. Prod: Loew's.
>   Dist: Films Inc.
>Cast: Greer Garson, Walter Pidgeon.
>A story about the problems of a Canadian couple living in a small town who
want to adopt an orphan.

MELVILLE, BAKER (see *Now and Forever* under KIRKLAND, JACK)

MELVILLE, HERMAN

Bartleby, the Scrivener

>*Bartleby*
>28 min.   color   1969
>Prod. and Dist: Encyclopaedia Britannica.
>Set in a nineteenth century law office. A young man clashes with his
employer, who wants to fire him.

Bartleby (Br.)
79 min.   color   1972
Dir: Anthony Friedman. Sp: Rodney Carr-Smith, Anthony Friedman. Prod:
    Maron.
Cast: Paul Scofield, John McEvery.
An updated version of the story in which the boss, although he empathizes
with Bartelby, must fire him. But Bartleby won't go.

Bartleby, the Scrivener
60 min.   color
Prod. and Dist: Maryland Center for Public Broadcasting.

The Happy Failure

The Happy Failure
15 min.   b&w   1955
Prod: Dynamic Films.
Cast: Monty Woolley.
An old man is taught by his nephew that material success is less important
than happiness.

The Lightning-Rod Man

The Lightning-Rod Man
16 min.   color   1975
Dir: John DeChancie. Dist: Pyramid Films (16 mm and video).
A heated debate between an aggressive lightning-rod salesman and a home-
owner who relishes rather than fears the excitement of an electrical storm.

MERIMEE, PROSPER

Carmen

Carmen was made into four silent films: *Carmen* (1913), *Carmen* (1915),
Us (with Charlie Chaplin), and *Carmen* (Fr., 1926).

Carmen
85 min.   b&w   1947
Prod: Scalera Films, Rome. Dist: Modern Sound Pictures, Alan Twyman
    Presents.
Cast: Vivan Romance, Jean Marias, Eli Parvo.
Carmen, a Spanish gypsy employed in a tobacco factory in Seville, is ruthless
and without conscience; she lives solely for her own pleasure.

The Loves of Carmen
98 min.   color   1948
Dir: Charles Vidor. Prod: Beckworth Corp.
Cast: Rita Hayworth, Glenn Ford.
The story of a soldier's love for a gypsy.

Carmen Jones
105 min.   1955
Dir: Otto Preminger. Prod: Caryle Prod.
Cast: Dorothy Dandridge, Harry Belafonte, Pearl Bailey.
An update of the Oscar Hammerstein play based on the story.

The Devil Made a Woman (Sp.; s.m. also "Carmen," a play by Georges Bizet,
     Henri Meilhac, and Ludovic Halevy)
90 min.   color   1962
Dir: Tulio Demicheli.
Cast: Sarita Montiel, George Mistral.
Antonio, a leader of the Spanish guerillas in 1812, takes refuge with Carmen.

Carmen, Baby (U.S., Yugoslavia, Ger.)
90 min.   color   1967
Dir: Rodley Metzger. Sp: Jesse Vogel.
Cast: Uta Leuka, Claude Ringer.
An updating of the story with rock and roll music and a good deal of sex.

Carmen
99 min.   color   1983
Dist: Media Home Entertainment (video).
Cast: Antionio Gades, Laura Del Sol, Paco Du Lucia.

MERRICK, LEONARD

Laurels and the Lady

Fool's Paradise
9 reels   b&w   1921   sil.
Dir: Cecil B. DeMille. Prod: Famous Players-Lasky.
Cast: Dorothy Dalton.
An ex-serviceman falls in love with Rosa; he is tricked by a dancer into
marrying.

Magnificent Lie
8 reels   b&w   1931
Dir: Berthold Viertel. Sp: Vincent Laurence, Samson Raphaelson. Prod:
     Paramount Publix.
Cast: Ralph Bellamy, Ruth Chatterton.
A cafe singer impersonates a French actress.

MICHENER, JAMES A.

Until They Sail

Until They Sail
95 min.   b&w   1957
Dir: Robert Wise. Sp: Charles Schnee. Prod: MGM. Dist: Films Inc.
Cast: Joan Fontaine, Sandra Dee, Piper Laurie, Jean Simmons.
A four-part soap opera about four sisters during wartime in New Zealand.

MILLER, ALICE DUER

The Adventuress

> *The Keyhole*
> 69 min.   b&w   1933
> Dir: Michael Curtiz. Prod: Warner Bros. Dist: MGM/UA Home Video (video).
> Cast: Kay Francis, George Brent.
> A jealous husband hires a detective and lives to regret it.

Are Parents People?

> *Are Parents People?*
> 5 reels   b&w   1925   sil.
> Dir: Malcolm St. Clair. Prod: Famous Players-Lasky. Dist: Em Gee Film
>   Library, Select Film Library, Willoughby-Peerless.
> Cast: Betty Bronson, Adolphe Menjou, Florence Vidor, Andre Beranger.
> Lita reconciles her parents by getting expelled from school after they file for
divorce.

The Charm School (in *Saturday Evening Post*)

> *The Charm School*
> 5 reels   b&w   1920   sil.
> Dir: James Cruze. Prod: Famous Players-Lasky.

The Princess and the Plumber

> *The Princess and the Plumber*
> 7 reels   b&w   1930
> Dir: Alexander Korda. Sp: Howard J. Green. Prod: Fox.
> Cast: Charles Farrell, Maureen O'Sullivan.
> An unsophisticated princess goes vacationing in the mountains with a rich
American and a Baron, and she falls in love with the American.

MILLER, ARTHUR

The Misfits (in *Esquire*)

> *The Misfits*
> 124 min.   b&w   1961
> Dir: John Huston. Sp: Arthur Miller. Prod: United Artists. Dist: CBS/Fox
>   Video (video), RCA VideoDiscs.
> Cast: Clark Gable, Marilyn Monroe, Montgomery Clift.
> The story of three sometime cowboys and a recent divorcee whom they meet
in Reno. Each sees the woman as an idealized image: mother, wife, sweetheart,
mistress. She herself is confused but loving and passionately desires freedom.

MILLER, MARY ASHE (jt. author) (see The Man Who Married His Own Wife
under WILSON, JOHN FLEMING)

MILLER, SETON I.

Public Enemy No. 1

> *"G" Men*
> 85 min.   b&w   1935
> Dir: William Keighley. Prod: United Artists. Dist: MGM/UA Home Video
>   (video).
> Cast: James Cagney, Lloyd Nolan, Margaret Lindsay.

A young man, raised and educated by an unknown gang leader, joins the
G-men to track down racketeers.

MILLHOLLAND, RAY

Island Doctor

> *Girl from God's Country*
> 54 min.   b&w   1940
> Dir: Sidney Salkow. Prod: Republic Pictures. Dist: Ivy Films.
> Cast: Jane Wyatt, Charles Bickford.

A nurse in Alaska helps a doctor in trouble with the law for the mercy
killing of his father.

MITCHELL, RUTH COMFORT

Into Her Kingdom (in *Redbook*)

> *Into Her Kingdom*
> 7 reels   b&w   1926   sil.
> Dir: Svende Gade. Adap: Carey Wilson. Prod: Corinne Griffith Prod.
> Cast: Corinne Griffith, Einar Hanson.

A Russian peasant is sent to Siberia for allegedly insulting the Grand Duchess
of Tatiana; when she is released seven years later, she joins the Bolsheviks.

MOFFITT, JACK

Hawk's Mate

> *Central Airport*
> 75 min.   b&w   1933
> Dir: William Dieterle. Prod: First National Pictures and Vitaphone. Dist:
>   MGM/UA Home Video (video).
> Cast: Richard Barthelmess, Sally Eilers.
> A love triangle in the aviation game.

MONTAYNE, CHARLES EDWARD

Her Night of Nights (in *Snappy Stories,* 10-25 October 1921)

> *Her Night of Nights*
> 5 reels   b&w   1922   sil.
> Dir: Hobart Henley. Prod: Universal.
> Cast: Marie Prevost, Edward Hearn.

Molly, a model, spurns the advances of the boss's son in favor of a shipping
clerk.

Judith

True Heaven
6 reels   b&w   1929   sd. effects.
Dir: James Tinling. Prod: Fox.
Cast: George O'Brien, Lois Moran.
A British soldier falls in love with a German agent.

MOONEY, MARTIN

Special Agent

Special Agent
76 min.   b&w   1935
Dir: William Keighley. Prod: Warner Bros. Dist: MGM/UA Home Video
     (video).
Cast: Bette Davis, George Brent.
A mystery melodrama about a newspaperman who plays ball with an evil
racketeer in order to obtain some incriminating evidence.

MOORE, OLGA

Quintuplets to You

You Can't Beat Love
84 min.   b&w   1937
Dir: Christy Cabanne. Sp: David Silverstein, Maxwell Stone. Prod: RKO.
     Dist: Don Bosco Films.
Cast: Joan Fontaine, Preston Foster.
The daughter of a mayoral candidate dares a playboy to become her father's
rival.

MORGAN, BYRON (see also *The Band Plays On* under STUHLDREHER, HARRY)

The Hell Diggers (in *Saturday Evening Post,* 2 October 1920)

The Hell Diggers
5 reels   b&w   1921   sil.
Dir: Frank Urson. Prod: Famous Players-Lasky.
Cast: Wallace Reid, Lois Wilson.
A construction superintendent falls in love with the daughter of a farmer
opposed to the destruction of the land.

Too Much Speed (in *Saturday Evening Post,* 28 May 1921)

Too Much Speed
5 reels   b&w   1921   sil.
Dir: Frank Urson. Prod: Famous Players-Lasky.
Cast: Wallace Reid, Agnes Ayres.
Pat retires from racing to please his father-in-law-to-be but eventually goes
back to it.

MORRIS, EDMUND

San Siandro Killings

> *The Savage Guns*
> 73 min.   color   1962
> Dir: Michael Carreras. Sp: Edmund Morris. Prod: MGM. Dist: Films Inc.
> Cast: Richard Basehart, Don Taylor.
> Bandits oppose a ranger in Mexico.

MORRIS, GORDON

Auf Widersehen (jt. author Morton Barteau)

> *Six Hours to Live*
> 78 min.   b&w   1932
> Dir: William Dieterle. Sp: Bradley King. Prod: Fox.
> Cast: Warner Baxter, Irene Ware, George Marion.
> A murdered diplomat returns to life and catches the murderer.

MORRIS, GOUVERNEUR

The Man Who Played God

> *The Man Who Played God* (s.m. also "The Silent Voice," a play based on
>   the story)
> 6 reels   b&w   1922   sil.
> Dir: Harmon White. Prod: Distinctive-United Artists.
> Cast: George Arliss.
> A musician loses his hearing, and his depression sorely tests his wife.

> *The Man Who Played God*
> 83 min.   b&w   1932
> Dir: John Adolfi. Prod: Warner Bros. Dist: MGM/UA Home Video (video).
> Cast: George Arliss, Bette Davis.
> A great musician who becomes deaf goes into a depression.

You Can't Get Away With It

> *You Can't Get Away With It*
> 6 reels   b&w   1923   sil.
> Dir: Rowland V. Lee. Prod: Fox.
> Cast: Percy Marmont, Malcolm McGregor.
> Jill enters into an illicit alliance with her employer when his wife refuses to
divorce him.

MORRIS, REBECCA

The Good Humor Man (in *The New Yorker*)

> *One Is a Lonely Number*
> 97 min.   color   1972
> Dir: Mel Stuart. Prod: MGM. Dist: Films Inc.
> Cast: Trish Van Devere, Monte Markham, Janet Leigh, Melvyn Douglas.

Suddenly abandoned by her husband, a young woman faces the lonely task of finding her own identity, earning a living, and seeking a new life.

MORROW, HONORE

Benefits Forgotten

> *Of Human Hearts*
> 110 min.   b&w   1938
> Dir: Clarence Brown. Prod: MGM. Dist: Films Inc.
> Cast: Walter Huston, James Stewart.
> A study of rural life in which a young man rebels against his religion.

MOSS, GEOFFREY MAJOR

Unidentified story

> *Isn't Life Wonderful*
> 99 min.   b&w   1924   sil.
> Dir: D.W. Griffith. Dist: MOMA.
> Cast: Carol Dempster, Neil Hamilton, Helen Lowell.
> The painful struggle for food is offset by the powerful love between Inga and Hans.

MUIR, AUGUSTUS

Ocean Gold

> *The Phantom Submarine*
> 7 reels   b&w   1940
> Dir: Charles Barton. Sp: Joseph Krumgold. Prod: Columbia Pictures.

MUMFORD, ETHEL WATTS

Everything Money Can Buy (in *Hearst's International Magazine,* 27 August 1924)

> *After Business Hours*
> 56 min.   b&w   1925   sil.
> Dir: Mal St. Clair. Prod: Columbia Pictures.
> Cast: Elaine Hammerstein, Lou Tellegen.
> June marries a wealthy young man in order to have whatever money can buy, but he refuses to give her money of her own.

MUNI, BELLE

Unwanted

> *The Deceiver* (jt. author Abem Finkel)
> 7 reels   b&w   1931
> Dir: Louis King. Adap: Charles Logue. Prod: Columbia Pictures.

MUNRO, ALICE

Boys and Girls

> *Boys and Girls*
> 25 min.　　　color　　　1984
> Dir: D. McBreaty. Dist: Beacon Films.
> A farm girl is stereotyped by her family into a traditional woman's role.

MUNSON, AUDREY

Studio Secrets (in *Hearst's Sunday Magazine*)

> *Heedless Moths* (s.m. "Life Story" and others)
> 6 reels　　　b&w　　　1921
> Dir: Robert Z. Leonard. Prod: Perry Plays.
> Cast: Holmes E. Herbert, Hedda Hopper.
> A model is asked to pose for a Greenwich Village painter whose intentions are not wholly artistic.

MURPHY, DUDLEY (see *Jazz Heaven* under FORNEY, PAULINE)

MUSSELMAN, MORRIS (see *She Had to Eat* under GRANT, JAMES EDWARD)

MYGATE, GERALD

Two Can Play (in *Saturday Evening Post,* 25 February-March 4 1922)

> *Two Can Play*
> 6 reels　　　b&w　　　1926　　　sil.
> Dir: Nat Ross. Prod: Encore Pictures.
> Cast: George Fawcett, Allan Forrest.
> A wealthy man who disapproves of his daughter's fiance tries to discredit him.

N

NAZARRO, RAY (jt. author) (see *Jimmy the Gent* under DOYLE, LAIRD)

NEBEL, FREDERICK

The Bribe

> *The Bribe*
> 98 min.   b&w   1949
> Dir: Robert Z. Leonard. Sp: Marguerite Roberts. Prod: MGM. Dist: Films
>   Inc.
> Cast: Robert Taylor, Ava Gardner.
> A war surplus racket in the tropics is broken up.

No Hard Feelings

> *Smart Blonde*
> 59 min.   b&w   1936
> Dir: Frank McDonald. Prod: Warner Bros. and Vitaphone. Dist: MGM/UA
>   Home Video (video).
> Cast: Glenda Farrell, Barton MacLane.
> A mettlesome reporter named Torchy Blane nabs the villain, aided by an
irate police lieutenant.

> *A Shot in the Dark*
> 60 min.   b&w   1941
> Dir: William McCann. Prod: Warner Bros. Dist: MGM/UA Home Video
>   (video).
> Cast: William Lundigan, Ricardo Cortez.
> A reporter tracks down a murderer.

NEIDIG, WILLIAM J.

The Snob (in *Saturday Evening Post,* 28 September 1918)

> *The Snob*
> 5 reels   b&w   1921   sil.
> Dir: Sam Wood. Prod: Realart.
> Cast: Wandy Hawley, Edwin Stevens.
> Kathryn snubs a poor boy working his way through college.

Tracked to Earth (in *Saturday Evening Post*)

Tracked to Earth
5 reels   b&w   1922   sil.
Dir: William Worthington. Prod: Universal.
Cast: Frank Mayo, Virginia Valli.
A railroad agent, although innocent, is arrested as a horse thief.

NEWHOUSE, EDWARD

Come Again Another Day

Shadow in the Sky
78 min.   b&w   1951
Dir: Fred M. Wilcox. Sp: Ben Maddow. Prod: MGM. Dist: Films Inc.
Cast: Ralph Meeker, Nancy Davis.
A war-shocked veteran disrupts the lives of the relatives who have given him a home.

Several unidentified stories

I Want You
102 min.   b&w   1952
Dir: Mark Robson. Prod: Metro-Goldwyn.
Cast: Dana Andrews, Dorothy McGuire.
The effect of the Korean War on the typical American family is dramatized.

NEWSOM, J.D.

The Rest Cure

We're in the Legion Now
8 reels   color   1937
Dir: Crane Wilburn. Sp: Roger Whately. Prod: Edward L. Alperson.
Cast: Reginald Denny, Esther Ralston.
Two confidence men join the Foreign Legion.

Sowing Glory

Trouble in Morocco
7 reels   b&w   1937
Dir: Ernest B. Schoedsack. Sp: Paul Franklin. Prod: Columbia Pictures.

NORRIS, KATHLEEN

Manhattan Love Song

Change of Heart
87 min.   b&w   1943
Dir: Albert Rogell. Prod: Twentieth Century Fox. Dist: Ivy Films.
Cast: Susan Hayward, John Carroll.
A midwest song writer thinks a young song publisher has stolen her song.

Poor, Dear Margaret Kirby

Poor, Dear Margaret Kirby

5 reels   b&w   1921   sil.

Dir: William P.S. Earle. Prod: Selznick.

Cast: Elaine Hammerstein, William B. Donaldson.

A society woman is forced to take in boarders when her husband, beset with financial difficulties, attempts suicide and becomes seriously ill.

OATES, JOYCE CAROL

In the Region of Ice

In the Region of Ice
38 min.   b&w   1977
Prod: A. Guttfreund, P. Werner. Dist: Phoenix Films (16 mm and video).
Cast: Fionnoulla Flanagan, Peter Lempert.

A brilliant but disturbed Jewish student seeks help from his college English professor, a Catholic nun named Sister Irene, but she is unable to help him.

Norman and the Killer

Norman and the Killer
27 min.   b&w   1982
Prod: Peggy King, Bob Graham, Kate Quillan. Dist: Coronet Films (16 mm and video).

Norman, a bachelor in his early 30s, lives a life of quiet desperation in a room in an old house.

O'CONNOR, FLANNERY

A Circle in the Fire

A Circle in the Fire
50 min.   color   1976
Dir: Victor Nunez. Dist: Coronet Films (16 mm and video).

The security of the Cope farm is shattered by a visit from three teenaged boys. Jealous of the farm's tranquility, the boys slowly destroy that which they cannot possess—first with petty vandalism and finally with cruel malice.

Comforts of Home

Comforts of Home
40 min.   color   1974
Dir: Jerome Shore. Prod: Leonard Lipson. Dist: Phoenix Films (16 mm and video).
Cast: Stockard Channing.

A seemingly happy mother-son relationship is disrupted by a young girl who enters the household and tragically affects the mother.

In the Region of Ice
Photograph courtesy of Phoenix Films

The Displaced Person

The Displaced Person
58 min.   color   1977
Dir: Glenn Jordan. Sp: Horton Foote. Dist: Coronet Films (16 mm and
    video).
Cast: Irene Worth, John Houseman.

The "displaced person" is a conscientious but driven Polish refugee who
arrives on a Georgia farm in the late 1940s. An elderly priest means well but fails
in his efforts to integrate the Pole with the people on the farm.

Good Country People

Good Country People
32 min.   color   1975
Dir., Prod., and Dist: Jeff Jackson.

A traveling salesman seduces an unattractive woman with a wooden leg,
who has returned to her hometown with a Ph.D. in philosophy and finds she is
out of place.

The River

The River
29 min.   color   1978
Dir. and Prod: Barbara Noble. Dist: Phoenix Films (16 mm and video).

A neglected four-year-old, who finds solace in his river baptism, returns to
the river.

O'CONNOR, FRANK

The Majesty of the Law

The Rising of the Moon (s.m. also "The Minutes Wait," a story by Martin
    J. McHugh, and "The Rising of the Moon," a play by Lady Gregory)
81 min.   b&w   1957
Dir: John Ford. Prod: Four Province Prod. Dist: Warner Bros.
Cast: Noel Purcell, Denis O'Dea.
Trio of Irish tales.

OLIVER, JENNIE HARRIS

Several unidentified stories

Mokey
9 reels   b&w   1942
Dir: Wells Root. Sp: Wells Root, Jan Fortune. Prod: MGM.
Cast: Bobby Blake, Donna Reed.
A child must get used to his stepmother.

The River
Photograph courtesy of Phoenix/BFA Films & Video

OPPENHEIM, E. PHILIPS

Numbers of Death

Monte Carlo Nights
70 min.   b&w   1934
Dir: William Nigh. Prod: Monogram Pictures. Dist: Mogull's Films.
Cast: Mary Brian, John Darrow.
A young man convicted of murder escapes, and with one club he is able to
find the real murderer.

OPPENHEIMER, GEORGE

Baby Face (jt. author George Bruce)

Killer McCoy
103 min.   b&w   1947
Dir: Roy Rowland. Prod: MGM. Dist: Films Inc.
Cast: Mickey Rooney, Brian Donlevy.
Story of a boxer whose father was an alcoholic. Remake of *The Crowd
Roars.* According to one source, *The Crowd Roars* was based on a short story by
George Bruce of the same title.

ORNITZ, SAMUEL

Tong War

Chinatown Nights
83 min.   b&w   1929
Dir: William Wellman. Prod: Paramount.
Cast: Wallace Beery, Florence Vidor.
A society woman caught in the midst of a Tong war in Chinatown is rescued.

ORR, GERTRUDE

Women Like Men (jt. author Doris Malloy)

Mad Parade
7 reels   b&w   1931
Dir: William Beadine. Sp: Henry McCarthy, Frank R. Conklin. Prod:
    Paramount.

ORR, MARY

The Wisdom of Eve

All about Eve (s.m. also a radio play)
139 min.   b&w   1950
Dir: Joseph L. Mankiewicz. Prod: Twentieth Century Fox. Dist: Films Inc.,
    CBS/Fox Video (video).
Cast: Bette Davis, Anne Baxter, George Sanders.
An older actress, near the end of her fabulous career, does battle with a
calculating, treacherous newcomer.

OSBOURNE, LLOYD

The Man Who (in *Saturday Evening Post,* 1 January 1921)

> *The Man Who*
> 6 reels   b&w   1921   sil.
> Dir: Maxwell Karger. Adap: Arthur J. Zellner. Prod: Metro Pictures.
> Cast: Bert Lytell, Lucy Cotton.

To protest the soaring price of shoes and to gain importance in the eyes of a rich girl, a poor bank clerk refuses to wear shoes on the street and causes a sensation in New York.

OXFORD, JOHN BARTON

The Man Tamer (in *Redbook,* April 1918)

> *The Man Tamer*
> 5 reels   b&w   1921   sil.
> Dir: Harry B. Harris. Prod: Universal.
> Cast: Gladys Walton, Rex De Roselli.

A female lion tamer is called on by a profligate millionaire to tame his hard-drinking son.

PACKARD, FRANK L.

The Iron Rider (in *Argosy All-Story Weekly Magazine,* 11 March-8 April 1916)

Smiles Are Trumps
5 reels   b&w   1922   sil.
Dir: George E. Marshall. Prod: Fox.
Cast: Maurice B. Flynn, Ora Carew.
A young man discovers that his boss is cheating the company.

The Wrecking Boss

The Crash
8 reels   b&w   1928   sil.
Dir: Eddie Cline. Prod: First National Pictures.
A man's jealousy and drinking cause his wife to leave him.

PADGETT, LEWIS (pseud. of Henry Kuttner)

Don't Look Now

Don't Look Now
20 min.   color   1983
Prod: Auburn Television. AIT.
Science fiction story in which a Martian ends up having a drink at a bar.

The Twonky

The Twonky
72 min.   b&w   1953
Dir. and Sp: Arch Oboler. Prod: United Artists.
Cast: Hans Conreid, Billy Lynn, Gloria Blondell.
A creature from the future invades a television set and tries to protect and serve the set's owner, but the owner kills it.

PAGONO, JO

Double Jeopardy

Murder without Tears
64 min.   b&w   1953
Dir: William Beaudine. Prod: Allied Artists. Dist: Ivy Films.
Cast: Craig Stevens, Joyce Holden.
A series of murders keep detective Stevens busy.

PALMER, STUART

The Riddle of the Dangling Pearl

The Plot Thickens
7 reels   b&w   1936
Dir: Ben Homes. Sp: Clarence Upson Young, Jack Townley. Prod: RKO.
Cast: ZaSu Pitts, Louise Latimer.
An unmarried schoolteacher foils the theft of a priceless museum piece.

The Riddle of the 40 Naughty Girls

Forty Naughty Girls
7 reels   b&w   1937
Dir: Edward Cline. Sp: John Grey. Prod: RKO.
Cast: James Gleason, Joan Woodbury.
A schoolteacher's friend solves two murders blundered by the police.

PARKER, DOROTHY (see *Horsie* under ASHWORTH, JOHN)

PARKER, GILBERT

The Lodge in the Wilderness

The Lodge in the Wilderness
6 reels   b&w   1926   sil.
Dir: Henry McCarthy. Prod: Tiffany Prod.
Cast: Anita Stewart, Edmund Burns.
Jim, a young engineer in a northwest logging camp, is convicted and jailed for a murder, even though he is innocent.

PARKER, GILBERT

She of the Triple Chevron

Over the Border
7 reels   b&w   1922   sil.
Dir: Penrhyn Stanlaws. Prod: Famous Players-Lasky.
Cast: Betty Compson, Tom Moore.
The daughter of a whiskey smuggler falls in love with a Canadian Mountie and must cope with divided loyalties.

PARKER, LOUIS NAPOLEON (see *Monkey's Paw* under JACOBS, WILLIAM W.)

PARKER, NORTON S.

The Walls of San Quentin

Prison Break
72 min.   b&w   1938
Dir: Arthur Lubin. Sp: Norton Parker, Dorothy Reid. Prod: Trem Carr.
Cast: Barton MacLaine, Glenda Farrell.
A tuna fisherman takes the blame for a murder, even though he is innocent.

PARKER, PHYLLIS

Unidentified story

> *Steel Fist*
> 72 min.   b&w   1952
> Dir: Wesley Barry. Prod: Monogram Pictures. Dist: Hurlock Cine-World.
> Cast: Roddy McDowell, Kristine Miller.
> A United States student is trapped in an Iron Curtain country.

PARROTT, URSULA

Love Affair

> *Love Affair*
> 63 min.   b&w   1932
> Dir: Thornton Freeland. Adap: Jo Swerling. Prod: Columbia Pictures.
> Cast: Humphrey Bogart, Dorothy Mackaill.

PATTEN, LEWIS B.

Back Trail

> *Red Sundown*
> 81 min.   color   1956
> Dir: Jack Arnold. Prod: Universal.
> Cast: Rory Calhoun, Martha Hyer, Dean Jagger.
> Western. A former gunslinger becomes a deputy.

PATTERSON, NEIL

International Incident

> *Man on a Tightrope*
> 105 min.   b&w   1953
> Dir: Elia Kazan. Prod: Twentieth Century Fox. Dist: Films Inc.
> Cast: Fredric March, Gloria Grahame.
> In a small traveling circus, a man loves an unfaithful wife.

Scotch Settlement

> *The Little Kidnappers* (Br. title *The Kidnappers*)
> 93 min.   b&w   1954
> Dir: Philip Leacock. Prod: United Artists. Dist: Janus Films.
> Cast: Adrienne Corri, Duncan MacRae.
> Two boys who can't have a dog kidnap a baby.

PATULLO, GEORGE

The Ledger of Life (in *Saturday Evening Post,* 4 March 1922)

> *Private Affairs*
> 6 reels   b&w   1925   sil.
> Dir: Renaud Hoffman. Prod: Renaud Hoffman Prod.
> Cast: Gladys Hulette, Robert Agnew.

The discovery of a five-year-old package of undelivered letters in a small-town post office disrupts the lives of the addressees.

PAYNE, STEPHEN

Tracks

Swiftly
61 min.   b&w   1936
Prod: Walter Futter. Dist: Video Connection (video).
Cast: Hoot Gibson.
Western.

PAYNE, WILL J.

Black Sheep (in *Saturday Evening Post*)

The Family Closet
6 reels   b&w   1921   sil.
Dir: John B. O'Brien. Prod: Ore-Col Films.
Cast: Holmes Herbert, Alice Man, Kempton Greene.
An editor hires McMurty to obtain evidence against a man who is suing him for libel.

PAYNTER, ERNEST

Maskee

Shipmates
6 reels   b&w   1931
Dir: Harry Pollard. Sp: Delmer Davis, Lou Edelman. Prod: MGM.
Cast: Robert Montgomery, Dorothy Jordan.
A formula Navy story of a young sailor who falls for the admiral's daughter.

PELLEY, WILLIAM DUDLEY

The Sunset Derby (in *American Magazine,* January 1926)

The Sunset Derby
6 reels   b&w   1927   sil.
Dir: Albert Rogell. Prod: First National Pictures.
Cast: Mary Astor, William Collier, Jr.
Former partners in a livery business have a falling out when one opens a service station.

PENTCOST, HUGH

If I Should Die

Appointment With a Shadow
72 min.   b&w   1958
Dir: Richard Carlson. Sp: Alex Coppel, Norman Jolley. Prod. and Dist: Universal.
Cast: George Nader, Joanna Moore.
The downfall of a former top reporter who becomes an alcoholic.

PERKINS, KENNETH

Bow Tamely to Me

Escape to Burma
87 min.　　　　color　　　　1955
Dir: Alan Dwan. Prod: RKO. Dist: Cinema Concepts.
Cast: Barbara Stanwyck, Robert Ryan.
The mistress of a Burmese teak plantation owner gives refuge to a murder suspect.

The Devil's Saddle (in *Argosy All-Story Weekly Magazine*)

The Devil's Saddle
6 reels　　　　b&w　　　　1927　　　　sil.
Dir: Albert Rogell. Adap: Marion Jackson. Prod: Charles R. Rogers.
Cast: Ken Maynard, Kathleen Collins.
The Hopi Indians' land is invaded.

PEARLMAN, VAN TERRYS

Scoop

That's My Story
63 min.　　　　b&w　　　　1937
Dir: Sidney Salkow. Prod: Universal.
Cast: Claudia Morgan, William Lundigan.
A fired reporter finds that the only way to get a job is to interview a gangster's moll, who is jailed in a small town. He gets himself thrown in jail and mistakes a female reporter for the moll.

PERROWNE, BARRY

Blind Spot

Blind Spot
73 min.　　　　b&w　　　　1947
Dir: Robert Gordon. Prod: Columbia Pictures.
Cast: Chester Morris, Constance Dowling.
A writer on a drunken binge is accused of the murder of his publisher.

PESTRINIERO, RENATO

One Night of 21 Hours

Planet of the Vampires
86 min.　　　　color　　　　1965
Dir: Mario Bava. Prod: American International. Dist: Kerr Film Exchange.
Cast: Barry Sullivan, Norma Begell, Angela Aranda.
The Argos and the Galliot spaceships land on the strange planet Aura in an effort to contact the inhabitants.

PETRACCA, JOSEPH

Four Eyes

> *It's a Big Country* (an eight-part film, three based on short stories; s.m. also "Interruptions, Interruptions" by Edgar Brooke and "Rosika the Rose" by Claudia Cranston)
> 89 min.   1952
> Prod: MGM.
> Cast: Gene Kelly, Janet Leigh, Frederic March.

PFALZGRAF, FLORENCE LEIGHTON (see LEIGHTON, FLORENCE [pseud.])

PHILIPS, JUDSON P.

The House of Death

> *House of Mystery* (s.m. also a radio show "Street and Smith's Detective Story Magazine Hour")
> 20 min.   b&w   1931
> Dir: Kurt Neumann. Sp: Samuel Freedman. Prod: Universal.
> A mystery-fantasy Shadow Detective short.

PHILLIPI, ERICH

Secrets of the Blue Room

> *Secrets of the Blue Room*
> 66 min.   b&w   1933
> Dir: Kurt Neumann. Sp: William Hurlbut. Prod: Universal.
> Cast: Lionel Atwill, Gloria Stewart, Paul Lukas.

Twenty-three years after death occurs in the castle's Blue Room, a beautiful girl's three suitors decide to spend the night there to prove their bravery to the girl.

> *The Missing Guest*
> 68 min.   b&w   1938
> Dir: John Rawlins. Sp: Charles Martin, Paul Perez. Prod: Universal.
> Cast: Paul Kelly, Constance Moore, William Lundigan.

A reporter poses as a psychic when a family reopens the mansion where a man was killed 20 years earlier.

> *Murder in the Blue Room*
> 61 min.   b&w   1944
> Dir: Leslie Goodwins. Sp: I.A.L. Diamond, Stanley Davis. Prod: Universal.
>   Dist: Mogull's Films.
> Cast: Anne Gwynne, Donald Cook.

A man tries to solve the mystery of his wife's first husband, who was killed in the Blue Room and as a result, more murders occur.

PIRANDELLO, LUIGI

The Fan (see *Of Life and Love* under **The Jar**)

The Jar

> *Of Life and Love* (It., s.m. also his short stories "The Fan," "The Lap Dog,"
>   and "The Night Tuxedo")
> 103 min.   b&w   1958
> Dir: Aldo Babrizi. Prod: Distributors' Corp.
> Cast: Anna Magnani.
> Several unrelated romantic plots.

The Lap Dog (see *Of Life and Love* under **The Jar**)

The Night Tuxedo (see *Of Life and Love* under **The Jar**)

POE, EDGAR ALLAN (see also *The Haunted Palace* under LOVECRAFT, H.P.)

The Black Cat (see also *Tales of Terror* under **The Facts in the Case of M.
      Valdemar**)

> *The Black Cat* (Br. title *House of Doom;* rereleased as *The Vanishing Body*)
> 65 min.   b&w   1934
> Dir: Edgar G. Ulmer. Prod: E.M. Asher. Dist: Swank, Alan Twyman Presents.
> Cast: Boris Karloff, Bela Lugosi.
> A mad architect-soldier builds a fantastic structure on the ruins of a castle
he betrayed in the first World War and stashes the corpses of young girls in glass
cases in its underground passages.

> *Maniac* (partly based on the story)
> 52 min.   b&w   1934
> Dir: Dwain Esper. Dist: Budget Films/Video.
> Cast: Bill Woods, Horace Carpenter.
> A mad doctor's assistant murders his boss, then impersonates the doctor and
treats a patient, whom he literally makes go "ape" in this low-budget horror film.

> *The Living Dead* (s.m. also "The System of Doctor Tarr and Professor
>   Fether," and "The Suicide Club" by Robert Louis Stevenson)
> 70 min.   b&w   1940
> Dir: Thomas Bentley. Dist: Thunderbird Films.
> Cast: Sir Gerald du Maurier.

> *The Black Cat*
> 70 min.   b&w   1941
> Dir: Albert S. Rogell. Prod. and Dist: MCA Home Video (video—coupled with
>   *The Raven*).
> Cast: Basil Rathbone, Bela Lugosi, Broderick Crawford.
> A real estate promoter and a goofy antique collector intrude on the reading
of a will in a gloomy old mansion and murder ensues.

The Black Cat
77 min.   b&w   1966
Dir: Harold Hoffman. Prod: Falcon International.
Cast: Robert Frost, Robyn Baker, Scotty McKay.
A man believes that a cat is the reincarnation of his murdered father.

The Cask of Amontillado (see also *Tales of Terror* under **The Facts in the Case of M. Valdemar**)

The Cask of Amontillado
15 min.   b&w   1955
Prod: Dynamic Films.
Cast: Monty Woolley.
Montressor lures Fortunato to his death in a walled-in wine cellar.

The Edgar Allen Poe Special (s.m. also his stories "The Tell-Tale Heart," "The Sphinx," and "The Pit and the Pendulum")
56 min.   color   1970
Dir: Ken Johnson. Prod: Roger Corman. Dist: Audio Brandon, Wholesome Film Center.
Narrator: Vincent Price.
Vincent Price interprets four stories.

A Descent into the Maelstrom

War Gods of the Deep (s.m. also the poem "The Doomed City")
85 min.   color   1965
Dir: Jacques Tourneur. Sp: Charles Bennett. Dist: Kerr Film Exchange, Modern Sound Pictures, Wholesome Film Center.
Cast: Vincent Price, Tab Hunter, Susan Hart.
A girl is kidnapped from her home on the Cornish coast, and two friends go to her rescue. Their search for her leads through secret doorways and subterranean passages to a strange city under the sea.

The Facts in the Case of M. Valdemar

Tales of Terror (s.m. also his stories "Morella," "The Black Cat," and "The Cask of Amontillado")
90 min.   color   1961 62
Dir: Roger Corman. Prod: American International. Dist: Audio Brandon, Warner Bros. Home Video (video).
Cast: Vincent Price, Peter Lorre, Basil Rathbone, Debra Paget.
"Morella" is a brief, morbid study of the obsession of Leonara's father for his wife. The second tale is about a stumbling drunk and an effete wine taster freely adapted from "The Cask of Amontillado." The last tale pits a medical hypnotist against a dying patient whose soul he's trying to command.

Awakening of the American Imagination: Edgar Allan Poe and Washington Irving
20 min.   color   1983

Prod: Auburn Television. Dist: AIT (video).

A dramatization coupled with Washington Irving's *The Adventure of the German Student.*

The Fall of the House of Usher

Fall of the House of Usher
55 min.   b&w   1927   sil.
Dir: Jean Edstein.
Cast: Margaret Gance, Jean Dubencourt, Charles Lamay.

The Fall of the House of Usher
12 min.   b&w   1928   sil. (sd. later added)
Dir: James Sibley Watson, Jr. Dist: MOMA.

The Fall of the House of Usher (Br.)
70 min.   b&w   1952
Dir: Ivan Barnett. Prod: L. Barry Bernard, Arthur Mason. Dist: Video
     Communications (video).
Cast: Kay Tendeter, Irving Steen, Lucy Pavey.
A lord's sister revives after being buried. Reissued in 1955 and 1961.

House of Usher
81 min.   color   1960
Dir: Roger Corman. Prod: American International. Dist: Audio Brandon,
     Warner Bros Home Video (video).
Cast: Vincent Price, Mark Damon, Myrna Fahey.

Roderick Usher, a man who fears being buried alive more than anything else, has accidentally buried his sister alive, and her spirit beckons him from the crypt.

The Fall of the House of Usher
30 min.   color   1969
Prod. and Dist: Encyclopaedia Britannica.

The events surrounding the mysterious Usher twins, the last survivors of an ancient family, build to a violent climax.

Fall of the House of Usher
101 min.   color   1979
Prod: Sunn Classic. Dist: Lucerne Films, Video Communications (video).
Cast: Charlene Tilton, Martin Landau, Ray Walston.

Gold Bug

Manfish (s.m. also "The Tell-Tale Heart")
76 min.   color   1956
Dir: W. Lee Wilder. Prod: United Artists.
Cast: John Bromfield, Lon Chaney, Jr., Victor Jory.
Bubbles reveal the location of a murdered diver.

Gold Bug
Dir: Robert Fuest. Dist: Simon & Schuster.

The Gold Bug
43 min. (edited to 31 min.)   color   1980
Prod: Learning Corp. of America. Dist: Simon & Schuster (16 mm and
   video).
Cast: Geoffrey Holder.
   A young boy finds a gold bug, a secret code, and an old man and his mute
servant, who are looking for treasure. An ABC Children's Weekend Special.

Hop Frog (see The Masque of the Red Death)

Ligeia

Tomb of Ligeia
81 min.   color   1965
Dir: Roger Corman. Prod: American International. Dist: Audio Brandon.
Cast: Vincent Price, Elizabeth Shepherd, John Westbrook.
   A fight for the possession of the body of Ligeia by the reluctantly deceased
wife.

The Masque of the Red Death

The Masque of the Red Death (s.m. also Poe's story "Hop Frog")
89 min.   color   1961
Dir: Roger Corman. Prod: American International. Dist: Budget
   Films/Video, Roa's Films.
Cast: Vincent Price, Hazel Court.
   Prince Prospero, advocate and leader of a devil cult, stays in his castle with his
houseguests while the Red Death, a plague, claims victims on the outside and then
comes into the castle.

The Masque of the Red Death
10 min.   color   1970
Dir. and Sp: Pavao Stalter. Dist: CRM McGraw-Hill.
   In this animated version, Count Prospero locks himself and his court inside
his castle to protect them against the plague that is devastating the countryside, but
the plague, disguised as a seductive woman, enters.

Metzengerstein

Spirits of the Dead (s.m. also Poe's stories "William Wilson" and "Never
   Bet the Devil Your Head")
118 min.   color   1969
Dir: Roger Vadim, Louis Malle, Frederico Fellini. Sp: Roger Vadim, Pascal
   Cousin Malle, Frederico Fellini, Bernadino Zapponi. Dist: Kit Parker
   Films, Wholesome Film Center.
   In "William Wilson," a medical student is involved in a game for his life
against a Don Juan double who returns to embarrass and taunt him. In "Toby

Dammit" (based on "Never Bet the Devil Your Head"), the hero makes a small bet with the devil in order to escape the world of cameras and microphones.

Morella (see *Tales of Terror* under **The Facts in the Case of M. Valdemar**)

The Murders in the Rue Morgue

Murders in the Rue Morgue
62 min.   b&w   1932
Dir: Robert Florey. Sp: Tom Reed, Dale Van Every. Prod: Universal.
Cast: Bela Lugosi, Sidney Fox.
Dr. Mirakle, a fanatically dedicated scientist, supports his experiments in evolution by his activities as a sideshow concessionaire in the Paris circus. He requires the blood of selected young women to prove his theory of man's kinship with apes.

Phantom of the Rue Morgue
84 min.   color   1953
Dir: Roy Del Ruth. Prod: Warner Bros. Dist: Budget Films/Video, Modern
     Sound Pictures, Wholesome Film Center.
Cast: Karl Malden, Claude Dauphin, Patricia Medina.
A series of unexplained murders occur in the Rue Morgue section of Paris, and the police are baffled. Dupin, an amateur detective, discovers the culprit.

Murders in the Rue Morgue
86 min.   color   1973
Dir: Gordon Hessler. Prod: American International. Dist: Swank.
Cast: Jason Robards, Jr., Herbert Lom, Christine Kaufmann.
The only clue to a series of murders is that all the victims were business associates of a theater owner.

The Mystery of Marie Roget

The Mystery of Marie Roget
60 min.   b&w   1942
Dir: Phil Rosen. Sp: Michael Jacoby. Prod: Universal.
Cast: Maria Montez, Mara Ouspenskaya, John Litel, Patrick Knowles.
A detective investigates the disappearance of a beautiful actress.

Never Bet the Devil Your Head (see *Spirits of the Dead* under **Metzengerstein**)

The Oblong Box

The Oblong Box
95 min.   b&w   1969
Dir: Gordon Hessler. Dist: Wholesome Film Center.
Cast: Vincent Price, Christopher Lee.
His face distorted by the curse of an African witch doctor, Sir Edward Markham is kept in cruel imprisonment in a dark English mansion by his tyrannical older brother. He is driven to the brink of insanity until he devises a bizarre plan to secure his freedom.

The Pit and the Pendulum (see *The Edgar Allan Poe Special* under **The Cask of Amontillado**)

The Raven (s.m. also the poem "The Raven")
62 min.   b&w   1935
Dir: Louis Friedlander (later Lew Landers). Sp: David Boehm. Prod:
     Universal. Dist: MCA Home Video (video; coupled with *The Black Cat*)
Cast: Boris Karloff, Bela Lugosi.
Obsessed with the writings of Poe, a mad doctor creates his own torture machines.

The Pit and the Pendulum
85 min.   color   1961
Dir: Roger Corman. Prod: American International. Dist: Audio Brandon,
     Swank, Warner Bros. Home Video (video).
Cast: Vincent Price, John Kerr, Barbara Steele.
Driven mad by hereditary insanity, Nicholas Medina reverts to the period of the Spanish Inquisition and uses instruments of torture perfected by his father and sadistic inquisitors.

The Blood Demon (W. Ger.)
85 min.   color   1967
Dir: Harold Reinl. Sp: Manfred R. Kohler.
Cast: Christopher Lee, Lex Barber.
A man is revived from the dead.

The Premature Burial

The Crime of Doctor Crespi
63 min.   b&w   1935
Dir: John H. Auer. Prod: Liberty Pictures. Dist: Budget Films/Video, Kit
     Parker Films.
Dr. Andre Crespi—master surgeon, hospital saint, and full-time madman—is embittered by the loss of the woman he loved to a former assistant. Crespi gets his chance to exact a warped revenge. When his rival is seriously injured in an auto accident, Crespi injects him with a drug that will make him appear dead.

Premature Burial
81 min.   color   1962
Dir: Roger Corman. Prod: American International. Dist: Budget Films/Video,
     Modern Sound Pictures, Alan Twyman Presents.
Cast: Ray Milland, Hazel Court.
Set in London during the 1860s. A medical student, suffering from a cataleptic fit, is haunted by a fear of being buried alive. He is treated by a friend, who suggests that they open the father's coffin to prove he was not buried alive. But he was.

The Sphinx (see *The Edgar Allan Poe Special* under **The Cask of Amontillado**)

The System of Doctor Tarr and Professor Fether (see *The Living Dead* under
The Black Cat)

The Tell-Tale Heart (see also *The Edgar Allan Poe Special* under **The Cask of
Amontillado** and *Manfish* under **The Gold Bug**)

The Avenging Conscience
60-80 min.   b&w   1914   sil.
Dir: D.W. Griffith. Prod: Reliance/Majestic. Dist: MOMA.
Cast: Henry B. Walthall, Blanche Sweet.
Drawn from various works of Poe, primarily "The Tell-Tale Heart." This
film is considered significant for showing the development of Griffith as a director.

Bucket of Blood (Br. title *The Tell-Tale Heart*)
49 min.   b&w   1934
Dir: Brian Desmond Hurst. Sp: David Plunkett Greene. Prod: Du World.
Cast: Norman Dryden, John Kelt.

Heartbeat
2 reels   b&w   1949
Dir: William Cameron Menzies. Prod: General TV Enterprises.
Made for television.

The Tell-Tale Heart
20 min.   b&w   1953
Prod: MGM. Dist: Films Inc.
An excerpt in which an apprentice kills his master and is then driven mad
by the sound of the dead man's heart beating.

The Tell-Tale Heart (Br.)
81 min.   b&w   1962
Dir: Ernest Morris. Prod: Danziger. Dist: Budget Films/Video, Penguin
    Video (video).
Cast: Laurence Payne, Adrienne Corri.
An author dreams he killed his rival and is driven mad. Reissued in 1972.

The Tell-Tale Heart
8 min.   color   1969
Prod: Stephen Bosustow. Dist: Simon & Schuster (16 mm and video).
Narrator: James Mason.
An animated version in which the eye of a man drove another to murder,
and the murderer is haunted by the beating of the dead man's heart.

The Tell-Tale Heart
26 min.   b&w   1973
Dir: Steve Carver. Prod: American Film Institute. Dist: Churchill Films
    (16 mm and video).
Cast: Alex Cord.

A manservant is driven to murder his elderly employer because of the man's sinister, clouded eye.

The Tell-Tale Heart
15 min.   color   1978
Prod: International Instructional Television Coop. Dist: Indiana University
      (16 mm and video).
A classic tale about the guilt of murder.

The Vampyre (suggestion for)

The Vampire's Ghost
54 min.   b&w   1945
Dir: Leslie Selander. Dist: Ivy Films.
Cast: Charles Gordon, Adele Mara.
A leader of the underworld on the West Coast of Africa is revealed to be a
400-year-old vampire, and not a traditional vampire at that.

William Wilson (see *Spirits of the Dead* under **Metzengerstein**)

PONTSEVREZ

The Ingenious Reporter

The Ingenious Reporter
25 min.   color   1977
Prod: Twentieth Century Fox. Dist: Encyclopaedia Britannica (16 mm and
      video).
A brash, young American reporter who works for a Paris scandal sheet devises
a clever way to improve his paper's circulation: he poses as a suspect in a murder,
only to learn that the victim is his sweetheart.

PORTER, KATHERINE ANNE

The Jilting of Granny Weatherall

The Jilting of Granny Weatherall
57 min.   color   1980
Dir: Randa Haines. Dist: Coronet Films (16 mm and video).
On her deathbed, a stubborn woman realizes that all her accomplishments
cannot make up for the day she was left at the altar.

POZNER, VLADIMIR

The Dark Mirror (in *Good Housekeeping,* September-October 1945)

The Dark Mirror
85 min.   b&w   1946
Dir: Robert Siodmak. Sp: Nunnally Johnson. Prod: Universal. Dist: Ivy
      Films.
Cast: Olivia De Havilland, Lew Ayres.
A story about twins, one good and one evil.

PRESSBURGER, EMERIC

Breach of Promise

Adventure in Blackmail
8 reels   b&w   1943
Dir: Harold Huth. Prod: Mercury.
Cast: Clive Brook, Judy Campbell.
Comedy about a girl who is more interested in money than marriage.

PUSHKIN, ALEXANDER

The Captain's Daughter

The Captain's Daughter
1959
Prod: Mosfilm Studios.

Mozart and Salieri

Requiem for Mozart (U.S.S.R.)
47 min.   b&w   1967
Prod: Riga Film Studio.
Cast: Innokentity Smoktunovskiy, Pyotr Glebov.
Composer Salieri envies Mozart in this operatic film.

Postmaster

Postmaster's Daughter
1946
Prod: Vog Films.

Queen of Spades

A number of silent foreign films were based on this story, including *Pique Dame* (Ger., 1927); *Queen of Spades* (U.S.S.R., 1916), and *La Pique Dame* (Fr.).

Queen of Spades
100 min.   b&w   1937
Dir: Fedor Ozep. Sp: Bernard Zimmer.
Cast: Pierre Blancher, Andre Luquet.

The Queen of Spades (Br.)
95 min.   b&w   1953
Dir: Thorold Dickinson. Prod: Stratford Pictures. Dist: Janus Films.
Cast: Anton Walbrook, Dame Edith Evans, Yvonne Mitchell, Ronald Howard.
An Army captain learns the art of gambling at the expense of his soul.

The Queen of Spades
15 min.   b&w   1954
Prod: Dynamic Films.
Cast: Monty Woolley.

A clerk's eagerness for success at the gambling tables leads him to force a supernatural secret out of an ancient countess, and her death is his undoing.

Pikovaya Dama (U.S.S.R.)
100 min.　　　　color　　　　1960
Dir: Roman Tikhomirov. Sp: Georgy Vassiliev. Prod: Artkino.
Cast: Oleg Strizhenov, Olga Krasina.
An operatic version adapted from Tchaikovsky.

The Queen of Spades
15 min.　　　　color　　　　1978
Prod: International Instructional Television Coop. Dist: Indiana University (16 mm and video).
A greedy gambler meets a fitting fate.

PUTNAM, NIN WILCOX

Doubling for Cupid (in *Saturday Evening Post,* 13 December 1924)

The Beautiful Cheat
7 reels　　　　b&w　　　　1926　　　　sil.
Dir: Edward Sloman. Prod: Universal.
Cast: Laura La Plante, Harry Myers, Bertram Grassby.
Press agent Jimmy Austin takes Mary Callahan, a shopgirl, to Europe, and she returns as Maritza Callahansky, a Russian actress.

The Grandflapper (in *Saturday Evening Post,* 23 October 1926)

Slaves of Beauty
54 min.　　　　b&w　　　　1927　　　　sil.
Dir: J.G. Blystone. Prod: Fox.
Cast: Olive Tell, Holmes Herbert.
A "clay" operation makes a woman beautiful.

Two Weeks with Pay (in *Saturday Evening Post,* 9 October 1920)

Two Weeks with Pay
5 reels　　　　b&w　　　　1921　　　　sil.
Dir: Maurice Campbell. Prod: Realart Pictures.
Cast: Bebe Daniels, Jack Mulhall.
At a resort hotel, a clerk mistakes Patsy for a movie star, and she goes along with it.

R

RAINE, NORMAN REILLY

Stories about Tugboat Annie

Tugboat Annie
88 min.   b&w   1933
Dir: Mervyn LeRoy. Sp: Zelda Sears, Eve Greene. Prod: MGM. Dist: Films Inc.
Cast: Wallace Beery, Marie Dressler.
   A story about husband-wife brawling and mother-son sentiment. Later films based on the character Tugboat Annie include *Tugboat Annie Sails Again* (Warner Bros., 1940) and *Capt. Tugboat Annie* (Republic Pictures, 1945).

RANKIN, WILLIAM (jt. author) (see *Be It Ever So Humble* and *Hi, Beautiful* under GRIFFIN, ELEANOR)

RAPHAELSON, SAMSON

The Day of Atonement

The Jazz Singer (s.m. was based on the play "The Jazz Singer," which in turn was based on the story)
89 min.   b&w   1927
Dir: Alan Crosland. Prod: Warner Bros. Dist: Swank.
Cast: Al Jolson, Warner Oland, May McAvoy.
   Story of a singer who chooses show business rather than following his orthodox Jewish father's wish that he become a cantor. Generally recognized as the first sound film, this picture won a Special Academy Award for "marking an epoch in motion picture history."

The Jazz Singer
110 min.   color   1980
Prod: Paramount. Dist: Paramount Home Video (video), RCA VideoDiscs (disc).
Cast: Neil Diamond, Laurence Olivier, Lucie Arnaz.
   A remake of the earlier film.

A Rose Is Not a Rose

Bannerline
81 min.   b&w   1951
Dir: Don Weiss. Sp: Charles Schnee. Prod: MGM. Dist: Films Inc.

Cast: Keefe Brasselle, Lionel Barrymore.
The story of a cub reporter.

REILLY, PATRICIA

Big Business Girl (jt. author H.N. Swanson)

Big Business Girl
75 min.   b&w   1931
Dir: William A. Seiter. Sp: Robert Lord. Prod: First National Pictures. Dist:
    MGM/UA Home Video (video).
Cast: Loretta Young, Frank Albertson, Ricardo Cortez, Joan Blondell.
Comedy about a secretary's adventures in New York.

REYNOLDS, QUENTIN

West Side Miracle

Secrets of a Nurse
75 min.   b&w   1938
Dir: Arthur Lubin. Sp: Tom Lennon, Lester Cole. Prod: Universal.
Cast: Edmund Lowe, Helen Mack, Dick Foran.
An ex-prizefighter is convicted of a murder he didn't commit.

RICE, ALBERT (jt. author) (see *Gay Blades* under GOODMAN, JACK)

RICHARDS, LAURA E.

Captain January

Captain January
75 min.   b&w   1936
Dir: David Butler. Prod: Twentieth Century Fox. Dist: Films Inc.
Cast: Shirley Temple, Guy Kibbee.
The law wants to take a small girl away from her loving guardians.

RICHLER, MORDECAI

The Summer My Grandma Was Supposed to Die

The Street
10 min.   color   1976
Dir: Caroline Leaf. Prod. and Dist: National Film Board of Canada.
Watercolor and ink animation. Family reactions to a dying grandmother as
seen from a child's point of view.

RIGDON, GERTRUDE

The Department Store

Hold Me Tight
65 min.   b&w   1933
Dir: David Butler. Sp: Gladys Lehman. Prod: Fox.
Cast: James Dunn, Sally Eilers.
Trouble begins when a husband is fired from his job without cause.

RILEY, J.W.

An Old Sweetheart of Mine

An Old Sweetheart of Mine
6 reels   b&w   1923   sil.
Dir: Harry Garson. Adap: Louis Duryea Lighton.
Cast: Pat Moore, Elliott Dexter.
A man reminisces about his first sweetheart, a woman business associate who prevented oil swindlers from cheating the town out of profits from its oil wells.

RINEHART, MARY ROBERTS

Affinities

Affinities
6 reels   b&w   1922   sil.
Dir: Ward Lascell. Prod: Ward Lascell Prod.
Cast: John Bowers, Colleen Moore, Joe Bonner, Grace Gordon.
Two couples spend a lot of time at a country club, and Fanny and Fred's spouses leave them alone so often that Fred suggests an "affinity" party.

Babs

Rinehart's character Babs was used in several films produced prior to 1920 by Famous Players-Lasky.

Her Majesty, the Queen

Her Love Story
7 reels   b&w   1924   sil.
Dir: Allan Swan. Prod: Famous Players-Lasky.
Cast: Gloria Swanson, Ian Keith.
Princess Marie of the Balkan kingdom of Viatavia falls in love with the captain of the guards, and they marry secretly. Then her father forces her to marry the king of another country.

In the Pavilion

The Glorious Fool (s.m. also "Twenty-Two in Love Stories")
6 reels   b&w   1922   sil.
Dir: E. Mason Hopper. Adap: J.G. Hawks. Prod: Metro-Goldwyn.
Billy Grant persuades his nurse to marry him so that his property will not be inherited by his relatives.

Mind Over Motor (in *Saturday Evening Post,* 5 October 1912)

Mind Over Motor
5 reels   b&w   1923   sil.
Dir. and Prod: Ward Lascell.
Cast: Trixie Friganza, Ralph Graves.
Tish unknowingly finances a crooked promoter of an auto race.

Mr. Cohen Takes a Walk

Mr. Cohen Takes a Walk
81 min.   b&w   1936
Dir: William Beaudine. Prod: Warner Bros.
Cast: Paul Graetz, Violet Farebrother.
A story of a lovable London merchant prince.

Seven Days (in *Lippincott's Magazine,* December 1908)

Seven Days
7 reels   b&w   1925   sil.
Dir: Scott Sidney. Prod: Christie Film Co.
Cast: Lillian Rich, Creighton Hale.
A divorced couple, assorted friends, and a cop are trapped inside a quarantined house.

Tish stories

Tish
8 reels   b&w   1942
Dir: S. Sylvan Simon. Sp: Harry Rusking. Prod: MGM.
Cast: Susan Peters, Marjorie Main, ZaSu Pitts, Aline MacMahon.
Village spinsters adopt a baby.

Twenty-Three and a Half Hours' Love

Twenty-Three and a Half Hours' Love
5 reels   b&w   1919   sil.
Dir: Henry King. Prod: Thomas H. Ince.
Cast: Douglas MacLean, Doris May.
A disgraced soldier vindicates himself by uncovering a spy ring, thereby winning the colonel's daughter.

23 ½ Hours' Leave
5 reels   b&w   1937
Dir: John G. Blystone. Sp: Harry Ruskin, Henry McCarty. Prod: Grand
    National.

Twenty-Two (see *The Glorious Fool* under **In the Pavilion**)

What Happened to Father (in *Lippincott's Magazine,* September 1909)

What Happened to Father
6 reels   b&w   1927   sil.
Dir: John G. Adolfi. Prod: Warner Bros.
Cast: Warner Oland, Flobelle Fairbanks.
An absent-minded professor is cowed by his wife, who is trying to arrange a marriage between their daughter and a wealthy man.

RITCHIE, JACK

The Green Heart

> *A New Leaf*
> 102 min.   color   1971
> Dir. and Sp: Elaine May. Prod: Paramount. Dist: Films Inc.
> Cast: Walter Matthau, Elaine May, Jack Weston.

A fastidious middle-aged bachelor playboy, running out of his inheritance, is forced to go to work or acquire a rich wife, and he finds an awkward, unsexy woman for the purpose.

ROBERTS, STANLEY

Riding Monte Christo

> *Galloping Dynamite*
> 58 min.   b&w   1936
> Prod: Maurice Conn Prod. Dist; Modern Sound Pictures, National Cinema
>   Service, Video Dimensions (video).
> Cast: Kermit Maynard.

ROCHE, ARTHUR SOMERS

Penthouse (in *Cosmopolitan Magazine*)

> *Penthouse*
> 90 min.   b&w   1933
> Dir: W.S. Van Dyke. Sp: Frances Goodrich, Albert Hackett. Prod: MGM.
>   Dist: Films Inc.
> Cast: Phillips Homes, Mae Clarke, Myrna Loy.
> Story about a murder frame-up.

> *Society Lawyer*
> 77 min.   b&w   1939
> Dir: Edwin Marin. Sp: Frances Goodrich, Albert Hackett, Leon Gordon,
>   Hugo Butler. Prod: MGM.
> Cast: Walter Pidgeon, Eduardo Ciannelli.
> A remake of *Penthouse.*

Rich but Honest (in *Hearst's International Magazine,* November 1926)

> *Rich but Honest*
> 6 reels   b&w   1927   sil.
> Dir: Albert Ray. Prod: Fox.
> Cast: Nancy Nash, Clifford Holland.

A department store clerk who wins a Charleston contest gets a job on the stage, only to alienate her steady sweetheart.

A Scrap of Paper (in *Saturday Evening Post*)

> *Living Lies*
> 5 reels   b&w   1922   sil.
> Dir: Emile Chautard. Prod: Mayflower Photoplay Corp.

Cast: Edmund Lowe, Mona Kingsley.

A reporter obtains documented evidence of the crooked deals of a band of high financiers, and he and his girl are kidnapped.

Wolf's Clothing (in *Hearst's International Magazine,* May-October 1926)

Wolf's Clothing
70 min.　　　　b&w　　　　1927　　　　sil.
Dir: Roy Del Ruth. Prod: Warner Bros.
Cast: Monte Blue, Patsy Ruth Miller.
In a dream, a man imagines himself being very tiny in a huge world.

ROECCA, SAMUEL

Salem Came to Supper

The Night Visitor
106 min.　　　　color　　　　1971
Dir: Laslo Benedek. Prod: Mel Ferrer. Dist: Audio Brandon, Kerr Film
　　Exchange, Video Communications (video).
Cast: Max Van Sydow, Liv Ullman, Trevor Howard.

A man escapes from a prison for the criminally insane and sets out to avenge himself on the husband and wife who committed the murder for which he was convicted.

ROONEY, FRANK

The Cyclists Raid

The Wild One
79 min.　　　　b&w　　　　1953
Dir: Laslo Benedek. Prod: Stanley Kramer Prod. Dist: Budget Films/Video,
　　Alan Twyman Presents.
Cast: Marlon Brando.

A leather-jacketed motorcycle gang vandalize and terrorize a small town, although their leader is attracted to a nice girl.

ROSTEN, LEO

The Dark Corner

The Dark Corner
99 min.　　　　b&w　　　　1946
Dir: Henry Hathaway. Prod: Twentieth Century Fox. Dist: Films Inc.
Cast: Lucille Ball, Clifton Webb, Mark Stevens.
A detective is framed for murder.

ROTH, PHILIP

Goodbye, Columbus

Goodbye, Columbus
105 min.　　　　color　　　　1969
Dir: Larry Peerce. Prod: Paramount. Dist: Films Inc., Paramount Home
　　Video (video), RCA VideoDisc (disc).

Story about the romance between a poor boy from the Bronx who works in a local library and a rich girl from Westchester.

RUNYON, DAMON

The Big Mitten

No Ransom
8 reels   b&w   1934
Dir: Fred Newmeyer. Prod: Liberty Pictures.

Bloodhounds of Broadway

Bloodhounds of Broadway
90 min.   color   1952
Dir: Harmon Jones. Prod: Twentieth Century Fox. Dist: Films Inc.
Cast: Mitzi Gaynor, Scott Brady.
A hillbilly turns into a Broadway babe in the city and becomes involved in a crime being investigated by a committee.

Butch Minds the Baby

Butch Minds the Baby
75 min.   b&w   1942
Dir: Albert S. Rogell. Sp: Leonard Spigelgass. Prod: Mayfair Prod.
Cast: Virginia Bruce, Broderick Crawford.
Zany things happen when a thug is forced to watch a small child.

Butch Minds the Baby
30 min.   color   1982
Prod: Highgate Pictures. Dist: Simon & Schuster (16 mm and video).
Set in New York during the Depression. Butch turns down a heist because he is babysitting.

A Call on the President

Joe and Ethel Turp Call on the President
7 reels   b&w   1939
Dir: Robert Sinclair. Prod: MGM.
Cast: Walter Brennan, Ann Sothern, William Gargan.
A couple takes their troubles right up to the White House.

Guys and Dolls

Guys and Dolls (s.m. the musical by Jo Swerling and Abe Burrows, which in turn was based on the story)
100 min.   b&w   1955
Dir: Joseph L. Mankiewicz. Prod: Metro-Goldwyn. Dist: Wholesome Film Center, CBS/Fox Video (video).
Cast: Marlon Brando, Frank Sinatra, Jean Simmons, Vivian Blaine.
A fable about gamblers and gangsters and the women who take them from their crap games to the marriage altar.

Hold'em Yale

Hold'em Yale
7 reels   b&w   1935
Dir: Sidney Lanfield. Sp: Paul Gerard Smith, Eddie Welch. Prod: Paramount.
Cast: Patricia Ellis, Cesar Romero.
Ticket scalpers are double-crossed.

Johnny One-Eye

Johnny One-Eye
78 min.   b&w   1950
Prod: Cahuenga Prod.
Cast: Pat O'Brien, Wayne Morris, Dolores Moran.
A gangster with a heart of gold is on the lam.

The Lemon Drop Kid

The Lemon Drop Kid
8 reels   b&w   1934
Dir: Marshal Neilan. Sp: Howard J. Green. Prod: Paramount.
Cast: Lee Tracy.

The Lemon Drop Kid
91 min.   b&w   1951
Dir: Sidney Lanfield. Prod: Paramount. Dist: Budget Films/Video, Ivy
    Films.
Cast: Bob Hope, Marilyn Maxwell.
When gangster Moose Moran loses $10,000 following a bid tip from a race-track tout, the heat is on, and the Lemon Drop Kid schemes to raise the money.

Little Miss Marker

Little Miss Marker
80 min.   b&w   1934
Dir: Alexander Hall. Prod: Paramount.
Cast: Shirley Temple, Adolphe Menjou.
A sentimental tale of a little girl who reforms a bookie.

Little Miss Marker
103 min.   color   1980
Dir: Walter Bernstein. Dist: Swank, MCA Home Video (video).
Cast: Walter Matthau, Julie Andrews.

Sorrowful Jones (s.m. the screenplay of the 1934 film)
88 min.   b&w   1949
Dir: Sidney Lanfield. Prod: Paramount.
Cast: Bob Hope, Lucille Ball, William Demarest, Bruce Cabot.

Little Pinks (in *Collier's Magazine,* 27 January 1940)

> *The Big Street*
> 88 min.   b&w   1942
> Dir: Irving Reis. Prod: RKO. Dist: Films Inc.
> Cast: Henry Fonda, Lucille Ball.

Gloria, a selfish singer, is loved by Little Pinks, who takes care of her when she becomes incurably crippled.

Madame La Gimp

> *Lady for a Day*
> 95 min.   b&w   1933
> Dir: Frank Capra. Prod: Columbia Pictures.
> Cast: May Robson, Warren William, Walter Connolly, Hobart Bosworth.

Apple Annie, a ragpicker, is put into a mansion for a week by a gambler to convince her daughter that she has a stately position in life.

> *Pocketful of Miracles* (s.m. the screenplay of *Lady for a Day*)
> 136 min.   color   1961
> Dir: Frank Capra. Sp: Hal Kantor, Harry Tugent (uncredited). Prod:
>   Franton.
> Cast: Glenn Ford, Bette Davis.

Money from Home

> *Money from Home*
> 100 min.   color   1954
> Dir: George Marshall. Sp: Hal Kanter. Prod: Paramount.
> Cast: Dean Martin, Jerry Lewis.

A slapstick comedy in which gangsters complicate a gambler's effort to recoup his losses at the track by arranging an illegal race.

The Old Doll's House

> *Midnight Alibi*
> 59 min.   b&w   1934
> Dir: Alan Crosland. Prod: First National Pictures.
> Cast: Richard Barthelmess, Ann Dvorak.
> A sweet old lady befriends a fleeing gambler.

Princess O'Hara

> *Princess O'Hara*
> 74 min.   b&w   1935
> Dir: David Burton. Sp: Doris Malloy, Harry Clark. Prod: Universal.
> A man tries to help the four children of a taxi driver who was killed.

> *It Ain't Hay*
> 80 min.   b&w   1943
> Dir: Erle C. Kenton. Sp: Allen Boretz, John Grant. Prod: Universal.
> Cast: Bud Abbott, Lou Costello.
> A champion horse is mistakenly given away. A remake of *Princess O'Hara.*

Three Wise Guys

Three Wise Guys
8 reels   b&w   1936
Dir: George B. Seitz. Sp: Elmer Harris. Prod: MGM.
Cast: Robert Young, Betty Furness.
A story about Broadway sharpies.

Tight Shoes

Tight Shoes
68 min.   b&w   1941
Dir: Albert S. Rogell. Prod: Mayfair Prod.
Cast: John Howard, Binnie Barnes, Broderick Crawford.
A gangster gets a shoe clerk started in a political career.

RUSSELL, JOHN

The Fire-Walker

Girl of the Port
8 reels   b&w   1930   sd. or sil.
Dir: Bert Glennon. Sp: Beulah Marie Dix. Prod: RKO.
Cast: Sally O'Neil, Reginald Sharland.
Love between a showgirl and an English war veteran.

The Lost God

The Sea God
b&w   1930
Dir: George Abbott. Prod: Paramount Publix.
Cast: Richard Arlen, Fay Wray.
Two traders seek the attentions of Daisy.

The Passion Vine

Where the Pavement Ends
8 reels   b&w   1923   sil.
Dir: Rex Ingram. Prod: Metro Pictures.
Cast: Edward Connelly, Alice Terey.
Pastor Spencer, trying to convert the natives, contends with the saloon
keeper.

The Red Mark

The Red Mark
8 reels   b&w   1928   sil.
Dir: James Cruze. Adap: Julien Josephson. Prod: James Cruze Inc.
Cast: Nina Quartaro, Gaston Glass.
The rival of Bibi-Ri on the penal island of Noumea is the executioner, whom
Bibi-Ri fears.

RYERSON, FLORENCE

Willie the Worm (in *American Magazine,* September 1926)

Love Makes 'em Wild
6 reels   b&w   1927   sil.
Dir: Albert Ray. Prod: Fox.
Cast: Johnny Harron, Sally Phipps.
   A spineless office plodder known as Willie the Worm is told by quack doctors that he has only six months to live, so he proceeds to get even with those who have bullied him.

S

ST. JOHN, ADELA ROGERS

Great God Fourflush

Woman's Man
80 min.   b&w   1934
Dir: Edward Ludwig. Prod: Monogram Pictures. Dist: Mogull's Films.
Cast: John Halliday, Wallace Ford.
A spoiled Hollywood movie star meets a prizefighter.

The Haunted Lady (in *Hearst's International Magazine,* May 1915)

Scandal
7 reels   b&w   1929   sil.
Dir: Wesley Ruggles. Prod: Universal.
Cast: Laura La Plante, Huntley Gordon.
When her family wealth is dissipated, socialite Laura Hunt goes to work and marries for money.

Love o' Women (in *Hearst's International Magazine,* February 1926)

Singed
6 reels   b&w   1927   sil.
Dir: John Griffith Wray. Prod: Fox.
Cast: Blanche Sweet, Warner Baxter.
Because Dolly loves Royce, an irresponsible chap, she backs an oil well in which he has an interest, but when he becomes wealthy, he leaves her.

Pretty Ladies (in *Cosmopolitan Magazine*)

Pretty Ladies
6 reels   b&w   1925   sil.
Dir: Monta Bell. Adap: Alice D.G. Miller. Prod: MGM.
Cast: ZaSu Pitts, Tom Moore, Ann Pennington, Lilyan Tashman.
A star comedienne helps a drummer become a successful songwriter and gives up her career to marry him.

The Worst Woman in Hollywood (in *Cosmopolitan Magazine,* February 1924)

Inez From Hollywood
7 reels   b&w   1924   sil.

Dir: Alfred E. Green. Adap: J.G. Hawks. Prod: Sam E. Rork Prod.

Inez, a vamp and Hollywood star, tries to protect her sister from men she considers dishonorable.

SAKI

The Lull

The Lull
15 min.   color   1978
Prod: International Instructional Television Coop. Dist: Indiana University (16 mm and video).

A politician seeking a respite from campaigning ends up tending barnyard animals in his room.

The Open Window

Open Window
12 min.   color   1971
Dir: Richard Patterson. Prod: American Film Institute. Dist: Pyramid Films (16 mm and video).

A young girl tells a ghost story to a visitor, who then flees.

SALE, RICHARD

The Doctor Doubles in Death

Embraceable You
80 min.   b&w   1948
Dir: Felix Jacoves. Prod: Warner Bros. Dist: MGM/UA Home Video (video).
Cast: Dane Clark, Geraldine Brooks.

A small-time crook falls for a girl he injured.

This Side of the Law
74 min.   b&w   1950
Dir: Richard L. Bare. Prod: Warner Bros.
Cast: Viveca Lindfors, Kent Smith, Janis Page.

A contribed plot in which a shady lawyer hires a man to impersonate a missing wealthy man.

SALINGER, J.D.

Uncle Wiggily in Connecticut (in *The New Yorker*, 20 March 1948)

My Foolish Heart
98 min.   b&w   1949
Dir: Mark Robson. Sp: Julius and Philip Epstein. Prod: Metro-Goldwyn.
Cast: Susan Hayward, Dana Andrews.

A wartime romance between a lonely girl (suburban lush in the story, a wronged lonely woman in the movie) and a pilot.

SANTLEY, JOSEPH

Murder in a Chinese Theatre

> *Mad Holiday*
> 8 reels   b&w   1936
> Dir: George B. Seitz. Sp: Florence Ryerson, Edgar Allan Woolf. Prod: MGM.
> Cast: Elissa Landi, Edmund Lowe, ZaSu Pitts.
> A comedy whodunit in the *Thin Man* style.

SAPPER (pseud. of H.C. McNeile)

Challenge

> *Bulldog Drummond in Africa*
> 70 min.   b&w   1938
> Dir: Louis King. Prod: Paramount. Dist: Hollywood Home Theater (video).
> Cast: John Howard, Heather Angel.
> Col. Nielson is kidnapped, and Drummond chases after him to Africa. Note:
The character of Bulldog Drummond appeared in many novels and some stories.

The Female of the Species

> *Bulldog Drummond Comes Back*
> 70 min.   b&w   1937
> Dir: Louis King. Prod: Paramount. Dist: Cable Films (video), Discount Video
>   Tapes, Penguin Video.
> Cast: John Howard, Heather Angel.
> Bulldog Drummond is hot on the trail of a clever criminal who has kidnapped
his fiance.

Thirteen Lead Soldiers

> *Thirteen Lead Soldiers*
> 64 min.   b&w   1948
> Dir: Frank McDonald. Sp: Irving Elman. Prod: Reliance Pictures.
> Cast: Tom Conway, Maria Palmer.
> Bulldog Drummond solves three murders with the aid of thirteen lead
soldiers, which hold the key to hidden treasure.

SAUNDERS, JOHN MONK

A Maker of Gestures (in *Cosmopolitan Magazine*, April 1923)

> *Too Many Kisses*
> 6 reels   b&w   1925   sil.
> Dir: Paul Sloane. Prod: Famous Players-Lasky.
> Cast: Richard Dix, Frances Howard.
> Because Richard puts pleasure before business, his father sends him to Spain,
where he falls in love with a Spanish girl.

SAUNDERS, KENNETH J.

The Devil's Playground

The Lady Who Dared
55 min.   b&w   1931
Dir: William Beaudine. Prod: First National Pictures. Dist: MGM/UA Home
    Video (video).
Cast: Billie Dove, Conway Tearle.
A diamond smuggler is forced to join in a crooked scheme.

SAYERS, DOROTHY L.

The Inspiration of Mr. Budd

The Inspiration of Mr. Budd
25 min.   color   1976
Prod: Twentieth Century Fox. Dist: Encyclopaedia Britannica (16 mm and
    video).
A meek, unsuccessful barber meets adventure when a fierce-looking, red-
haired man demands that his hair be dyed and talks as though he has murdered his
wife. The barber dyes his hair brown but with a slow-working chemical that turns it
green.

SAYRE, JOEL

Man on the Ledge

Fourteen Hours
91 min.   b&w   1951
Dir: Henry Hathaway. Prod: Twentieth Century Fox. Dist: Films Inc.
Cast: Paul Douglas, Richard Basehart, Grace Kelly.
Chronicles the fourteen hours a man spends on a 15th floor New York
window ledge, threatening to jump.

SCHAEFER, JACK

Jeremy Rodock

Tribute to a Bad Man
95 min.   color   1956
Dir: Robert Wise. Prod: MGM. Dist: Films Inc.
Cast: James Cagney, Irene Papas.
Set in Wyoming in 1875. A vengeful rancher takes the law into his own hands
when horse thieves steal some of his breeding stock.

SCOTT, EWING

Arctic Manhunt

Narana of the North
b&w   1948
Cast: Mikel Conrad, Carol Thurston.
Story about an ex-convict's flight to Alaska to cash in on some armored car
loot.

Gaitor Bait

Untamed Fury
65 min.   b&w   1947
Dir: Ewing Scott. Prod: Pathe. Dist: Institutional Cinema Service.
Cast: Mikel Conrad, Leigh Whipper.

Shadow of the Curtain

Arctic Flight
75 min.   b&w   1952
Prod: Monogram Pictures. Dist: Hurlock Cine-World.
Cast: Wayne Morris, Lola Albright.
Bush pilot battles foreign agents in the Arctic.

SCOTT, LEROY

In Borrowed Plumes

In Borrowed Plumes
6 reels   b&w   1926   sil.
Dir: Victor Hugo Halperin. Prod: Welcome Pictures.
Cast: Marjorie Daw, Niles Welch.
A penniless society girl passes herself off as the Countess D'Autreval.

Little Angel

Lady of Chance
8 reels   b&w   1928   sil.
Dir: Robert Z. Leonard. Sp: A.P. Younger. Prod: MGM.
Cast: Norma Shearer, Lowell Sherman.
The heroine lures men to her apartment in order to blackmail them.

The Mother (in *Cosmopolitan Magazine,* February 1914)

The Poverty of Riches
6 reels   b&w   1921   sil.
Dir: Reginald Barker. Prod: Metro-Goldwyn.
Cast: Richard Dix, Beatrice Joy.
A woman yearns to have children, but her husband wants to achieve financial and social success first.

SHAFFER, ROSALIND KEATING

Finger Man

Lady Killer
76 min.   b&w   1933
Dir: Roy Del Ruth. Prod: Warner Bros. Dist: MGM/UA Home Video (video).
Cast: James Cagney, Margaret Lindsay, Mae Clark.
A mobster becomes a Hollywood actor.

SHAFTEL, JOSEPH

The Bliss of Mrs. Blossom

> *The Bliss of Mrs. Blossom* (s.m. "A Bird in the Nest," a play by Alec Coppel,
>   which in turn was based on the story)
> 93 min.   color   1968
> Dir: Joseph McGrath. Prod: Paramount. Dist: Audio Brandon.
> Cast: Shirley MacLaine, Richard Attenborough.
> A brassiere manufacturer keeps a lover in the attic.

Notorious Tenant (in *Collier's Magazine,* 3 February 3, 1956)

> *Notorious Tenant*
> 123 min.   b&w   1962
> Dir: Richard Quine. Prod: Columbia Pictures. Dist: Budget Films/Videos,
>   Roa's Films.
> Cast: Kim Novak, Jack Lemmon.

A young American diplomat stationed in London rents an apartment in the
fashionable private home of a beautiful young woman suspected by Scotland Yard
of having murdered her husband.

SHAW, DAVID (jt. author) (see *Take One False Step* under SHAW, IRWIN)

SHAW, IRWIN

In the French Style

> *In the French Style* (s.m. also "A Year to Learn the Language")
> 105 min.   1963
> Dir: Robert Parrish. Prod: Gasanna-Orsay Films.
> Cast: Jean Seberg, Stanley Baker.

A post-World War II female expatriate becomes involved in a series of brief,
meaningless love affairs.

Night Call (jt. author David Shaw)

> *Take One False Step*
> 94 min.   b&w   1947
> Dir: Chester Erskine. Prod: Universal.
> Cast: William Powell, Shelley Winters.

An innocent college professor becomes entangled with the police when a
blonde from his past runs into him.

Then There Were Three

> *Three*
> 102 min.   color   1969
> Dir. and Sp: James Salter. Prod: United Artists. Dist: MGM/UA Home Video
>   (video).

Three Americans just out of college during the 50s wind up a vacation in
Europe.

Tip on a Dead Jockey (in *The New Yorker,* 6 March 1954)

> *Tip on a Dead Jockey*
> 129 min.　　　b&w　　　1957
> Dir: Richard Thorpe. Prod: MGM. Dist: Films Inc.
> Cast: Robert Taylor, Dorothy Malone.
> A pilot is involved with smugglers.

A Year to Learn the Language (see *In the French Style*)

SHER, JACK

Memo to Kathy O'Rourke (in *Saturday Evening Post,* 23 November 1946)

> *Kathy-O*
> 99 min.　　　color　　　1958
> Dir: Jack Sher. Prod. and Dist: Universal.
> Cast: Patty McCormack, Dan Duryea, Jan Sterling.
> A temperamental child star who makes life miserable for her public relations man is kidnapped.

SHERDEMAN, TED

Latitude Zero Stories

> *Latitude Zero* (Japan)
> 99 min.　　　color　　　1970
> Dir: Ishiro Hondo.
> Cast: Joseph Cotten, Cesar Romero.
> A science fiction adventure about an underwater civilization where benevolent geniuses battle the legions of Malic, who are out to rule the world.

SHEW, EDWARD SPENCER

Hands of the Ripper

> *Hands of the Ripper* (Br.)
> 85 min.　　　color　　　1972
> Dir: Pete Sasdy. Sp: L.W. Davidson, Rel: Universal. Dist: Swank.
> Cast: Eric Porter, Angharad Rees.
> A thriller set in Victorian England, where a series of murders occur soon after a psychiatrist takes custody of a seventeen-year-old.

SHIPMAN, SAMUEL (jt. author) (see *Law of the Underworld* under HYMER, JAMES)

SHORE, VIOLA BROTHERS

On the Shelf (in *Saturday Evening Post,* 22 July 1922)

> *Let Women Alone*
> 6 reels　　　b&w　　　1925　　　sil.
> Dir: Paul Powell. Adap: Frank Woods. Prod: Peninsula Studios.

Cast: Pat O'Malley, Wanda Hawley, Wallace Beery.

An interior decorator whose husband was lost at sea plans to remarry until he shows up.

The Prince of Headwaiters (in *Liberty Magazine,* 9 April 1927; jt. author Garrett Fort)

> *The Prince of Headwaiters*
> 7 reels   b&w   1927   sil.
> Dir: John Francis Dillon. Prod: Sam E. Rork Prod.
> Cast: Lewis Stone, Priscilla Bonner.

The headwaiter at the Ritz Hotel saves a college boy from a notorious gold digger and finds out the boy is his son.

SHORT, LUKE (pseud. of Fred Dilley Glidden)

Hurry, Charlie, Hurry

> *Hurry, Charlie, Hurry*
> 65 min.   b&w   1941
> Dir: Charles E. Roberts. Prod: RKO. Dist: Films Inc.
> Cast: Leon Errol.

A henpecked husband who gets into trouble is abetted by his Indian friends.

SHRANK, JOSEPH (see *He Couldn't Say No* under MATSON, NORMAN)

SIMENON, GEORGES

A Life in the Balance

> *A Life in the Balance*
> 74 min.   b&w   1955
> Dir: Harry Horner. Prod: Twentieth Century Fox. Dist: Films Inc.
> Cast: Ricardo Montalban, Anne Bancroft.
> Murders in Mexico.

SINGER, ISAAC BASHEVIS

The Beard

> *Isaac Singer's Nightmare and Mrs. Pupko's Beard*
> 30 min.   color   1973
> Dir: Bruce Davidson. Dist: New Yorker Films.

The story features the famous writer intercut with a dramatization about a writer married to a bearded woman. The writer invests in the stock market and becomes rich, and Pupko urges Singer to write about him, but Singer refuses.

Short Friday

> *Isaac Bashevis Singer*
> 40 min.
> Prod. and Dist: Authors on Videotape.
> Singer reads his love story.

Yentl

Yentl
134 min.   color   1983
Dir. and Prod: Barbra Streisand. Dist: CBS/Fox Video (video).
Cast: Barbra Streisand.
A young woman disguises herself as a boy in order to study at the yeshiva.

SLESINGER, TESS

The Answer on the Magnolia Tree

Girl's School
80 min.   b&w   1938
Dir: John Brahm. Sp: Tess Slesinger. Prod: Columbia Pictures. Dist: Kit
     Parker Films.
Cast: Anne Shirley, Nan Grey.
Two roommates clash over romance and school rules.

Mousie Baby

Mousie Baby
25 min.   color   1978
Dir. and Prod: Anne Shanks. Dist: Phoenix/BFA (16 mm and video).
During the Depression, a young secretary, is unsure about striking with her
co-workers at an advertising agency.

SLODE, CHRISTINE J.

Caretakers Within (in *Saturday Evening Post,* 5 February 1921)

Life's Darn Funny
6 reels   b&w   1921   sil.
Dir: Dallas M. Fitzgerald.
Cast: Viola Dana, Gareth Hughes.
A young couple goes into business designing clothes.

SMITH, FRANK LEON

Bells of Waldenbruck

Melody in Spring
8 reels   b&w   1934
Dir: Norman McLeod. Sp: Benn W. Levy. Prod: Paramount.
Cast: Lanny Ross, Charles Ruggles.
A young man who wants a job as a soloist on the Blodgett Radio Hour agrees
to elope with Blodgett's daughter.

SMITH, GARRETT

Old Hutch Lives Up to It

Old Hutch
8 reels   b&w   1936
Dir: J. Walter Ruben. Prod: MGM.
A ne'er-do-well finds $100,000 but can't spend it because everyone knows
he's never earned a penny.

SMITH, HAROLD JACOB

The Highest Mountain

The River's Edge
87 min.   color   1957
Dir: Allan Dwan. Prod: Twentieth Century Fox. Dist: Films Inc.
Cast: Anthony Quinn, Ray Milland, Debra Paget.
A killer menaces his old girlfriend and her husband.

SMITH, MAXWELL

Dated (in *Saturday Evening Post,* 3 July 1920)

The Last Card
6 reels   b&w   1921   sil.
Dir: Bayard Veiller. Prod: Metro Pictures.
Cast: May Allison, Albert Roscoe.
A criminal lawyer murders his wife's lover and frames a friend, who hires him.

SMITH, WALLACE

The Grouch Bag (in *Hearst's International Magazine*)

Not Quite Decent '
5 reels   b&w   1929   sd. effects and talking sequences
Dir: Irving Cummings. Prod: Fox.
Cast: Louise Dresser, Jane Collyer.
An aging nightclub singer meets an actress, who turns out to be the daughter from whom she had been separated years before.

Little Ledna

Big Time
8 reels   b&w   1930
Dir: Kenneth Hawks. Adap: Sidney Lanfield. Prod: Fox.
Cast: Lee Tracy, Mae Clark.
A vaudeville husband and wife team breaks up when a schemer named Gloria slips into the act.

New York West (in *Blue Book,* March 1926)

West of Broadway
6 reels   b&w   1926   sil.
Dir: Robert Thornby. Adap: Harold Shumate. Prod: Metro Pictures.
Cast: Priscilla Dean, Arnold Gray.
The golf instructor hired by a rancher turns out to be a woman.

The Snake's Wife (in *Hearst's International Magazine,* May 1926)

Upstream
6 reels   b&w   1927   sil.
Dir: John Ford. Prod: Fox.

Cast: Nancy Nash, Earle Foxe.
An actor becomes the victim of his own conceit.

A Woman Decides (in *Cosmopolitan Magazine*)

The Delightful Rogue
7 reels   b&w   1929   sil. or sd.
Dir: Lynn Shores. Prod: RKO.
Cast: Rod LaRocque, Rita La Roy, Charles Boyer,
A tropical seas romance between a pirate and an American dancer.

SOMERVILLE, A.W.

No Brakes (in *Saturday Evening Post*, 8 December 1928)

Oh, Yeah!
85 min.   b&w   1930
Dir: Tay Garnett. Prod: Pathe. Dist: Film Classic Exchange.
Cast: James Gleason, ZaSu Pitts.
Two drifters blow into town and each finds a sweetheart.

SOUTAR, ANDREW

On Principle (in *Snappy Stories*, 2 April 1918)

Love's Redemption
6 reels   b&w   1921   sil.
Dir: Albert Parker. Prod: Norma Talmadge Prod.
Cast: Norma Talmadge, Harrison Ford.
A young woman raised in Jamaica marries a rich Englishman and returns
with him to England, only to become disillusioned with the upper crust.

SPAULDING, SUSAN MARR

Two Shall Be Born

Two Shall Be Born
6 reels   b&w   1924   sil.
Dir: William Bennett. Prod: Twin Pictures.
Cast: Jane Novak, Kenneth Harlan.
Mayra is entrusted with important international papers and is then
kidnapped.

SPEARMAN, FRANK HAMILTON

The Nerve of Folly

The Runaway Express
6 reels   b&w   1926   sil.
Dir: Edward Sedgwick. Dist: Mogull's Films.
Cast: Jack Daugherty, Blaine Mehaffey.
Joe commandeers an engine to get cattle to market and is offered a job on
the railroad.

Whispering Smith Rides

The Lightning Express (a ten-part serial)
2 reels ea.   b&w   1930
Dir: Henry McRae. Prod: Universal.
Cast: Land Chandler, Louise Lorraine.
Permission is needed for the Lightning Express, a train, to cross land owned by a pretty girl, but her unscrupulous guardian fights the railroad.

Whispering Smith
88 min.   b&w   1949
Dir: Leslie Fenton. Prod: Universal.
Cast: Alan Ladd, Robert Preston, Brenda Marshall.
A western remake of the above serial. A railroad detective finds his best friend mixed up with bandits.

SPRINGER, NORMAN

Then Hell Broke Loose

Shanghaied Love
7 reels   b&w   1931
Dir: George B. Seitz. Adap: Roy Chancellor, Jack Cunningham. Prod: Columbia Pictures.

SPRINGS, ELLIOT WHITE

The One Who Was Clever (in *Redbook,* August 1929)

Young Eagles (s.m. also the story "Sky-High" in *Redbook,* July 1929)
6 reels   b&w   1930   sd. or sil.
Dir: William A. Wellman. Prod: Paramount.
Cast: Charles Rogers, Jean Arthur.
The romance of a lieutenant and an American is cut short when he must return to the front.

SQUIER, EMMA LINDSAY

The Angry God and the People of Corn

The Angry God
57 min.   color   1948
Dir: Van Campel Heilner. Prod: Arlisle Prod.
Cast: Alicia Parla, Casimiro Ortega.
The god of the Mexican Indians is personified.

Glorious Buccaneer

Dancing Pirate
80 min.   color   1936
Dir: Lloyd Corrigan. Prod: RKO. Dist: Ivy Films, Mogull's Films.
Cast: Charles Collins, Frank Morgan.
The romantic adventures of a dancing instructor shanghaied in Boston in the early part of the nineteenth century.

STAFFORD, JEAN

The Scarlet Letter

Pardon Me for Living
30 min.   color   1982
Prod: Highgate Pictures. Dist: Simon & Schuster (16 mm and video).
Cast: Margaret Hamilton.
Set in the early 1930s. Story about school friendships among sixth graders.

STARRET, VINCENT

Recipe for Murder

Great Hotel Murder
53 min.   b&w   1935
Dir: James Tinling. Sp: Bess Meredyth. Prod: Fox.
Cast: Edmund Lowe, Victor McLaglen.
A detective lives in a hotel where a dead man is discovered.

STEELE, WILBUR DANIEL

Ropes (in *Harper's Monthly,* January 1921)

Undertow
60 min.   b&w   1930
Dir: Harry A. Pollard. Adap: Winnifred Reeve, Edward T. Lowe. Prod:
     Universal.
Cast: Mary Nolan, Johnny Mack Brown.
A young man in the Coast Guard steals away the wife of the lighthouse
keeper.

STEINBECK, JOHN

Flight

Flight
81 min.   b&w   1961
Prod: San Francisco Films, re. Columbia Pictures. Dist: Kit Parker Films.
Cast: Efrian Ramirez.

STELLA, ENRICO

A Girl Named Francesca

Crazy Desire (It.)
108 min.   b&w   1962
Dir: Luciano Salce. Prod: Isidoro Broggi, Renato Libassi.
Cast: Ugo Tognazzi, Catherine Spaak.
A forty-year-old businessman falls prey to the teasing of a sixteen-year-old
girl and willingly undergoes all sorts of indignities.

STEPHENSON, CARL
Leiningen Versus the Ants

The Naked Jungle
95 min.   color   1953
Dir: Byron Haskin. Prod: Paramount. Dist: Films Inc.
Cast: Charlton Heston, Eleanor Parker.
Convinced that his mail-order bride is too beautiful to be useful, Christopher urges her to leave his South American plantation, but she refuses and helps him in a struggle to survive.

STERN, PHILIP VAN DOREN
The Greatest Gift

It's a Wonderful Life
130 min.   b&w   1947
Dir: Frank Capra. Sp: Frances Goodrich, Albert Hackett, Frank Capra.
Prod: RKO. Dist: Ivy Films, Kit Parker Films, Hollywood Home Theater
    (video).
Cast: James Stewart, Donna Reed.
A hard-working man whose business fails attempts to commit suicide but is shown the value of life by a lovable guardian angel.

STEVENSON, ROBERT LOUIS
The Body Snatcher

The Body Snatcher
77 min.   b&w   1945
Dir: Robert Wise. Sp: Philip MacDonald, Carlos Keith. Prod: RKO. Dist:
    Films Inc., Nostalgia Merchant (video).
Cast: Boris Karloff, Bela Lugosi.
Set in nineteenth century Edinburgh. A distinguished surgeon falls into the power of the man who supplies cadavers for his medical classes.

The Rajah's Diamond

The Tame Cat
4,943'   b&w   1921   sil.
Dir: William Bradley. Prod: Dramafilms.
Cast: Ray Irwin, Marion Harding.
A story about a fabulous gem and the people who desperately want to possess it.

Silverado Squatters

Adventures in Silverado
75 min.   b&w   1948
Dir: Phil Karlson. Prod: Columbia Pictures. Dist: International Cinema
    Service, Modern Sound Pictures.
Cast: William Bishop, Forrest Tucker.

A drama of the California frontier in 1880 when settlers attempt to settle in the wilderness.

Sire de Maletroit's Door

The Strange Door
81 min.   b&w   1951
Dir: Joseph Pevney. Prod: Universal International.
Cast: Boris Karloff, Charles Laughton, Sally Forrest.
An insane French nobleman vows revenge on his dead sweetheart by imprisoning members of her family.

The Suicide Club (see also *The Living Dead* under POE, EDGAR ALLAN)

Three silent versions were made of this story, one in 1910, another in France in 1912, and a third in Britain in 1914.

Suicide Club (Br.)
1932
Dir: Maurice Elvey.

Trouble for Two (s.m. also "The Young Man With the Cream Tart")
80 min.   b&w   1936
Dir: J. Walter Ruben. Sp: Manuel Seff, Edward Paramore, Jr. Prod: MGM.
    Dist: Films Inc.
Cast: Robert Montgomery, Rosalind Russell.
Chilling adventure tale.

The Treasure of Franchard

The Treasure of Lost Canyon
82 min.   color   1951
Dir: Ted Tetzlaff. Sp: Brainerd Duffield, Emerson Crocker. Prod: Universal.
Cast: William Powell, Julia Adams.
A young orphan, adopted by a middle-aged couple, stumbles onto a buried treasure and brings havoc into their lives.

The Young Man With the Cream Tart (see *Trouble for Two* under **The Suicide Club**)

STOCKTON, FRANK R.

The Lady or the Tiger

The Lady or the Tiger
10 min.
Dir: Fred Zinnemann. Prod: MGM. Dist: Wholesome Film Center.
A Roman gladiator, faced with a life-and-death dilemma, must choose his fate. Behind one door is a beautiful woman and behind the other is a ferocious tiger.

The Lady or the Tiger?
16 min.   color   1969
Prod. and Dist: Encyclopaedia Britannica (16 mm and video).
Reset in the space age.

STONE, PETER

The Unsuspecting Wife

Charade
113 min.   color   1963
Dir: Stanley Donen. Prod: Universal. Dist: Alan Twyman Presents, MCA
   Home Video (video).
Cast: Cary Grant, Audrey Hepburn.
A suspenseful, elegant thriller about a preposterous and deadly chase through
Paris complete with five corpses and red herrings.

STRAKOSCH, AVERY

I Married An Artist

She Married an Artist
8 reels   b&w   1938
Dir: Marion Gering. Sp: Gladys Lehman, Delmar Davies. Prod: Columbia
   Pictures.

STREET, JAMES

The Biscuit Eater

The Biscuit Eater
83 min.   b&w   1942
Dir: Stuart Heisler. Prod: Paramount.
Cast: Billy Lee, Cordel Hickman, Helen Millard, Richard Lee.
A Georgia youngster takes an outcast puppy, names him Promise, and
tries to make him a champion hunting dog.

The Biscuit Eater
90 min.   color   1972
Dir: Vincent McEveety. Prod: Walt Disney Prod.
Cast: Earl Holliman, Johnny Whitaker, Lew Ayres, Godfrey Cambridge.

Letter to the Editor

Nothing Sacred
80 min.   b&w   1938
Dir: William Wellman. Prod: United Artists. Dist: Mogull's Films, Budget
   Films/Video (video), Cable Films, Discount Video Tapes, Penguin Video.
Cast: Carole Lombard, Fredric March.
Drama about a girl with a short time to live who is given a good time for two
weeks. But it's nothing except a publicity stunt.

Living It Up (s.m. also the screenplay of *Nothing Sacred* and the play
   "Hazel Flagg" by Ben Hecht, which in turn was based on the story)
94 min.   color   1954
Dir: Norman Taurog. Prod: York Pictures. Dist: Films Inc.
Cast: Dean Martin, Jerry Lewis, Janet Leigh
A story about a railroad attendant with sinus trouble.

Mr. Bisbee's Princess

So's Your Old Man
6,347'   b&w   1926   sil.
Dir: Gregory La Cava. Prod: Famous Players-Lasky.
Cast: W.C. Fields.
A comedy about the invention of unbreakable glass.

You're Telling Me
70 min.   b&w   1934
Dir: Erle C. Kenton. Prod: Paramount. Dist: Swank.
Cast: W.C. Fields.
A remake of *So's Your Old Man.*

Weep No More, My Lady

Weep No More, My Lady (made for television)
54 min.   color   1979
Dist: MTI Teleprograms (video).
Skeeter finds a dog, which he trains to hunt. He later finds out she belongs
to someone else.

STRINGER, ARTHUR

The Coward (in *Hearst's International Magazine*)

The Coward
6 reels   b&w   1927   sil.
Dir: Alfred Raboch. Prod: R-C Pictures.
Cast: Warner Baxter, Sharon Lynn.
A young, rich idler must prove his worth.

Fifth Avenue (in *Saturday Evening Post,* 19 September 1925)

Fifth Avenue
6 reels   b&w   1926   sil.
Dir: Robert G. Vignola. Sp: Anthony Coldwey. Prod: Belasco Prod.
Cast: Marguerite De La Motte, Allan Forrest.
When her cotton crop is burned, Barbara goes to New York, where she is
mistaken for a whore.

Manhandled (in *Saturday Evening Post,* 29 March 1924)

Manhandled
50 min.   b&w   1924   sil.

Dir. and Prod: Allan Swan. Sp: Frank W. Tuttle. Dist: Em Gee Film Library,
Alan Twyman Presents.
Cast: Gloria Swanson, Tom Moore, Frank Morgan.

Tessie is a New York department store salesgirl whose boyfriend, a mechanic,
leaves for Detroit to demonstrate a new carburetor he invented. During his absence,
Tessie dresses up as a Russian countess and becomes casually involved with several
rich men.

Snowblind (in *Hearst's International Magazine,* March 1921)

Unseeing Eyes
9 reels   b&w   1923   sil.
Dir: E.H. Griffith. Prod: Cosmopolitan Pictures.
Cast: Lionel Barrymore, Seena Owen.

Miriam flies to Canda to help her brother with his silver mine, and the plane
crashes en route.

White Hands (in *Saturday Evening Post,* 30 July-20 August 1927)

Half a Bride
6,238'   b&w   1928   sil.
Dir: Gregory La Cava. Sp: Doris Anderson. Prod: Paramount.
Cast: Esther Ralston, Gary Cooper.

Thrill-seeker Patience Winslow enters a trial marriage, which is not
consummated because her father kidnaps her.

The Wilderness Woman (in *Saturday Evening Post,* 16-30 January 1926)

The Wilderness Woman
8 reels   b&w   1926   sil.
Dir: Howard Higgin. Prod: Robert Kane Prod.
Cast: Arleen Pringle, Lowell Sherman.

A miner finds gold and heads for New York with his daughter. En route
they run into confidence men.

Womanhandled (in *Saturday Evening Post,* 2 May 1925)

Womanhandled
7 reels   b&w   1925   sil.
Dir: Gregory La Cava. Prod: Famous Players-Lasky.
Cast: Richard Dix, Esther Ralston.

Society playboy Bill must prove to Mollie that he's a man, so he goes out
West.

Buck Benny Rides Again
86 min.   b&w   1940
Cast: Jack Benny, Ellen Drew.
An adaptation based on the radio character Buck Benny.

STRONG, HARRISON

Saddle Mates (in *Western Story Magazine,* 12 January 1924)

> *Saddle Mates*
> 5 reels   b&w   1928   sil.
> Dir: Richard Thorpe. Prod: Action Pictures.
> Cast: Wally Wales, Hank Bell.
> Western. Two ranchers track down the crook who cheated them out of their

land.

STUART, JESSE

Split Cherry Tree

> *Split Cherry Tree*
> 26 min.   color   1984
> Prod: Learning Corp. of America. Dist: Simon & Schuster (16 mm and
>   video).
> Cast: Colleen Dewhurst, Will Newman.
> To pay for breaking a limb off a cherry tree, a young boy has to stay after

school, which upsets his poor, uneducated father.

STUHLDREHER, HARRY

The Gray Game

> *The Band Plays On* (s.m. also "Backfield" by Byron Morgan)
> 89 min.   b&w   1934
> Dir: Russel Mack. Sp: Bernard Schubert, Ralph Spence, Harvey Gates.
>   Prod: MGM.
> Cast: Una Merkel, Stuart Erwin.
> Story of a football player.

SUDERMANN, HERMANN

Trip to Tilsit

> *Sunrise*
> 10 reels   b&w   1927   sd. effects or sil.
> Dir: F.W. Murnau.
> Cast: George O'Brien, Janet Gaynor.
> Infatuated with another woman, who encourages him to kill his wife, a

farmer tries but cannot do it.

SULLIVAN, WALLACE

No Power on Earth

> *Behind the High Wall*
> 85 min.   b&w   1956
> Dir: Abner Biberman. Prod: Universal.
> Cast: Tom Tully, Sylvia Sidney.
> A prison warden who has a paraplegic wife finds $100,000 of an escaped

prisoner's loot.

The Big Guy
80 min.   b&w   1939
Dir: Arthur Lubin. Prod: Universal.
Cast: Victor McLaglen, Jackie Cooper, Ona Munson
A prison warden is forced to choose between keeping $25,000 or returning it and saving a man from the electric chair.

SURDEZ, GEORGES

A Game in the Bush (in *Adventure Magazine*)

South Sea Love
5 reels   b&w   1923   sil.
Dir: David Soloman. Prod: Fox.
Cast: Shirley Mason, J. Frank Glendon.
Dolores falls in love with her guardian, who is already married.

SWANSON, NEIL H.

The First Rebel

Allegheny Uprising
81 min.   b&w   1939
Dir: William A. Seiter. Prod: RKO. Dist: Films Inc., Blackhawk (video).
Cast: John Wayne, Claire Trevor.
American frontiersmen battle the British for their civil rights—a preamble to the American Revolution.

SWARTHOUT, GLENDON F.

A Horse for Mrs. Custer

Seventh Cavalry
75 min.   color   1956
Dir: Joseph Lewis. Prod: Producers Actors Corp. Dist: Kit Parker Films.
Cast: Randolph Scott, Barbara Hale.
"Avenge General Custer" is the order that sends the Seventh Cavalry charging against the Indians despite the tremendous odds.

SYLVESTER, ROBERT

China Valdez

We Were Strangers
106 min.   b&w   1949
Dir: John Huston. Prod: Columbia Pictures.
Cast: Jennifer Jones, John Garfield.
A story about political intrigue and revolution in Cuba during the 1930s.

T

TAGORE, RABINDRANATH
The Postmaster

Two Daughters (India; s.m. also "The Conclusion")
114 min.   b&w   1961
Dir: Satyajit Ray. Dist: Janus Films.
Cast: Anil Chatterjee, Chandana Bennerjee; in the second part of the film,
   Aparna Dad Gupta, Soumitra Chatterjee.

A young man who is assigned as the postmaster in a small village forms a
strong bond with a ten-year-old orphan. In the second half of the film, Amulya
refuses to marry his chosen wife because he wants to marry a tomboy he loves.

TARKINGTON, BOOTH
Father and Son

Father's Son
b&w   1931
Dir: William Beaudine. Prod: Warner Bros.
Cast: Lewis Stone, Leon Janney, Irene Rich.

A sentimental family story. Note: There are conflicting views on these films.
One source lists the story as "Old Fathers and Young Sons"; still another source
claims that the second film was based on an unpublished story.

Father's Son
57 min.   b&w   1941
Dir: Ross Lederman. Prod: Warner Bros.
Cast: John Litel, Frieda Inescort.

Penrod stories

Penrod was a character who appeared in several novels and stories. Original
screenplays based on this character also were written, including *Penrod and His
Twin Brother* and *Penrod's Double Trouble*.

Penrod and Sam
8 reels   b&w   1931
Dir: William Beaudine. Prod: Warner Bros.
Cast: Leon Janney.

Penrod and Sam
64 min.   b&w   1937
Dir: William McGann. Prod: Warner Bros.
Cast: Billy Mauch, Frank Craven, Spring Byington.
Penrod gets into wild escapades with G-men and bank robbers.

On Moonlight Bay
95 min.   b&w   1951
Dir: Roy Del Ruth. Prod: Warner Bros.
Cast: Doris Day, Gordon MacRae.
A musical romance.

TATE, SYLVIA

Man on the Run (in *American Magazine,* April 1948)

Woman on the Run
77 min.   b&w   1950
Dir: Norman Foster. Sp: Alan Campbell, Norman Foster. Prod: Universal.
Cast: Ann Sheridan, Dennis O'Keefe.
A beautiful woman tries to find her husband, who witnessed a gangland killing, before the mobsters do.

TAYLOR, GRANT

Riders of the Terror Trail

The Terror Trail
58 min.   b&w   1933
Dir: Armand Schaefer. Prod: Universal.
Cast: Tom Mix, Naomi Judge.
Western. A crooked sheriff aids horse thieves.

TAYLOR, KRESSMAN

Address Unknown

Address Unknown
72 min.   b&w   1944
Dir: William Menzies. Prod: Columbia Pictures. Dist: Kit Parker Films.
Cast: Paul Lukas, Carl Esmond.
A businessman in Germany embraces the Nazi party, and his partner in America takes his revenge.

TAYLOR, MATT

Safari in Manhattan

More than a Secretary
77 min.   b&w   1936
Dir: Alfred E. Green. Prod: Columbia Pictures.
Cast: Jean Arthur, George Brent.
The secretary to the publisher of a health magazine falls for him.

TAYLOR, SAMUEL W.

Fever

Bait
79 min.   b&w   1954
Dir: Hugo Haas. Sp: Taylor. Prod: Columbia Pictures. Dist: Kit Parker
    Films.
Cast: Hugo Haas, Cleo Moore, John Agar.
An old prospector married to a sexy blonde tries to kill his partner.

The Man Who Came to Life

The Man Who Came to Life
6 reels   b&w   1941
Dir: Lew Landers. Sp: Gordon Rigby. Prod: Columbia Pictures.
Cast: John Howard.
A man leaves town to get a fresh start but later learns that someone is on
trial for supposedly murdering him.

A Situation of Gravity (in *Liberty Magazine*)

The Absent-Minded Professor
97 min.   b&w   1961
Dir: Robert Stevenson. Prod: Walt Disney Prod. Dist: Cine Craft, Roa's
    Films, RCA VideoDiscs (video and LV, CED)
Cast: Fred MacMurray, Nancy Olsen.
A lovable but bumbling science teacher accidentally invents an incredible
antigravity substance, which he calls "flubber." When he uses it in his Model T,
he finds it can fly. *Son of Flubber* (1962) is the sequel to this film.

TELLEZ, HERNANDO

Just Lather, That's All

Just Lather, That's All
21 min.   color   1976
Dir: John Sebert. Sp: Joan Overaker. Dist: Simon & Schuster (16 mm and
    video).
A Latin American army captain strolls into a barber shop for a shave and
begins discussing killing revolutionaries, and it becomes clear that the barber is one.

TERHUNE, ALBERT PAYSON

Driftwood (in *Redbook,* September 1918)

Daring Love
6 reels   b&w   1924   sil.
Dir: Roland G. Edwards. Adap: Roland West, Willard Mack.
Prod: Hoffman Prod.
Cast: Elaine Hammerstein, Huntley Gordon.
John, a heavy drinker, divorces his wife, reforms, and marries again.

Grand Larceny (in *Cosmopolitan Magazine,* December 1920)

> *Grand Larceny*
> 6 reels   b&w   1922   sil.
> Dir: Wallace Worsley. Prod: Metro-Goldwyn.
> Cast: Claire Windsor, Elliott Dexter.

After finding his wife in the arms of another man, John divorces her without getting an explanation.

The Hero

> *Whom the Gods Destroy*
> 7 reels   b&w   1934
> Dir: Walter Lang. Adap: Fred Niblo, Jr. Prod: Columbia Pictures.
> Cast: Robert Young, Walter Connolly, Doris Kenyon.

A theatrical producer believed dead secretly helps his son become a producer.

The Hunch (in *Redbook,* September 1920)

> *Knockout Reilly*
> 7 reels   b&w   1927   sil.
> Dir: Malcolm St. Clair. Sp: Pierre Collings, Kenneth Raisbeck. Prod: Famous Players-Lasky.
> Cast: Richard Dix, Mary Brian, Mack Renault.

A New Jersey steelworker named Dundee falls in love with Mary, sister of a defeated boxer, who then trains Dundee.

TERRETT, COURTENAY

Public Relations

> *Made on Broadway*
> 7 reels   b&w   1933
> Dir: Harry Beaumont. Sp: Gene Markey. Prod: MGM.
> Cast: Robert Montgomery, Madge Evans.

A story about the manufacture of a star through effective publicity.

TERRILL, LUCY STONE

Clothes (in *Saturday Evening Post,* August 25, 1928)

> *Clothes*
> b&w   1929
> Prod: Pathe.

Face (in *Saturday Evening Post,* 26 January 1924)

> *Unguarded Women*
> 6 reels   b&w   1924   sil.
> Dir: Alan Crosland. Prod: Famous Players-Lasky.
> Cast: Bebe Daniels, Richard Dix.

Douglas, guilt ridden for allowing his buddy to die during the war, offers to marry the dead man's widow.

THIERY, JACQUES

Yoland and the Thief (jt. author Ludwig Bemelmans)

Yoland and the Thief
110 min.　　　color　　　1945
Dir: Vincente Minelli. Prod: MGM. Dist: Films Inc.
Cast: Fred Astaire, Lucille Bremer.
The story of a con man and a little girl.

THOM, ROBERT

The Day It All Happened, Baby (in *Esquire,* December 1966)

Wild in the Streets
95 min.　　　color　　　1968
Dir: Barry Shear. Dist: Films Inc.
Cast: Christopher Jones, Shelley Winters, Ed Begley.
A liberal Congressman seeks youngsters' support, and when he wins, he offers to get the voting age lowered. But the kids pour LSD into the water supply in Washington, D.C.

THOMPKINS, JULIET WILBUR

Fanny Foley Herself

Fanny Foley Herself
1931
Prod: RKO.

THOMPSON, HAMILTON

The Ark Angel (in *Saturday Evening Post*)

The Rowdy
5 reels　　　b&w　　　1921　　　sil.
Dir: David Kirkland. Prod: Universal.
Cast: Rex Roselli, Anna Hernandez.
A retired skipper raises a child found in a storm.

THOMPSON, MARY AGNES

A Call from Mitch Miller

Loving You
101 min.　　　1957
Dir: Hal Kanton. Prod: Paramount. Dist: Warner Bros. Home Video (video).
Cast: Elvis Presley, Lizabeth Scott, Wendell Corey.
A small-town boy becomes an overnight sensation when he is signed to sing with a band.

THOMPSON, MORTON

Lewie, My Brother Who Talked to Horses

My Brother Talks to Horses
93 min.　　　b&w　　　1946

Dir: Fred Zinnemann. Sp: Morton Thompson. Prod: MGM. Dist: Films Inc.
Cast: Butch Jenkins, Peter Lawford.

A child's gift for talking to animals proves lucrative when he talks to race horses.

THURBER, JAMES

The Catbird Seat

The Battle of the Sexes
83 min.   b&w   1960
Dir: Charles Crichton. Prod: Continental. Dist: Budget Films/Video.
Cast: Peter Sellers, Constance Cummings, Robert Morely.

The Old World head of the accounting department of a Scottish firm is discomforted by a female efficiency expert.

Mr. Preble Gets Rid of His Wife

Mr. Preble Gets Rid of His Wife
17 min.   color   1982
Prod: Middlemarch Films. Dist: Direct Cinema.

Mr. Preble's daily flirtation with his secretary is finally taken seriously by both of them, and he decides to kill his wife, with humorous results.

The Night the Ghost Got In

James Thurber's The Night the Ghost Got In
16 min.   color   1977
Dir: Robert Stitzel. Dist: Phoenix Films.

While taking a bath, young James hears a noise, which his brother believes is a ghost.

The Secret Life of Walter Mitty

The Secret Life of Walter Mitty
110 min.   color   1947
Dir: Norman Z. McLeod. Prod: Metro-Goldwyn.
Cast: Danny Kaye, Virginia Mayo.

Henpecked by his mother and a finicky fiancee, Mitty dreams of sailing the Seven Seas, dogfighting the Red Baron, facing down gunmen, and other heroic feats.

Suggested by the writings of Thurber and his cartoons

The War between Men and Women
110 min.   color   1972
Dir: Melville Shavelson. Dist: "The" Film Center.
Cast: Jack Lemmon, Barbara Harris, Jason Robards.

A gruff, grumpy cartoonist who dislikes women, children, and dogs meets an attractive divorcee with three kids and a pregnant dog.

A Unicorn in the Garden

A Unicorn in the Garden
8 min.   color   1953
Prod: UPA. Dist: Simon & Schuster.
The whimsical tale of a domineering wife who tries to get her meek husband carted off to the booby-hatch because he saw a unicorn in the garden.

TILDESLEY, ALICE L.

What Can You Expect?

Short Skirts
5 reels   b&w   1921   sil.
Dir: Harry B. Harris. Prod: Universal.
Cast: Gladys Welton, Ena Gregory.
A seventeen-year-old girl tries to ruin the election of her mother's fiance.

TINSLEY, THEODORE A.

Five Spot

Panic on the Air
6 reels   b&w   1936
Dir: D. Ross Lederman. Sp: Harold Shumate. Prod: Columbia Pictures.
   Dist: Kit Parker Films.
Cast: Lew Ayres, Florence Rice.
A farfetched comedy about a sports announcer with a flair for uncovering mysteries.

Manhattan Whirligig

Manhattan Shakedown
6 reels   b&w   1937
Dir: Leon Barsha. Sp: Edgar Edwards. Prod: Warwick Pictures.
Cast: John Galloudet, Rosalind Keith.
A columnist wants to run a blackmailing doctor out of town.

TITUS, HAROLD

Stuff of Heroes

The Great Mr. Nobody (a.k.a. *Bashful Hero*)
71 min.   b&w   1941
Dir: Ben Stoloff. Prod: Warner Bros. Dist: MGM/UA Home Video (video).
Cast: Eddie Albert, Joan Leslie.
Comedy about a salesman who is perpetually in hot water.

How Baxter Butted In
7 reels   b&w   1925   sil.
Dir: William Beaudine. Adap: Julien Josephson. Prod: Warner Bros.
Cast: Dorothy Devore, Matt Moore.
A shy clerk in the circulation department of a large newspaper dreams of performing heroic deeds and falls in love with a pretty stenographer.

TOLSTOY, LEO

Father Sergius

Father Sergius (U.S.S.R.)
81 min.   b&w   1917   sil.
Dir: Yakov Protazanov. Sp: Alexander Volkow. Dist: MOMA.
Cast: Ivan Mozhukhin, Vera Dzheneyeva.
On the eve of his wedding to a beautiful woman, a handsome officer at the court of Czar Nikolai I breaks off his engagement, gives up his estate, and becomes a monk.

Martin the Cobbler

Martin the Cobbler
28 min.   color   1977
Prod: Frank Moynihan. Dist: Billy Budd Films, Mass Media.
A cobbler who has lost his family loses all interest in life and hopes to die. In a dream he hears a voice, which he assumes is the Lord's, promising to come and visit him the next day. Done in three-dimensional clay animation and available in French and Spanish.

The Three Questions

The Three Questions
14 min.   color   1984
Prod: Will Vinton. Dist: Billy Budd Films.
How a king finds the answers to three questions: Who are the most important people? What action is the best? When is the most opportune time to act? Done in animation and available in French.

TOMPKINS, JULIET

Once There Was a Princess

Misbehaving Ladies
75 min.   b&w   1931
Dir: William Beaudine. Prod: First National Pictures.
Cast: Louise Fazenda, Lila Lee, Ben Lyon.
A girl returns home incognito.

TOOHEY, JOHN PETER

On the Back Seat (in *Collier's Magazine,* 12 September 1925)

Outcast Souls
6 reels   b&w   1928   sil.
Dir: Louis Chaudet. Prod: Sterling Pictures.
Cast: Pricilla Bonner, Charles Delaney.
A husband's father and his wife's mother meet and fall in love after trying unsuccessfully to live with their children.

TORS, IVAN

Jumpin' Joe

> *Below the Deadline*
> 7 reels   b&w   1946
> Dir: William Beaudine. Sp: Harvey H. Gates, Forrest Judd. Prod: Monogram
>   Pictures.
> A returning G.I. gets involved in the rackets.

TRAVEN, BRUNO

The Third Guest

> *Macario* (Mex.)
> 90 min.   1960
> Dir: Roberto Gavaldon. Prod: Azteca Films.
> Cast: Ignacio Lopez Tarso, Pina Pellicer.

A hungry peasant refuses to share food with God and the Devil but shares it
with Death, who cures the dying when willing. Nominated for an Academy Award
in 1960 in the Foreign Language Film Category.

TREYNOR, ALBERT

Highway Robber

> *It's a Small World*
> 7 reels   b&w   1935
> Dir: Irving Cummings. Sp: Gladys Lehman, Sam Hellman. Prod: Fox.
> Cast: Spencer Tracy, Wendy Barrie.

Two St. Louis big-timers who smash their cars near a small Louisiana town
are stranded there.

TRUMBELL, WALTER (see *Bits of Life* under WILEY, HUGH)

TUPPER, TRISTRAM

Four Brothers (in *Saturday Evening Post*, 7 April 1928)

> *First Kiss*
> 6 reels   b&w   1929   sil.
> Dir: Rowland V. Lee. Prod: Paramount/Famous Players-Lasky.
> Cast: Fay Wray, Gary Cooper, Land Chandler.

The Talbot family is going downhill, so to finance an education for his
brothers, the second son decides to rob ships in the Chesapeake Bay.

Three Episodes in the Life of Timothy Osborn (in *Saturday Evening Post*,
     9 April 1927)

> *Lucky Star*
> 10 reels   b&w   1929   sil. or sd.
> Dir: Frank Borzage. Prod: Fox.
> Cast: Charles Farrell, Janet Gaynor.

After World War I, a farm girl chooses a disabled veteran over a war hero
against the wishes of her mother.

TURGENEV, IVAN
Bezhin Meadow

Bezhin Meadow
30 min.   b&w   1935
Dir: Sergei Eisenstein. Dist: Audio Brandon.
Cast: E. Vitka, Boris Zakhava, Yelena Teleshova.
A story about the gallant work of Russian youths on a collective farm and one who is shot down by his father, a mad saboteur.

First Love

First Love
90 min.   color   1970
Dir: Maximillian Schell. Prod: Maximillian Schell, Barry Levinson. Dist: Audio Brandon, Video Communications (video).
Cast: Maximillian Schell, Dominique Sanda, John Moulder Brown.
During an era of social decay and impending revolution, a sixteen-year-old boy becomes infatuated with an impoverished princess.

Mumu

Mumu
71 min.   b&w   1960
Dir: Anatoli Bobrovsky, Yevgeni Teterin. Dist: Audio Brandon.
Cast: Afanasi Kochetkov, Nina Gregeshkova, Leonid Kmit.
Gerasim, the huge, powerful deaf mute, is a village serf who loves the land, his work, and the people around him. When his mistress decides to take him to Moscow, he is lonely and seeks out the company of Vanya, a laundress, and takes comfort in his puppy Mumu, which is taken from him.

TURNER, GEORGE KIBBE
Compassionate

Half Marriage
7 reels   b&w   1929   sil. or sd.
Dir: William J. Cowen. Prod: RKO.
Cast: Olive Borden, Morgan Farley.
Following a party, Judy Page elopes with Dick Carroll, who is employed by her father.

A Passage to Hong Kong

Roar of the Dragon (s.m. also a story by Marian C. Cooper and Jane Bigelow)
8 reels   b&w   1932
Dir: Wesley Ruggles. Sp: Howard Estabrook. Prod: RKO.
The American captain of an Oriental steamship defends the foreign population from a murderous bandit.

The Street of Forgotten Men (in *Liberty Magazine,* 14 February 1925)

The Street of Forgotten Men
7 reels   b&w   1925   sil.
Dir: Herbert Brenon. Prod: Famous Players-Lasky.
Cast: Grace Fleming.
Charlie disguises himself as handicapped.

TUTTLE, W.C.

Baa, Baa Black Sheep

Black Sheep
5 reels   b&w   1921   sil.
Dir: Paul Hurst. Prod: Chaudet-Hurst Prod.
Cast: Neal Hart, Ted Brooks.
A complicated western about cattlemen versus sheepmen.

The Devil's Dooryard (in *Adventure Magazine,* 3 May 1921)

The Devil's Dooryard
5 reels   b&w   1923   sil.
Dir: Lewis King. Prod: Ben Wilson Prod.
Cast: William Fairbanks, Ena Gregory.
Western melodrama. Paul Stevens recovers stolen money.

Fate of the Wolf (in *Short Stories,* 25 June 1925)

Driftin' Sands
5 reels   b&w   1928   sil.
Dir: Wallace W. Fox. Adap: Oliver Drake. Prod: FBO Pictures.
Cast: Bob Steele, Gladys Quartaro.
Western. A wealthy Mexican hires Driftin' Sands to guard his daughter.

Henry Goes to Arizona

Henry Goes to Arizona (a.k.a. *Spats to Spurs*)
7 reels   b&w   1939
Dir: Edwin Marin. Sp: Florence Ryerson, Milton Merlin. Prod: Loew's.
Cast: Frank Morgan.
Henry is a rent-beating vaudevillian who heads West.

The Law Rustlers (in *Adventure Magazine,* 1 September 1921)

The Law Rustlers
5 reels   b&w   1923   sil.
Dir: Lewis King. Prod: Ben Wilson Prod.
Cast: William Fairbanks, Edmund Cobb.
On their way to Alaska, a pair of drifters help a young woman stand up to a corrupt town council.

Peaceful (in *Short Stories*)

Peaceful Peters
5 reels   b&w   1922   sil.
Dir: Lewis King. Prod: Ben Wilson Prod.
Cast: William Fairbanks, Harry La Mont.
Western. The last words of a dying prospector bring danger, excitement, romance, and fortune to Peaceful Peters.

The Redhead from Sun Dog

The Red Rider (a 15-part series)
2 reels ea.   b&w   1934
Dir: Lew Landers. Prod: Universal.
Cast: William Fairbanks.
Western. A sheriff sacrifices his job when he lets his friend, a convicted murderer, out of jail and sets off to find the real killer.

The Sheriff of Sun Dog (in *Adventure Magazine*, 30 November 1921)

The Sheriff of Sun Dog
50 min.   b&w   1922   sil.
Dir: Lewis King. Prod: Berwilla Film.
Cast: William Fairbanks, Robert McKenzie.
Western. Sheriff "Silvent" Davidson is framed.

Sir Piegan Passes

Cheyenne Kid
6 reels   b&w   1933
Dir: Robert Hill. Sp: Jack Curtis. Dist: Penguin Video (video).
Cast: Tom Keene.
Western. A danger-loving cowboy is mistaken for a killer.

The Fargo Kid
64 min.   b&w   1940
Prod: RKO.
Cast: Tim Holt.
Western. The Fargo Kid outwits a professional gunman.

Spawn of the Desert (in *Short Stories*, 10 May 1922)

Spawn of the Desert
5 reels   b&w   1923   sil.
Dir: Lewis King. Prod: Berwilla Film.
Cast: William Fairbanks, Florence Gilbert.
Western. Le Saint searches for the man who destroyed his home.

Straight Shooting (in *Short Stories*)

The Border Sheriff
56 min.   b&w   1926   sil.

Dir: Robert North Bradbury. Prod: Universal. Dist: Em Gee Film Library.
Cast: Jack Hoxie.

After leaving a conference on drug smuggling in Washington, Cultus Collins, the sheriff of Cayuse County, goes to San Francisco to rescue a millionaire rancher from a Chinatown dive.

The Yellow Seal (in *Liberty Magazine,* 10 January 1925)

The Prairie Pirate
50 min.   b&w   1925   sil.
Dir: Edmund Mortimer. Adap: Anthony Dillon. Dist: Film Classic Exchange.
Cast: Harry Carey, Jean Dumas.

Western tale of murder, revenge, and romance as a bandit and a gambler battle over a woman.

TWAIN, MARK

The Celebrated Jumping Frog of Calaveras County

The Best Man Wins
75 min.   b&w   1948
Prod: Columbia Pictures.
Cast: Edgar Buchanan, Anna Lee.

A man who returns home after many years raises money by jumping his
frog.

The Jumping Frog
24 min.   color
Dist: MTI Teleprograms (video).
A modern-day version.

The Legend of Mark Twain
32 min.   color   1969
Prod: ABC News. Dist: Benchmark Films.

Recounts the life of Twain and includes a dramatization of this story and segments of "The Adventures of Huckleberry Finn."

Mark Twain
20 min.   color   1983
Prod: Auburn Television. Dist: AIT (video).

Sketches of his life, the story, and scenes from "The Adventures of Huckleberry Finn" and "The Innocents Abroad."

The Diary of Adam and Eve

The Diary of Adam and Eve
15 min.   color   1978
Prod: Instructional Television Coop. Dist: Indiana University (16 mm and video).
A humorous retelling of the Biblical story.

The Diary
26 min.   color   1981
Dir: Will Vinton. Dist: Billy Budd Films.
Clay animation in which Adam is not fond of Eve until they are expelled.

The Man That Corrupted Hadleyburg

The Man That Corrupted Hadleyburg
40 min.   color   1980
Dir: Ralph Rosenblum. Dist: Coronet Films (16 mm and video).
A stranger rebuffed by the townspeople decides to get even by showing them that they are not as honest as they claim.

The Million Pound Bank Note

Man With a Million (Br.)
90 min.   color   1953
Dir: Ronald Neame. Sp: Jill Craigie. Prod: Group Film Prod. Dist: MGM/UA
     Home Video (video).
Cast: Gregory Peck, A.E. Matthews.
An impoverished American stranded in London comes into possession of a million-pound bank note that no one can change.

U

ULMAN, WILLIAM A., JR.

A Gun in His Hand

Sergeant Madden
8 reels   b&w   1939
Dir: Josepf von Sternberg. Sp: Wells Root. Prod: MGM. Dist: Films Inc.
Cast: Wallace Beery, Laraine Day.
A bad cop story.

UPDIKE, JOHN

The Music School

The Music School
30 min.   color   1977
Dir. and Sp: John Korty. Dist: Coronet Films (16 mm and video).
A contemporary writer struggles during a 24-hour period to find meaning in his life and then takes his daughter to music school.

UPSON, WILLIAM HAZLETT

A series of unidentified stories (in *Saturday Evening Post*)

Earthworm Tractors
69 min.   b&w   1936
Dir: Ray Enright. Prod: First National Pictures and Vitaphone.
Cast: Joe E. Brown, June Travis.
Salesman Alexander Botts blunders into trouble.

V

VADNAI (a.k.a. VADNAY), LADISLAUS

Josette

> *Josette* (s.m. "Jo and Josette," a play by Paul Frank and George Fraser,
> which in turn was based on the story)
> 63 min.   b&w   1938
> Dir: Allan Swan. Sp: James Edward Grant. Prod: Twentieth Century Fox.
> Cast: Simone Simon, Robert Young, Don Ameche.
> Two brothers pressure the wrong girl.

VANCE, HENRY C.

Pin Money (in *Snappy Stories*, 2 December 1921)

> *Diamond Handcuffs*
> 6,070'   b&w   1928   sil.
> Dir: John P. McCarthy. Adap: Willis Goldbeck. Prod: Cosmopolitan Pictures.
> Cast: Lena Malena, Charles Stevens, Conrad Nagel.
> Three episodes about a cursed diamond.

VANCE, LOUIS JOSEPH

Lone Wolf in Paris

> *Lone Wolf in Paris*
> 7 reels   b&w   1938
> Dir: Albert S. Rogell. Sp: Arthur T. Horman. Prod: Columbia Pictures.
> Cast: Francis Lederer, Francis Drake.

Rival Thieves. Note: The Lone Wolf, a jewel thief, was a character who
appeared in a number of novels and stories as well as in original screen stories. The
Lone Wolf films include *Last of the Lone Wolf, The Lone Wolf and His Lady,
The Lone Wolf in London, The Lone Wolf in Mexico, The Lone Wolf Meets a Lady,
The Lone Wolf Returns, Lone Wolf Spy Hunt, The Lone Wolf Strikes, The Lone
Wolf Takes a Chance,* and *The Lone Wolf's Laughter.*

VAN LOAN, CHARLES E.

Scrap Iron (in *Saturday Evening Post*)

> *Scrap Iron*
> 7 reels   b&w   1921   sil.
> Dir: Charles Ray. Adap: Finis Fox. Prod: Charles Ray.
> Cast: Charles Ray, Lydia Knott.

A mill worker gives up amateur boxing at the request of his invalid mother and is ostracized by co-workers and his girlfriend.

VAN RIPPER, DONALD

Dying Lips

Sealed Lips (s.m. the radio show "Street and Smith's Detective Story Magazine Hour")
17 min.   b&w
Dir: Kurt Neuman. Sp: Samuel Freedman. Prod: Universal. Dist: Ivy Films.

VONNEGUT, KURT, JR.

Next Door

Next Door
24 min.   color   1975
Dir: Andrew Silver. Dist: Phoenix Films (16 mm and video).
The parents of an eight-year-old boy forget to call the sitter and go to the movies anyway.

VROMAN, MARY ELIZABETH

See How They Run

Bright Road
69 min.   b&w   1953
Dir: Gerald Mayer. Prod: MGM. Dist: Films Inc.
Cast: Dorothy Dandridge, Harry Belafonte.
A story about a problem pupil.

Next Door
Photograph courtesy of Phoenix/BFA Films and Video

WALLACE, EDGAR

Criminal at Large (s.m. also the play by Wallace)

> *Criminal at Large* (Br. title *The Frightened Lady*)
> 70 min.   b&w   1932
> Dir: T. Hayes Hunter. Prod: Gainsborough and Helber.
> Cast: Emlyn Williams, Cathleen Nesbit, Norman McKinnel.
> A man commits murder during spells of insanity.

Death Watch

> *Before Dawn*
> 60 min.   b&w   1933
> Dir: Irving Pichel. Sp: Garret Fort, Marian Dix, Ralph Block.
> Cast: Stuart Erwin, Dorothy Wilson, Warner Oland.
> A clairvoyant girl is mixed up in murders.

The Feathered Serpent

> *The Menace*
> 70 min.   color   1932
> Dir: Roy Chanslor. Adap: Charles Logue. Prod: Columbia Pictures.
> Cast: Bette Davis.

The Greek Poropulos

> *Born to Gamble*
> 8 reels   b&w   1935
> Dir: Phil Rosen. Prod: Liberty Pictures.

WALPOLE, HUGH

The Silver Mask (s.m. based on the play "Kind Lady" by Edward Chodorov, which in turn was based on the story)

> *Kind Lady*
> 78 min.   b&w   1951
> Dir: John Sturges. Prod: MGM. Dist: Films Inc.
> Cast: Ethel Barrymore, Maurice Evans, Angela Lansbury, Keenan Wynn.
> A wealthy old lady befriends a charming artist, who, by a clever ruse, gets
into her home and with several of his friends keeps her prisoner while they sell off
her possessions.

WALSH, MAURICE

Green Rushes

The Quiet Man
129 min.   color   1952
Dir: John Ford. Prod: Republic Pictures. Dist: Blackhawk (video).
Cast: John Wayne, Maureen O'Hara, Barry Fitzgerald, Ward Bond.
A boxer returns to Ireland and courts a fiery woman. Nominated for an Academy Award as the Best Written American Comedy.

WALSH, THOMAS

Homecoming (suggestion for)

Don't Turn 'em Loose
65 min.   b&w   1936
Dir: Ben Stoloff. Sp: Harry Segall, Ferdinand Reyher. Prod: RKO.
Cast: Lewis Stone, Bruce Cabot, Betty Grable.
Parole board member watches his own son become a criminal.

Husk

We're Only Human
7 reels   b&w   1936
Dir: James Flood. Sp: Rian James. Prod: RKO.
Cast: Preston Flood, Jane Wyatt.
A detective loses his job when he lets a bandit escape, but he eventually clears himself.

WARE, LEON

The Search

In Self-Defense
1947
Prod: Monogram Pictures.

WATKINS, MARY T.

Stolen Thunder (in *Saturday Evening Post,* 7 June 1930)

Oh, for a Man!
9 reels   b&w   1930
Dir: Hamilton MacFadden. Prod: Fox.
Cast: Jeanette MacDonald, Reginald Denny.
An opera singer falls for and marries a former burglar with the intention of making a singer out of him.

WAUGH, ALEX

Small Back Room in St. Marylebone (in *Esquire,* March 1953)

Circle of Deception (Br.)
100 min.   b&w   1961

Dir: Jack Lee. Prod: Twentieth Century Fox. Dist: Select Film Library, Willoughby-Peerless.
Cast: Bradford Dillman, Suzy Parker.
An intelligence agent on a dangerous mission in Germany gets caught.

WEBB, JAMES R.

A Baby for Midge

Close to My Heart
90 min.   b&w   1951
Dir: William Keighley. Prod: Warner Bros.
Cast: Gene Tierney, Ray Milland, Fay Bainter.
A soap opera about a couple who adopt the child of a convicted murderer.

Fugitive from Terror (magazine serial)

Woman in Hiding
92 min.   b&w   1950
Dir: Michael Gordon. Sp: Oscar Saul. Prod: Universal.
Cast: Ida Lupino, Howard Duff.
A woman pretends she was killed in a car crash in order to prove that her husband killed her father.

WEIDMAN, JEROME

R.S.V.P.

Invitation
84 min.   b&w   1952
Dir: Gottfried Reinhardt. Sp: Paul Osborn. Prod: MGM. Dist: Films Inc.
Cast: Van Johnson, Dorothy McGuire.
A rich father bribes a young man to marry his daughter, who has only one year to live.

WEIMAN, RITA

Curtain (in *Saturday Evening Post*)

Curtain
5 reels   b&w   1927   sil.
Dir. and Adap: James Young. Prod: Katharine MacDonald Picture Corp.

Footlights (in *Saturday Evening Post,* 17 May 1919)

The Spotlight
5 reels   b&w   1927   sil.
Dir: Frank Tuttle. Prod: Paramount/Famous Players-Lasky.
Cast: Esther Ralston, Neil Hamilton.
Romantic drama about an obscure actress who rises to stardom by pretending to be an exotic Russian.

On Your Back (in *Liberty Magazine,* 22 February 1930)

> *On Your Back*
> 8 reels   b&w   1930
> Dir: Guthrie McClintic. Prod: Fox.
> Cast: Irene Rich, Raymond Hackett.
> A college student becomes engaged to a showgirl who is having an affair
with a powerful broker in business with his mother.

One Man's Secret

> *Possessed*
> 108 min.   b&w   1949
> Dir: Curtis Bernhardt. Prod: Warner Bros. Dist: MGM/UA Home Video (video)
>   (video).
> The dramatic story of a pretty schizophrenic who is entangled in a love
triangle and becomes involved in a murder case.

The Stage Door

> *After the Show*
> 6 reels   b&w   1921   sil.
> Dir: William De Mille. Prod: Famous Players-Lasky.
> Cast: Jack Holt, Lila Lee, Charles Ogle, Eve Southern.
> Pop O'Malley, a stage doorkeeper, takes a paternal interest in Eileen, a
chorus girl, and objects when the millionaire backer of the show also takes an
interest in her.

To Whom It May Concern (in *Cosmopolitan Magazine,* February 1922)

> *The Social Code*
> 5 reels   b&w   1923   sil.
> Dir: Oscar Apfel. Prod: Metro-Goldwyn.
> Cast: Viola Dana, Malcolm McGregor.
> A girl saves her lover from the electric chair.

WELCH, DOUGLAS

We Go Fast

> *We Go Fast*
> 59 min.   b&w   1941
> Dir: William McGann. Prod: Twentieth Century Fox.
> Cast: Marjorie Weaver, John Hubbard.
> Ten people sign a pact whereby $200,000 goes to the last survivor.

WELLS, H(erbert) G(eorge)

The Man Who Could Work Miracles

> *The Man Who Could Work Miracles* (Br.)
> 82 min.   b&w   1937
> Dir: Alexander Korda. Prod: London Film Prod. Dist: Budget Films/Video,
>   Mogull's Films.

Cast: Roland Young, Joan Gardner.

An obscure little clerk in a small English country town discovers he has the power to work miracles. When this power is abused, the world is on the brink of disaster.

WEST, REBECCA

Abiding Vision

A Life of Her Own
108 min.   b&w   1950
Dir: George Cukor. Sp: Isobel Lennart. Prod: MGM. Dist: Films Inc.
Cast: Lana Turner, Ray Milland, Ann Dvorak.

A story about two photographic models—one on her way up, the other on her way down.

WEST, WALTON

Big Bend Buckaroo

Riding Avenger
50 min.   b&w   1936
Dir: Harry Fraser. Prod: Walter Futter.
Cast: Hoot Gibson.
Western.

WESTMAN, LOLITA ANN

Lawless Honeymoon

The Perfect Clue
7 reels   b&w   1935
Dir: Robert G. Vignola. Adap: Albert De Mond. Prod: Majestic Producers.
Cast: David Manners, Skeets Gallagher.
A too-perfect clue almost thwarts the detectives.

WESTON, GARNETT

Mounted Patrol (a serial in *Saturday Evening Post,* 7-14 April 1951)

Pony Soldier
82 min.   b&w   1952
Dir: Joseph M. Newman. Prod: Twentieth Century Fox. Dist: Films Inc.
Cast: Tyrone Power, Cameron Mitchell, Robert Horton.
A Mountie tries to stop a tribe of rebellious Indians from waging war.

WESTON, GEORGE

The Open Door (in *Saturday Evening Post,* 8 January 1921)

Is Life Worth Living?
5 reels   b&w   1921   sil.
Dir: Alan Crosland. Prod: Selznick Pictures.
Cast: Eugene O'Brian, Winifred Westover.

A man on parole for a crime he didn't commit becomes a salesman, but he can't succeed and thinks about killing himself.

Taxi! Taxi! (in *Saturday Evening Post,* 25 July-8 August 1925)

> *Taxi! Taxi!*
> 7 reels   b&w   1927   sil.
> Dir: Melville W. Brown. Prod: Universal.
> Cast: Edward Everett Horton, Marian Nixon.
> Romantic farce in which a murder is committed in a taxi.

WETJEN, RICHARD ALBERT

Wallaby Jim of the Islands

> *Wallaby Jim of the Islands*
> 7 reels   b&w   1937
> Dir: Charles Lamont. Sp: Bennet Cohen, Houston Branch. Prod: Edward L.
>   Alperson. Dist: Mogull's Films.
> Cast: Ian Keith, George Houston.
> Pearl pirates roam the waters of the South Seas.

WHARTON, EDITH

The Dilettante

> *The Dilettante*
> 15 min.   color   1978
> Prod: International Instructional Television Coop. Dist: Indiana University
>   (16 mm and video).

A look at the "life of manners" characteristic of the upper class at the turn of the century.

WHEELIS, ALLEN

The Illusionless Man and the Visionary Maid (in *Commentary,* May 1964)

> *The Crazy Quilt*
> 80 min.   b&w   1967
> Dir: John Korty. Prod: Continental. Dist: Budget Films/Video, Kit Parker
>   Films.
> Cast: Tom Rosqui, Ina Mela.

A story about the 50-year marriage of a pragmatic man and a romantic dreamer.

WHITE, E.B.

A Preposterous Parable

> *The Family That Dwelt Apart*
> 8 min.   color   1973
> Prod: National Film Board of Canada. Dist: Simon & Schuster (16 mm and
>   video).

A tall, salty, animated Yankee story about a family done in by do-gooders. The Pruitt family, seven members strong, lives in euphoric independence on an island off the New Hampshire coast until they are marooned by a winter freeze and the mainlanders mount a massive campaign to save them.

WHITE, LESLIE T.

Five Thousand Trojan Horses

Northern Pursuit
94 min.   b&w   1942
Dir: Raoul Walsh. Prod: First National Pictures.
Cast: Errol Flynn, Julie Bishop.
A Canadian Mountie pursues a Nazi.

Six Weeks South of Texas (a.k.a. Trouble in Paradise, a magazine serial)

The Americano
85 min.   color   1954
Dir: William Castle. Sp: Guy Trosper. Prod: Robert Stillman Prod. Dist: Budget Films/Video, Ivy Films.
Cast: Glenn Ford, Frank Lovejoy, Cesar Romero.
A Texan delivering three bulls to cattlemen in Brazil becomes involved in a feud.

WHITE, NELIA GARDNER

The Little Horse

Sentimental Journey
55 min.   b&w   1946
Dir: Walter Land. Prod: Twentieth Century Fox. Dist: Films Inc.
Cast: Maureen O'Hara.

The Gift of Love
105 min.   color   1958
Dir: Jean Negulesco. Prod: Twentieth Century Fox. Dist: Films Inc.
Cast: Lauren Bacall, Robert Stack.
After the death of his wife, a man adopts a precocious child who tries desperately to fill the void in his life.

WHITE, STEWART EDWARD

Leopard Woman

Leopard Woman
77 min.   b&w   1920   sil.
Dir: Wesley Ruggles. Dist: Em Gee Film Library.
Cast: Louise Glaum.
An epic of passion, intrigue, and espionage in the Equatorial jungle.

The Shepper-Newfounder (in *Saturday Evening Post,* 29 March 1930)

Part-Time Wife
6,500'   b&w   1930

Dir: Leo McCarey. Prod: Fox.

Cast: Edmund Lowe, Leila Hyams.

A husband who is married to his business activities is reunited with his estranged wife on the golf course.

The Two Gun Man (in *Famous Story Magazine,* October 1925)

Under a Texas Moon
8 reels   tinted   1930
Dir: Michael Curtiz. Sp: Gordon Rigby. Prod: Warner Bros.
Cast: Frank Fay, Raquel Torres.
Western. A dashing Mexican adventurer captures rustlers and wins the heart of his girl.

WHITFIELD, RAOUL

Inside Job

High Tide
70 min.   b&w   1947
Dir: John Reinhardt. Prod: Monogram Pictures.
Cast: Don Castle, Lee Tracy, Anabel Shaw.
A newspaperman combats corruption.

WHITTAKER, WAYNE

Chicago Lulu

The Bamboo Blonde
67 min.   b&w   1946
Dir: Anthony Mann. Prod: RKO. Dist: Films Inc.
Cast: Frances Langford.
A South Pacific pilot names his bomber after a nightclub singer, bringing her fame.

WHITTIER, JOHN GREENLEAF

The Barefoot Boy

The Barefoot Boy
6 reels   b&w   1923   sil.
Dir: David Kirkland. Prod: Mission Films.
Cast: John Bowers, Marjorie Daw, Sylvia Breamer.
Mistreated by his stepfather and wrongly accused of setting fire to the school, Dick runs away.

WHITTINGTON, HARRY

Wyoming Wildcatters

Black Gold
98 min.   color   1961
Dir: Leslie Martinson. Prod: Warner Bros.
Cast: Philip Care, Diane McGain, James Best.
An adventurer stakes everything on the chance of striking oil.

WILBUR, RICHARD

A Game of Catch

A Game of Catch
7 min.   color   1974
Dir: Steven K. Witty. Dist: Audio Brandon.
Two young boys exclude one another from their games.

WILDE, OSCAR

The Canterville Ghost

The Canterville Ghost
95 in.   b&w   1944
Dir: Jules Dassin. Prod: MGM. Dist: Films Inc.
Cast: Robert Young, Charles Laughton.
Condemned for his cowardice, a ghost must haunt the ancestral castle until someone in the family line performs a heroic act.

The Canterville Ghost
15 min.   b&w   1955
Prod: Dynamic Films.
Cast: Monty Woolley.
A modern version of the story about a weary ghost and children.

The Happy Prince

The Happy Prince
25 min.   color   1974
Pood: Reader's Digest. Dist: Pyramid Films (16 mm and video).
A swallow strips the gold off a statue of a prince to help the poor.

Lord Arthur Saville's Crime (s.m. also two unidentified stories, one by Laslo Vadnai and the other by Ellis St. Joseph)

Flesh and Fantasy
94 min.   b&w   1942
Dir: Julien Duvivier. Prod: Universal. Dist: Alan Twyman Presents.
Cast: Edward G. Robinson, Charles Boyer, Barbara Stanwyck, Robert Benchley, Robert Cummings, Betty Field, Thomas Mitchell.
The theme of superstition links three stories: one depicts the ugly duckling fable; in another, a man is obsessed by murder; and the third concerns the inner struggle of a superstitious circus performer.

The Nightengale and the Rose

The Nightengale and the Rose
14 min.   color   1967
Dir: Joseph Karbert.
A two-dimensional animated version.

The Remarkable Rocket

The Remarkable Rocket
25 min.   color   1975
Prod: Reader's Digest. Dist: Pyramid Films (16 mm and video).
Narrator: David Niven.
A witty animated story about the fireworks ready to be set off during a royal wedding ceremony.

The Selfish Giant

The Selfish Giant
27 min.   color   1972
Prod: Reader's Digest. Dist: Benchmark Films, Pyramid Films.
A giant won't let the children play in his garden; therefore, Spring is kept away.

WILDE, PERCIVAL

The Extreme Airiness of Duton Lang

The Rise of Duton Lang
7 min.   color   1955
Dir: Osmond Evans. Prod: Bosustow.

WILEY, HUGH

Hop (s.m. also the short story "The Man Who Heard Everything" by Walter Trumbell in *Smart Set*, April 1921)

Bits of Life
6 reels   b&w   1921   sil.
Dir: A. Marshall Neilan. Prod: First National Pictures.
Cast: Wesley Barry, Rockliffe Fellowes.
Four episodes about good versus evil.

James Lee Wong stories and character

Doomed to Die
67 min.   b&w   1940
Dir: William Nigh. Prod: Monogram Pictures. Dist: Budget Films/Video,
     Reel Images, Cable Films (video), Discount Video Tapes, Penguin Video.
Cast: Boris Karloff, Marjorie Reynolds, Grant Withers.
James Lee Wong joins the police in solving a murder in order to prevent a Tong war while tracking down stolen bonds.

The Fatal Hour
68 min.   b&w   1940
Dir: William Nigh. Prod: Monogram Pictures. Dist: MGM/UA Home Video
     (video).
Cast: Boris Karloff.

Mr. Wong, Detective
69 min.   b&w   1938
Dir: William Nigh. Prod: Monogram Pictures. Dist: Budget Films/Video,
    Hollywood Home Theater (video).
Cast: Boris Karloff, Grant Withers.
Wong traps a killer who acts guilty to avoid suspicion.

Mr. Wong in Chinatown
70 min.   b&w   1939
Dir: William Nigh. Prod: Monogram Pictures.
Cast: Boris Karloff, Grant Withers.

The Spoils of War (in *Saturday Evening Post,* 9 May 1925)

Behind the Front
50 min.   b&w   1926   sil.
Dir: Edward Sutherland. Prod: Paramount. Dist: Em Gee Film Library.
Cast: Mary Brian.
Misadventures at the front, where a couple of wise guys try to make the war
go the way they want it to go.

WILKINSON, RODERICK (see *Three Cases of Murder* under MAUGHAM, W.
    SOMERSET)

WILLIAMS, BEN AMES

More Stately Mansions (in *Good Housekeeping,* October-November 1920)

Extravagance
6 reels   b&w   1921   sil.
Dir: Philip E. Rosen. Prod: Metro Pictures.
Cast: May Allison, Robert Edeson.
A young lawyer finds that his wife's extravagant tastes are beyond his
financial means and forges a check to obtain money.

Prodigal's Daughter

Someone to Remember
8 reels   b&w   1943
Dir: Robert Siodmak. Sp: Frances Hyland. Prod: Republic Pictures.

Johnny Trouble
80 min.   b&w   1957
Dir: John H. Auer. Prod: Clarion Enterprises, rel. Warner Bros.
Cast: Stuart Whitman, Ethel Barrymore.
A guy on the road turns over a new leaf when he meets a woman who has
never given up hope that her long-lost son will return. A remake of *Someone to
Remember.*

Three in a Thousand (in *Argosy All-Story Weekly Magazine,* 20 October 1917)

The Fighting Lover
5 reels   b&w   1921   sil.
Dir: Fred Leroy Granville. Prod: Universal.
Cast: Frank Mayo, Elinor Hancock.
Andrew bets his friend $10,000 that he will fall in love with one of three girls.

A Very Practical Joke (in *Saturday Evening Post,* 5 December 1925)

Man Trouble
8 reels   b&w   1930
Dir: Berthold Viertel. Adap: George M. Watters, Marion Orth. Prod:
    Fox.
Cast: Milton Sills, Dorothy Mackaill.
Against the wishes of her bootlegger boyfriend, a cabaret singer falls in love with a newspaper columnist.

Inside Story
87 min.   b&w   1938
Dir: Allan Swan. Prod: Twentieth Century Fox.
Cast: William Lundigan, Marsha Hunt.
On a bank holiday during the Depression, a $1,000 bill is suddenly put into circulation.

WILLIAMS, GENE

Sticky My Fingers, Fleet My Feet (in *The New Yorker*)

Sticky My Fingers, Fleet My Feet
23 min.   color   1973
Prod: American Film Institute. Dist: Time-Life Video.
Norman, a fortyish executive addicted to Sunday touch football, is drawn to New York's Central Park to engage in ritual combat with his friends. But their dreams of glory turn to dust when a fifteen-year-old boy is allowed to join the game. Academy Award nomination.

WILLIAMS, JESSE L.

Not Wanted (s.m. also "Too Many Parents," an unpublished story by George
    Templeton)

Too Many Parents
75 min.   b&w   1936
Prod: Paramount.
Cast: Frances Farmer, Billy Lee.
Story about a group of boys at a military academy.

WILLIAMS, MONA

May the Best Man Win

> *Woman's World*
> 94 min.   color   1954
> Dir: Jean Negulesco. Prod: Twentieth Century Fox. Dist: Films Inc.
> Cast: Lauren Bacall, Clifton Webb, June Allyson.
> A story about the world of fashion.

WILLIAMS, TENNESSEE

Man, Bring This Up Road (s.m. based on the play, "The Milk Train Doesn't Stop Here Anymore," which in turn was based on the story)

> *Boom* (It.)
> 110 min.   color   1968
> Dir: Joseph Losey. Prod: Universal.
> Cast: Elizabeth Taylor, Richard Burton, Noel Coward.

In her private kingdom on an unnamed Mediterranean Island, Flora Goforth, who has driven six husbands to the grave, builds a fortress against death, and then in comes Chris Flander, nicknamed the "Angel of Death."

WILLIAMSON, ALICE MURIEL

Honeymoon Hate (in *Saturday Evening Post,* 9-16 July 1927)

> *Honeymoon Hate*
> 6 reels   b&w   1927   sil.
> Dir: Luther Reed. Prod: Paramount/Famous Players-Lasky.
> Cast: Florence Vidor, Tullio Carminati, William Austin.

The impetuous daughter of a wealthy steel magnate demands the Imperial Suite in a hotel in Venice, and she is escorted around the city by a prince.

WILLSON, DIXIE

God Gave Me Twenty Cents (in *Cosmopolitan Magazine*)

> *God Gave Me Twenty Cents*
> 7 reels   b&w   1926   sil.
> Dir: Herbert Brenon. Adap: John Russell. Prod: Famous Players-Lasky.
> Cast: Lois Moran, Jack Mulhall.
> The story of the whirlwind courtship and marriage of a sailor.

Help Yourself to Hay (in *Hearst's International Magazine*)

> *Three-Ring Marriage*
> 6 reels   b&w   1928   sil.
> Dir: Marshall Neilan. Prod: First National Pictures.
> Wealthy Ann joins the circus.

Here Y' Are Brother

Here Y' Are Brother
7 reels   b&w   1927   sil.
Dir: Millard Webb. Prod: First National Pictures.
Cast: Lewis Stone, Billie Dove, Lloyd Hughes.
An inventor returns to his wife with the help of his friend.

WILSON, JOHN FLEMING

The Man Who Married His Own Wife (in *Hearst's International Magazine*) (jt. author Mary Ashe Miller)

The Man Who Married His Own Wife
5 reels   b&w   1922   sil.
Dir: Stuart Paton. Prod: Universal.
Cast: Frank Mayo, Sylvia Breamer.
A disfigured sea captain married to the heiress he once rescued undergoes plastic surgery, only to find that his wife loved him as he was.

The Salving of John Somers (in *Everybody's Magazine*)

The Bonded Woman
6 reels   b&w   1922   sil.
Dir: Philip E. Rosen. Prod: Famous Players-Lasky.
Cast: Betty Compson, John Bowers.
Angela rehabilitates a drunken first mate and gives him money to buy a ship.

WINTER, LOUISE

The Mad Dancer (in *Young's Magazine,* December 1924)

The Mad Dancer
7 reels   b&w   1925   sil.
Dir: Burton King. Prod: Jans Prod.
Cast: Ann Pennington, Johnny Walker.
A woman's romance with the son of a U.S. senator is threatened when a sculptor unveils a nude statue of her.

WITNER, H.C.

Cain and Mabel

The Great White Way
10 reels   tinted   1924   sil.
Dir: E. Mason Hopper. Prod: Cosmopolitan Pictures.
Cast: Anita Stewart, Tom Lewis.
A press agent links romatically the names of his two most popular clients, a fighter and a Follies dancer, and they later really fall in love.

Cain and Mabel
90 min.   b&w   1936
Dir: Lloyd Bacon. Prod: Warner Bros. Dist: MGM/UA Home Video (video).

Cast: Clark Gable, Marion Davies, Allen Jenkins.
A musical comedy star tangles with a boxing champion over a publicity stunt.

WODEHOUSE, P.G.

The Small Bachelor (in *Liberty Magazine,* 18 September-25 December 1926)

The Small Bachelor
7 reels   b&w   1927   sil.
Dir: William A. Seiter. Prod: Universal.
Cast: Barbara Kent, Andre Beranger.
Molly's mother plots to break up her marriage plans.

The Watchdog (suggestion for)

Dizzy Dames
9 reels   b&w   1935
Dir: William Nigh. Sp: George Waggner. Prod: Liberty Pictures.

WOHL, LUDWIG VON

Jimmy the Crook

Century Daredevil
b&w   1929
Prod: American General.

WONDERLY, WILLIAM CAREY

The Viennese Charmer

Street Girl
9 reels   b&w   1929
Dir: Wesley Ruggles. Prod: RKO.
Cast: Betty Compson, John Harron.
A Hungarian violinist rescued by a band later teams up with them and they become well known.

That Girl from Paris
105 min.   b&w   1937
Dir: Leigh Jason. Prod: RKO.
Cast: Lily Pons, Gene Raymond.
An opera star flees from her wedding and follows a band.

Four Jacks and a Jill
68 min.   b&w   1941
Dir: Jack Hively. Prod: RKO.
Cast: Ray Bolger, Desi Arnaz.
The trials and tribulations of a band and a girl.

WOODBURY, HERBERT A.

A Fool and His Gold

Riders in the Sky
70 min.　　　　b&w　　　　1949
Dir: John English. Prod: Gene Autry.
Cast: Gene Autry.
A singing country investigator tracks down evidence that convicts a murderer.

WOOLRICH, CORNELL

The Boy Cried Murder (in *Mystery Book Magazine,* March 1947)

The Window
73 min.　　　　b&w　　　　1948
Dir: Ted Tetzlaff. Prod: RKO. Dist: Films Inc., Nostalgia Merchant (video).
Cast: Bobby Driscoll, Barbara Hale.
Because ten-year-old Tommy has a reputation for telling tales, no one believes that he really witnessed a murder except the killers.

The Boy Cried Murder
88 min.　　　　color　　　　1966
Dir: George Breakston. Sp: Robin Estridge. Prod: Universal. Dist: Cousino Visual Ed. Service.
Cast: Veronica Hurst, Frasher (Fizz) MacIntosh, Phil Brown.
A young boy witnesses a murder, but no one believes him except the killer.

Children of the Ritz

Children of the Ritz
b&w　　　　1929　　　　sd. effects and mus.
Dir: John Francis Dillon. Prod: First National Pictures.
Cast: Dorothy Mackaill, Jack Mulhall.
A rich girl amuses herself by trying to seduce the chauffeur.

Cocaine

Fall Guy
63 min.　　　　b&w　　　　1947
Dir: Reginald Le Borg. Prod: Monogram Pictures. Dist: Hurlock Cine-World.
Cast: Robert Armstrong, Clifford Penn.
A man is the fall guy for a murder he didn't commit.

Face Work

Convicted
6 reels　　　　b&w　　　　1938
Dir: Leon Barsha. Sp: Edgar Edwards. Prod: Columbia Pictures.
Cast: Rita Hayworth, Marc Lawrence.
A detective convicts a boy of murder and is later convinced that the boy is innocent.

Nightmare

Fear in the Night
72 min.   b&w   1947
Dir. and Sp: Maxwell Shane. Prod: Paramount.
Cast: Paul Kelly, De Forrest Kelly, Ann Doran.
A man, hypnotised and forced to commit murder, recalls the murder in a nightmare.

Rear Window

Rear Window
122 min.   b&w   1954
Dir: Alfred Hitchcock. Sp: John Michael Hayes. Prod: Patron. Dist: MCA
    Home Video (video).
Cast: James Stewart, Grace Kelly, Raymond Burr.
A photographer laid up in his apartment watches his neighbors through binoculars and suspects a murder. Nominated for an Academy Award for Best Written American Drama.

Two Men in a Furnished Room

The Guilty
70 min.   b&w   1947
Dir: John Reinhardt. Prod: Monogram Pictures.
Cast: Don Castle, Bonita Granville.
Two friends are in love with the same girl, who has a twin, and one of them is murdered.

WORMSER, ANNE

The Baby's Had a Hard Day

West Point Widow
64 min.   b&w   1941
Dir: Robert Diodmak. Prod: Paramount.
Cast: Anne Shirley, Richard Carlson.
A nurse secretely marries an Army football star, but her pregnancy jeopardizes the secret.

WORMSER, RICHARD

It's All in the Racket

Sworn Enemy
8 reels   b&w   1936
Dir: Edwin Marin. Sp: Wells Root. Prod: MGM.
Cast: Joseph Calleia, Robert Young, Florence Rice.
Crime drama.

Right Guy

The Frame-Up
6 reels   b&w   1937

Dir: D. Ross Lederman. Sp: Harold Shumate. Prod: Columbia Pictures.
Cast: Paul Kelly, Jacqueline Wells.
A strong-arm romance between a track sleuth and a secretary.

The Road to Carmichaels

The Big Steal
70 min.   b&w   1949
Dir: Don Siegel. Prod: RKO. Dist: Films Inc., Nostalgia Merchant (video).
Cast: Robert Mitchum, Jane Greer.
A robbery caper and romance set in the Southwest and Mexico.

WORMSER, RICHARD

Sleep All Winter (in *Esquire*) (jt. author Dan Gordon)

Showdown
86 min.   b&w   1950
Dir: Darrell McGowan. Prod: Republic Pictures. Dist: Ivy Films.
Cast: Walter Brennan, Leif Ericson.
A former state trooper looks for his brother's killer and finds the suspect
in a gambling house.

WORTS, GEORGE FRANK

Out Where the Worst Begins (in *Argosy All-Story Weekly Magazine,* 5 January-
2 February 1924)

Where the Worst Begins
6 reels   b&w   1925   sil.
Dir: John McDermott. Prod: Co-Artists Prod.
Cast: Ruth Roland, Alec B. Francis.
A young lady kidnaps Donald, and he falls in love with her.

Red Darkness (in *Argosy All-Story Weekly Magazine,* 18 November-9 December
1922)

Madness of Youth
5 reels   b&w   1923   sil.
Dir: Jerome Storm. Prod: Fox.
Cast: John Gilbert, Billie Dove.
A youthful crook poses as an evangelist when pulling jobs.

WRIGHT, RICHARD

Almos' a Man

Almos' a Man (American Short Stories Series)
39 min.   color   1977
Dir: Stan Lathan. Sp: Leslie Lee. Dist: Coronet Films (16 mm and video).
Cast: LeVar Burton.

Set in the Deep South during the late 1930s. David's parents protectively deprive him of independence, yet he persuades his mother to give him part of his earnings for a used handgun. While practicing, he accidentally kills a mule and is bonded by the landowner to work 25 months without pay.

WYLIE, EDA ALEXA ROSS

The Gay Banditti (in *Saturday Evening Post,* 26 February 1938; s.m. also a novel "The Young in Heart")

The Young in Heart
86 min.   b&w   1938
Dir: Richard Wallace. Prod: Selznick International Pictures. Dist: Mogull's Films.
Cast: Douglas Fairbanks, Jr., Janet Gaynor.
A dizzy family of cardsharps and fortune hunters is reformed by the kindness of a sweet old lady.

Grandma Bernie Learns Her Letters (in *Saturday Evening Post,* 11 September 1926)

Four Sons
100 min.   b&w   1928   mus. and sd. effects
Dir: John Ford. Prod: Fox.
Cast: Margaret Mann, James Hall.
A Bavarian widow with four sons loses them one by one until only Joseph is left. He migrates to America, and after World War I asks his mother to join him.

Four Sons
89 min.   b&w   1940
Dir: Archie Mayo. Prod: Twentieth Century Fox.
Cast: Don Ameche.
A Czech family is torn apart by the Nazi invasion. Far removed from the original story.

Jungle Law (in *Good Housekeeping*)

A Man Must Live
7 reels   b&w   1925   sil.
Dir: Paul Sloane. Prod: Famous Players-Lasky.
Cast: Richard Dix, Jacqueline Logan.
A scandal sheet reporter finds a story when an old war buddy gets arrested on narcotics charges. But when he falls in love with his buddy's sister, he tries to kill the story.

Pilgrimage

Pilgrimage
90 min.   b&w   1933
Dir: John Ford. Prod: Fox. Dist: Films Inc.
Cast: Henrietta Crossman, Heather Angel.

An old woman who breaks up her son's romance by sending him off to war lives to regret it.

Vivacious Lady (published later as a three-act comedy)

Vivacious Lady
90 min.   b&w   1938
Dir: George Stevens. Prod: RKO. Dist: Films Inc.
Cast: James Stewart, Ginger Rogers.
A college professor marries a nightclub singer and then has trouble getting his family to accept her.

Why Should I Cry

Torch Song
90 min.   color   1953
Dir: Charles Walters. Sp: John Michael Hayes, Jan Lustig. Prod: MGM. Dist: Films Inc.
Cast: Joan Crawford, Michael Wilding.
A singer/dancer falls in love with a blind pianist.

Young Nowheres (in *Saturday Evening Post,* 16 April 1927)

Young Nowheres
7 reels   b&w   1929   sil. or sd.
Dir: Frank Lloyd. Prod: First National Pictures.
Cast: Richard Barthelmess, Marion Nixon.
A poor boy takes his sick girlfriend to the luxurious apartment of his employer.

That Man's Here Again
58 min.   b&w   1937
Dir: Louis King. Prod: Warner Bros. Dist: MGM/UA Home Video (video).
Cast: Hugh Herbert, Tom Brown.
An apartment dweller furthers a romance.

WYLIE, PHILIP

Death Flies East

Death Flies East
7 reels   b&w   1935
Dir: Phil Rosen. Prod: Columbia Pictures.

Death in Paradise Canyon

Fair Warning
68 min.   b&w   1937
Dir: Norman Foaster. Prod: Twentieth Century Fox.
Cast: Jay Edward Bromberg, Betty Furness, John Payne.
A fashionable winter resort turns into bedlam when a mysterious death puts the guests under suspicion.

Murderess Welcome

Under Suspicion
63 min.   b&w   1937
Dir: Lewis D. Collins. Prod: Columbia Pictures.
Cast: Jack Holt, Katherine De Mille, Craig Reynolds.
Auto magnate plans to retire and is almost killed.

Worship the Sun (suggestion for)

Springtime in the Rockies
91 min.   color   1942
Prod: Twentieth Century Fox.
Cast: Betty Grable, John Payne.
Musical about show people and a broken promise.

WYNDHAM, JOHN

Random Quest

Quest for Love (Br.)
91 min.   color   1971
Dir: Ralph Thomas. Sp: Bert Batt. Prod: Peter Rogers Prod.
Cast: Joan Collins, Tom Bell, Denholm Elliott.
A man finds himself in a world where disasters don't occur.

YERKOW, CHARLES

Island Freighter

Sea Tiger
75 min.   b&w   1952
Dir: Frank McDonald. Prod: Monogram Pictures. Dist: Ivy Films.
Cast: Marguerite Chapman, John Archer.
A man cleared of collusion with the Japanese becomes a murder suspect.

YOUNG, GORDON RAY

Hurricane Williams stories

Hurricane Smith
90 min.   b&w   1952
Dir: Jerry Hopper. Prod: Paramount.
Cast: John Ireland, Yvonne de Carlo.
A fugitive on a South Seas island captures a ship.

Z

ZANGWILL, ISRAEL

Merely Mary Ann

> *Merely Mary Ann*
> b&w   1931
> Prod: Fox.

ZILAHY, LAJAS

The General

> *The Virtuous Sin*
> 81 min.   b&w   1930
> Dir: George Cukor, Louis Gasnier. Prod: Paramount Publix.
> Cast: Walter Huston, Kay Francis.
> The wife of a Russian medical student bribes her way into a brothel
in order to persuade a general to exempt her husband from military service.

ZOLOTOW, MAURICE

Little Boy Blue

> *Let's Dance*
> 112 min.   color   1950
> Dir: Norman Z. McLeod. Prod: Paramount.
> Cast: Fred Astaire, Betty Hutton.
> An ex-actress and her former partner fight her wealthy mother-in-law
when she tries to take her son away.

Directory of Distributors

AIT
Agency for Instruction Television
Box A
Bloomington, IN 47402

Admit One Video
311 Adelaide St. E.
Toronto, Ontario, Canada M5A IN2

Alba House
7050 Pinehurst (Box 40)
Dearborn, MI 48126

Almi
1585 Broadway
New York, NY 10036

Argus Films
1225 Broadway
New York, NY 10001

Audio Brandon
733 Green Bay Rd.
Wilmette, IL 60091

Authors on Videotape
1619 Broadway
New York, NY 10019

Beacon Films
1250 Washington St.
Box 575
Norwood, MA 02062

Benchmark Films
145 Scarborough Rd.
Briarcliff Manor, NY 10510

Billy Budd Films
235 E. 57th St.
New York, NY 10022

Blackhawk
One Old Eagle Brewery
Box 3990
Davenport, IA 52808

Brigham Young University
AV Services
Provo, UT 84602

Buchan Pictures
254 Delaware Ave.
Buffalo, NY 14202

Budget Films/Video
4590 Santa Monica Blvd.
Los Angeles, CA 90029

CBS/Fox Video
1211 Sixth Ave.
New York, NY 10036

CRM/McGraw-Hill
110 Fifteenth St.
Del Mar, CA 92014

Cable Films
Country Club Station
Box 717
Kansas City, MO 64113

Carousel Films
241 E. 34 St.
New York, NY 10016

Center for the Humanities
Communications Park
Box 1000
Mount Kisco, NY 10549

Charard Motion Pictures
2110 E. 24th St.
Brooklyn, NY 11229

Churchill Films
622 N. Robertson Blvd.
Los Angeles, CA 90069

Cine Craft
1720 W. Marshall
Portland, OR 79209

Cinema Concepts/Cinema Eight
2461 Berlin Turnpike
Newington, CT 06111

Classic Film Museum
6 Union Sq.
Dover-Foxcroft, ME 04426

Clem Williams Films
2240 Noblestown Rd.
Pittsburgh, PA 15205

Corinth Films
410 E. 62 St.
New York, NY 10021

Coronet Films
108 Wilmot
Deerfield, IL 60051

Cousino Visual Ed. Service
1945 Franklin Ave.
Toledo, OH 43624

Direct Cinema
Box 69589
Los Angeles, CA 90069

Discount Video Tapes
37113 W. Clark Ave.
Box 7122
Burbank, CA 91510

Walt Disney Ed. Media
500 S. Buena Vista St.
Burbank, CA 91521

Walt Disney Home Video
500 S. Buena Vista St.
Burbank, CA 91521

Don Bosco Films
48 Main St.
Box T
New Rochelle, NY 10802

Educational Communications
2814 Virginia
Houston, TX 77098

Embassy Home Entertainment
1901 Ave. of the Stars
Los Angeles, CA 90069

Em Gee Film Library
6924 Canby Ave. (Suite 103)
Reseda, CA 91335

Encyclopaedia Britannica Ed. Corp.
425 N. Michigan Ave.
Chicago, IL 60611

Film Classic Exchange
1914 S. Vermont Ave.
Los Angeles, CA 90007

FilmFair Communications
10900 Ventura Blvd.
Box 1728
Studio City, CA 91604

Films Inc.
733 Green Bay Rd.
Wilmette, IL 60091

Glenn Video Vistas
6924 Canby Ave. #103
Reseda, CA 91335

Griggs-Moviedrome
263 Harrison St.
Nutley, NJ 07110

Hollywood Home Theater
4590 Santa Monica Blvd.
Los Angeles, CA 90029

Hurlock Cine-World
13 Arcadia Rd.
Old Greenwich, CT 06870

Images
300 Phillips Park Rd.
Mamaroneck, NY 10543

Indiana University
AV Center
Bloomington, IN 47405

Institutional Cinema Service
10 First St.
Saugerties, NY 12477

International Film Bureau
332 S. Michigan Ave.
Chicago, IL 60604-4382

Ivy Films
165 W. 46 St.
New York, NY 10036

Jackson, Jeff
124 Woodgate
Battle Creek, MI 49107

Janus Films
888 Seventh Ave.
New York, NY 10016

Kerr Film Exchange
3034 Canon St.
San Diego, CA 92106

Killiam Collections
6 E. 39th St.
New York, NY 10016

King of Video
3529 S. Valley View Blvd.
Las Vegas, NV 89103

Kit Parker Films
1245 Tenth St.
Monterey, CA 93940

LSB Productions
1310 Monaco Dr.
Pacific Palisades, CA 90272

Lewis Film Service
1425 E. Central
Witchita, KS 67214

Lucerne Films
37 Ground Pine Rd.
Morris Plains, NH 07950

MCA Home Video
70 Universal City Plaza
Universal City, CA 91608

MGM/UA Home Video
1350 Sixth Ave.
New York, NY 10019

MOMA
Museum of Modern Art
11 W. 53rd St.
New York, NY 10019

MTI Teleprograms
108 Wilmot Rd.
Deerfield, IL 60015

Maryland Center for Public
    Broadcasting
11767 Bonita Ave
Owings Mill, MO 21117

Mass Media
2116 N. Charles St.
Baltimore, MD 21218

Media Home Entertainment
116 N. Robertson Blvd.
Los Angeles, CA 90048

Modern Sound Pictures
1402 Howard St.
Omaha, NE 68102

Mogull's Films
1280 North Ave.
Plainfield, NH 07062

Monterey Home Video
7920 Alabama Ave.
Canoga Park, CA 91304-4991

NTA Home Entertainment
12636 Beatrice St.
Box 66930
Los Angeles, CA 90066

National Cinema Service
Box 43
Ho-Ho-Kus, NJ 07423

National Film Service
14 Glenwood Ave.
Raleigh, NC 27602

National Film Board of Canada
1251 Ave. of the Americas
New York, NY 10020

New Line Cinema
853 Broadway
New York, NY 10003

Newman Film Library
1444 Michigan Ave.
Grand Rapids, MI 49503

New Yorker Films
16 W. 61st St.
New York, NY 10023

Nostalgia Merchant
6255 Sunset Blvd.
Hollywood, CA 90028

Paramount Home Video
5451 Marathon St.
Hollywood, CA 90038

Penguin Video
3500 Verdugo Rd.
Box 65157
Los Angeles, CA 90065

Perspective Films and Video
108 Wilmot
Deerfield, IL 60051

Phoenix/BFA Films and Video
470 Park Ave. S.
New York, NY 10016

Pyramid Films
Box 1048
Santa Monica, CA 90406

RCA/Columbia Pictures Home Video
2901 W. Alameda Ave.
Burbank, CA 91505

RCA VideoDiscs
1133 Ave. of the Americas
New York, NY 10036

Reel Images
456 Monroe Turnpike
Monroe, CT 06468

RKO
15840 Ventura Blvd.
Encino, CA 91436

Roa's Films
1696 N. Astor St.
Milwaukee, WI 53202

Select Film Library
902 Broadway
New York, NY 10010

Sheik Video
1823-25 Airline Highway
Metairie, LA 70001

Simon & Schuster Communications
108 Wilmot
Deerfield, IL 60051

Swank
201 S. Jefferson Ave.
St. Louis, MO 63116

Sylvan Films
Box 622
Brevard, NC 28712

"The" Film Center
938 K St. NW
Washington, DC 20001

Thorn EMI
1370 Ave. of the Americas
New York, NY 10019

Thunderbird Films
3500 Verdugo Rd.
Los Angeles, CA 90065

Time-Life Video
Time-Life Bldg.
1271 Ave. of the Americas
New York, NY 10020

Trans-National Film
48 W. 69th St.
New York, NY 10023

Trans-World
332 S. Michigan Ave.
Chicago, IL 60604

Alan Twyman Presents
592 S. Grant Ave.
Columbus, OH 43206

Universal
445 Park Ave.
New York, NY 10022

Vestron Video
1011 High Ridge Rd.
Box 4000
Stamford, CT 06907

VidAmerica
235 E. 55th St.
New York, NY 10022

Video Communications
6535 E. Skelly Dr.
Tulsa, OK 74145

Video Connection
1920 Sylvania Ave.
Toledo, OH 43613

Video Dimensions
110 E. 23 St.
New York, NY 10010

Video Yesteryear
Box C
Sandy Hook, CT 06482

Viewfinders
Box 1665
Evanston, IL 60204

Walter Reade 16
241 E. 34 St.
New York, NY 10016

Warner Bros. Home Video
4000 Warner Blvd.
Burbank, CA 91522

Weiss Global Enterprises
2055 Saviers Rd., Suite 12
Oxnard, CA 93030

Welling Motion Pictures
454 Meacham Ave.
Elmont, NY 11003

Westcoast Films
25 Lusk St.
San Francisco, CA 94107

Wholesome Film Center
20 Melrose St.
Boston, MA 02116

Willoughby-Peerless
115 W. 31st St.
New York, NY 10001

Xerox Films
Communications Park
Box 4000
Mt. Kisco, NY 10549

Film Title Index

Penthouse, 235
People Versus Dr. Kildare, 33
People Will Talk, 159
Perfect Clue, 286
Perfect Crime, 58
Perfect Flapper, 133
Perfect Specimen, 5
Personal Maid's Secret, 77
Petticoat Brigade, 124
Pettigrew's Girl, 40
Phantom Patrol, 70
Phantom of the Rue Morgue, 225
Phantom Submarine, 204
Pikovaya Dama, 230
Pilgrimage, 300
Pin-Up Girl, 28
Pit and the Pendulum, 226
Plaisir, 193
Planet of the Vampires, 219
Platinum High School, 36
Plot Thickens, 216
Pocketful of Miracles, 239
Poker Faces, 105
Pony Soldier, 286
Poor, Dear Margaret Kirby, 208
Port of Shadows, 186
Portable Phonograph, 58
Possessed, 285
Postmaster's Daughter, 229
Poverty of Riches, 246
Prairie Pirate, 275
Prairie Schooners, 106
Prelude to Fame, 145
Premature Burial, 226
Pressure Point, 176
Pretty Ladies, 242
Price of a Party, 185
Pride of the Marines, 19
Prince of Headwaiters, 249
Prince Who Was a Thief, 86
Princess and the Plumber, 200
Princess O'Hara, 239
Priory School, 82
Prison Break, 216
Private Affairs, 119, 217
Private Life of Sherlock Holmes, 82
Proud Rebel, 117
Prowlers of the Sea, 180
Proxies, 4
Pursued, 93
Pursuit to Algiers, 82

Quartet, 190
Queen of Spades, 229
Quest for Love, 302
Quiet Man, 283
Quiet Please, Murder, 28

Race for Number One, 179
Race Street, 74
Rachel and the Stranger, 94
Racing Blood, 166
Rain, 191
Rainmaker, 17
Ransom of Red Chief, 135
Rappaccini's Daughter, 129
Rarin' to Go, 69
Raven, 226
Ready, Willing and Able, 185
Real Thing, 151
Rear Window, 298
Recoil, 15
Red-Headed League, 82
Red Mark, 240
Red Rider, 274
Red Sundown, 217
Referee, 17
Reformer and the Redhead, 47
Remarkable Rocket, 291
Requiem for Mozart, 229
Restless Souls, 78
Return, 24
Return from the Sea, 188
Return of Boston Blackie, 30
Return of Sherlock Holmes, 83
Return of Sophie Lang, 8
Return of the Cisco Kid, 134
Return of Wild Bill, 60
Revenge, 23
Rich But Honest, 235
Rich Man, Poor Girl, 105
Ride on Vaquero, 134
Riders in the Sky, 297
Riding Avenger, 286
Riding High, 131
Riding the California Trail, 134
Right That Failed, 188
Rikki-Tikki-Tavi, 162
Rim of the Canyon, 49
Rio Grande, 20
Rio Grande Romance, 167
Rip Roarin' Roberts, 139
Rip Van Winkle, 147
Rise of Duton Lang, 291
Rising of the Moon, 211
Risky Business, 31
River, 211
River's Edge, 251
Road to Alcatraz, 7
Road to Denver, 121
Roar of the Dragon, 272
Rocking-Horse Winner, 173
Rollerball, 124
Romance of the Redwoods, 181
Rose for Emily, 95
Rose of Kildare, 19

Short Story Title Index